THE
DIAMOND
CONSPIRACY

NICOLAS
KUBLICKI

SOURCEBOOKS LANDMARK™
AN IMPRINT OF SOURCEBOOKS, INC.®
NAPERVILLE, ILLINOIS

Published by Sourcebooks, Inc.
P.O. Box 4410, Naperville, Illinois 60567-4410
(630) 961-3900
FAX: (630) 961-2168
www.sourcebooks.com

Library of Congress Cataloging-in-Publication Data

Kublicki, Nicolas M.
    The diamond conspiracy : a novel / Nicolas M. Kublicki.
        p. cm.
    ISBN 1-4022-0226-1 (Paperback)
    1. Diamond mines and mining—Fiction. 2. Conspiracies—Fiction. 3. Arkansas—Fiction. I. Title.
    PS3611.U27 D43 2002
    813'.6—dc21

2002009775

Printed and bound in the United States of America
QW 10 9 8 7 6 5 4 3 2 1

To my parents
Tadeusz and Marie
who taught me right from wrong.

Every contract, combination in the form of trust or otherwise, or conspiracy, in restraint of trade or commerce among the several States, or with foreign nations, is declared to be illegal….Every person who shall monopolize, or attempt to monopolize, or combine or conspire with any other person or persons, to monopolize any part of the trade or commerce among the several States, or with foreign nations, shall be deemed guilty of a felony, and, on conviction thereof, shall be punished by fine not exceeding $10,000,000 if a corporation, or, if any other person, $350,000, or by imprisonment not exceeding three years, or by both said punishments, in the discretion of the court.

—Sherman Antitrust Act of 1890
15 United States Code
Sections 1 and 2, as amended

PROLOGUE

Arkansas, 1920

The United States Geological Survey team set out in August. Unrelenting heat, suffocating humidity, and deafening choruses of crickets ruled the Arkansas countryside. They traveled in a convoy of Model T Fords weighed down by camping equipment, delicate surveying tools, crates of canned food, pickaxes, shovels, and dynamite. Despite their hardy construction, the Model Ts became bogged in mosquito-infested swamps created by the torrential summer downpours. Veteran geological surveyors, they had experienced conditions far worse. Besides, they had been sent by Washington on an official mission, and Washington paid well. They pressed on.

Their efforts yielded utter disappointment. Explode and dig and sift through mounds of dirt as they might, the geologists could not locate their quarry. Hours stretched into days, days into weeks. After a month's toil under the beating summer sun, supplies dwindled to a few meager boxes. The hired hands were exhausted, covered with chigger bites, on the verge of walking off the job. The rickety cars could barely move. Morale was at a low point, the contract nearly expired. Exhausted and dejected, team leader Samuel Osage called off the expedition.

On the swampy road back to Murfreesboro, one of the Model Ts again overheated in a deep pool of mud. The team decided to let the engine cool off and broke out the last few cans of beans and chipped beef for lunch. As Osage negotiated his way through the sticky substance around the car, he misjudged the depth of the mud and lost his balance. He thrust an arm out to break his fall, but it plunged deep into the ooze. Osage fell face forward into the muck. He fought to prop himself up amid the roaring laughter of the men. After several failed attempts, he managed to stand. He shook dollops of heavy mud from his body, scooped handfuls of dark slime from his face and arms. The clay stuck to his arms and hands. But it wasn't smooth. He could feel rocks embedded in the mud scrape his fingers. He cleaned himself as best he could and looked at his filthy hands.

Suddenly, Osage went rigid.

A rough pebble was stuck between two fingers of his left hand. Still partially caked with mud, it stood out to Osage's trained eye. He picked it from his fingers, carefully wiped it on the only remaining clean part of his shirt, and lifted it to the burning sun between two grimy fingers. The translucent pebble glowed in the sun. Osage's dirty face creased into a wide grin. In his fingers was the object of their quest.

A diamond.

Washington wasted no time. Within two months of the team's report, the USGS constructed a mine. It immediately produced a large number of carats. Washington directed Osage and his fellow geologists to determine the exact extent of the diamondiferous deposits. Their findings surpassed Osage's wildest expectations. What originally had been thought a remote deposit was an underground ocean of diamonds.

Despite the fact Washington kept the operation heavily under wraps, news of the surprising discovery managed to find its way to South Africa, where the domestic discovery of vast diamond deposits had been big news for forty years. News of the Arkansas deposits sounded an ominous tone to South Africa's Waterboer Mines Limited.

Since the discovery of diamonds at Kimberley in South Africa's Orange Free State in 1871, South African diamond miners had used every conceivable strategy to consolidate the legion ad hoc diamond mines into a single efficient operation. After years of cutthroat tactics, shady deals, and backroom politics, Waterboer Mines Limited had emerged the victor. Waterboer controlled diamond production in South Africa, then on a global scale. The Arkansas discovery spelled disaster for the Waterboer monopoly. An immense diamond deposit outside its control would send prices plummeting. Waterboer had to act. Fast.

Head of the world's largest monopoly, Cecil R. Slythe was a force. The diamond monopoly brought wealth. Wealth brought influence. Influence brought power. In South Africa and Europe. In America as well. Particularly in Arkansas.

Cecil R. Slythe arrived in Washington in the autumn of 1920. Within one hour of his meeting with his clique of financial and political power brokers in the nation's capital, Osage and his team were split up and sent on urgent expeditions in faraway lands. The Murfreesboro diamond mine was fenced in, boarded up, and shut down. The Arkansas diamond miners were transferred to high-paying jobs in different parts of the country. Journalists and politicians were silenced. The USGS report was sealed in a vault in the basement of a nameless edifice in Washington, never again to see the light of day.

Upon his return to his native Arkansas in 1932 from an unusually perilous emerald expedition in Colombia, Osage decided to pay a visit to what he still thought of as his Arkansas mine. Not because of financial interest—he had received no stake in the government mine—but out of professional, nearly paternal interest.

Where hundreds of carats of diamonds had been excavated daily at the time of his departure now stood creaking wooden boards and rusting machinery. Why? He himself had plotted the vast diamond deposits, millions of carats. The mine could not possibly have exhausted the deposits. So why was it closed?

He decided to investigate.

He started in the most logical place, the Washington headquarters of the USGS. The official response astounded him. They were sorry, but they had no records of any diamond deposits in Arkansas. They vaguely remembered a diamond mine in Arkansas, but it had been shut down twelve years ago. He knew it had been shut down, but why? No one would give him a straight answer. Befuddled, Osage traveled to Arkansas and contacted state and local authorities. They, too, evaded his questions and pleaded ignorance. Back in Washington he tried to meet with the members of Congress who oversaw the

USGS. None had time to speak with him. Finally, he decided to speak with members of his original geology team, the men who had struggled through the mud with him. He had lost track of them over the years, while each went from dig to dig in often remote locations. They would know.

Not one was alive. Each had perished under mysterious circumstances during faraway expeditions.

Anguished, Osage tried to convince himself his colleagues had died accidentally. He could not. He tried to believe the mine had depleted the diamond deposits, but could not. He tried to forget about the mine altogether, but the diamonds haunted him. There had to be an explanation.

Finally, Osage resigned himself to the only option that remained. He contacted the press. In the midst of the greatest depression the country had ever experienced, news of diamond deposits in Arkansas was bound to constitute front page material. One by one, large, then medium, then small newspapers brushed him off as a senile lunatic. But Osage was a tenacious old bird. His resolve strengthened, he made it his personal mission to contact each newspaper in the country. After several weeks, when it appeared no journalist would speak with him, a young rookie reporter from a low-circulation Little Rock rag agreed to listen to his story the very same day. Osage set course for Little Rock, a hundred miles away, in his battered black Model A Ford.

Roads in 1932 Arkansas were far from safe. Potholes, mud, and rocks conspired to destroy automobiles unfortunate enough to attempt the dirt paths that masqueraded as roads. At thirty miles per hour on the rough path, the Model A's rattling frame shook Osage to near numbness. He began to think the car might fall apart.

The sun had begun its dip below the horizon, and Little Rock was still over forty miles away. If he didn't make it before dark, he'd have to cut his speed by half and risk losing his opportunity—his only opportunity, he reminded himself—to tell his story to someone who would actually listen.

Between his concentration on the road and the flurry of thoughts in his mind, Osage had little attention left for the world around him, or behind him. Muted by the roar from Osage's shorn muffler and hidden from view by a missing rearview mirror, a car approached. Also a Model A, it was very different from Osage's. Although the two cars shared body style, even color, the car behind hid a massive Duesenberg eight-cylinder engine that drove its wheels far faster than Osage's Ford engine. So fast, in fact, it was not until the car was twenty or thirty feet from Osage's rear bumper that he noticed its square radiator and round headlights in his side mirror.

Where had this maniac come from? The driver wanted to pass. Disadvantaged in the horsepower department, Osage eased back on the accelerator. As the Model A slowed, he edged toward the right side of the dirt road to let the crazed driver pass.

Instead of unleashing the "Duesie" engine, the driver inched forward, matched speeds with Osage. Thinking the driver lacked sufficient width to pass, yet careful not to fall into the ditch that paralleled the road, Osage stared ahead, gestured for the driver to pass.

The driver continued matching speeds with Osage, inches from his door. Concluding the driver lacked the power to pass, Osage slowed further. Still, the car did not pass.

Genuinely angered, Osage turned to glare at the driver. Before he could discern the man's face, he felt a sharp pain in his head.

And everything went black.

Because of the execrable conditions of the country roads, it did not strike local residents or police as strange when Osage's Model A was found burned to the ground on the side of the road, its front end wrapped around a large tree trunk. Sad, perhaps. Certainly not strange. Without even a glance at the body, the local coroner assumed the driver had perished as a result of the accident and so avoided the hassle of an autopsy. Had he performed his duty, the coroner would have discovered that Samuel Osage had been killed by a bullet fired at close range. Further inquiry would have revealed the bullet was manufactured exclusively for the Federal Bureau of Investigation. Even further inquiry would have revealed that a rookie reporter had met an identical fate on his way to Little Rock. Assiduous inquiry would have revealed that not all of Osage's Arkansas diamond surveys were locked away in a vault in Washington.

PART I
COLOR

"Important facts to know about buying a diamond are
the 4Cs: Cut, Color, Clarity, and Carat-weight.
These are the characteristics that determine
the quality and value of a diamond."

—*"Shadows of Love," the diamond engagement ring pamphlet,*
Jewelers of America, Inc.

———

"Diamonds are beauty."
—*Waterboer Mines, Ltd. slogan*

1 ASSIGNMENT

Present Day
United States Department of Justice (DOJ)
Robert F. Kennedy Main Justice Building
Washington, D.C.
10:20 A.M.

Patrick Carlton rushed into Justice Department headquarters through the main entrance of the marble-and-granite federal fortress, beneath an immense American flag that waved ponderously in the cold wind. A late night's work and rush-hour gridlock had conspired to make him late for work. Again. He slid his identification card into the electronic turnstile, waved to the guard pulling morning duty, and hurried past the seal of the fabled agency, the largest law firm in the world.

Qui Pro Domina Justitia Sequitur was its motto.

He who seeks to rule follows justice.

Carlton shunned the slow elevators, bolted up the graceful staircase to the third floor. The tap-tap of his cowboy boots reverberated through the marble corridors as he strode past the offices that lined interminable hallways. Despite his exhaustion, a smile tugged at the corners of his eyes as he approached his office. *United States v. Global Steel* was Carlton's first serious assignment after three grueling years of paying dues in the DOJ trenches. It was an important case because of its substance and because it was his case. He was lead counsel. He made the strategic decisions. He called the shots.

One of the new lawyers straight out of law school walked toward him down the hall. He had not formally met her yet. She was very attractive, but to entertain romantic thoughts, far less act upon them, regarding subordinates at DOJ was more than against policy; it was punishable by immediate termination. Carlton was about to wish her a polite good morning when he noticed an expression of anxiety on her face, her gaze darting toward his office. He stopped, stared at his office door in confusion as she walked past, trailing a wisp of Calandre perfume.

The reason for her grimace was clear as soon as he opened the door. Harry Jarvik, director of the Antitrust Division's Economic Litigation Section, was seated in Carlton's chair, feet propped on the desk.

"Well, well. Good morning, Carlton. Or should I say good afternoon?" He glanced at his pocket watch, nodded theatrically. "How good of you to join us. Is this what they taught you in that white-shoe law firm of yours?"

Jarvik was short in stature and temper, a man who made himself appear taller by cutting others down. The staff of the Antitrust Division referred to him as Stalin. A corpulent man, his thick mustache and piercing gaze gave him a sinister look. He looked over Carlton head to toe with beady eyes, his gaze lingering on Carlton's trademark spit-shined cowboy boots.

"Good morning, sir," Carlton said. "There is a reason. I worked very late on *Global Steel* last ni—"

"Of course, of course. Tomorrow another excuse." He stood, all five-feet-four bristling. "Do I really look that stupid?"

Carlton decided sincerity would only aggravate matters. "I'm sorry, sir."

Jarvik grunted, he pointed a thick finger at the visitor's chair next to Carlton's desk. "Sit down."

Carlton peeled off his overcoat and scarf, hung them on a battered hat rack. He removed a pile of legal publications from the cracked leather chair and sat. He awaited his sentence, a visitor in his own office.

"Now," Jarvik sat and reclined, "tell me what you know about diamonds."

"Diamonds?" Carlton wondered if the question was designed to lead to further humiliation, then decided Jarvik was serious. "I don't know anything about diamonds, sir. Except that they're very expensive."

"Just as I thought. Most people don't, but Rothenberg loves them." He referred to the deputy assistant attorney general in charge of DOJ's Antitrust Section. Jarvik's boss. "She's nuts about them, and for some reason, she got it into her mind to prosecute a local mom-and-pop diamond mining outfit in Arkansas for antitrust violations."

"Diamonds in Arkansas? I though diamonds came from Afri—"

"It's a miniature deposit. A freak of nature, from what the geologists say. Strictly mom and pop. Raymond Mines, the outfit is called. Nuts, if you want my opinion. There's hardly any evidence, but Rothenberg's got this crazy idea the Raymonds accepted money to shut down operations, asked me to make sure it gets followed up. You're the lucky one. I'm taking you off of *Global* and putting you on Raymond Mines."

Carlton's jaw dropped. "What?" The word cracked in his throat.

"You heard me."

Had he been standing, the blow would have knocked him to the ground. "Off *Global*? Sir, I've been working on *Global* for six months. I've done all the trial prep. The witnesses. The strategy. The questions on direct and cross. Everything." He stood, fought to retain his composure. "The trial is in a week. One week, sir. And *Global* is a corporate maze. Dozens of witnesses. It'll take another attorney weeks to figure out what's going on." He stood. "I'm going to—"

"Sit down! The case is closed, Carlton. Literally. You're off *Global*. On Raymond Mines." He stood, indicating the finality of his ruling. "I'll send down the Raymond Mines file." He walked to the door, turned. "One more thing. I want you to wrap this up quickly. I know Rothenberg wants it prosecuted, and she's the boss, but Justice has never won a diamond case. Ever. Raymond Mines won't be different. The last thing this Section needs is another embarrassment in the press. Rothenberg or no Rothenberg, you are not to risk Section credibility by taking this to trial. Get a little settlement for show. Move on."

"Sir, I—"

"Settle!" he shouted, then lowered his voice to a whisper. "Then move on. Do I make myself clear?"

Carlton paused, still in shock. "As a diamond, sir."

"Good." Jarvik walked out and slammed the door.

Carlton sat for a long moment, trying hard to contain his anger, then walked to the window across the room. The thick glass was stained with the deposits of countless rains. Outside, dark clouds loosed freezing rain onto the red tile roof.

Global Steel. Carlton had come too close to being able to win the case so many others thought unwinnable. With a victory, Carlton would shine, brightly enough to raise the level of cases assigned to him after two years in the trenches, brightly enough to outshine Jarvik. Something Jarvik's pride could not, would not, tolerate. By giving *Global* to another lawyer right before trial, Jarvik could simultaneously prevent Carlton from shining and blame his unlucky replacement for the loss. Tidy. No matter to Jarvik the real losers would be those harmed by Global Steel: the American public.

Raised by parents slightly south of middle class and graduating from parochial high school with a perfect GPA and attendance record, Carlton moved from his parents' home in El Centro, California, to attend UCLA. He worked his way through college doing odd jobs on boats in the marina. He worked hard. He had a goal, and he stuck to it. His goal was money. The 1980s, Carlton's formative years, was the Decade of Greed. For him, like so many others, a big salary, a German sports car, and a condo in a coveted zip code were all that mattered. His hard work paid off. He earned a full scholarship to George Washington University law school in D.C. Three grueling years later, he attained his goal: a six-figure job in a top-ten Washington law firm.

But private practice in a D.C. megafirm did not live up to his image. Neither the status of the firm nor the bloated salary made up for its shortcomings. It took only two months for him to christen the firm the "Merchants of Pain" and begin to question his choices. The firm name and money were great, the work unspeakably stressful, tedious, and repetitious. His questioning coincided with a spiritual quest for the faith he'd considered an obstacle to success and abandoned ten years before.

Was this all there was? Had he endured the repeated mental beatings of law school for such meaningless work? Day after dreary day, meaningless memos to faceless clients. Dilatory depositions. Endless research. Scant hours of sleep punctuated by anxiety attacks. The rumors in law school had been true. As clichéd as it sounded, he had traded his life, his health, his soul, for a salary. After three years, Carlton gave up the fat paycheck and made the lateral hop to Justice, hoping law practice there would be different. But at Justice nothing changed except the salary, which was now a pittance.

A soft knock at his door shook him out of his sullen introspection. He turned. "Yeah."

The rookie lawyer with green eyes peeked through the half-open door. "You okay?"

He tried hard to smile, failed. "No, actually. But thanks for the warning." He stood and offered his hand. "We've never met. I'm—"

"Patrick Carlton." Her eyes were smiling now. "I'm Erika Wassenaar."

Carlton was surprised by her strong grip. And by the thumping in his chest.

At five-feet-eight, the young redhead in her mid-twenties was slim but not starved. A first-year lawyer, her demeanor suggested a confidence rarely attained without a few years of practice. Her lively eyes shone with curiosity. Professionally dressed in a smart navy blue suit and white blouse, she exuded freshness. She smiled with bright white teeth, slightly crooked, that added a girlish quality to her impish, mischievous charm.

Carlton forced his thoughts to professional matters. "You're new in the department, right?"

"Two weeks. The ink is still wet on my Bar certificate." She laughed genuinely, like a child.

"Congratulations. That's impressive." DOJ hired only the elite of law students directly out of school.

"Thanks, Mr. Carlton."

"Mr. Carlton sounds like my dad's in the room. We're a bit more informal around here. Pat'll do just fine," he paused. "Wassenaar. Dutch?"

"That's pretty good. Most people can't pin it down."

"Beginner's luck." He motioned to a chair. "Grab a seat."

Erika's gaze wandered over the framed photographs, diplomas, and awards on the office wall. Bar of the Supreme Court of the United States. Federal District Court here, Federal District Court there. Court of Appeals for this and that Circuit. California Bar. District of Columbia Bar. George Washington University National Law Center. University of California at Los Angeles.

"I went to UCLA undergrad," she said.

"Aces. I could use another Bruin in this Ivy League prison. Where did you go to law school?"

"Pepperdine."

"We've got a couple good lawyers from there."

The phone rang. "Excuse me," Carlton said as he reached for the receiver.

Erika assessed the man facing her. He seemed genuinely friendly, a bit nervous around her, which she found refreshing. Despite black hair worn in a crew cut, his strong nose, intense blue eyes, and angular jaw, Carlton was not exactly handsome. Nor was he particularly fit, brilliant, or wealthy, from what she'd heard. The word at DOJ was he smoked cigars with a vengeance, but never Cubans, because they were illegal. He had a temper, but lost it rarely. He wore conservative navy blue suits with white shirts to work, always with spit-shined cowboy boots. But the buzz didn't quite get it, didn't point to the intensity she sensed in him.

When he hung up, she pointed to a grainy discolored photograph on the wall, an elderly man and a teenager smiling next to a dusty biplane. "Who's that in the picture?"

"My grandfather and I. He was a crop duster in El Centro back in California. He taught me to fly when I was a kid."

"You still fly?"

"Not since he passed away. I've moved on to boats," he announced, picking up a small wooden model of a gray boat with white lettering on its side from the edge of his desk.

She cocked her head. "You're in the Navy?"

"Lieutenant Carlton, Navy Reserves. I skipper this little guy on the Chesapeake two weekends a month. After this morning, I may be doing it full time real soon."

They chuckled. After a moment of silence, she stood. "I have to go. Please let me know if you need any research. I hope we can work together sometime."

So did Carlton, and that rang alarm bells. He stood, nearly knocking a pile of documents off the desk in the process. "Thanks again for the warning."

2   RAID

Mirny Diamond Processing Center
1,300 miles Northeast of Irkutsk
Mirny, Siberian Republic of Yakut-Sakha (formerly Yakutia)
Russian Federation
2:37 A.M.

They approached like wraiths in the searing cold of the black Siberian night.

Without fear.

Without sound.

Without mercy.

Thirty members of the *Volki*—the Wolves—crept to the entrance of the Mirny diamond processing center on the outskirts of town where the lion's share of Russia's diamond yield was processed. Over ten million carats a year.

Thick fireproof jumpsuits protected the former Red Army's elite *Spetsnaz* commandos with synthetic fiber mesh. Helmets and breathing apparatus protected their eyes and lungs. They removed the Baigish night vision gear that had washed the darkened compound in an eerie green glow during their approach. Armed with titanium knives and flamethrowers, they now lay flat against the Siberian permafrost and awaited their leader's signal.

Ulianov waved a luminescent stick. One of the commandos responded by squirting a stream of liquid onto the ground. The substance reacted almost instantly with the chemical sprayed over the compound minutes before by gliders, unleashing a firestorm. Flames leapt hundreds of feet into the air. Balls of fire engulfed wood buildings whole. Vehicles exploded. Following Ulianov's second signal, a series of Semtex charges exploded and shattered the armored entrance gate.

Befuddled guards screamed in crazed flight from matchstick barracks. Guards who moments before sat and shivered in their frigid entrance pillbox yelled in short-lived deliria, rolled on the frozen ground, trying to extinguish the flames that tore at their flesh. The Volki stormed past them all.

A pack of six Volki reached the natural gas supply lines elevated above the impenetrable permafrost. Soon, additional Semtex charges exploded, cracking the heavy metal tubes like so much brittle glass, sending their cargo into a fireball hundreds of feet into the glacial air.

Four simultaneous offensives hammered the barracks strategically located at each of the four cardinal points of the compound. Another pack of Volki stood guard at the entrance gate, engulfing escaping guards in fire with flamethrowers.

The Volki splintered the doors of the four barracks with swift kicks, sprayed their prey with inflamed gel from flamethrowers, most members of the half-naked garrison too stunned to react. The maelstrom asphyxiated screams and lives as it devoured oxygen.

Several guards in the barracks valiantly brandished Kalashnikov AKSU-47 submachine guns resting near their cots. Most were immersed in baths of inflamed gel before they could squeeze off a single round at the strangely masked enemy blurred by the turbulent heat. A few courageous young guards in the eastern barracks managed to switch off their safeties, shove their selector levers into full automatic position, and pepper several Volki with a half dozen rounds before they succumbed to the flamethrowers. One of the plastic-encapsulated 5.45 millimeter steel core rounds found its target in the cranium of one of the Volki. His finger muscles contracted, pulling back the flamethrower trigger. Flames enveloped two of his comrades, quickly dissolving the fibers of their mesh suits. They rolled on the ground to extinguish the flames, but their movements ceased before their comrades could drag them clear of the burning structure.

In the western barracks, an alert young officer emptied an entire magazine of nine-millimeter rounds from his Stechkin handgun into an unsuspecting Volki's chest. He slammed another magazine into the gun and was about to continue his attack when another Volki slit his throat from behind. The guards in the other barracks met similar fates.

Although pockets of resistance erupted, the guards were no

match for the Volki's training and the element of surprise. The devastating attack was over almost immediately after it began. The Volki reassembled and counted off. They could not allow a single trace of the attack to remain. They recovered all their dead. Although the civilian work force had returned home hours earlier, guards could have sought refuge in the diamond processing and storage buildings. Though it was only a matter of minutes before the compound's flames would decrease sufficiently for the town's emergency teams to enter, the processing and storage structures had to be searched.

Upon Ulianov's signal, twenty Volki rushed into the diamond processing plant. Unlike the cheaply erected barracks, it was constructed of steel-reinforced concrete. Bunkerlike, it was badly charred but unharmed by the searing flames. The Volki split into smaller packs, wound through the maze of corridors. All seemed empty as they neared the pens that held the uncut diamonds. They could see hundreds of thousands of carats of dull white diamond roughs in piles behind armored padlocked fences. Suddenly, the contingent was met with a barrage of rounds from Makarov handguns. Two Volki were killed instantly and fell to the ground. The other three scrambled for cover behind the concrete corner. They threatened the defending guards with bursts from their flamethrowers but could not use them. Doing so would incinerate the room and evidence the attack. One Volki unclipped a small canister from his belt, twisted its top, flung it along the ground at the defending guards, and ran for cover. The two other Volki mimicked their comrade, dragged the injured to safety. Within seconds, the diamond pens filled with a cloud of gas. Unlike their colleagues, the defending guards were unconscious when they were dragged out of the bunker and set aflame. Breathing apparatus firmly in place, the Volki reentered the storage area now free from defending guards. In others less trained and less motivated, the temptation to grab million-dollar handfuls of diamonds would be great. The former Spetsnaz commandos were fanatically disciplined. They left the diamond pens untouched, busied themselves with the removal of the guards' shell casings from the floor. To the Volki's advantage, none of the rounds had lodged in concrete.

Ulianov signaled a full retreat as the wail of sirens pierced the din of the inferno. The Volki sprayed fire on a swath of ground thirty feet wide and retreated over it as a convoy of fire trucks, ambulances, and militia vehicles converged on the Mirny diamond processing compound.

Carrying dead and injured comrades, the Volki jogged to two military personnel trucks a mile distant. As the trucks sped away into the night, headlights off, the commandos peeled off their insulation suits, drank liters of sodium-laced water to counter the massive dehydration suffered during the raid, and changed into Russian military uniforms.

Ulianov looked at his watch. The entire operation had lasted only six minutes.

Perfect. Molotok would be pleased.

At precisely 2:45 A.M. local Mirny time, a United States National Reconnaissance Office (NRO) 8X satellite traveled through the Van Allen radiation belts in orbit thousands of miles above the darkened face of the Earth's Eastern hemisphere. A result of years of Strategic Defense Initiative research and a $1.5 billion development budget, the satellite had evolved from the "Keyhole" KH-12. Unlike its older brother, the twenty-ton 8X provided intricate detail and live digital information return of areas as wide as one thousand miles. More important was that the 8X detected infrared radiation—heat. Each object has a specific temperature colder or warmer than its ambient environment. By measuring relative heat, the satellite could pinpoint nearly any object, even in complete darkness. Because heat signatures did not vanish immediately, the 8X infrared detectors viewed the position of objects even after they had moved.

The 8X could view the past in the black of night.

3 BILLIONAIRE

Castel MacLean
Beverly Hills, California
8:30 A.M.

Maximillian MacLean, billionaire founder and owner of MacLean Inc., a global food concern, swept out of his palatial bedroom, enveloped in a robe of deep blue silk. While generally men of his wealth were passionate only about acquiring yet more wealth and power, MacLean was occupied by an entirely different passion. It was the central focus of his existence, the meaning in his life, the fire in his soul. He was obsessed with it.

Beauty.

Though his name no longer betrayed the fact, Maximillian MacLean had come into the world as the son of Don Giancarlo Innocenti, one of the last of the great American mafia dons, the *uomini di rispetto*—men of respect. Unlike other dons, who continued to believe the American branch of the Cosa Nostra, its lavish lifestyle and free reign would grow forever, Giancarlo Innocenti had detected the subtle winds of change. Despite the mafia's cooperation with the American government during Operation Underworld in World War II, when in exchange for leniency—and a blind eye to black marketeering—the American Cosa Nostra protected the mafia-controlled American ports against Axis saboteurs, helped the American Army find its way through the Sicilian countryside, and restored post-Mussolini order in the villages, and despite the mafia boom of the early '50s, Innocenti divined the organization's future. Amid the powerful families, his was the lone voice that predicted their fall at the hands of the federal government. As the other dons buried their heads in the sands of Las Vegas, Miami Beach, and Atlantic City, Giancarlo Innocenti prepared for the end.

First and foremost, Innocenti made sure to protect his only son. His family name could only harm his son's new life, so Don Innocenti gave him a new name: MacLean, which he pronounced "Mac-Lane." For Maximillian MacLean, no numbers, no prostitution, no drugs, no rackets, no violence, no murders. For him the finest schools in the East and England, the Church, ROTC, summers in Europe. For him charity work to learn humility. For him the gift of a legitimate business when he turned twenty-one: an Italian restaurant in Los Angeles at the very onset of the Italian food craze.

Until then, MacLean's life had been choreographed by his father. Soon thereafter, his father died. He was on his own. Maximillian became "Max." Although he knew more about history, classics, and table manners than about money and business, his father's blood flowed in his veins. As ordained by his father, Max forever gave up his family share in illegal activities. Yet he maintained channels of communication with the other families in the United States and the rest of the world. He did legal favors for the other families, and they did favors for him. As Max MacLean grew wealthy, he gave and accepted big favors. For this reason, and because he left his slice of the Cosa Nostra pie to the other families, they were pleased to oblige him.

As the Italian food craze intensified, with the patronage of his father's friends, Max's Italian restaurant became two, then three. He opened restaurants in other cities, other countries. Then came a café chain. Product licensing. Frozen foods. Import-export. Food transportation—domestic, then international. A local, national, international cooking school. A magazine. Websites. A television food channel. A gourmet spa. Then a hotel around it. Then several hotels. An Atlantic City casino—a legitimate one. Ever-increasing real estate holdings. Finally, his diversified food products company devoured others to dominate the market. In twenty years, MacLean had built a fortune. At forty, he married for the first time, to Claire Des Eaux, a beautiful and young French marine biologist. He shielded her from even the slightest knowledge of his past, and kept all his old family connections at bay. They looked forward to children.

Svelte and tall, with a patrician aquiline nose, an accent halfway between the East Coast and England reminiscent of Cary Grant's, and a quiet, self-assured manner, MacLean's appearance was more that of a senior European banker, a managing partner of an international law firm, or an Ivy League university president than the son of a mafia don.

After a few moments of sartorial reflection in his warehouse-sized dressing closet, MacLean selected a three-button, solid navy Brioni suit, a light blue Charvet French-cuffed shirt, a deep blue Etro tie, and black Gucci loafers with shiny silver buckles. He chose slightly eccentric red and blue–lacquered gold cufflinks in the form of bees—the symbol of Napoléon—and the subdued elegance of a roman-numeraled Chaumet Aquila watch.

Satisfied with his regal appearance in the stand-up mirror, MacLean turned and descended the brushed aluminum and frosted glass spiral staircase, trailing the 1930s scent of Acqua di Parma. Dan Wenzel, his lawyer, paced in the vast entry hall below, puffing on his tenth cigarette of the morning.

"Ah, Dan." He consulted his watch. "Always early."

They shook hands. "Morning, Max. Thanks for seeing me on short notice."

"Good God, man. You sound as though I'm doing you a favor. You're the one with the diamonds. Come on up."

They ascended to the second floor, walked down a black marble hallway, and emerged in an antique Italianate room with a shiny marble bar. Floor-to-ceiling plate glass windows provided a panoramic vista of Beverly Hills below.

MacLean walked behind the bar, leaned back against a rack of dusty claret bottles. "So, Dan. What's all this excitement about diamonds?"

Wenzel, curly haired, large but not muscular, propped himself up on a black leather barstool, lit another John Player Special cigarette, and squinted in concentration behind his oval wire-rimmed glasses. "Here's the story. Two days ago I went to the South to finalize the leases on the restaurants in Tennessee and Mississippi. I could have sent an associate, but I needed the break."

MacLean nodded.

Wenzel smiled. "Don't worry. I charged you the associate rate."

"I don't doubt it." As opposed to his father's lawyers, Wenzel was a straight arrow. His honesty was legendary in California's legal and business communities.

"I was flying around in a tiny twin engine jobbie, on my way from Texarkana to Little Rock. The plane developed a glitch, and the pilot landed at this tiny airstrip in Murfreesboro. Ever hear of the place?"

"Never."

"It's a one-stoplight town about a hundred miles south of Little Rock. About fifty miles from where Bill Clinton was born." Wenzel exhaled a puff of smoke. "The pilot says it's going to be a couple of hours, so I head for the nearest restaurant. Hamburgers, chili. That type of thing."

MacLean flinched. "I can imagine." His lips tightened.

"So I sit down and order a burger. Have a beer and a smoke. Big blondie waitress with a beehive hairdo says there's a phone call for me. The pilot tells me it's going to take another couple of hours. Fuel line problem. I decide to watch some TV at this old bar next to the restaurant. It's dark, only one person in the place besides the bartender. An older guy in overalls, Theodore Osage. He's a little trashed, but coherent. I order a beer. This bass fishing show comes on TV. Well, you know how I love fishing."

MacLean wrinkled his nose. "Indeed."

"Well it turns out this guy loves fishing too. We started talking. After a few more beers—man, could he drink—we're on a first-name basis. I ask him what he's doing all alone in this bar in the middle of the day. He tells me he's a farmer and the bank is foreclosing on his land. I asked him how much he owed. He says two thousand dollars. A lousy two thousand bucks, Max! So I give him some tips about what he can do to stall the foreclosure. He asks me if I want to see his place. Great for bass fishing, he says, jabbing me in the ribs. It's seven miles north on a river near this lake. I don't know why, but I'm completely taken by this old guy. Against all better judgment, I get into his truck and we drive up there."

"You're nuts."

"I know. I just had this urge. We bonded, I guess."

"Bonding over a bass fishing show," MacLean taunted.

"We get out there, and it's nothing like what I expected. It's gorgeous. A cabin. Some farm land. A kind of lake or pond. None of the rusting hulks of cars in the backyard type of stuff

I had expected in the rural South. About a hundred acres total. I fell in love with the place."

"And?"

"I offered Osage two thousand bucks for an option to buy the entire place, and he gets to keep living there."

"Very civil of you. Now—"

"No, no. As it turns out, very civil of him. Here's where it gets interesting." He leaned forward. "Osage was thrilled I put up the money, said he knew I was doing it just to be nice and that it was great to see a young city slicker like me had enough values to care about old timers like him—his words exactly. So I cut him a check. I was going to draft a contract, but he said his word was his bond. You know the type."

"I thought we were extinct."

Wenzel agreed with a nod. "Osage hands me an old survey done in the 1920s by a team of government geologists that included some of his land. Apparently, they concluded that the area contained a large diamond deposit."

MacLean smiled. "Diamonds in Arkansas?"

"Osage's father was one of the geologists. He disappeared in 1932, a few years after mining stopped cold, supposedly after a visit by a South African diamond corporation. Never found him. Osage thinks his father was killed because he knew the land had diamond deposits and refused to keep quiet. Later Osage found his father's copy of the geological report. He was terrified of the people who killed his father so he never mined the land. Some random mining occurred nearby, but in 1952, an area south of Osage's land was turned into a tourist attraction. In 1972, the land was purchased by the State of Arkansas. Today it's called the Crater of Diamonds State Park. Osage said he wanted me to know everything about the land since I had been so nice helping him out."

"What about this park?"

"A tourist attraction. I contacted the park. Apparently you pay a fee to enter the property and can keep any diamonds you find. No machine tools allowed. Only about six hundred carats of small diamonds are found there each year."

"Small potatoes."

"I knew you'd say that. But look at these." Wenzel reached into his pocket, let three small stones fall on the bar top.

MacLean leaned over, pushed them around with a manicured finger, picked one up, held it up to the bright halogen beam, then examined the other two. "Beautiful." Each stone was the size of a coffee bean, uncut, but its glow announced that in the hands of an adept diamond cutter the stone would yield an attractive jewel. Perhaps two.

"Where did you get these diamonds?"

"Osage gave them to me after I cut him the check. They're from his land. He showed me where."

MacLean replaced the stone on the bar top. "But you don't own the land, just have an option to buy it later."

"That's the great part. Osage will let us mine. Right now. That's why he gave me the geological report. Here's the deal, Max. You develop the mine. I do the legal work." He extinguished the cigarette and smiled. "Merry Christmas, Gatsby."

MacLean stared at his lawyer, again amazed at the man's loyalty. "You could have kept quiet, developed the mine for yourself."

"No," he shook his head. "I was in Arkansas on your dime. It would be unethical to keep this deal for myself." He lit another cigarette. "Besides, I'm a lawyer, not a businessman."

"As always, I'm amazed by your sense of ethics, but the legal work isn't enough. If we do this, you'll get a percentage of the profits." Wenzel was about to protest, but MacLean held up his hand. "I insist."

"Thanks," Wenzel whispered, thinking of the glee of his greedy law partners, with whom his partnership agreement required he share such a profit—technically, a legal fee.

"What are we talking about, in carats?"

"About 250,000 carats a year. But remember, that's from a 1920s report, based on 1920s mining technology. With today's equipment, it's got to be way more."

Far more than dollar signs, MacLean imagined the thousands of beautiful diamonds coming out of the Arkansas mine. "Did Osage give you a copy of the report?"

Wenzel removed a folded piece of paper from his coat pocket. "Right here. It's a photocopy of the copy Osage's father made." The print was small, faded, but still legible. MacLean and Wenzel leaned over the photocopied report and read in silence. At times, it was difficult for the two laymen to understand the meaning of the geologic terminology. *Intrusive peridotite. Volcanic breccia. Tuff and fine-grained breccia.* The terms were Greek to them, but it was clear there were diamond deposits on Osage's land.

MacLean looked up. "You think it's legit? Not a con?"

"Believe me, I've thought about it. Ordinarily, there's no way I'd buy it. However," he began to count off on his fingers, "when you consider the history of the area, the fact diamonds were mined there in the 1920s, the fact there's a state park next door that produces diamonds, the fact Osage showed me the report after—not before—I gave him the two thousand bucks, it seems to add up."

MacLean stared at Wenzel for several moments, flashed a broad smile. "When do we start mining?"

4 CASE

Main Justice Building
Washington, D.C.
8:07 A.M.

Carlton arrived early and found a slim file bucket marked *U.S. v. Murfreesboro Mining Corporation, Raymond Mines, et al* on his chair.

Stalin's diamond case.

He reclined in the brown cracked leather chair. Outside, thick gray clouds jockeyed in front of a pale winter sun. Carlton clicked on his battered green glass-and-brass lamp. Photocopies of statutes and cases, memo pads filled with hand-written questions for direct and cross-examination of witnesses, and scribbled notes on yellow stickies stared back at him from every nook and cranny of his desk, forcing him to face the fact Jarvik had destroyed the *Global Steel* case. His case.

The jerk.

Carlton cleared his desk of all paperwork related to *Global Steel* before turning his attention to the new file. He removed the manila folders from the bucket, each stamped by the file department to keep the file organized. Notes and Memoranda. Correspondence. Legal research. Background.

To Carlton, a diamond was a sparkling stone, necessary precursor to a couple's engagement. He was surprised that his thoughts strayed to Erika and quickly forced them back on track. He still pined for the *Global Steel* case. Now that was an antitrust case. A huge conglomerate cornering the market on industrial steel, the raw material of the American industrial juggernaut.

But wishing would not bring *Global Steel* back, and he had a job to do. He selected the file marked "Background" and read the U.S. Attorney Office's interview of Jim Higgins, the man who had brought the case to light. Carlton sighed and started to read.

The Raymond Mines company was owned by the Raymonds, an elderly couple who lived near Murfreesboro, Arkansas. Their ten-year-old grandson fell in a ditch at the edge of their farm and found a strange stone in the mud, which he showed Raymond. Raymond compared the stone to pictures in a handbook on minerals and gems. According to the book, the stone was a diamond. Still in doubt, Raymond asked the advice of Jim Higgins, a local geologist, who confirmed that the stone was in fact a diamond. Raymond hired a few local men who dug several deep holes near the ditch where the stone had been found. The dirt was washed through a sieve and some garnets—diamond indicator stones—and then a few small diamonds were discovered. Reasoning that the diamonds had to have broken off of a main diamond deposit through erosion, Higgins recommended that borings be performed. One boring eventually led to the suspected diamondiferous kimberlite pipe. A solid citizen, Raymond easily obtained local mining permits and a line of credit from his bank. After three months, the operation began to produce approximately two hundred carats per month, with Higgins as a supervising partner. Almost all of the diamond roughs were industrial quality stones, mostly yellowish in color.

Four months after the mine's opening, a man named Mr. Lester visited the Raymonds. Lester stated that he was a lawyer who represented the Murfreesboro Mining Corporation, a large mining concern out of Murfreesboro. Lester offered to purchase the Raymonds' land, but the Raymonds refused, because their farm had been in the family since before the Civil War. Lester then offered to purchase the Raymonds' entire diamond production. The Raymonds again refused out of concern that Murfreesboro Mining Corporation would impose quantity and quality requirements on the mine. Finally, Lester offered to pay the Raymonds $3 million not to mine any diamonds. The Raymonds agreed, considering the proposal profitable and free from effort.

The Raymonds offered Higgins $1 million as a fee for discontinuing operations. Higgins did not like the offer. His long-term profit was greater than $1 million. And as the mine manager with twenty employees working under him, he had found a renewed purpose in his career. But the Raymonds were adamant about closing the mine, which, after all, was on their land. Higgins called his son-in-law, an attorney in Little Rock, who informed him that the agreement between the Raymonds and the Murfreesboro Mining Corporation was probably illegal under federal antitrust laws.

Higgins informed the Raymonds. The Raymonds contacted Lester, who convinced them that the transaction was not illegal in any way. On that basis, the Raymonds refused to rescind their agreement with Murfreesboro Mining Corporation. Higgins threatened to litigate. Higgins' son-in-law filed a complaint with the U.S. Attorney in Little Rock. The U.S. Attorney's Office interviewed Higgins, but was overloaded and pushed the case up to DOJ's Antitrust Division in D.C., where the information filtered up to Gail Rothenberg, deputy assistant attorney general for Antitrust.

Carlton stared at his scant notes and sifted through the rest of the thin file. "That's it?" He needed more information. He found a number in his electronic Rolodex, dialed.

"Josh Stein," the familiar voice answered.

"Josh? Pat Carlton."

"Patty boy! Long time no hear, buddy. What's up at Justice?"

They had gone through law school together. Stein had opted for the government track directly, and had recently been ordained senior trial attorney at the Securities and Exchange Commission. "I can't stand the sandbox politics."

"Welcome to government service. Listen, we should get together soon, but right now I'm swamped."

"Sorry to catch you at a bad time. I was calling to see if you could dig up some background on a corporation."

"*No problemo*." Carlton heard him rummaging papers. "Shoot."

After obtaining Stein's assurance he would keep the conversation confidential, Carlton thumbnailed the few facts he knew about Murfreesboro Mining Corporation.

"Get back to you A-S-A-P."

"Thanks, Josh."

Carlton stared at his notes. There would be depositions, expert witnesses to interview, but it seemed rather cut and dry. He clicked off his brass desk lamp and was thrust into near total darkness. As his eyes adjusted to the dim glow from streetlights outside, he stumbled to find his scarf and wool overcoat on the hat rack. In the hall, he shoved the key in the lock under the old door handle and secured his little cave, hoping against reason it would keep Jarvik out, knowing such security was an illusion.

Carlton lay on his sofa at home, reading the *Washington Post* and smoking a CAO L'Anniversaire maduro when the black 1930s-style telephone rang. He turned down Frank Sinatra before picking up.

"Pat Carlton."

"Pat. It's Josh. I've got your info."

"That was quick."

"The SEC aims to please."

"Apparently. Shoot."

"It's a bit convoluted, even by SEC standards. As you suspected, Murfreesboro Mining Corporation is incorporated in Arkansas. Apparently in good standing. Seems clean. No litigation pending or on the books. Current on their taxes. Up to date on all their filings at SEC and in Arkansas. One class of stock. Capitalization of about thirty million. Five mil of debt."

"So they're solvent. Good. I was afraid they'd be a shell corp." Carlton scribbled notations on a yellow memo pad.

"Sounds legit, but it gets complicated from there."

"How's that?"

"Murfreesboro Mining is owned by Hamilton Mines Incorporated, incorped in Delaware. Seems to be a holding company for a few mining concerns in Arkansas and Alaska. Their stock is controlled by Stone Holdings Inc., also out of Delaware. Stone Holdings also owns an Arkansas real estate company and part of an Arkansas savings and loan called Little Rock S&L. It nearly went bust in the late '80s, but somehow got saved and seems to be in good standing now. Their stock is wholly owned by an outfit called Cleveland Metals Inc., also incorped in Delaware. All have only one class of stock except for Cleveland Metals. Quite a maze if you ask me."

"Sure is."

"My opinion is worth exactly what you're paying for it, but I think it's pretty bizarre to create a solvent entity on the bottom of such a stack of corporation pancakes for a small mining outfit. Even if it is violating antitrust laws."

"Stranger things have happened."

"True. I'll fax you what I have."

"Great. Love to Elizabeth."

Murfreesboro Mining was legit and solvent. Unless Murfreesboro Mining filed for bankruptcy protection, which did not appear likely, the company could pay damages to DOJ. That was all Carlton needed to know, but Josh did have a point. The corporate maze seemed overly complicated for comfort. Even for a deliberate antitrust violator.

Stalin's words rang in his ears. "Just get a settlement and move on." That's exactly what he'd do.

"Open and shut," he said out loud.

5 THREATS

Shaughnessy, McGuire & Wenzel LLP
Century Park East
Century City, California
1:37 P.M.

As a name partner of Shaughnessy, McGuire & Wenzel LLP, Dan Wenzel rated a corner office on the thirty-fifth floor of the law firm's granite and glass building. He faced the floor-to-ceiling tinted plate glass window, hands thrust deep into the pockets of his navy-blue-suit trousers suspended by black and burgundy braces. He sipped his after-lunch espresso and surveyed the expansive greens of the Los Angeles Country Club golf course below. Golf addicts arrayed in the gaudiness of pale yellows, baby blues, and contrived plaids dotted the course, antlike when seen from his privileged height.

Since his meeting with MacLean, Wenzel had applied himself to the Arkansas diamond venture fervently. He'd formed a new company for MacLean, purchased the land from Osage, recorded a deed to MacLean's new company, and signed a $1 a year lease with Osage that allowed the farmer to live on the land until his death. He contracted with a trusted geological consultant to draw up preliminary mining and environmental impact plans with the express proviso of complete secrecy until the necessary public hearings. He obtained an application from Macon Grove City Hall for a mining permit, which he was currently filling out with the consultant's help. The geological consultant was also performing a boring survey of the deposits. Judging the operation too secret at the moment, Wenzel held off negotiating a line of credit to finance the mine's initial development. For now, MacLean would have to use his own considerable funds.

Things were going smoothly, he thought, finishing the contents of his lilliputian espresso cup. The intercom beeped loudly as he ensconced himself in his soft leather swivel chair.

Gertrude bellowed from outside the closed doors of his office, where she stood guard duty. "A Geraldine Forest on line one. From the National Trust for Historic Preservation in Washington, D.C."

Wenzel stabbed at the button next to the flashing light.

"Dan Wenzel."

"Mr. Wenzel, my name is Geraldine Forest. I'm with the National Trust for Historic Preservation in Washington." Not a hint of warmth in her hard voice, Ms. Forest sounded like she might be a lawyer.

"Good afternoon."

"I'll come right to it, Mr. Wenzel. The Trust has learned that one of your clients intends to conduct mining operations in Murfreesboro, Arkansas."

"Mining, you say?" How the heck had the Trust found out so quickly? MacLean's new company name was on the deed, but how had they learned about the mining? They hadn't discussed the mining with Macon Grove or even filed the mining permit application.

"I don't know if you are aware of this, sir, but the property is a historic site. No mining can be allowed on the property."

Wenzel's due diligence of the property had not revealed any historical status.

"I don't recall the property being listed in the National Historic Register, or any state or local list of historic properties, for that matter."

"Well, it's not actually listed, but it qualifies for listing."

"I see." He didn't. "How so, if you don't mind my asking?"

"The property has very important ties to our nation's history, Mr. Wenzel," she said, in a tone that made it sound as though even a first-grader would have known.

"It does? Don't tell me you found Jimmy Hoffa."

Not as much as a snicker. "The site played a key role in the Civil War."

"Really? I had no idea." Not at all. "Exactly what role did this land play during the Civil War, if you don't mind my asking?"

"The Confederate Army used the land in 1864."

"Used? You mean a fort? Like at Valley Forge during the Revolutionary War?"

"Not exactly, no."

"Well what connection—exactly—did the Confederate Army have with my client's land?"

"Confederate soldiers camped on the land during the Civil War."

"Camped? That's it? No fort? No battlefield?"

"That is correct."

"And the Trust is going to try to prevent mining on my client's land because a bunch of soldiers made a campfire over a hundred years ago?"

"Yes."

"You've got to be joking."

"I assure you, I am not."

"I've got to hand it to you. You've got chutzpah."

"Pardon me?"

"*Chutzpah*, Ms. Forest. *Chutzpah*. Yiddish for 'guts'." Chutzpah nothing. Something was not kosher here. "Do you realize how ridiculous this is? A fort or battlefield I understand. But a campsite? Do you have any idea how many square miles of land were marched on and camped on by soldiers during the Civil War? Almost every plot of land from Massachusetts to South Carolina. Do you intend to make the entire eastern U.S. a historical preserve? It's absurd."

"Nonetheless, sir, we must list the land as a historic site. It's…it's our duty."

"And it's my duty to inform you, Ms. Forest, that listing by your group does not in any way bar development on private land. Good day."

He slammed the handset into the receiver and stared at it, fuming.

Gertrude beeped his intercom at nearly the exact same time on the following day. "A Roger Mackie from the Bureau of Land Management in D.C."

Oy. Wenzel punched the flashing green light. "Dan Wenzel."

"Good afternoon, sir. Roger Mackie with the Bureau of Land Management at the Department of the Interior in Washington, D.C." One heck of a long intro. "How are you this afternoon?"

"You tell me," Wenzel said.

Mackie ignored the ribbing. "Let me come directly to the point, sir. The records in Pike County, Arkansas, list your client Mr. MacLean's company as the owner of a parcel of land that adjoins the Little Missouri River south of the Narrows Dam and south of Lake Greeson."

"I think that's correct, yes."

"Good. The records are correct, then. You have no idea how many of these county records are all topsy-turvy," he chuckled, a dry, forced sound.

"I can imagine."

"Yes, well, records are important because BLM has to notify all adjoining landowners whenever it redesignates a river."

"Redesignates a river? I'm afraid you've lost me."

"Are you familiar with the Wild and Scenic Rivers Act?"

"Never heard of it." A small fib, really.

"The Act protects rivers from pollution."

"I see. And?"

"There are three possible designations for rivers under the Act. The BLM has jurisdiction over the Little Missouri River adjacent to your client's land in Pike County and can designate the river as a wild river, a scenic river, or a recreational river.

"Almost all activity whatsoever is prohibited on wild rivers. The designation as a scenic river allows a certain amount of activity. Recreational rivers are preserved, except for recreational use."

"I see. And into what category does the BLM intend to list the Little Missouri River?"

"As a wild river, of course."

"Of course." He refrained from anger and craved a cigarette—illegal in his building. "Well that certainly sounds like a wonderful idea. Thank you for informing me. My client will be delighted to hear that he can look forward to pollution-free fishing in the river. He's a big fisherman, you know. Very serious about it. I can't wait to call him." Having befuddled Mackie into several seconds of silence was satisfying, more satisfying than ranting.

"You're…you're not upset about the designation?"

"Upset? Why should I be? Thanks to you, my client's land will increase in value. People pay a premium for pollution-free water and fishing, you know."

"Yes, but…but that designation will prevent your client from obtaining a waste discharge permit…for his mining operations."

Now it was Wenzel who was reduced to silence. He suddenly remembered crazy old Osage's story about his father being murdered by the government. The tall tale had just shrunk to credible size. He recovered quickly. "Of course, but my client will accept an additional cost. If necessary, he will be pleased to keep the water pure and pristine by simply disposing waste elsewhere than in the river. Is that satisfactory to BLM?"

Mackie's stammering evidenced his shock. "Why…maybe. I don't know."

"Excellent. Good day, Mr. Mackie." He replaced the handset in its cradle.

What the hell? First the NTHP. Now the BLM. And there was still the specter of Osage's father. What's next?

The intercom buzzed mid-morning for the third day in a row.

"Mr. Wenzel. A woman named Perry Trask is on the telephone. Says she's from some group in Arkansas and it's urgent." Gertrude's voice was a rock in the storm. Where would he be without her?

He jabbed at the telephone line. "Dan Wenzel."

"Mr. Wenzel, Perry Trask. Counsel for MRPG, the Mineral Rights Protection Group of Arkansas."

Her voice was cold, nasal, with a complete absence of Southern drawl.

They must be recruiting Bostonians to protect the Arkansas environment. "Pardon me. The Mineral Rights what?"

"Protection Group. The Mineral Rights Protection Group. MRPG for short."

"Forgive me, ma'am, but I've never heard of your group."

"Quite simply, we oppose mining."

"All mining?"

"Particularly open-pit mining. We are an ideological organization. We believe minerals have rights. Like animals and plants. Inalienable rights."

It was just too much for Wenzel. "Really? Do they have the right to vote? That would give a whole new meaning to 'Rock the Vote'." He chuckled.

She ignored the barb. "We discovered you were going to mine the land below Lake Greeson. We cannot allow such action. Arkansas has already been devastated by poor environmental policy. We cannot—we will not—allow this to continue."

"I see."

"We are a radical organization. We don't deny this. We will do whatever is necessary to stop your client from mining." A bit like Mackie the day before, but more on edge. More willing to do something…illegal.

"Is that a threat, Ms. Trask? Are you threatening my client?"

"No, of course not. I'm merely being courteous in giving you some advice."

"Advice that sounds like a threat."

"Of course, we are more than willing to litigate the issue. And as you know, litigation has a way of tolling mining permits. Litigation and…other actions."

"I see. Then perhaps you can answer a question for me."

"Yes?"

"How is it that seventy-two hours after a deed is recorded for the purchase of a property remarkably similar to a thousand other properties in Arkansas, your completely unknown organization contacts the owner's attorney directly after a pathetic series of failed efforts by the NTHP and the BLM to stop any mining. Care to cut the bullshit and fill me in on what's going on here, exactly?"

"I don't have a duty to explain how our group operates. The fact is your client did purchase the land, the deed was recorded as a public document, and our group virulently opposes mining. Please take this as notice, advice, warning, or any other way you wish. Good afternoon, Mr. Wenzel."

Wenzel slammed the handset into its cradle for the third day in a row and walked to the plate glass window. A faint drizzle descended on Los Angeles. He recalled Theodore Osage's ramblings about how his father was murdered when he tried to go public with information about Arkansas diamonds and shivered.

Dressed in black tie, white Pal Zileri dinner jacket with matching black slacks and black suede Gucci loafers, MacLean again found Wenzel pacing the green marble floor, black Taiga Louis Vuitton attaché case firmly clutched in his right hand. "Good God, man. Don't you have a home? You're always here." His smile tightened as he noticed the worried lines on Wenzel's face.

Wenzel stared through his spectacles at MacLean. "Something's very wrong, Max. I'm completely stumped. I have absolutely no idea what these people want. I've held my own in vicious negotiations for as long as I can remember. I've always understood the other side's motivations, however unreasonable. But I just don't get this. Why do these people want to stop a diamond mining operation? It's not for environmental reasons. There are other mines nearby, ore for example, and the geological consultant tells me we can build the mine without much of an impact on the environment anyway."

MacLean ushered him into a pale green suede Roche Bobois sofa in one of Castel MacLean's many salons.

"But you know what the real quirk is?"

MacLean eyed Wenzel, played with his blue diamond cufflink.

"The first two calls were from the National Trust for Historic Preservation and the Bureau of Land Management, the third some loony new age environmental group that actually threatened us. I had one of my associates check them out. The ink on their nonprofit incorporation papers is still wet. Whoever they are, I think it's safe to assume they were pulled in by the feds."

"That goes without saying."

Wenzel grasped a cigarette between index and middle finger, smoothed his red and blue tie. "So why haven't the state authorities said anything? Arkansas may not be number one on the list of environmentally conscious states, but if the feds are so riled up, you'd think the state and local authorities would have something to say."

"Quite. But I don't understand why the feds are even interested. The operation will create jobs, bring capital into the local economy. God knows Arkansas needs it. It won't pollute, no matter what the environmentalists say."

"And," Wenzel said, "it's not as though there aren't any diamond mines in Arkansas. That Crater of Diamonds State Park right next door brings more people into the area than this mine ever would." He gestured wildly with his cigarette, exhaled. "After all, it's the locals who have to approve this—not the feds—and they have every interest in opening a mine."

MacLean nodded. He'd seldom seen Wenzel wound this tight.

"Problem is, I haven't heard peep out of them. Not like I haven't tried. I've called everyone down there. Planning. Building and safety. The city council. The mayor's office. No one is ever in. They won't talk to me at all."

"What about the seller?"

"Osage?"

"Have we asked him about this? After all, he's the one who told us about the diamonds in the first place. He lives there. Maybe he let the information leak."

Wenzel shook his head, pushed back his unruly hair. "No. I don't think so. He's still obsessed with his big diamond conspiracy theory, convinced it goes back to his father. He only told me after I agreed to buy his land."

"I don't believe in conspiracy theories. They're simplistic."

"Neither do I, Max. But let me tell you, this just might make a convert of me." He crushed out his cigarette and reclined. "Maybe I'll get answers if I go down there and snoop around."

"In a small town like that, you'll only generate more suspicion, shut them off. Why not attack the problem head-on?"

"What do you suggest?"

"Instead of asking questions, get them on our side. If the feds want to give us a hard time, fine. They're pretty much immune to local sentiment about a diamond mine. No one's going to lose their job in D.C. because of one less business in Macon Grove. Ultimately, the decision is up to the local residents, their local representatives. If we can sell them on the idea, we can bypass the problems with the feds. The locals are going to want this mine. Unemployment is too high down there for them to pass up this project, no matter what Washington thinks. And you know how much Southern locals like the feds."

Maxfield, MacLean's English butler, set two espresso cups painted dark blue with small lemons on the coffee table in front of them. Wenzel lifted one tiny cup with his large hand and drained its contents.

"Tell the local residents the truth. Tell them that we're going to hire and train local labor, offer good benefits, share profits, the whole nine yards. Tell them we'll set up an environmental preserve in the area, clean up some land. Heck, it's only fair. Crunch some numbers. Get a petition going so the local authorities take stock of what their electorate thinks. Even if they're coerced by the feds, once they see the voters want a mine, they'll support the project and issue permits. Once the local residents get riled up, the federal government may not have the inclination to stop the mine."

"Might work. I'll give it a shot. Besides, it'll be good to see Osage again. Maybe he'll cook some more of his fried chicken."

MacLean winced. "On my end, I'll have a chat with Abe Cohen."

6 DEFENDANT

Carlton struggled to find the telephone receiver under the draft documents, memo pads, and federal case reporters that papered his desk. Remnants of the complaint against Murfreesboro Mining Corporation he had filed in Arkansas federal district court and served on the defendant the day before. Knowing that the government wouldn't recover much from the elderly Raymonds, and that the media would have a field day against DOJ if it sued them, he decided not to include them in the complaint, but sent them a copy so they could see what Mufreesboro Mining was doing.

He followed the trill and fished out the instrument milliseconds before voicemail cut in. "Pat Carlton."

"Mr. Carlton, Jonathan Black at Fox, Carlyle, Ashton, Chase, Whitfield & Whyte." A haughty nasal voice enunciated the entire string of name partners, then paused to allow the statement to impress Carlton. "In Manhattan."

Carlton immediately disliked him. Not because Black was hiding behind the name of his mega firm, not because he emphasized Manhattan to give Carlton notice that Black was a tough bastard, but because Fox, Carlyle had a well-founded reputation for unnecessarily litigious, scorched-earth, underhanded, and just plain unethical practices. He had dealt with Fox, Carlyle when he was with the Merchants of Pain. As far as Carlton was concerned, they were the devil, which should have tipped him off.

"Is that so? Well, what can I do for you, Jonathan Black of Fox, Carlyle, Ashton, Chase, Whitfield & Whyte in Manhattan?"

"Our firm represents the Murfreesboro Mining Company."

"I see." The fact that Fox, Carlyle represented Mufreesboro Mining automatically lowered Carlton's opinion of the defendant.

"We received your summons and complaint and wanted to discuss the possibility of settlement."

Carlton stood, stunned. *Already?* Instinct forced him to snap out of it. Knowing Fox, Carlyle, it was probably a prelude to a slimy trick. He decided to take the bait. "Great! I'm so pleased your client will save me a lot of work. I propose twenty million." The handset buzzed through a long pause. "Hello?"

"Twenty million?"

"Correct. I think it's a reasonable sum, don't you?"

"You're not serious."

"I am serious. Twenty million."

"No...I don't think so, Mr. Carlton. My client has only authorized me to offer a settlement of one million dollars. Far more than the case is worth."

Black had anticipated surprising Carlton with a quick settlement offer that he would have felt compelled to accept. But that had assumed Black made the opening offer, take it or leave it. If he had done so, $1 million would have appeared a generous settlement offer. Unrefusable, even. But Carlton beat him to it. Black hadn't counted on it. The young toughie was now perplexed.

"One million?" Carlton asked incredulously. "Oh come on, Jonathan. No. Listen, between you, me, and the wall, Justice is looking at this antitrust violation very carefully. *Very* carefully. My hands are tied. Department policy and all that jazz. Twenty million."

"But that's ridiculous. The maximum proscribed by the Sherman Act is ten million."

"Of course. But that's just the criminal portion of the statute. Remember, civil antitrust violations carry treble damages." Under the rule of treble damages, the amount of actual damages was multiplied threefold to discourage future violations. "Plus, criminal violations carry jail time."

"My client is a corporation. There can be no jail time."

"Corporate veils can be pierced. I'm certain that the Murfreesboro Mining Corporation has made some mistake with its corporate formalities or its capitalization that would convince the court to bring the individual principals to justice."

"It has not." As if he knew. "Regardless, twenty million is excessive. I cannot in good faith recommend such an amount to my client. It's simply excessive."

"I'm sorry to hear that," Carlton announced sadly, sitting down. "But if that's the way you feel, the United States will be happy to go to trial on this case." Jarvik may have told Carlton to settle, but Carlton had far more respect for Deputy AAG Rothenberg's opinion than his. "But that really wouldn't be good press for your client, especially now that the environmental crowd has begun to scrutinize your client's mining techniques," he pushed, having read that one of Murfreesboro Mining's parent companies recently was forced to clean up one of its former mines. "By the time all of this useless paperwork got investigated, researched, served, mailed, filed, and tried, your client would lose and be hit with treble damages. Not to mention your firm's massive legal fees. Is that what you want to recommend to your client?"

"But twenty million. It's simply too high. Too high."

Carlton sharpened his tone. The fact was, he didn't like Fox, Carlyle and he didn't like this weasel Black. The result was that he transferred all his rage concerning Jarvik and *Global Steel* against Murfreesboro Mining and Black. "Listen, Jonathan. This isn't personal. I have nothing against you personally. I'm certain you don't go around deceiving little old ladies into antitrust violations. But Murfreesboro Mining does. Your client, Mr. Black. Not mine."

"Now see here. My client never—"

"Let's just cut the crap, Jonathan." He jabbed at the air with his finger, as if Black could see him. "Your client is guilty. As sure as God made little green apples, your client is guilty of civil and criminal violations under the Sherman Act. Guilty of manipulating the free market. This case is about as open and shut as they come. I know that, and you know that. We've both seen the evidence," he bluffed. The evidence was about as strong as wet toilet paper. "I'm sure you're a terrific attorney, Jonathan. After all, you're with Fox, Carlyle. In Manhattan. And I know you're supposed to push this settlement amount down to the lowest amount possible. But it won't wash. Not with me. Not with Justice. In addition to the fact your client conned an elderly couple—a particularly appetizing fact for jurors—your client interfered in the free market price of diamonds. The free market. The heart and soul of America. I'm sure most jurors have purchased an overpriced diamond engagement ring. Or didn't because they couldn't afford it. How do you think they're going to react to a defendant who helped keep the price of those shiny little rocks sky high?"

"I—"

"I'm reasonable. And so is Justice. Take your time. Discuss it with your client. I'm certain the Murfreesboro Mining Corporation will see the wisdom of the government's settlement offer."

Silence on the other end. "I'll call you back."

"I look forward to hearing from you."

Carlton stared at the telephone dumbfounded.

A settlement proposal only one day after serving the defendant? What was going on? His instinct told him there was something else here. What it was, he had no clue.

7 HELICOPTER

Ninety Miles West of Cuba
2:16 A.M.

"Damn this machine!" Leonid Pyashinev howled. "Can't it go any faster?"

"No, comrade," replied his pilot, Major Esposito of the Cuban Air Force. "We will be there soon. Have patien—"

"Patience? Don't talk to me about patience! I've been traveling for ten days! In cars and airplanes and boats and submarines! I have no more patience! Go faster, damn you!"

"The helicopter can only go so fast. I can't push it beyond its—"

"Push it, damn you! *Skoryie, skoryie!* Go faster!"

"It would be unwise."

"God damn you! *Skoryie!*"

"As you wish." Pompous Russian ass. *Hijo de puta.* Esposito swore under his breath as he forced the two throttles further into their metal grooves. The twin Allison turbines screamed overhead. Needles on backlit gauges crept into the red. An oil pressure warning light buzzed, immediately followed by another.

"One hundred sixty-two knots. We're going too fast. The engines can't handle it." Esposito switched off the alarms, gripped the stick with sweaty fingers.

In the passenger compartment, Pyashinev patted his sweaty forehead with a dirty handkerchief. After a journey of nearly ten thousand miles, he was beyond exhaustion. He panted with fear and nervous exhaustion, he peered through the large window of the compartment. Pitch darkness. Not a sliver of light on this cloudy night. He could see nothing. Not even whether they had reached the mainland. For a man who detested flying, it was not a reassuring thought.

He removed a creased cigarette nervously from a crumpled pack of Marlboros in his pocket. The flame from his lighter momentarily cast wild shadows about the padded cabin. He inhaled deeply. Just a little longer. Just a little longer and I will be rich.

A wicked smile curled on his lips. His expensive Italian double-breasted suit and the silk shirt under it could not mask the toll greed and fear and exhaustion had taken. Dark craters sagged under his gray eyes. Matted hair and a ten-day beard emphasized his haggard face. He smelled of sweat, of the urine he expelled during the takeoff and maneuverings of the fighter jet that had flown him out of Russia several days before. He shifted uneasily in his seat, hacked violently into a sweaty palm. Ash fell from the tip of the burning cigarette, drifted to the floor.

Rich. I will be rich. Just a little longer. Just a little—

The helicopter shuddered violently. Pyashinev was rammed against the hull. *"Shto eta?"* he shouted at Esposito. "What is it? What is happening?"

Esposito's arms and hands flailed crazily among the forest of switches. Then, as suddenly as it arrived, the turbulence ceased. The only sound that remained was of air that curled around the airframe in a high-pitched whine. It bored into the Russian's skull.

A second series of sirens wailed.

"Damn you, Major! What—"

"We've lost turbine two! And the rotor's leaking oil! It's going to—"

Blinding red lights flashed in the dark. Needles spun madly in their gauges.

"We've lost pressure on the rotor! *Madre de Dios!* We're going to crash! You fat Russian pig! We're going to crash!"

Esposito began to pray as he fought to steady the directional stick.

Pyashinev was paralyzed. Terror bolted him to his seat. Sweat trickled from his forehead and stung his eyes. His mind and body went numb. He could not even feel the stomach-churning loss of altitude. The numbness prevented any thought of using the parachute stowed under the seat, even if the helicopter had been high enough to use the contraption. Seconds later, amid deafening sounds that seemed very far away, Pyashinev plunged into unconscious darkness.

Pyashinev awoke in excruciating pain. His head throbbed wildly. His legs were broken. The pain assured him of that. His blurred vision and the darkness of the crash site made it difficult to discern anything in the interior of the cabin. He opened his mouth to suck in air. Blood and saliva splattered onto the floor below.

He stared at the sight for several seconds before understanding. His seat belt had kept him alive through the crash and now cradled him in a precarious hanging position above the floor and port side window of the helicopter. In pain, he lifted his head and looked toward the cockpit. Branches and trees grew where glass once stood as a barrier between pilot and sky. Major Esposito was dead. Of that Pyashinev was also certain. The human body simply could not remain in working condition contorted into the former pilot's position.

Pyashinev was nothing if not a realist. He would die as well. The hemorrhaging was simply too profuse to prevent it. Perhaps if there were an ambulance. Or a doctor. But there was no one. Nothing but the sounds of jungle fauna nearby. As a security precaution, the Russian had ordered the pilot to disconnect the helicopter's radio. Esposito would never have been able to send a distress call.

He would die on this miserable spot.

In pain.

In sin.

Alone.

He could feel the life ebbing from him now. With each wheeze of his injured lungs he felt less energy, more numbness. Though Pyashinev was an atheist, he experienced regret and guilt. The diamonds. The government would never find them without him.

With extreme difficulty, Pyashinev removed a pen from his pocket, tore a scrap of paper that hung from the ripped lining of the ceiling. For what seemed like hours, he scrawled letters on the paper, barely readable through his increasingly blurred vision.

Finished, he let the pen and note drop to the floor.

If there is a God, forgive me.

8 KREMLIN

The Kremlin
Moscow, Russia
5:25 P.M.

Russian President Vasili Illych Orlov observed the glacial Muscovite winter from the warm confines of his office in the distinctly Russian, yellow-and-white eighteenth-century building inside the Kremlin compound. The weak glow of the setting sun cast the frozen trees and the snow-capped crenelated walls in a golden hue.

Orlov turned his worried face away from the window, reached into an ornate lacquered box with thick fingers, and pulled out a cigarette. He lit it, reclined, and scanned his office, the eighteenth-century porcelain stove in the corner of the room reminding him of the tsars.

The tsars. No pollsters, approval ratings, or elections. Their word was law. In Russia today, law had little meaning. Law wasn't a rule anymore, merely a suggestion.

A loud knock sounded at the door.

"*Da.*" Orlov's mood improved when he saw his political aide peek through the heavy carved wood door. "Vladimir Petrovich. Come in, come in. *Sieditiest.* Sit down." It was his first smile of the day.

"I have good news." The thin man bore a look of happy urgency as he strode briskly toward Orlov. "As of this afternoon, the Mirny diamond processing plant is back on line. The main portion of the plant was made of concrete, so it was not harmed. Diamond shipments will resume shortly. As you ordered, Marshall Aleksakov has been promoted to commander of the Eastern Ground Forces. He is supervising the rebuilding and the replacement garrison." Orlov had ordered the promotion to replace Marshall Ogarkov, who had been found murdered along with his chauffeur one week earlier, in a bullet-riddled Mercedes on Moscow's frozen Tverskaya Prospekt.

"*Harasho*." Excellent. "I was worried. To have our largest diamond production center at a standstill during the negotiations with Waterboer would have been devastating. The South Africans are already stealing from us. It would have been an excellent excuse for that bastard Slythe to offer us an even lower price for our diamonds than Waterboer already pays." He blew a trail of smoke that billowed into a gray cloud. "Now if Kovanetz would only shed some light on Pyashinev's disappearance, we should be in good shape for the negotiations."

"He should be here at any moment."

The disappearance of Leonid Pyashinev bothered Orlov almost as much as the Mirny fire. Absent any demand for ransom by the *mafiya*, the man's disappearance did not make sense. Over a week had passed since his family had reported him missing. No one had heard from him since. If Pyashinev had been an ordinary citizen, such a disappearance would not have attracted much attention. But Leonid Pyashinev was no ordinary citizen. Pyashinev was the director of Komdragmet, the committee in charge of the Russian diamond industry. His disappearance was a serious matter.

Yet Orlov had not reached his present position of power without considering every crisis as an opportunity. Like many of the other Russian industries whose control—if not its ownership—Orlov had wrested from the oligarchs, he had wanted the Kremlin to assume control of the diamond, other gems, and metals industries. Until now it had been politically risky because those industries were the last real sources of the oligarchs' profit—particularly diamonds and palladium. But now, the imposition of real Kremlin control seemed possible. He had a legitimate excuse. *It was about time,* he reflected. God only knew how many billions of dollars were bleeding away from Russia to offshore accounts the world over.

As if on cue, another knock sounded at the door, far more military in tenor than that of the aide.

"*Da*." Orlov looked up to see the chiseled face of Colonel Kovanetz, without rising from the seat.

The colonel held an olive green officer's hat firmly between his left arm and ramrod-straight torso. His wiry frame was draped in the double-breasted olive green suit, black tie, and ocher "scrambled eggs" lapels of the GRU—military intelligence. The combination of his sharp angular features and flat jade green eyes revealed a soul that had witnessed a great deal of pain, much of it inflicted by himself, and knew little of kindness.

"So, Nikolai Konstantinovitch. What news of your search for Pyashinev?"

Orlov opened the cigarette box and held it out to Kovanetz, who selected a cigarette. "Thank you, *tovarish prezidyent*." He lighted the cigarette with a silver lighter emblazoned with a gold hammer and sickle encircling a red enamel star. Orlov disliked officials who continued to favor the red flag and hammer and sickle, particularly military officers. And they knew it. To Orlov, such displays signified that they considered the present political organization of Russia merely temporary, transitory to a future right- or left-wing bloody and enslaving empire. But he had bigger fish to fry and let it slide.

"The news is disquieting, *tovarish prezidyent*." Kovanetz descended uneasily into his seat. "Director Pyashinev is dead."

Orlov was unfazed. "How and where?"

"Mexico."

"Mexico? Now that's a surprise."

"With your permission, *tovarish prezidyent*, I would like to start from the beginning. It will make more sense that way."

Orlov nodded.

"We…interrogated both the director's family and his staff at Komdragmet."

Orlov winced at the thought of overturned books, broken glass, smashed porcelain, and a wife and children locked in cold, filthy cells in the Lubyanka prison. Russian leaders could and did rename the secret organs of the Russian state, but whether they were referred to as Okhrana, Cheka, GPU, OGPV, NKVD, NKGB, MGB, KGB, the new FSB/SVR, or its military counterpart, the GRU, their methods remained the same. However, as much as Orlov disliked the GRU, never for a moment did he doubt its efficiency.

"His family truly had no idea where he was. But through his staff we were able to trace Pyashinev to Murmansk. He drove there himself, from his dacha. He traveled from the Murmansk Military Air Field to the carrier Kuznetzov on a MiG-31 Foxhound. From there he took a Navy helicopter to London, commercial flights to Mexico, then a Cuban military helicopter to Havana. The helicopter crashed in the Yucatan jungle nearly two hundred kilometers west of Cuba. Apparently, there were no survivors."

Orlov sat up slowly. "But why all these flights? Pyashinev had a state Tupolev at his disposal. Why would he use a succession of military and commercial aircraft? And why would he go to Cuba, of all places? I can think of few countries as little associated with diamonds as Cuba."

"*Tovarish prezidyent*, we believe that Pyashinev did not want anyone to know that he had left the country."

"Come on, Colonel. Pyashinev was no imbecile. He knew we would find out."

"*Da*. It does not make any sense unless Pyashinev thought by the time we discovered he had fled the country the discovery would no longer matter."

Kovanetz was efficient. A brilliant orator he was not. "In Russian, Colonel."

"The diamond contract negotiations with Waterboer."

"What about them?" Orlov winced, sensing the worst.

"Pyashinev assumed we would not discover his disappearance until after the contract was renegotiated. By that time, he could return and invent whatever explanation he could think of to explain his absence, and the contract with Waterboer would be already in place."

"But why would he?"

"Sir, we dug into his finances. Pyashinev was bribed by Waterboer."

"*Solkin sin*." Son of a bitch. Orlov wasn't naïve. He understood Russian corruption, which had reached institutionalized status in the 1970s under Leonid Brezhnev. Unlike the de-intellectualization undertaken by Stalin after Lenin's death and the de-Stalinization undertaken after Stalin's death, Russia had never undergone "de-corruptization" after Brezhnev, mostly because the Communist *nomenklatura* benefited from it. Orlov had begun a de-corruptization, but doing so was taking much time, mostly because he couldn't afford to piss off the West with the massive executions necessary to eliminate the problem. It was for that reason he made sure significant officials like Pyashinev earned—and actually received—very large salaries and substantial government perks. Unfortunately, Orlov had underestimated Pyashinev's greed. He had suspected Pyashinev of stealing from state coffers, but not of bribery.

"Waterboer deposited five million dollars in an offshore South Pacific bank account in Pyashinev's name just last week. Russians generally send funds offshore to Cyprus. Pyashinev was being very careful."

"My God. He knew everything. The real diamond production figures. The real reserves."

"We found his crashed helicopter, *tovarish prezidyent*. Pyashinev and his pilot were dead." Kovanetz removed a folded paper from from his uniform jacket and handed it to Orlov. "And we also found this."

Orlov unfolded the paper, stared at the handwritten words:

"*Rossiya, trieti sloi. Nie dopustit im wziat eto*." Russia, third layer. Must not let them get it. "What the hell does it mean?" Orlov looked up at Kovanetz, confused.

"I'm afraid we don't know, *tovarish prezidyent*."

Orlov leaned back, pointed to the door. "I suggest you start thinking hard, colonel. You have only one day until the negotiations with Waterboer begin."

9 SETTLEMENT

Main Justice Building
Washington, D.C.
1:05 P.M.

"Pat Carlton."

"Mr. Carlton. Jonathan Black."

That was quick. Just one day since his previous discussion with the haughty lawyer. "Good afternoon."

Black sighed. "I've discussed your settlement proposal," he paused, obviously waiting for Carlton to speak. He was met by silence. "I have been instructed to accept your offer of $20 million."

Once again, Carlton had the wind knocked out of him. "Well, I'm very pleased," he managed to say several seconds later. "Very pleased. I'll draft our form of settlement agreement and a consent decree and email them to you by the end of the day."

"There is one contingency, however, and my client was most adamant on this point."

"Yes?"

"Otherwise there can be no deal."

"I'm all ears."

"Murfreesboro Mining Corporation will not admit to any liability and will agree to the settlement only—I repeat, only— if the Justice Department agrees not to publicize it."

"The consent decree must be approved by the court, Jonathan. It will be a public document."

"I understand. But a public document does not have to be publicized."

"I'll check with my superiors, but I don't think that should be a problem."

"Very well, then."

"Thank you." Carlton replaced the handset in its cradle, fell back into his chair in shock.

Twenty million. They agreed to $20 million. In just twenty-four hours. For a worthless case. No answer to the complaint. No motion on the pleadings. No motion for failure to state a claim. No motion to strike. No motion for summary judgment. No depositions or document requests or interrogatories. Nothing. A $20-million settlement accepted inside twenty-four hours.

What is going on?

Even if DOJ could have won the case, it wasn't worth more than $6 million. Ten tops. And DOJ may not have won. Carlton had dirt for evidence. Jonathan Black would have discovered that if he had waited. Carlton might have understood if it came from a small law firm intimidated by the Justice Department, but not Fox, Carlyle. Those guys ate federal litigators for lunch. He felt a sneaking suspicion that, somehow, he had been had.

Carlton propped his boots on his desk, gazed up at the yellowed ceiling. The only logical explanation Carlton could think of was that Murfreesboro Mining's bosses were intent on keeping the company out of the press. After all, Black had made the settlement contingent on confidentiality. But that kind of reasoning couldn't apply to this case. Murfreesboro Mining Corporation was an unknown corporation. No one would care.

He grabbed his DOJ mug, grimaced at the congealed brown contents. As he walked down the corridor to pour himself a fresh mug of government brew, still in shock, he spotted Erika. "Hey, Erika!"

She turned toward him, and cocked her head. "You okay, Pat?"

"Yeah, I'm great." He looked up and down the corridor suspiciously, back at Erika. "You got a couple minutes?"

"Sure. What's up?"

He led the way back to his office, ushered her inside, closed the door behind them.

"What is it?"

"I need a reality check." He sat on the edge of his desk, pointed to one of the guest chairs. "Where to start?" He ran his hand over his buzz cut, forced himself to calm down. "Less than a week ago, Gail Rothenberg assigned me what was supposed to be a simple case. Remember when Stalin was in my office?"

"Sure."

"That's when he pulled me off *Global Steel* and gave me this new case. *U.S. versus Murfreesboro Mining Corporation.* I filed a complaint in Arkansas federal court and served the defendants. Twenty-four hours later, just five minutes ago, the defendant agreed to a huge settlement."

"Is that…is that strange?"

"That's what I'm trying to figure out. I've never heard of a settlement agreement so fast in a case with so little evidence. First, they had no idea what evidence we had—and we had almost zilch. They didn't bother to go through discovery to find that out. That's particularly strange for Fox, Carlyle. Those guys can tie up a parking ticket in court for years. Second, they agreed to a $20 million settlement, without even really negotiating."

"That's more than three times the criminal penalty."

Carlton nodded. "I'm impressed you know that. But then if you made it into DOJ straight out of law school, you're sharp enough to cut glass."

Erika blushed. "So, congratulations."

"No, no. No. Not congratulations. It's weird, don't you see? It's too much, too quickly." He stood and paced, looking down at his boots, running his hand over his hair.

"I guess it's weird. But does it really make a difference? I mean, you won big, right? So, congratulations. Plus, it should put you up several notches with Jarvik."

He gazed down at the floor, lost in thought. "Which makes it even stranger. Jarvik asked me not to make a big deal out of it, just get a settlement. But twenty million? Within a day of filing the case?"

"Maybe they wanted to avoid a public fight in court."

"I thought of that, too, but twenty million is a boatload of cash to keep yourself out of court. Especially for an unknown company. Merill Lynch, maybe. But this company is totally unknown. What would they lose by having a courtroom fight? Certainly less than twenty million dollars."

"So what are you going to do?"

"I don't know, but I'll tell you one thing. Stalin or no Stalin, I'm going to look into this."

10 DEALER

Via Rodeo Shopping Center
Rodeo Drive
Beverly Hills, California
10:05 A.M.

MacLean's chauffeured British racing-green Bentley Arnage limousine deposited him at the street level of the Via Rodeo Shopping Center in Beverly Hills. He walked past tourists up the playful cobblestone reproduction of a European pedestrian street to a red brick building across from Tiffany & Co.'s display cases of breathtaking diamond jewelry, where men and women pined for the sparkling embodiments of love. Hair combed straight back, wrapped in a tan cashmere Gucci topcoat, dark blue Etro wool scarf, his feet coddled by shiny black Ferragamo cap-toed oxford lace-ups, MacLean looked more like a 1930s movie star than the scion of a multinational corporation. People looked at him oddly. He was confident they thought they should know who he was but didn't.

The elevator whisked him to the quiet offices of Cohen Diamonds, LLC on the third floor. He gave his name to an attractive receptionist, who whispered it into her headset microphone. A short elderly man with wisps of white hair appeared, greeted him with open arms.

"Maximillian! Come in. Come in." The words were heavily accented with Polish intonations, the English flawless.

"Abe." He grasped Abraham Cohen's soft wrinkled hand and was pulled into a strong hug. MacLean was glad to feel such energy from a man eighty-five years of age.

"I am so happy to see you. You look well. Always the dapper gentleman." His warm smile reached pale blue eyes. "Come, come. Let us make ourselves comfortable, shall we?"

Cohen walked in a slightly hunched posture in short rapid steps. The effect was not unlike that of the stereotype of an eccentric professor. They walked down a short hallway, past several small offices. Men in black suits, white shirts, many of them wearing yarmulkes, looked up curiously from illuminated magnifying lenses, then back down at the sparkling stones before them.

At the end of the hall, Cohen motioned to a wooden chair in front of a white desk and shut the door behind MacLean. "Please sit down. Would you like some tea? How is Claire?"

"Yes, thank you. Claire is as wonderful as ever."

"She's a wonderful woman." Cohen radiated an aura of stern authority and deep wisdom. His smiling face and endearing mannerisms masked them only partially. MacLean watched Cohen pour tea. Strangely for a man his age, Cohen did not need eyeglasses. Like his office, he had a style of refined simplicity that indicated a devotion to his work, a refusal to become distracted by useless material adornments. He was dressed in dark gray slacks, a white shirt, the top button unfastened, his shirt sleeves rolled up to his elbows. A simple black Uniball Micro pen was tucked into his breast pocket. Except for an old Omega watch on his wrist and a simple gold band he still wore despite his wife's death several years ago, Cohen did not wear any jewelry. MacLean's gaze came to rest on a group of black letters and numbers on Cohen's arm. The tattoo came from Dachau.

He had seen the tattoo many times before. It never failed to immerse him in sadness. Six million Jews exterminated by Nazis, along with millions of non-Jewish Poles, Gypsies, homosexuals, physically and mentally disabled, and others. And so many of the present generation do not even know. Or worse: deny.

In 1945, when the American Army liberated the Dachau concentration camp in Germany, MacLean's father Giancarlo Innocenti was doing his duty as a very young captain in the Army. Giancarlo was proud to fight for his country but was not so stupid as not to use a few favors to get a captain's commission. He realized certain of the prisoners still alive at the camp would die if they did not receive medical attention immediately. And it would be several days before the small army of doctors and nurses could arrive. Against his superiors' orders that the prisoners not be moved until higher authority arrived,

Innocenti personally ordered the worst cases airlifted to an Army hospital, where most recuperated. Many others did not. He took a particular interest in the young Abraham Cohen, first noticing him because he was the only Pole at the camp. The Nazis generally had murdered Poles at Auschwitz. They were the same age. Innocenti later facilitated Cohen's passage to America.

"May God bless you and your family." Cohen's warm smile dissolved MacLean's sadness. "I'm happy you're here. Claire comes by to say hello and give me cookies once in a while. Don't tell her but I give them to the office—too much sugar at my age is bad. And you? It's been a long while."

"Nearly a year. Right after our honeymoon. It's been so busy."

"No need to explain. What about children? Any children on the way?"

"We're thinking about it."

"You should think less and do more." Cohen chuckled, reclining into his seat. "So, what can I do for you?" He tapped his head with a finger. "Something tells this old mind this is a business matter. Am I right?"

MacLean smiled. "Nothing gets past you."

"Very little."

MacLean placed his cup on the desk. "Last week, Dan Wenzel came to me with some rather extraordinary information."

MacLean removed a black velvet pouch from his jacket pocket, spilled its contents into his palm, placed them on top of the pouch, and slid it carefully across the desk.

Cohen silently lifted the pouch and moved it back and forth under an illuminated magnifying glass, observing the three coffee bean-sized rough diamonds tumble from side to side. He looked up at MacLean without raising his head. "Where?"

"Arkansas."

"Murfreesboro? Crater of Diamonds park?"

"Close, but no. Dan bought some land in Arkansas from a local farmer. Afterwards, the farmer showed Dan an old geological map of the area."

"How old?"

"1920s."

"U.S. Geological Survey map?"

"Yes. How did—"

"Go on."

"The map shows substantial diamond deposits on the land. Dan didn't believe him, so the farmer showed him those." He pointed to the diamonds. "We did some testing and decided to start a mining operation."

Cohen reclined, looked at MacLean. He tightened his lips and shook his head in serious concern. "No, Maximillian. No."

"What do you mean, no?"

"Diamond dealers are a secretive lot. We are paranoid. By nature, training, and experience. We distrust outsiders. We are open only with our own families. To me, all Innocentis and MacLeans are family. And while you may be a good business-man and like beautiful gems, knowing gems and knowing the gem business are two separate things. We have a saying in the diamond industry. 'If you don't know diamonds, know your diamond dealer.' And you and I know each other well, do we not? Like family?"

"Of course, yes."

"You are a rich man. Restaurant chains, an import-export company, food products, hotels."

"Yes."

"And such a beautiful wife. On the verge of having little MacLeans."

"Abe, I—"

Cohen leaned over his desk and grasped MacLean's hand. "You are like a son to me, you know that." Cohen stared at MacLean. "I would give you only good advice. The best advice I could give." He paused and gave MacLean a stern look under-scored with concern. "Do you trust me, Maximillian?"

"Of course I trust you."

"Then forget about this mine in Arkansas or anywhere else. Keep the land if you want, but drop the project." Cohen released MacLean's hand. "You don't need the money. Let it go."

"But why? I don't understand. All those beautiful diamonds."

"If it's diamonds you want, diamonds I'll get you. As cheap as I can get them." Cohen took a deep breath. "I can't give you specifics, Maximillian. It would only place you in greater harm than you are already in."

"Harm?" A shiver of fear shot up his spine.

Cohen nodded. "Grave harm."

"Because I want to mine diamonds in Arkansas? How could—"

"Things are not always as they seem. You of all people know this. Arkansas may seem poor, simple, quiet, but it has been a diamond battleground since the 1920s. Since the time of your map. How can I say this for you to understand? I don't even understand myself. There are certain…certain interests at work in Arkansas. Diamond interests. No one knows exactly what they are. Exactly who is involved. Frankly, I don't want to know. For many years, there have been threats to diamond miners, diamond dealers who dig a little too deep in Arkansas, if you'll forgive the pun. Quiet and subtle at first, then severe. People have disappeared, never to be heard from or seen again."

MacLean nodded. "That explains the telephone calls."

"Calls? From whom?"

MacLean explained.

"So it has already started."

MacLean had never seen Abraham's face so serious.

"I can't tell you what not to do. You are a powerful man. You are cautious and wise. I know that people do not toy with you. What I tell you is between an old diamond dealer who has seen a great deal and a man who is like my own son. Abandon the project, Maximillian."

"But I can't. Not now. All those beautiful stones." He visualized them in his mind's eye. "Such beauty."

Cohen stared at MacLean in silence, then sighed. "In that case, *mazeltov*. And be very careful."

"Thank you. I will."

Cohen stood and smiled broadly. "Enough gloom. Life is too short. Come, I have something to show you." He opened a large safe behind his desk and removed a tray filled with small white envelopes. He ran a finger along the tray and selected an envelope. "This, you will find of unparalleled beauty." He unfolded the envelope with great care. He reverently picked up a large stone with a tweezer and dropped it in MacLean's palm.

MacLean gasped. The little glowing stones from Arkansas he had shown Cohen were dull granite pebbles compared to the fiery brilliant-cut gem that sparkled pink in his palm. The synergy of God's hand and man's industry. The gem in his palm surpassed all other stones he had seen, diamond or otherwise. Even the six-figure D flawless diamond in Claire's engagement ring. MacLean lifted the gem up to the light, turned it reverently between two fingers. Shards of rose, crimson, magenta, and blood red light shot out from the stone and made it dance before his eyes.

Cohen smiled. "A thirty-carat brilliant-cut Argyle pink. From Australia. Absolutely flawless. One of the rarest diamonds in the world. I just received it back from the cutter in Antwerp yesterday."

MacLean stared at the diamond in breathless silence, finally tore his gaze away. He held out his open palm to return it. Cohen closed MacLean's palm over the diamond. "I told you I would give you and Claire a wedding present when I found something worthy of you both." He leaned close. "For you and Claire, Maximillian." He stared into MacLean's eyes. "In your marriage and in all you do, particularly in your dangerous venture: *mazal u'bracha*. Luck and blessing."

11 HISTORY

Carlton would never have dreamed to ask a subordinate female employee to meet him alone outside of the office at night. In a bar, of all places. His sense of professional propriety forbade it. But this was different, he reasoned, trying to reconcile professional ethics with his growing fondness for her.

Erika had called the meeting, chosen the time, the location. Carlton didn't know why she had asked him to meet her, but she had sounded excited.

As usual, he was late. Snow fell from the sky in large flakes on Carlton's white 1958 Cadillac Eldorado Biarritz convertible he'd nicknamed "the Shark." The stereo gushed Sinatra as he made the short run from Main Justice to Capitol Hill. While other cars slipped and slid wildly in the accumulated slush, the Shark weaved in and out of traffic with impunity thanks to the concrete blocks Carlton had placed in the trunk before the onset of winter. He spotted a parking space at the corner of the block and gunned the massive engine. Carlton had great luck with parking spaces, even if they were generally far too small for his land-yacht.

He locked the car, thrust his hands into his overcoat pockets, and bent forward to avoid the falling snow. He walked past a group of homeless men bundled in filthy blankets, far too frozen to panhandle. He took a five-dollar bill out of his pocket, handed it to one of them, and whispered a silent prayer. Most Washington residents grew accustomed to the daily sight of the homeless on the streets. But Carlton never did. Homeless people in the richest, most powerful nation on earth baffled him. He shook his head and continued down the block.

The Hawk and Dove greeted him with its characteristic smells of hamburgers, beer, and cigarette smoke. The Hawk, as the Hill crowd referred to the pub, was packed with the usual suspects: legislative and agency staffers, interns, consultants, and those lobbyists not yet working the elected-official watering holes of

La Colline and the Monocle. Carlton had no problem spotting Erika by the bar. In contrast to the cookie-cutter Washington crowd, Erika glowed. He felt himself suppress a skipped heart-beat as she smiled and waved a glass of white wine.

"How's it going?" Carlton asked, squeezing between loud bar patrons.

"Great. I love this place. It's so...I don't know, political?"

"You chose well. It's one of my favorite D.C. haunts." He should caution her about professional propriety, but was far too happy to be with her. He ordered his favorite drink instead.

"Bombay Sapphire and tonic. Lots of ice and plenty of lime, please."

"I know it's kind of weird, asking you to meet me here, but you mentioned how paranoid Jarvik was about stopping after you got your settlement."

Settlement? He felt a prick of disappointment realizing that she had called him for professional, not romantic reasons. He retreated behind his professional armor. "You learn fast."

"After you told me what happened, I saw a diamond ad in a magazine. You know, 'Diamonds Are Beauty'?"

"I've seen them."

"The ad was put out by Waterboer Mines Limited of South Africa. I started doing some research on them, and the stuff was so interesting that, well, it sucked me in. I got carried away. A half hour of research during lunch ended up being six hours." Large green eyes smiled up at him over the wine glass. "I thought I'd fill you in."

A harried waitress with a beehive hairdo interrupted them and herded them to a newly vacated table. They quickly selected items from an oily laminated menu and ordered. The woman scribbled pub hieroglyphics on a tiny pad, all the while mashing on gum. Burger and fries for Carlton. Grilled chicken sandwich and salad for Erika. No butter, no mayo, dressing on the side.

She took a deep breath and organized her thoughts. "I've gone through history books, documentary videotapes, and news articles I pulled up on Lexis-Nexis. This is going to sound a bit like a lecture, so I apologize in advance. I don't want to come off...you know..."

"Patronizing? After Stalin, I'm immune. Lecture away. You're the one who did the research." He drained his gin and tonic, motioned for another.

"Thanks." She took a deep breath and concentrated.

"Okay. So a whole mess of diamonds were discovered in late nineteenth-century South Africa. Not just discovered, discovered big. By a man named Nicholas Waterboer. He and his young partner, Cecil R. Slythe, chained dozens of black laborers together—slaves, really—each with a can around his neck. The laborers formed a long line, on their hands and knees, and picked rough diamonds directly from the ground, putting them in the cups as they moved across the field. Alluvial diamonds found in dry river beds. Then Waterboer and Slythe found underground diamond deposits formed by old volcanic activity. That's when they really hit the jackpot. The diamond rush began. Miniature mines popped up all over the place, mostly in the Orange Free State."

"Where all those white supremacist crazies are."

Their food arrived. Carlton chomped into his burger. Erika was too engrossed to eat, pushing her plate aside. "At the time, the market for diamonds wasn't very large. Not nearly large enough for the flood of diamonds coming from South Africa. Until then, most diamonds had come from dry river beds in India. Now they were being mined by the ton, and new underground deposits were being discovered all over the place. The big mines figured out that diamond mining could be profitable only if it was monopolized. So big mines started buying up little mines. Major mines merged. One company came out on top."

"Let me guess. Waterboer?"

"Bingo. Waterboer Mines Limited. Although it was Slythe who led the way. A complete monopoly of South Africa's diamond industry. Eventually, Slythe forced Waterboer out and took firm control of the company and South Africa's diamonds. South Africa had no antitrust laws, so the monopoly was legal. As it is today, from what the articles said."

"That's right. No antitrust laws. Not the way we understand antitrust, anyway. But the new Boiko government is talking about it from what I hear. Go on."

"Well, from what I read, it was Slythe who made sure South Africa has no antitrust laws. But all that's just South Africa. Diamond fever spread worldwide. Everyone started mining for diamonds. The world supply of diamonds shot up. Slythe realized the key to maintaining Waterboer's preeminence in the diamond trade was to control the world supply, and they set up purchasing agencies all over the place, bought up mines like crazy. For huge sums of money. If they couldn't buy a mine, they got contracts to buy the mine's entire supply. If they couldn't get that, they simply paid the mine not to produce."

Carlton stopped mid-chew, blinked.

"Sound familiar? The Waterboer empire—it really is an empire—was untouchable. If a third-world government gave them trouble, they bribed officials, incited revolution, or simply assassinated the troublemakers. No scruples."

Carlton was taking her very seriously.

"Little by little, Waterboer gained control of world production. During the independence movements of the 1960s, Waterboer forged alliances with dictators who would control their countries' production with iron hands. During the Angolan civil war in the late '70s and early '90s, even today, the mines were overrun. Waterboer spent hundreds of millions of dollars however and wherever they could to protect the market."

"But if supply grew, prices had to drop."

"You would think. But by then Waterboer controlled the supply of diamonds and began stockpiling."

"Didn't they have any competitors?"

"They did in the beginning. But Waterboer had such a large stockpile they were able to manipulate the market and kill off competitors. Like starting a small car manufacturer if GM, Ford, and Chrysler were all rolled into one company and there weren't any antitrust laws. Just not possible, like the Tucker car company found out fifty or sixty years ago."

Carlton demolished the remainder of his burger, worked on the greasy french fries.

Tension, Erika guessed, as she sipped her Chardonnay.

"But that's just one side of their operation. Until the twenties, really, there wasn't much demand for diamonds. They were pretty stones, but compared to emeralds and rubies and sapphires, people considered diamonds pretty dull. Waterboer had to increase demand, and they used every gimmick in the book to push diamonds. In reality, they wrote the book."

"For instance?"

"All the strategies still used today in one form or another. They gave free diamonds to Hollywood producers to display prominently in films. They paid screenwriters to write scripts that gave diamonds an aura of ultimate elegance, of romance, of desirability. They gave diamonds to the wealthy and famous so the society pages would be filled with pictures of America's elite wearing diamonds. They launched a huge advertising campaign to brainwash people into believing it was necessary to buy a diamond at each important marker in a relationship: engagement, wedding, anniversary."

"Diamonds Are Beauty?"

"Right. They made people believe a man had to give a woman a diamond engagement ring if he really loved her." She held up her left hand. "Can you imagine what would happen if you gave your fiancée an engagement ring without a diamond?"

"Fiancée?" He smiled. "I don't even have a girlfriend."

Erika grinned. "Well, it's pretty much just assumed. Ask yourself why. Why would you automatically buy a diamond engagement ring? Why not a ruby, red like the color of love?"

"I never really thought about it. Tradition, I guess."

"Right, that's the feel of it. But that tradition didn't exist a hundred years ago. Before that, men readily purchased an emerald, sapphire, or ruby ring. Those stones are far more rare. Just as beautiful, more beautiful, even. Men automatically buy diamonds, don't even look at other stones. Women expect and demand diamonds, even if they esthetically prefer sapphires, rubies, or emeralds, because the world tells them that diamonds are a girl's best friend. Also because they couldn't make their girlfriends jealous by sporting an emerald engagement ring or really believe their fiancée loves them if he doesn't buy a diamond, even though the sapphire may be more expensive. Waterboer's ad campaign in action."

Erika sipped her water. "But Waterboer didn't stop there. It financed gem museums all over the world, donated fancy diamonds to display, emphasized how rare a diamond is, how durable, what a great investment diamonds are. They gave diamonds to royal families all over the world knowing they would be imitated. And it worked. People who would otherwise never have thought of buying a diamond now spend two months' salary to purchase a rock of pure carbon. The two-months'-salary rule is also a Waterboer contrivance, by the way."

"What are you saying, then? That diamonds aren't rare?"

"I thought so, but apparently they're not. They're carbon. Pressed carbon. So many diamonds are mined that Waterboer can barely buy and store them fast enough to prevent a flood on the market, and more mines are coming on line all the time. Just recently in Canada. Waterboer keeps billions of carats in storage to make them rare, because rare means expensive. Supply and demand. That's why they can charge so much more than diamonds are really worth.

"Waterboer has eliminated competition from the resale market. You can buy diamonds, but you can't sell them back. Unless they're so out of the ordinary they really are rare, like the ones sold at auction for millions."

"I don't follow."

"You can't sell diamonds back to jewelers. Not for the price you paid, anyway. Only about one hundred sixty people are allowed to buy rough diamonds directly from Waterboer. Waterboer holds a dozen sales to these people in London every year—in London to avoid U.S. antitrust laws. Most of these people are cutters who sell to retail establishments. Some are brokers who sell to cutters who can't buy direct. Waterboer also sells precut diamonds. Everyone else has to buy from these people. Try to sell a diamond back to a big jewelry house for its purchase price. They'll laugh. Politely, of course. But they'll laugh. They laughed at me when I asked."

"A car dealer would do the same."

"But a car really does become used. Its lifespan is limited. Parts wear down. Models change. Safety, emissions, and gas mileage improve. Diamonds are stones. They stay the same as the day you buy them."

"But that's capitalism and advertising. I mean, you could say the same thing about dishwashing liquid, too."

Erika leaned forward, pushed her plate still farther away. "But unless you eat off of paper plates, you really do need Palmolive. Plus, the company may soften peoples' hands, but it doesn't enslave them."

He stared at her. "Enslave?"

She nodded. "That's where this Waterboer thing really gets ugly. From what I found out, when diamond mining really boomed in South Africa, Waterboer needed unskilled labor to work in the mines, thousands of feet down. South Africa didn't have much unskilled labor. Whites would demand high wages, so Waterboer targeted the blacks. Most blacks were subsistence farmers on family farms who had no incentive to work in the mines. Waterboer forced the government to pass prohibitive taxes on black farmers to get them off the farms. They knew that black farmers did business through a barter economy and didn't have any cash. They were forced to find work to get the cash. But who would employ unskilled black farmers? Guess what? Waterboer was hiring.

"They left their wives and children behind, and when they got to the mines, they were stuck in concrete barracks with other miners for up to a year at a time. In filthy conditions. Slop for food. Like animals."

"Slavery."

"Sometimes worse, the laborers weren't allowed to leave the compounds for the duration of their mining contract. They couldn't have any contact with women. They had no civil rights. They could be publicly strip-searched and body cavity–searched at any time."

"The joys of apartheid." He shook his head in disgust.

"And all this stuff continued up to a few years before Mandela became president."

"I'm amazed. I had no idea."

Erika removed a bulging folder from her nearly new briefcase and placed it on the table. "Here you go. All my research.

I didn't have time to read all of it, so I indexed and tabbed it."

"That's quite a doorstop," he said, impressed.

"I just printed everything out."

"Indexed and tabbed? Do you ever sleep?"

"Very little." And alone, she wanted to add, but didn't. One step at a time, girl.

"This is above and beyond, you know. Thanks." He saw her blush before looking away. "I'll go through it."

Back home, it took Carlton nearly four hours to read through Erika's research material. How had he missed all of this? He was angry at himself for not having done more research. The complaint he filed was so simple, he had not felt research necessary. Sloppy. All because Stalin said the case was unwinnable.

The young woman was not only intelligent and beautiful, but also thorough. Her material was well researched and well organized. But the problem with research, Carlton remembered, was that it was never finished. The more Carlton read about Waterboer, the more questions and concerns he developed. They sprang to mind and prevented him from sleeping. He finally gave in to his curiosity. A few minutes past 1:30 A.M., he got dressed, drove to his office and scoured the Main Justice Building's 1930s Art Deco library until he found nearly everything he thought he wanted. Books could not be checked out of the main DOJ library, but he desperately wanted to read through the material away from prying eyes, especially Stalin's. So he scribbled a note to his friend Donna, one of the librarians, assuring her he would return the materials ASAP.

Back in his one-bedroom apartment, in the total calm of the winter night, he brewed a full mug of espresso, clipped and lit an Ashton maduro cigar, and plunged into the new material on the intriguing South African monopoly. Far more than the caffeine and nicotine, what he discovered gave him insomnia.

Waterboer was and still remained a global empire. During World War II, the Nazis needed industrial-grade diamonds for weapons, optics, and other engineering devices geared to the massive Nazi war effort. Germany didn't have any diamond deposits. No one knew where they got their industrial diamonds until, little by little, American OSS agents discovered the Nazis obtained their diamonds from one of the Waterboer mines in the Belgian Congo. The OSS told Waterboer about the leak. Waterboer knew if it shut down the mine for only a few months the Nazi war effort would collapse. No more war. No more Holocaust. Waterboer refused. Too much money would be lost.

Carlton cursed.

The amazing thing, he discovered, was that Waterboer refused to sell the diamonds to the American war effort until much later in the war, even though America was a South African ally. Their disturbed logic was that even though Nazi Germany, Imperial Japan, and fascist Italy were taking over the world, America wouldn't use the quantity it ordered and the oversupply would hurt prices. Only after massive pressure did Waterboer finally relent and sell America diamonds, but at bloated prices.

That was the Nazi connection. But there was also a Soviet connection. An inter-agency memorandum from CIA to Justice written by an analyst named Thomas Pink summarizing the history of diamonds in the Soviet Union stated that immense diamond deposits were discovered in Siberia in the late 1950s. The common misperception was that only Africa had diamonds when, in fact, Russia possessed the largest supply. Waterboer went ballistic. If Russia sold a large enough amount of diamonds on the market, the world market would tank. Waterboer sent its representatives to Moscow and offered the Communists hard currency for their entire output of diamonds. In the '60s, '70s, and '80s, when the U.S. and the rest of NATO were spending trillions on defense to crush communism, Waterboer was selling millions of carats of Soviet diamonds to the West. Basically, according to Pink's memo, Waterboer enabled the U.S. consumer market to finance a large portion of the Soviet defense buildup. This at a time when it was illegal for a South African to visit the Soviet Union.

The new Russian diamond supply was still a big problem for Waterboer. The diamonds out of Siberia were too small to send to the big cutters in Antwerp, Tel Aviv, or New York. Waterboer had to set up new cutting facilities, but traditional diamond cutters were too expensive to use on little stones. So Waterboer taught Third World children to cut diamonds for pennies apiece. Mostly in the slums of Bombay. Little kids. In filthy conditions. The practice continued today.

Carlton swore under his breath and stared at the pages of his research, dumbfounded. "How did I miss all this?"

After Mandela was elected president in South Africa, several people who worked for Waterboer came clean to the new government and its Reconciliation Committee. They confessed to kidnappings, torture, even assassinations, all against people who dealt in the diamond trade behind Waterboer's back. Two months later, two of them were found dead. The police ruled their deaths suicides.

On the U.S. side, DOJ had been trying to nab Waterboer for over fifty years, but the investigations hadn't gotten anywhere. Waterboer was a South African corporation and was too smart to do any business directly on U.S. soil, which is why it sold its diamonds in London. The U.S. had no jurisdiction. The two or three times the U.S. did get Waterboer, the penalties amounted to no more than slaps on the wrist.

Who could do such things? Carlton wondered. He dug for the material he had found about those who managed the Waterboer monopoly. Whoever they were, they were brilliant. Twisted and repulsive, but definitely brilliant.

The Slythe family had been running Waterboer ever since Cecil R. had usurped his mentor and the company's founder Nicholas Waterboer, in the late 1800s. Today, Waterboer was headed by his descendant Piet Slythe. A real piece of work. Fifty-five. Educated in England. Sharp as a tack. The Slythes were raised from birth to think, eat, breathe, and sleep diamonds. They were a paranoid bunch who considered themselves to be the trustees of the world's diamonds, who battle any and all who threaten their empire. Like a religion with their family as keepers of the flame. From the articles Carlton read, on the outside Piet Slythe appeared as a typical run-of-the-mill businessman. Happily married. Churchgoer. Gave money to orphanages. But the man was reputed to do whatever it took—no matter how evil—to maintain his family's control of diamonds.

Waterboer's pockets were just as deep as its market share of diamonds was broad. Five billion dollars of annual gross revenue from the monopoly of an international market by a single corporation not subject to U.S. laws. In an age when young kids killed each other over sneakers in the street, Carlton did not want to imagine how far a giant like Waterboer would go to protect such a monopoly.

The next revelation shot a shiver up his spine. One memorandum hinted that Waterboer had shut down a mine in Arkansas in the 1920s.

"So that's where they come in."

If Waterboer had been in Arkansas as far back as the 1920s, then maybe they were behind the Murfreesboro Mining case. It stood to reason. Twenty million dollars was huge for a small or even medium-sized Arkansas business concern, but it amounted to no more than a drop in the bucket for a global monopoly like Waterboer. If Murfreesboro Mining was part of the Waterboer diamond cartel, they were glad to accept the $20 million settlement offer, as overpriced as it may have seemed to Carlton. *They stalled so I'd be happy when they agreed to $20 million,* he concluded. And their tactic worked. *You were happy, Carlton.* He squinted angrily, feeling frustrated and deceived, realizing that Jonathan Black really had pulled the wool over his eyes. He relaxed. *They didn't expect you to continue the investigation, did they?*

He searched diligently but could not find anything more substantive to confirm Waterboer's involvement in Arkansas other than the one instance of rumor and innuendo. He'd have to call the CIA analyst. He looked for his name. Right. Thomas Pink. He leaned back in his chair and removed his cigar from the ashtray. It had gone cold. He lifted his mug only to remember that it was empty. The clock on his desk read 5:32 A.M.

"I have got to get some sleep."

He walked to his bed, set his alarm for 8:00 A.M. and fell asleep with all his clothes on. His dreams were as unpleasant as the research he had read.

12 COMPANY

Headquarters
United States Central Intelligence Agency (CIA)
Langley, Virginia
5:58 A.M.

As was his habit, Thomas Pink arrived at work early—after working until 2:00 A.M. the previous night. Pink was clean-cut and a workaholic. Though his early morning schedule prohibited any real night life, it afforded him a rapid commute before the Northern Virginia highways clogged with rush-hour traffic. This morning the drive had taken him nine minutes. He navigated his dark blue Mercury Sable through the gigantic parking lot that took up a large chunk of the CIA's 258-acre complex. Even at this early hour, the lot was nearly full with cars of other workaholic insomniacs. As a junior-grade analyst, Pink did not rate special parking privileges. He scouted through row after row of conspicuously nondescript American sedans and finally found a slot far from the main entrance. He locked his car and braced himself for the biting cold. Outside, neither his tan overcoat nor conservative navy blue suit offered much protection against the chill wind. His red tie flapped against his starched white button-down shirt as he walked briskly to the main entrance of the New Headquarters Building, the more recent of the two main Agency buildings that totaled over 2.5 million square feet of space. Each building was shielded in copper, enveloped in an outer shell, and acoustically defended by white-noise generators, all to protect against enemy eavesdropping technology so refined it could detect individual computer keystrokes from window vibrations.

Men and women in similarly conservative suits scurried about the warm lobby on their individual missions to protect the United States against its all-too-real foreign enemies. The black and white Company seal dominated the granite floor: fierce eagle head atop a shield that enclosed the rays of a star. Large white letters curved around the shield.

UNITED STATES OF AMERICA—
CENTRAL INTELLIGENCE AGENCY

As he did each morning, Pink bowed his head reverently as he walked past a marble wall of fifty stars, one for each Agency employee who had given his or her life for the United States. Only a handful of stars were accompanied by names, the missions of the other victims so secret they had taken even their identities to the grave. He negotiated a maze of hallways, each lined with acoustic baffles to prevent information from being overheard by passers-by. He walked to the Intelligence Directorate, then to the Russian Section, where his tiny office was located.

He hung his overcoat next to his framed vintage poster of *From Russia with Love*, poured himself a cup of Company java from the hall coffee-maker, sat at his immaculately neat desk and speed-read the still-warm Russian AM Report, a collage of news clippings on Russia gleaned from the Russian, national, and international press. Hardcopies from Russian news services. Transcripts of news stories and interviews that touched on Russia from major television and radio stations. Official government communiques. Copies of *Izvestia*, *Pravda*, and *Krasnaya Zvesda*. *Izvestia* was Russian for "news." *Pravda* meant "truth." Under the late communist regime, it was a running joke that there was little *izvestia* in *Pravda*, absolutely no *pravda* in *Izvestia*. As for the accuracy of the articles in *Krasnaya Zvesda*—"Red Star," the publication of the Russian military—it was anyone's best guess.

Pink's telephone warbled a series of single long buzzes, indicating an internal call.

"Pink."

"In early this morning, Tom," his boss said.

"What can I say? Analysis is my life."

"Well, take a break from your life and come to my office."

"On my way."

Pink walked down the hallway, wondering what assignment awaited him. Despite the thinly avoided coup by the GRU two years ago and the country's present economic and military mess, Russian affairs had become a touch routine since Orlov had acceded to power. Same news stories. Same reports. Since the passing of the cold war and in the aftermath of September 11, the Agency had focused on the more unstable countries of Eastern Europe, the rogue nations in the Middle East, and the countries harboring terrorists. The Soviet analysis staff had previously constituted 50 percent of the Agency's personnel, most of whom had been reassigned or laid off. The Aldrich Ames and Guatemalan disasters certainly had not endeared the Agency's Russian Section to a Congress wanting the Agency to focus nearly all of its classified—but widely discussed—$30 billion annual budget on counter-terrorism, regardless of the country's other very real threats.

Deborah Gold was the director of the Russian Section, one of the several subsections under the DI—Directorate of Intelligence. The DI was tasked with the central purpose for which President Harry Truman created the Agency in 1947 as a reaction not to the communist threat but to the surprise Japanese attack at Pearl Harbor. The DI predicted the actions of foreign governments and organizations through a meticulous analysis of information obtained by the Agency and prepared the *President's Daily Brief*, the most expensive and least distributed newspaper in the world, delivered each morning to the president and approximately fifteen other government officials on a strict need-to-know basis. Within the DI, Pink and Gold had developed a close working relationship based on the mutual respect of their talents.

He knocked on her door.

"Come in."

Gold crossed her hands on the table, smiled warmly. "Morning, Tom." She motioned to a seat.

Dressed in a smart professional gray suit and white blouse, she peered at him through thin-wire framed spectacles that perched on a nose becomingly "fixed" several years before, her only concession to vanity.

Her smile disappeared as she leaned forward. "I just spoke with Malcolm." She referred to the DDI, the deputy director for intelligence, second in line to the director of the Agency.

His real name was Randall Forbes, but the analysis staff referred to him as Malcolm because of his family wealth, despite the lack of any relation to the late financier, Malcolm Forbes. "Our dear Mr. Slythe is going to Moscow."

"Waterboer strikes again. To renegotiate the Russian diamond contract, no doubt."

"Exactly, probably a preliminary negotiation."

"Scumbags." An African-American, Pink harbored a particular enmity toward Waterboer and the monopoly's notorious former apartheid practices. As for the Russia-Waterboer Mines contract, it hardly qualified as classified information. Its existence was public knowledge. The *Wall Street Journal* and other financial newspapers regularly published articles about the contract. Public knowledge, but of little public interest. One of the beauties of a monopoly was its lack of competitors. No competitors, no news.

"You recall the fire at one of their Siberian diamond processing plants?"

"Mirny. I read Jerry Delpin's report from DST." He referred to his counterpart in the Directorate for Science and Technology, responsible for initial satellite imagery analysis, among other things. After initial analysis, DST transferred satellite imagery to the DI analysis staff, who analyzed information collected by all four directorates. "If I recall correctly, he concluded it was a natural gas fire."

"Exactly. The combination of the fire with Slythe's arrival in Moscow and Pyashinev's disappearance seems to have given Malcolm the Waterboer-Russia-diamond bug. He's convinced there's something brewing that we're not quite seeing. He wants a full analysis on the current Waterboer-Russia relationship. With predictions." She reclined, removing her eyeglasses. "It's yours."

Pink stood, cocked his head quizzically. "But why don't you…"

Gold rubbed her temples, shook her head. "I'm off to Moscow. Conference with their Crimes Department about the terrorist and mafia problems. FBI Moscow Section, Interpol, us." She jutted her chin forward after each name. "The usual gang. You're on your own." She sat forward, gathered papers, signifying the end of the meeting. "This is your big chance to impress Malcolm, Tom. But of course there's a catch. He wants the whole thing inside twenty-four."

"Hours?"

"You'd better get cracking."

Pink looked at his watch, sighed. Six-twenty-five. "Nothing like an arbitrary deadline to get the adrenaline up."

He walked to the door and turned. "Give Lenin the finger for me, will you?"

"Always do," she said, without looking up from her documents.

13 LINK

Shaughnessy, McGuire & Wenzel, LLP
Century City, California
3:03 P.M.

"Gail Rothenberg's office, please."

"May I ask who is calling, sir?"

"Dan Wenzel. We were in law school together."

"One moment, sir." The secretary placed him on hold. The Muzak nearly put him to sleep.

Wenzel stared out at the tufts of clouds above the privileged residential neighborhoods of Beverly Hills and the Hollywood Hills. Shadows covered and uncovered the white letters of the Hollywood sign on a distant green hill.

The calls from NTHP, BLM, and the loony new-age environmental group annoyed Wenzel. But having practiced real estate and corporate law for over twenty years, they did not distress him. What pushed him over the edge was the story Osage told combined with Cohen's warning, which MacLean had relayed. No matter how powerful MacLean might be as a private individual, Wenzel reasoned he needed government help from someone he trusted. Hence, his call to Gail Rothenberg.

"Dan?" Rothenberg's voice sounded loudly through the handset. "I haven't talked to you since my appointment party. How are you? I read about you in the Harvard bulletin."

"Ditto. How's government life?"

"No more billable hours, just politics. Marriage prospects are even worse than in private practice, if you can believe it."

"The grass is always greener, Gail."

"Still, I wouldn't mind grazing on your side of the fence. What can I do for you? Or is this a social call?"

"I'm afraid it's not. Ordinarily I wouldn't ask you this, but frankly, I'm stumped, and you're the only person I trust who I could think of on this."

"I'm flattered. If only you weren't married," she chuckled. "So, how can I help?"

Wenzel recounted the facts of the Arkansas diamond project,

the calls, and Cohen's warning, careful not to mention any names. "At first I thought it was just environmental pressure. Call me paranoid, but now it looks like someone is trying to block diamond production in Arkansas. Who, I've got no idea. As the antitrust enforcer, I thought you might know something. Unless it's privileged, of course."

"Well, you can rest safely."

"No one's trying to stop diamond mining?"

"No. You're not paranoid."

"That's less comforting."

"I hate to hand you over to someone else, but this someone else is better positioned to help you. I assigned an Arkansas diamond antitrust case less than a week ago to our Econ Lit section. He gave it to one of our young up-and-comers."

"Sounds like too much of a coincidence."

"Right. His name is Pat Carlton. Not much of a savvy political player, but he's smart and down to earth. I'll tell him you'll be calling."

Wenzel took down the number. "Thanks, Gail."

"It's quite simple, really," Carlton said to the Beverly Hills lawyer, a Daniel Wenzel. "Gail Rothenberg assigned a case that dealt with a diamond mine in Arkansas. I can't divulge names or locations, of course. A mining company tried to buy a family mining operation, but the farmer wouldn't sell. So they just paid him not to produce. The farmer was happy, the mining company was happy. It violated antitrust laws, but never went to trial because the defendant settled, on the condition of non-admission and no publicity, of course. The weird thing is they settled almost immediately for an astronomical amount. Plus, their corporate structure is a maze. I'm not quite certain how this affects you, if at all."

"It may or may not. My client recently purchased a property in Arkansas. In Macon Grove. From an old Arkansas farmer by the name of Osage. Anyway, we did him a small favor, letting him live on his land for the rest of his life. In turn, Osage informed us of a diamond deposit under the land. We were very excited. After some preliminary geological and environmental work, my client decided to mine the deposits.

"Here is where it gets weird. We didn't contact a single soul about this project, just recorded the deed. No mining permit application yet or even a declaration of intent to mine. Before all that, I received telephone calls from the National Trust for Historic Preservation, the Bureau of Land Management, and from some cockeyed environmental group. All within three days. Calls telling us not to mine. Not just asking us or telling us, but threatening us. And every one of those callers knew that we were going to mine."

Wenzel also told him about the warning from Cohen, without revealing his name.

A shiver crawled up Carlton's spine. He thought about the sinister results of his and Erika's research. "Are you sure no one spilled the beans?"

"Quite certain. We have long relationships with our contractors, Mr. Carlton."

"It's Pat."

"Thanks. Please call me Dan," Wenzel said in return.

"Have you spoken with the seller since all of this started? Osage, was it?"

Wenzel sniffed. "He showed us a geology report that substantiated the diamond deposits. He thinks it's some big government conspiracy, that the government murdered his father when he tried to publicize the report after the government buried it."

"The geology report—is it credible?"

"Apparently. Done in the 1920s by the U.S. Geological Survey."

"To be candid, although we've negotiated a settlement, I'm digging a bit further into our case. Something doesn't sit well with me. More so now that you've told me about your client's situation. Let me call you back in a few days when I've got more information."

"Thanks. I'd appreciate that."

"No. Thank you, Dan. I'll be in touch."

Carlton swiveled around to face his desk, returned the phone to its cradle.

Curiouser and curiouser.

But as they said at DOJ, to catch a criminal, know his business. Based on that adage, his next destination was clear.

14 JEWELER

Cartier
Connecticut Avenue, NW
Washington, D.C.
10:31 A.M.

"Pat Carlton, Department of Justice." Carlton said, pleased by the woman's firm handshake. He despised limp handshakes.

"Therese de la Pierre. Welcome to Cartier, monsieur Carlton," she replied with a heavy French accent.

Any man would have found the fortyish de la Pierre attractive. She had olive skin, an angular face from which ardent dark eyes smiled with Gallic sensuality. Her black hair was held in a ponytail with a gold clasp. Carlton found her stunning, but a touch too hard and cold, especially compared to Erika's warmth and spontaneity, her air of childlike mischievousness. He felt de la Pierre size him up.

"Thank you for seeing me on such short notice."

"You are welcome, monsieur. I was informed you wished to discuss diamonds. Are you getting engaged?"

"No, I have a case that involves diamonds, and I've realized I don't know the first thing about them. I thought perhaps someone from the venerable house of Cartier could give me a crash course."

"*Certainement, monsieur*. We are happy to be of service to the Department of Justice. Please sit down. May I offer you some coffee?"

"That would be great. Thanks."

Carlton scanned the photographs of 150 years of Cartier masterpieces that adorned the walls while de la Pierre requested coffee from her assistant.

"Cartier has been involved with diamonds since Louis Cartier founded the house in 1847, even before they were discovered underground in South Africa. For some reason, diamonds fascinate people. Since I don't know what you know or don't know, I will give you a general overview. Forgive me if my explanations are too elementary.

"First, what makes diamonds unique other than their hardness is that they are ranked according to a strict scale. No other gemstone is. Diamonds are judged by the four Cs—color, clarity, cut, and carat."

De la Pierre leaned back in her swivel chair as her assistant arrived with two tiny cups of espresso in Cartier porcelain on a silver Cartier tray.

She looked up and smiled. "*Merci*, François." She stirred sugar into her espresso. "Rabbi Nahman of Braslov once said, 'God never repeats Himself.' This is so with diamonds. Each diamond is unique, and because diamonds can be ranked, that uniqueness can be translated into specific monetary value, again unlike other gemstones.

"The clarity of a diamond refers to the type and quantity of flaws in the stone. Almost every diamond has a flaw of some sort." She gestured gracefully with her long fingers. "Bubbles. Black and brown spots. Small slivers called 'feathers.' Clouds called 'carbon spots.' Fluorescent concentrations. All of these are flaws, or 'inclusions.' Most of these inclusions aren't visible to the naked eye, even if you look very closely. Determinations must be made under ten-times magnification. That's the industry standard." She took a sip of coffee. "Are you with me so far?"

"As sure as God made little green apples."

She laughed. "I love that expression. Clarity, in diamonds, not apples, is divided into seven categories. A flawless diamond is the best, a diamond that has absolutely no flaws. These are extremely rare. Extremely expensive. 'Internally flawless' describes a diamond that is almost flawless, but has small surface imperfections. An extra number of facets, perhaps. Lines on its surface. These are also very rare stones. The next categories of clarity we call VVS1, VS1, and VS2. These are acronyms. Generally, they are very slight inclusions that can be seen only under magnification. The next level of clarity is SI. These are diamonds that have inclusions visible from the back of the diamond with the naked eye." She turned her palm up to emphasize the point. "But that can only be seen under magnification from the front of the stone. It's an awkward grouping, frankly. The last category we call I—imperfect. Imperfect diamonds have inclusions that are visible to the naked eye and can also affect the stone's durability. Still with me?"

"Yes." Carlton remembered his coffee, drained the small cup.

"*Bien*. Now, color. Normal diamonds are white. Fancies, as we call them, come in bright yellows, blues. Even pinks. But let's concentrate on white diamonds, the most common. The color standard set by the GIA—the Gemological Institute of America—slides from D to Z, D being the best. It denotes what we call a colorless white stone. From L on down, the diamonds are more and more yellow. Less valuable. These distinctions are difficult to make, so color should always be judged against a set of master stones. Even though Cartier buys diamonds daily, we never buy diamonds without comparing them to a master set. Eyes become tired. Even working with a master set of stones, diamond sorters compare color for no more than an hour at a time. Background light is also very important. Diamonds must be compared in a particular light. Once a diamond is judged, its color is noted on the GIA certificate. Disreputable retail jewelers won't give you a real certificate. They'll try to—how do you say in English?—swindle you? They'll say their diamonds are certified by 'GIA trained' gemologists or by 'GIA standards' and so on. This is always a bad sign.

"Now for the cut. There are many types of cuts. Here, let me show you." She took a memo pad from her desk and drew different shapes of diamond cuts with a sharp pencil, announcing each designation. Marquise. Emerald. Oval. Heart. Pear. Single. Baguette. "The most common cut, and the most valuable, is the brilliant cut. This is your standard diamond with fifty-eight facets." She drew the familiar round top, conical profile shape on a piece of paper. "But all of these," she motioned to the shapes on the pad, "are not really cuts. Just shapes. The real cut of a diamond is as important as its clarity and color. A good cut will yield maximum brilliance. In optical terms, it will maximize the return of white light to the eye.

This is the sparkle effect of a well-cut diamond. Too deep or too shallow and you miss the maximum brilliance of the stone. Does all this make sense?"

Carlton nodded. "You make it sound logical, but I have a feeling that law school may be easier than diamond school."

She smiled. "And now for carat. Spelled with a *C* for stones, with a *K* for gold. One carat corresponds to a fifth of a gram. The word comes from India. Before the South African discoveries in the late nineteenth century, India was the largest producer of diamonds. In ancient times, Indians believed that diamonds grew in the ground. Like seeds. So the carob seed became the standard of measurement. Of course, seeds in Greece, England, and Rome were different, so there were discrepancies in carats. *Les Anglais*—the English—for example, used to measure a carat by the middle grain of an ear of corn." The Frenchwoman chuckled at the foolish Brits. "Today, the system is precise. There are one hundred points to a carat, five carats to a gram. Each point corresponds to two one-thousandths of a gram. Extremely small. A difference of one point can make a large difference in price. An interesting convention is that although most people round numbers up, diamond dealers round points down. So 99.8 points does not round up to a carat, but down to ninety-nine points."

"Very conservative and very complicated."

"Diamond dealers are."

"The devil is definitely in the details, isn't he? What about value? How is that established?"

"I was wondering when you would ask." She allowed a sly smile to draw across her pouted lips. "Generally, it's the first question people ask. Value and price, of course, depend on the four *C*s. But it also depends on the relative size of the diamond."

"Clearly."

"Not for the obvious reason you think. Not size, but relative size. With diamonds, one plus one equals three."

"I might mention that I became a lawyer because I flunked math."

She grinned. "Let me explain. A stone costs more than two

stones of half its size. Larger stones are more rare than smaller stones. What is known as Jeffreys' and Tavernier's rule of squares links carat price and carat weight." She leaned forward, jotted down a simple formula with flourish.

"To determine the price of a stone, you must multiply the square of the number of carats in the stone by the price of a one-carat stone of that particular cut, color, and clarity. For example. Let us say that one-carat costs two dollars. A two-carat stone will cost the square of two—four—times two dollars—which is eight dollars. A three-carat stone would cost, let's see…"

"Eighteen dollars."

"*Très bien*. I think your math teacher was unfair."

Carlton decided it was time to fish for information closer to the bone. "But are diamonds really so rare? There are diamond deposits even in Arkansas."

"I've never heard about diamonds in Arkansas."

De la Pierre paused, obviously weighing her response. "Most people believe diamonds are valuable because they are rare. They are led to believe this. Made to believe it." Her voice became a whisper, as if others at Cartier were listening in. "The high price of diamonds is not based on the free market; it is imposed by the diamond syndicate. Diamonds aren't rare at all. They don't line the fields like gravel, of course, but they certainly are not as rare as the industry wishes people to believe. The syndicate stockpiles vast quantities of diamonds every year to maintain the price of diamonds at an inflated rate." She paused and lowered her gaze. "That is all I can say on the subject, you cannot quote me on it. I know you will not." Her tone was final, but Carlton noticed a flash of nervousness cross her face.

"Of course not." He rose. "Thank you for your time, ma'am. If you think of anything else important, you can reach me here." Uneasy about Jarvik, he handed her his personal card rather than his DOJ business card. "*Il n'y a pas de quoi, monsieur*. It is my pleasure. *Au revoir*. Call me if you need anything else." She smiled. "Anything at all."

The woman who answered the telephone had an ebullient voice heavily accented with a Southern twang. "Senator Bigham's office. Good morning."

"Good morning," Carlton said. "Could you please tell me the name of the LA who handles mining issues for the Senator?" Senator Bigham was the senior senator representing Arkansas. The legislative assistant—LA—handling mining issues for him might shed some light on things.

"Certainly, sir. That would be David Mazursky."

"Could you patch me through to him? My name is Pat Carlton. I'm over at Justice." The short statement informed the receptionist this was a government call, not a constituent call, which she would have directed to a legislative correspondent, or a press call, which she would have directed to the press secretary, no matter what the caller requested.

"Certainly, sir. One moment please."

"This is Dave Mazursky." The voice was friendly but decidedly not Southern.

"Good morning. My name is Pat Carlton. I'm an attorney in Antitrust over at Main Justice."

"Hi. What can I do for you?"

"I'd like to pick your brain about a bizarre mining case I'm involved in out of Murfreesboro."

"I'll be glad to help. If I can."

Carlton recounted the basic facts about Raymond Mines, Murfreesboro Mining Corporation, and the uncanny settlement without mentioning names or places. He also left out any mention of Wenzel's plans and unsettling telephone calls.

"Well it certainly seems unusual. But frankly, I'm amazed any diamond mining occurred at all. It's part of state folklore that there are oceans of diamonds in Arkansas, especially under Murfreesboro, but I have yet to see any proof. The closest I've seen is the Crater of Diamonds State Park down there. Tourist attraction. It's been open for years. People find diamonds there, but they're few and far between, industrial grade at best as far as I know. So I also find it strange that someone would settle so quickly for a large sum."

"Does the name Murfreesboro Mining Corporation ring any

bells?" He realized he had just blurted out the defendant's name, tried to convince himself it was okay because he didn't actually say they were involved.

"Murfreesboro Mining Corporation. Murfreesboro Mining Corporation. No. I can't say it does."

"Thanks for your time, David."

"You bet. If you need any more info, call me on my direct line." He recited it. "I'm often on the floor or in Arkansas, so leave a voicemail."

"Thanks a lot."

"You bet."

Carlton hung up. Another dead end. Of course, Mazursky could have been snowing him, but Carlton thought his lack of knowledge genuine. Still, something about the settlement and Wenzel's information kept gnawing at him.

He knew there was a link between the Raymond Mines case and the problems Dan Wenzel's client was having with his mining project, just didn't know what it was.

Both cases involved diamonds, the same hamlet in Arkansas, and serious efforts to squash mining. For Carlton, a ridiculously large settlement. For MacLean, threatening calls from the federal government and obscure groups. There were simply too many coincidences.

Carlton was all too aware coincidences rarely occurred. Besides, the information about Waterboer troubled him far too much and provided too obvious an opportunity for investigation for him to walk away now. He could, maybe should look away, drown himself in another case. Others would, particularly given Stalin's orders. But Waterboer's history of misdeeds was too strong for him to ignore, even if he didn't know how or even if the monopoly was involved. It was the first time he'd disobeyed explicit orders at DOJ, but then Jarvik didn't have to know, did he?

Further investigation began with a second call to Stein at the SEC. On a hunch, Carlton asked him to obtain the incorporation papers of the Mineral Rights Protection Group, the officious group that had threatened MacLean's operation. As expected, Carlton did not find anything in the documents other than what Wenzel had already divulged: that the shady group had been formed as a corporation only several days earlier. But incorporations for tax-exempt, nonprofit corporations were not prepared by concerned citizens on a whim. They were prepared by lawyers. Likely an attorney would be listed as the corporation's agent for service of process on the articles of incorporation that Stein faxed to Carlton's office. Carlton scanned the document. There it was: Perry Trask, Esquire.

Carlton punched a five digit internal DOJ extension and waited.

"Library."

"Donna? Hi. It's Pat Carlton."

"Hi, Pat. Hey, thanks for your note, but I need those books and periodicals back, you know. Even a man as charming as you can't just—"

"Okay, okay. Listen. I just need a favor."

"Name it."

"Thanks. Would you check Martindale Hubbell for an attorney named Perry Trask?" The national directory listed nearly every practicing lawyer in the United States by individual name, firm, city, and state. He told Donna he didn't have a firm or state or city. "Sorry. I know I'm a pain, but you librarians love challenges, right? Plus, you're the research maven. This should be a walk in the park for you."

"Sure, feed my ego." She laughed. "I'll buzz you back."

"Thanks." He hung up and dialed another internal number.

"Henri Monet speaking." The Frenchman's accent was as heavy as the battery of DOJ computers under his care.

"Henri. Pat Carlton."

"Ah, Monsieur Carlton. *Comment ça va?* How are you doing?"

"Fine. Listen, do you have some time for a little project?"

"No," Henri replied unequivocally. "But for you, of course, I will make an exception. What do you need?"

"*Merci.* I'm looking for something that's not supposed to exist." One had to challenge the quirky Frenchman's talents to interest him.

"Ah! My *spécialité*. And what is this thing that does not

exist?"

"A diamond mine."

"A diamond mine?" Henri repeated with a Gallic overload of emotion.

"In Arkansas."

"I did not know there were diamonds in Arkansas, Monsieur Carlton."

"Neither did I, but apparently, there are. Or were at one time." Carlton explained the rumor about the mine in Murfreesboro Nicholas Waterboer supposedly shut down in the 1920s. Carlton hoped it might provide a link between Murfreesboro Mining and MacLean's venture, whether it existed now or had existed at any time in the past. "I'll drop off a geological survey I have."

"*Très bien*. I will call you *immédiatement* when I find something."

"*Merci*, Henri."

The handset had barely made contact with its cradle when a voice boomed behind Carlton.

"Carlton!"

Carlton jerked in his seat, seconds away from a coronary. He did not have to look at the outline in the doorway to know it was Stalin.

"Sir?" Blotches of light appeared in Carlton's vision as he stood to face his boss.

Jarvik stretched his short frame to full height in front of Carlton's desk. His unusually friendly smile only reinforced Carlton's unease.

"Carlton. I never thought I'd say it, but congratulations on a job well done. You settled quickly, high, and discretely. Good show." Jarvik offered his hand across the desk. Confused, Carlton shook it. Never before had he received praise from Jarvik.

"Thank you, sir." The pleasure he might have felt he experienced as suspicion.

"You're welcome. Sit down, Carlton. Sit down." Jarvik sat in the guest chair. "Since you performed so brilliantly on Murfreesboro Mining, I have a reward for you. I'm assigning you a case in Hawaii." He beamed as though he had just handed Carlton the Keys to the Kingdom.

"Hawaii?"

"That's right. Ever hear of the Kobayashi Corporation?"

"Who hasn't?"

Jarvik's smile grew to never-before-observed proportions. Carlton feared that the man's lips might split.

"We've gotten word that Kobayashi has been engaged in some pretty major antitrust violations in Hawaii. High profile stuff. This could be very big for you, Carlton. Very big. Far more important than *Global Steel*." He paused. "You see? I deliver on my promises. I told you you'd get a better assignment if you did well. Pleased?" Eyebrows arched, he awaited waves of gratitude.

The case was exactly the type of assignment Carlton had wanted. Like *Global Steel*, it carried meaning and impact. A Japanese company that committed antitrust violations meant high-powered opposing counsel and real challenge. Perhaps even press. Hawaii. Far away from the dark, arid winter cold of Washington. Only a couple weeks ago, Carlton would have jumped at the opportunity, but now he felt annoyance rather than joy. Carlton's real duty was to stay in Washington.

"What's the matter, Carlton, don't you like Hawaii? You don't think it would be a great place to spend Christmas?"

"Well…yes, sir."

"Or is it too close to the hoi-polloi? Not white shoe enough for you? Is that it?"

"Not at all, sir."

"My God, Carlton, I don't understand you. A week ago you were bitching and moaning about *Global Steel*. Now I assign you to a case bigger and better than *Global*, in Hawaii of all places, and you look like I sentenced you to hard labor in Siberia. What's the matter with you?"

"I just…I'm sorry, sir. I guess I'm just a little tired today." He forced a smile. "Hawaii will be terrific. Thank you."

"That's better. Pick up the files on Kobayashi in the research department and fly out to Honolulu first thing. Report directly to the FBI office. They'll fill you in. You can use the DOJ apartment there as a bonus. Ever been there? Right on the beach. The travel office has all your paperwork. Enjoy."

"Thank you, sir."

Jarvik nodded and walked to the door. Before stepping into the hallway, he turned and stared at Carlton. "By the way, I wouldn't take old geological surveys too seriously if I were you. Very unreliable." Jarvik smiled. "Just some friendly advice."

Ice crept up Carlton's spine.

How did he know about Wenzel's geological survey?

"Pat Carlton."

"Pat, it's Donna." She waited for recognition. "From the library?"

"Right. Sorry, I—"

"How soon they forget. Anyhow, I found the info of that Perry Trask lawyer."

"Aces!"

She recited a telephone number with a 212 area code.

"You wouldn't happen to have the name of the law firm, would you?"

"Manhattan. It's Fox, Carlyle, Ashton, Chase, Whitfield & Whyte. On Fifth Avenue."

Son of a bitch. The ice returned to his spine.

"You want the address?"

"Pat? Dan Wenzel. The plot thickens. I just received an offer to buy MacLean's land in Arkansas. An outrageous amount of money from an outrageously aggressive lawyer."

"And?"

"MacLean refused, of course, not after all the trouble we've had with the government and the fake greenies. The lawyer had a heck of a difficult time taking no for an answer. Very aggressive."

"Let me take a guess. He was from Fox, Carlyle. In Manhattan."

"How did you know?"

"I'll call you back."

Thicker and thicker. As much as Carlton wanted to avoid involving another agency, maybe it was time to see what CIA knew. Or at least what it would be willing to tell DOJ. What was the man's name? Pink? Yeah. Ironic for a guy at CIA.

It took a while for Carlton to negotiate the telephonic barriers. Luckily, DOJ dissolved most of them.

"Tom Pink."

"Good afternoon, Mr. Pink. My name is Pat Carlton. I'm an attorney in DOJ's antitrust division."

"Good afternoon."

"I'm sure you're a busy man, so I'll get right to the point. I was informed you're an expert on Waterboer Mines Limited." Just enough nervous silence resulted for Carlton to know he had struck a nerve.

"Whoever told you that greatly overestimated my knowledge of Waterboer, I'm afraid." Carlton knew his unlisted office telephone number flashed on Pink's computer screen, together with the words "Department of Justice, Washington D.C.," confirming he was for real. "What exactly are you looking for?"

"To tell you the truth, I'm not quite sure. I'm involved in a lawsuit involving diamonds. Diamonds mined here in the U.S." Carlton was not about to risk giving detailed information after his conversation with Jarvik, even to CIA. "Almost immediately after I filed suit, I received a settlement offer that was very big from a virtually unknown corporation that must of course remain nameless."

"Where is the mine?"

"I'd rather not get into that right now."

"What makes you think that there is a connection with Waterboer?"

"If the settlement wasn't strange enough, I also received word from an unrelated party who recently acquired diamond-bearing land near my defendant's property. Before his client started mining, he received strange calls—threats, really—to stop mining. The same law firm represents both my defendant and one of the groups trying to stop the diamond mining. Too much of a coincidence. Since I know Waterboer tries to prevent diamond mining they don't control, I became suspicious that Waterboer—"

"Fox, Carlyle?"

It was Carlton's turn for a moment of nervous silence. "How did you know?"

"Fox, Carlyle is Waterboer's principal law firm in the United States."

"But Waterboer isn't allowed to conduct business in the United States."

"Not directly and not legally. But it does have interests in U.S. subsidiaries, through legal processes I'm sure you understand far better than I do. And believe me, those interests are well-guarded by Fox, Carlyle. Have you determined that one of Waterboer's subsidiaries is involved in your two cases?"

"I'm pretty sure." Fox, Carlyle hadn't revealed the identity of the company that wanted to buy MacLean's land, but Carlton was relatively certain it was somehow linked to Waterboer.

"I see." Pink paused. "May I suggest something, Mr. Carlton? If I were you, I would forget about it and move on. You said you got a large settlement. That case is settled. As much pressure as Waterboer places on the other party not to mine diamonds—if it is Waterboer—there is nothing that Waterboer can legally do to stop them from mining."

Carlton hadn't told him about the different federal agencies and still didn't feel comfortable doing so.

"So there really is no reason," Pink continued, "for you to hypothesize or delve into the possibility of Waterboer's involvement."

"Perhaps, but I'd like to know—"

"Trust me, Mr. Carlton. You don't. I don't know how much you know about Waterboer, but nothing about it is pretty. Piet Slythe, the present head of Waterboer, packaged and sugarcoated for the press, has an army of thugs that operates without risk of retribution from law enforcement. As an antitrust lawyer, I realize you must be focused on Waterboer's illegal monopolistic activities. But I assure you, monopoly is a tiny offense compared to other things Waterboer's involved in. It's always been a ruthless company—supported the Nazis and the

Soviets in the past. But with new diamond mines coming on line every few months, it's gotten even worse. They're a sick bunch. Their only goal is controlling diamonds. Believe me, if you don't have to get involved with these people, don't."

Carlton probed with silence.

"I feel bad pushing you off your path, especially since we're both feds on the same side, but trust me, it's for your own good."

"Thanks for your candor. I appreciate it."

"You betcha. Have a good one."

Carlton hung up, wondering if the warning had been well intentioned or if he had been royally hosed by yet another acronym in the thickening alphabet soup of federal agencies. Pink sounded friendly enough, but with the other federal agencies ganging up on MacLean, Pink's refusal didn't sit well with Carlton.

15 MONOPOLY

Johannesburg
Republic of South Africa
7:47 A.M.

The midsummer December sun beat down from a cloudless azure sky on the silver Jaguar XJ16L Sovereign as it sped from the posh residential district to Waterboer's stone-faced fortress in the business district of South Africa's financial and industrial capital. The two escort cars fell back only when the armored Jag passed through the steel-reinforced concrete entrance gate and disappeared into the underground parking structure.

The stretch Jag came to a halt opposite an open elevator door and a uniformed guard brandishing a Boer BXP submachine gun. The man's darting eyes and stance indicated preparation to use his weapon. The corporation took no chances with the Jag's passenger.

Two armed bodyguards emerged from the sedan, one from the front passenger door, the other from the opposite rear door. The elevator door slid shut as soon as the tall passenger and his cocker spaniel puppy were safely inside. It reopened several seconds later, thirteen floors up, to an office suite furnished with Victorian antiques and hand-woven scarlet wool throw rugs on glossy hardwood floors. Polished gold letters above a wide hallway entrance heralded the corporation: WATERBOER MINES LIMITED.

Underneath was the company's trademark: Diamonds Are Beauty.

On each side of the hallway entrance stood plexiglass cases illuminated by recessed spotlights. One protected an octahedronal, 120-carat champagne-colored diamond rough as it had emerged from Waterboer's first mine. The stone seemed to glow from within as if endowed with magical powers. The other case enclosed a flawless D-color 205-carat brilliant-cut diamond whose 291 facets had required eight months of painstaking cleaving, cutting, and polishing in Antwerp to cast its kaleidoscopic shards of fire. Beside each display case stood a man dressed in a conservatively styled business suit, black oxfords, white shirt, and tie. They could have passed as corporate executives or barristers except for the butts of Heckler & Koch P7s protruding from brown leather shoulder holsters that shone from years of use.

Piet Slythe cradled his puppy Kimberley in his left arm, dismissed the guard with a friendly wave of his right hand. He walked through the wood-paneled hallway, past the desks of two middle-aged secretaries. "Good morning, ladies."

A balding man in his late forties with odd-colored eyes—one black, one blue—opened a heavy carved door at the end of the hallway. "Good morning, sir." He bowed slightly.

"Morning, Ian." Slythe grinned, stopped and placed his hand on his personal assistant's shoulder. "How was Freddy's rugby match yesterday?" He sniffed.

"They won. Thank you, sir. Two games from the Cup."

"I won't miss that one."

"You honor us, sir."

Slythe bent down, set Kimberley on a red velvet pillow near his desk, walked to a gleaming sterling silver tea tray and poured himself a cup. He breathed deeply, admired the view from his office. "Beautiful day, isn't it, Ian?"

"Most definitely, sir."

The fifty-five-year-old patriarch of the Slythe clan, ruler of Waterboer Mines Limited, was almost always in good spirits. Endowed with an IQ off the charts and a photographic memory, he had been educated at Harrow, then "read" geology at Eton, as the British termed taking a major. He quickly grew bored and paid greater attention to more stimulating pursuits—legal at first, then mostly illegal—than dusty old rocks. Accustomed to enormous wealth and influence since childhood, Slythe quickly assumed the corporate reins after his father's passing at an early age.

With perfectly styled gray hair, dressed in a pink Dunhill shirt, glen plaid Burberry slacks, and black John Lobb moccasins, he would have looked at home in any English manor. In his position, Slythe was, however, far more than a simple landed English lord. Waterboer Mines Limited controlled 95 percent of the world diamond trade, and as Slythe ruled Waterboer with an iron grip, he de facto controlled the world diamond trade. Enormous power for one man. The responsibility, stress, and pressure were enormous, but Slythe almost always appeared as cool as the cucumbers he fancied in his very British tea sandwiches. But stress has to come out somehow. In Slythe, it came out in psychologically deviant ways.

Slythe's office suite reflected the character of the man. Each surface was perfectly dusted and polished to a deep luster. A series of six impressionist landscapes from the master hand of Jacob Hendrick Pierneef hung on the walls.

Ian Witsrand waited for his master, for Slythe was no less, to seat himself behind his massive desk before sitting in an armchair across the desk. His oddly colored right blue eye twitched ever so slightly.

"So. Down to business. What news this morning?" He sniffed. Born of years of cocaine use, the respiratory reflex had become more than a nervous tick.

"Lester's people settled with the American Justice Ministry."

Slythe flashed perfect white teeth. "Smashing. Thank God for our dear Lester Churchman. How much?"

"Twenty million." Ian's Afrikaaner accent betrayed his far more informal education.

"A large sum. But still a bargain."

Ian hesitated momentarily. "I'm afraid there's more, sir. A wealthy American by the name of MacLean recently purchased land near the Raymond Mine. The farmer who sold it to him apparently knew about the diamond deposits and told him. Somehow he also got hold of the original 1920s geology report. Lester discovered MacLean intends to begin a diamond mining operation."

For the first time that morning, concern pulled at Slythe's tan face. He sniffed. "Are the two related? The Raymond Mine and this...what's his name?"

"MacLean, sir. Apparently not. But Lester isn't taking any chances. He's already contacted some of our people and organized a coalition of government agencies and environmentalists against MacLean's proposed mine."

Slythe leaned over the oak table, the smile now a scowl. "Tell Lester to make this problem disappear. Fast and whatever the cost. The idiot. He should never have allowed the sale to happen in the first place. What is he doing? He's supposed to be buying everything in that area."

"According to Lester, the land wasn't for sale publicly."

"Nothing can be discovered in Arkansas! Not a single tiny, low-grade stone! Can you imagine the disaster if the Americans knew the true size of the deposit? They would mine it and we'd never be able to stanch the flow of stones from there. Waterboer and the family have kept it hidden for a hundred twenty years and I won't let them get one over on the family now."

"Yes, sir."

He flashed another smile, sniffed again. "While you're at it, make Harry Weinberg disappear. I've always liked Harry—friends at school and all that kind of thing—but he made another substantial diamond purchase outside Waterboer channels. He knew the rules. Set an example, and do it publicly."

"With pleasure."

Despite his generally pleasant demeanor, brilliance, vast wealth, and his family's near-dictatorial control of the world diamond trade since the discovery of diamonds at Kimberley in the late 1800s, Slythe was convinced governments, political groups, even Waterboer's most trusted diamond dealers, like Weinberg, were involved in an ongoing conspiracy to destroy Waterboer's and the Slythe clan's control of the diamond trade. To Slythe, diamonds were more than a 120-year-old family global business, they were a religion; the Slythe family its high priests. Many who knew of Slythe's stress and cocaine habit hypothesized their combination induced his paranoia, others that his paranoia was a byproduct of his intellectual brilliance. Whatever the cause, his paranoia was real.

"Publicly, not personally." He lifted his index finger in warning. "You are not to go to the United States, Ian. We can't risk having you take one step on their land. Send Ulianov or another of Molotok's goons. We need to curry favor with them;

they need money. Pay them well. They'll be happy with the assignment."

Disappointment lined Ian's face. "Yes, sir."

"Speaking of our Siberian crazy, what news about Molotok?" Again, he sniffed.

"Everything is in place, sir. Our man at CIA classified the Siberian fire at Mirny as a natural gas explosion. And as Molotok assured us, Molotok's man was appointed as commander of the new garrison to replace Marshal Ogarkov. They should be starting deliveries again inside the week."

"Smashing. Anything else? I'm getting bored already."

"Your meeting with Riebeeck later today, and don't forget you're opening the new wing of the children's hospital this afternoon, meeting with the black women's business group after that."

At precisely 2:00 P.M., an unmarked Bell 230 twin-turbine helicopter bearing the name "OFS Realty" swooped down from the clear blue South African sky, unfolded its landing gear, and crouched onto the roof of a small building in Kimberley, the capital of the South African diamond mining industry in the Orange Free State. Slythe and a bodyguard emerged and walked down a dark stairway into a hallway of empty offices. The building was advertised for sale by OFS Realty, as it had been for the past twenty years. Although it appeared unused and dilapidated, the building was, in fact, guarded around the clock and effectively sound-proofed. Slythe used it for sensitive discussions and clandestine meetings when Waterboer's corporate headquarters would draw unwanted attention.

In one of the abandoned offices, a portly man in his forties removed a cheap cigar from between stained teeth. His tangled hair became one with a thick, unkempt beard. His rumpled powder-blue suit was a full size too small for his considerable girth and contrasted sharply with muddy jodhpur boots. Wim Voerwold was more comfortable in paramilitary khakis than business attire. In truth, he had changed into the suit at the last minute, not wanting to attract attention.

Despite his appearance, he managed to exude the overconfidence he derived from leadership of thousands of white supremacist Afrikaaner Volksfront troops. Out of sheer mega-lomania, Voerwold had adopted the name of Jan van Riebeeck, the shipwrecked Dutch sailor who first proposed that the Dutch East India Company occupy the Cape region in 1649, twenty-nine years after an English captain failed to convince the dull English crown to do the same. Based on his five years' previous military service in the South African forces, he had appointed himself to the rank of general.

Riebeeck tried hard to maintain his composure. This meeting could propel him to the forefront of South African politics, or it could consign him to imprisonment and, far worse, that ignominious group of failed revolutionaries.

"Mr. Slythe. It is a great honor," Riebeeck said with a deep Afrikaaner accent.

Slythe shook his hand vigorously. "The honor is mine, General. But if you don't mind, let us make this a rapid meeting. I would rather avoid suspicion from the government."

"The government," Riebeeck hacked. "Those *kaffir* vultures are too stupid to suspect anything."

The mostly peaceful transition from white to black rule orchestrated by the first democratically elected black government of Nelson Mandela in 1994 after decades of unspeakable humiliation and violence suffered at the hands of the apartheid government had not opened the hearts of the Afrikaaner Volksfront. They continued to claim title to the land in the Orange Free State. The elections of 1994 had been but a set-back to the group, which had managed to garner only a few seats in the four hundred-member legislative assembly, even less in the succeeding elections. Since then, they had used every means available to regroup and train as a fighting force. The mounting corruption, sloth, patronage, and disorganiza-tion of the new Boiko administration had pushed more whites into the Volksfront camp. But before it could take action, the Volksfront needed more weapons, more mercenaries. And weapons and mercenaries were expensive.

"I am afraid I do not share your confidence, General. But be that as it may, I have come to offer you my proposal personally."

Riebeeck could not help himself from breaking into an

anticipatory grin. Slythe had refused to tell him the nature of his proposal when he had arranged their clandestine meeting, but whatever it was, Riebeeck was certain if it involved Waterboer, it involved money. A lot of money.

"I know the Volksfront will soon demand possession and control of the Afrikaaner homeland in the Orange Free State."

"Your information is excellent, sir. We have a legitimate claim to this land by virtue of the British crown's recognition of Afrikaaner farms in 1848 and in 1854. We had hoped the *kaffir* government would recognize our rightful claim, but they are too drunk with their power. Their power over us. Us! The Boers who built this country with our own sweat and blood. We have no choice but to fight for our land. We have done it before. We are not afraid to die for our country, Mr. Slythe."

"As you say, General. Our land is in danger, and that means Waterboer is in danger. The two are inextricably tied as one. Under pressure from the Americans using economic aid as an incentive, as usual, Boiko is on the verge of passing sweeping antitrust legislation. The black American president has him convinced more blacks can be employed in the mining industry if Waterboer is split into myriad companies. He is right, of course. But it would destroy Waterboer. I cannot allow—we cannot allow—the irreplaceable Waterboer monopoly to be destroyed by antitrust laws of the childish black government."

"The Volksfront will never allow harm to Waterboer. It is the bedrock of our Afrikaaner homeland." Riebeeck paused, shifted his wet cigar to the other side of his mouth. "What do you propose?"

"To pay."

Riebeeck cocked his head. "Pay whom? Pay the government? But it's—"

"No, General. Pay the Volksfront. The Volksfront needs money if it is to reclaim the Orange Free State. For weapons, soldiers, supplies, propaganda. The world does not readily or kindly take to separatism. Especially not white separatism, as you know only too well. It will take money. A lot of money, and money is something Waterboer has a great deal of."

"Do you mean—"

"I propose to finance the Volksfront's efforts."

Riebeeck's cigar nearly fell to the ground as his mouth dropped open in shock. He quickly recovered. "What would be wanted in exchange?" Waterboer had always practiced apartheid in its mines, even though it denounced the practice publicly, but it had never been a supporter of the Volksfront. "You are a powerful man, Mr. Slythe. Waterboer is a powerful company. Can't you pressure the government? Your family has done so successfully many times in the past. Why finance us?"

Slythe stared hard at the grubby self-important militia leader. A caricature, he was nonetheless necessary to Waterboer's future. Slythe closeted condescension. "There was a time when Waterboer could. When the Slythes could. My father and grandfather could. I cannot. Not since the blacks have the vote. No matter how corrupt Boiko's administration has become, he himself is not. Some people simply cannot be bought. Boiko is legislating ideology, not pragmatism.

"For our financing your efforts, there are two conditions. First." Slythe raised a finger. "Volksfront troops will protect the Waterboer diamond mines from government and civilian attacks and will not disrupt operations. Second." He raised another finger. "There will be no antitrust legislation in the Orange Free State once the Volksfront takes over. Kill all the *kaffirs* you want, but these two requirements are absolute."

"Those are large demands."

"They are non-negotiable."

"How much do you propose to pay the Volksfront in exchange for its generosity?"

"Ten percent of Orange Free State diamond production within the Volksfront's protection. Once a month. In American dollars deposited in the banks of your choice outside South Africa and England."

Riebeeck paused, weighing pro and con. The proposal was far more advantageous than he'd hoped. Without the funds, the Volksfront could not possibly wage its secessionist campaign. Now, the secession could—would—move from theory to practice. Even the method of payments itself would facilitate the purchase of weapons and influence.

"The Volksfront is prepared to protect the Waterboer mines from the *kaffirs*, but that kind of protection will draw many troops away from the fighting, where they will be sorely needed. And the protection of the Waterboer monopoly will require many payoffs in the Afrikaaner camp." He paused. "Fifteen percent." Riebeeck seemed almost apologetic. Slythe was elated by the low counter proposal, but he hid his pleasure, squinted at the Volksfront leader. "You are certain, General? Not 20 or 30 percent? Or will a reevaluation of your figures come later? I do not take kindly to renegotiation."

"No." Riebeeck feigned insult. "I am a man of my word, Mr. Slythe. Some in the Volksfront will want to ask for a greater share than 15 percent, but anything greater than 15 percent would be extortion. Extortion is not what the Volksfront wishes from the Waterboer diamond mines, the glory of the Orange Free State. Fifteen percent it is and 15 percent it will remain."

"Very well then. We have an agreement. The first payment will be made today, in this account, so you can purchase what you need." He handed Riebeeck a typed piece of paper. "The second payment will only be made once your forces have begun their attack and secured the mines."

Riebeeck did not hide his joy. Tears welled in his eyes. He placed a meaty hand on Slythe's shoulder. "I don't know if you realize the importance of Waterboer's contribution. Finally, after 150 years, the Volksfront will finally be able to make the Orange Free State into the independent nation it always should have been."

Slythe tolerated Riebeeck's hand and placed his own hand on the man's shoulder. "We are trusting you not only with our heritage, but with our preeminence in the world diamond market, General. Let's hope you can keep it independent."

He flashed a smile, glanced at his watch. It wouldn't do to arrive late for the opening of the new children's hospital.

16 NATIONALIST

Vladivostok, Primorskaia
Russian Federation
3:02 P.M.

The change was as abrupt as it was swift. The collapse of Soviet Communism and the dissolution of the Soviet Union marked the end of ideological repression, police-state intrusions, organized atheism, and government-controlled social, economic, and geographic mobility. Initially greeted as gifts from heaven, the reforms that followed, then stopped, then started again in earnest under Orlov, ushered in myriad requirements to work, and therefore, myriad problems. Competition. Taxes. Risk. A work ethic. Democratic participation. Instability. Accountability.

Once the maritime gem in the Soviet crown, within a few years after the Soviet collapse, Vladivostok disintegrated into a corrupt, impoverished town controlled by the *krestnii otets*, the Russian *mafiya's* godfathers. The massive Soviet Pacific fleet that once had projected Soviet naval power from its home port of Vladivostok into the Pacific and the South China Sea rusted with disuse. Legions of sailors, aviators, and other soldiers were laid off, the records of their service to the motherland, the *rodina*, filed away on mimeographed sheets, slid into forgotten folders, stored in molding wood cabinets, locked in abandoned basements. Those who remained in the military were paid subsistence wages—when they were paid at all. Forced to survive without government assistance, many had no choice but to sell their services and weapons to the highest bidder, often terrorist countries, such as Iran.

Corruption became institutionalized. Smuggling was not only tolerated but actively encouraged. The value of the ruble plunged to such depths that *Amerikanskii* dollars became the only form of acceptable tender. Roads were not maintained. Public buildings peeled and crumbled in disrepair. Public transportation was cannibalized for spare parts. Despite the growing economy under Orlov, many harsh reforms still had several years to run before the economic pain would pass.

In Vladivostok, as in many other cities in the Russian Federation, the people—the *narod*—were in utter despair. They had waited too long. Since the tsar, under Lenin, Stalin, Khrushchev, Brezhnev, Andropov, Chernenko, Gorbachev, then under the so-called reformers, the *narod* had been told to wait. To be patient. To endure just a little longer. To bear the pain like good Russians. But the *narod* had had enough. Enough patience. Enough pain. Although willing to suffer more painfully and longer than almost any other people in the world, the Russian *narod* was fed up. It wanted action, not promises. It craved a real Russian leader, a man with a grip of steel. One who would yank Russia out of the quagmire into which she had been sinking since Peter the Great. One who would destroy the evil outside forces that strangled the *rodina*. An ardent patriarch to comfort the *narod*. A hammer to pound a former empire, a former global superpower, back into Holy Mother Russia.

It was with this in mind that Yevgeni Vilinovsky made his way through the Vladivostok fish market. No one knew Vilinovsky by his real name. They knew him as Molotok, the "Hammer." Like Stalin—"Steel"—Molotok was a name to which the people responded. He was a giant of a man. Tall, muscular, like a hardened stevedore who lifted superhuman weights, performed backbreaking work, and devoured red meat, potatoes, bread, and vodka. His long black hair waved back and forth in the brisk wind. He wore a thick black mustache. His veined, red nose was testament to his taste for the national beverage. He dressed in simple peasant clothes— coarse dark wool pants tucked into heavy leather boots, a fur-lined, rough leather coat.

Molotok's origins were a mystery. He seemed simply to have always existed, as if he originated from the protean depths of the Russian soul; from the fertile earth of the Russian countryside; from the vast and ancient national consciousness. There was a sense of dark mysticism about this man with the smoldering black eyes. Though most Russians were familiar with

Molotok's *Russkost* party, "Russianness," few had seen its leader. He was not visible like other politicians, who danced like puppets and whores before television cameras. Molotok appeared and disappeared, each time voicing the pain of the *narod* in a way that no one else could. Many of the suffering, impatient, longing Russian people believed Molotok had been unleashed by the wild and desolate vastness of Siberia to reclaim the very soul of Holy Mother Russia from its domestic and foreign enemies.

On this gray afternoon, Molotok stood on a crude wooden table identical to others laden with fresh fruits of the sea. Behind him the pale blue hulls of the once-mighty Pacific fleet lay still.

"Skyward soar the whirling demons," Molotok's voice boomed.

"Shrouded by the falling snow.

"And their plaintive, awful howling,

"Fills my heart with dread and woe."

The immortal words of Alexander Pushkin resonated through speakers placed around the makeshift market by his local Russkost supporters. People immediately recognized the words of their beloved poet. Who is this giant man who quotes Pushkin?

No visible aides. No bodyguards. No tailored suit. No eyeglasses. No Zil or Chaika or Mercedes limousine. It could not be a politician. Could it be him?

"What to do?

"We have lost our way.

"From afar, the Demon cries out,

"He is leading the way!"

The familiar words, this huge man's hypnotic plaintiveness drew people to the marketplace like fire sucked in oxygen.

"I love Russia!

"I love the Russian people!

"I love the Russian countryside!

"I love the Russian forests and snow and ice and plains!

"I love the Russian spirit!

"I love the Russian soul!"

Molotok paused.

"But where is Russia? Russia has disappeared! Where is the Russia we knew? The Russia of strength and warmth and comfort? The Russia who cared for us, fed us, clothed us, educated us? The motherland. The *rodina*!"

It must be him, they concluded. Molotok.

Sailors wrapped in black overcoats congregated on the rusty railings of the few functioning naval vessels behind the makeshift podium, tilted their shaved heads to hear the man who spoke to their souls.

"We have lost our empire!

"We have lost our pride!

"We have lost our respect!

"The West plunders our resources! The *mafiya krestnii otets*, godfathers for the devil, eat at the fabric of our beloved *rodina!* Plunder our treasures! Our glorious capital! Our agriculture! They corrupt our children and demoralize our families! We are being colonized!"

Molotok paused and scanned the crowd, making repeated eye contact. He saw the Russian soul in the collective gaze, saw pain swell from behind the hardened masks of daily life.

"Where is Holy Mother Russia? I will tell you! It has gone to the *Amerikanskii* demons! They suck our lifeblood! Our natural resources! Our pride and glory! It has passed into the hands of the greedy, money-grubbing Jews, the corrupt Roman Church! The *zhidomasonstvo*, the Jewish freemasonry! They control our economy! They control our once-noble institutions! Our government!" He paused again and looked into the eyes of the crowd. "They have brought about *gibel Rossii*—the ruin of Russia. Who else could benefit from Russia's ruin? From our pain? From our suffering? From our weakness?"

Many stood on tables to get a better glimpse of the near-mystical figure.

"The great veterans fought for the *rodina*! Against the Nazis! They pushed them back!" Molotok roared. "In the snows and ice of Stalingrad! Without food, with their bare hands!" His right hand tightened into a fist. "Our government has forgotten them! Their sacrifices! Glory and pride has been stolen from

our children! They have never seen the great *rodina* as it once
was! Under Stalin! When the world trembled at our armies! At
our warships! At our fighters! At our bombers! At our rockets!
Our children have been robbed of their inheritance! We have
been robbed of our birthright!"

The crowd's shouts became angrier.

"And us? What do we have? What have the corrupt Western
reforms brought us? Where have the public services gone? The
roads? The buses? I cannot afford a loaf of bread. I could
afford *benzina* for my car, then it was stolen by the mafia. My
pay goes into the pockets of the capitalist Western demons! To
the Jews! To the Roman Church! My countryside and farms
and pastures are blackened by their pollution. Russian soldiers.
Sailors. Aviators. Those who protect our great *rodina*. They
have been decimated by the bureaucrats! They are not paid!
Their equipment stands idle!" He pointed to the ships in the
harbor. "Cannibalized! Why do they do this to us?" he cried
out, almost in tears. "What have we done to them? We spilled
our blood to liberate them in the Great Patriotic War! We have
become the slaves of the West! Where is our country? Where
is the *rodina*? Where is Holy Mother Russia?"

The shouts escalated to a frenzy.

Molotok paused, stared hard at the people. "We must rescue
the *rodina*. We must rescue the *rodina* by force! The force it
craves. The pure force of the Russian soul. We must destroy all
that destroys the *rodina*."

A unified roar of approval rose from the crowd. Pain, fear,
anger, and desperation had found the easy path of expression
provided by Molotok. The path of hatred.

"We must reclaim what is ours! Not by weak and corrupt
Western elections. We have seen how that works."

"It doesn't!" screamed a portly *babushka*, scarred with the
pain of her seventy years.

"No Western democracy! No human rights! No Roman
Church! No Jews!" He spat the words with disdain. "Lies and
liars all. Leeches on the lifeblood of the *rodina*! Elections and
democracy are for the weak. We are strong. We must take over
the *rodina* by force!" He continued to shake his fist. "We must

cut out the Western cancer! We must reclaim our imperial borders! The traitorous breakaway republics! Poland! Alaska! We must be hammers on rotten wood!"

He paused.

"And we will do it! Together, as one. Russkost will do it. We will lead the patriotic ones. The patriotic Russian farmers. The patriotic workers. The patriotic unemployed. The brave patriotic Russian soldiers of the army and navy and rocket forces. Together we will be the force of salvation for the *rodina*! This is our campaign for Russia's soul!

"The battle will soon begin! Join me, my Russian brothers and sisters! Long live the *rodina*! Long live Holy Mother Russia!"

Raw emotion thundered from the crowd like demons loosed in the glacial cold. Following the prompts of Molotok's people scattered through the crowd, the people began to chant. "Mo-lo-tok! Mo-lo-tok! Mo-lo-tok!"

Hatred and anger and fear pumped nationalism through their veins. Now flowing freely, Molotok knew it could be summoned at a moment's notice.

Before the crowd could reach him, Molotok rushed into a dirty olive-green Moskvitch sedan and sped off in a cloud of mufflerless exhaust. He had three more speeches to deliver in Vladivostok that afternoon. One large city per week. One small town per day. The development of name recognition imposed a difficult schedule, but the thick wads of cash soon to tumble into Russkost coffers would finally transform his words into action.

17 FRAME

Macon Grove, Arkansas
1:00 P.M.

The national economic slowdown was quick to reach the tiny town of Macon Grove, Arkansas. And as the rest of America's economy leveled for a break in its seemingly unstoppable expansion, Macon Grove had fallen into a deep recession. Jobs held by villagers working in nearby Murfreesboro were eliminated by nameless, faceless men in dark suits far away who had neither visited Macon Grove nor broken bread with their employees. Many had gone to the large cities in search of work.

It was against this backdrop that a crowd of residents filed down Main Street to Martha and Ed Jameson's coffee shop. One of the neon letters above the double doors was burned out. The sign read COF-EE SHOP. Each of the five hundred villagers had been personally invited to lunch by simple mailed invitation through the work of MacLean's public relations consultants. The lunch was free. People piled their plates with barbecued ribs, chili, and corn on the cob. Dressed in blue jeans, a white shirt, a bolo tie, and cowboy boots, Dan Wenzel stood on the formica counter top. A microphone squawked in his hand as he smiled at the guests who could hardly contain their curiosity.

"How're you all doin' today?"

A low volume rumble of "fine," "good," and "great" emanated from the crowd.

"Food all right?"

A louder rumble of approval. A few shouts and catcalls.

"I know you're all wondering what this is about, so I'll get right to the point. First off I'd like to thank Martha and Ed Jameson and their wonderful kids Jeanie and Tom for letting me invite you here today. How 'bout a round of applause for them? Let's give 'em a hand."

The crowd liked the Jamesons, was happy about the free food. The applause was sincere.

Wenzel deep-sixed the fake Southern accent. "Let me introduce myself. You may have seen me around town this week. Many of you I've had the pleasure of meeting personally. For those of you I've missed, my name is Dan Wenzel. I'm not from here, but I guess that's pretty obvious."

People chuckled.

"I work for a man named Max MacLean. A little while ago, Mr. MacLean bought a piece of land two miles up the road. It belonged to Theodore Osage, who still lives there." People nodded. Old man Osage was part of the town. Curiosity increased. "Mr. MacLean has decided to open a mining operation on the land, and he's going to need workers. He sent me down here to see if anyone would be interested in working there."

Three dozen men and women shouted "yes" in unison and stretched their arms as high as they would reach.

Wenzel smiled. "That's great. That's great. Now Mr. MacLean realizes that some people might not have the particular training necessary to work in a mine, but he's willing to train new employees. While paying them a starting salary, of course. For starters, we'll need about forty men and women for drilling, digging, sorting, accounting. The works. There'll be a signup sheet on your way out and jobs enough for everyone." He let it sink in. Husbands and wives spoke in hushed tones. Single men and women smiled and clapped.

"Now, that's the good news. But you know how it works. If there's good news, there's also bad news. So here's the bad news. It seems that some politicians up in Washington aren't too happy about the mine." A series of grunts rose from the crowd. "I have no idea why, really, but it's a fact. Mr. MacLean has been personally threatened to stop the mine and sell the land. Frankly, he doesn't give a hoot what Washington thinks. He thinks the mine is going to make him a lot of money and bring a whole bunch of jobs to Macon Grove for a long time. The feds can't really do anything about it because the mine is legal and this is your town." He jabbed at the air. "You're going to decide, not a bunch of politicians in D.C."

The room applauded.

"The thing is this, people, and I'm going to lay it on the line here. Before we can get this mine off the ground and hire people, we're going to need permits that depend entirely on your city government here." Wenzel pointed at the crowd. "But last time I checked, America was a democracy and you're the town. You decide."

He paused and looked down at the counter. "I'd like to tell you what it is we're going to mine, but I can't do that just yet, other than we're mining rock. What I can tell you in case you're worried is that there'll be no chemical processes involved other than washing rocks with water. No pollution. And all our reports will be public, right there for you to see at City Hall anytime you want to read them. Again, you're the town. You decide if you want this.

"There is one last thing I'd like to add. If we can get this mine off the ground, we'd like to hire local companies to build the mine itself. Not outside companies. The Japanese may do it cheaper, but Americans can do it better."

Cheers erupted. People stood and clapped enthusiastically. His ear always firmly to the political ground, Mayor Jack Billings concluded that the political winds were howling in Wenzel's direction. He made a brief speech supporting the mine, which Wenzel had discussed with him earlier in the week, then everyone dove into the large frosted cakes brought out by the Jameson children. The crowd mobbed Wenzel as he made his way across the room. They slapped him on the back, laughed and introduced wives, husbands, and children. They were good people. Wenzel was convinced that the mine could not possibly be constructed in a better place.

His immediate mission in town accomplished, Wenzel drove his rented light-blue Mercury Sable back to Osage's farm to pick up his bags before catching his commercial flight out of Little Rock airport. The gravel crunched loudly under the Sable's tires as Wenzel drove up to Osage's house near the lake fed by the Little Missouri River. The setting sun glowed orange in the West. Clouds hung low in the air. A brisk wind blew from the Northeast. Osage's new bright red Chevy pickup—a gift from MacLean—was parked under a carport Osage had built especially for it. He doted on the vehicle, only drove it on special occasions. His dented clunker remained his main method of daily transportation. Wenzel smiled. Osage was a neat old bird. He would have made someone a perfect grandpa.

Wenzel walked to the two-story wood house. Smoke puffed from the chimney. The lights were on. The steps creaked as he walked up the stairs to the front porch. He knocked on the peeling paint of the battered door and waited for Osage's familiar bellow. A minute passed. He tried again.

Still no answer.

Wenzel looked at both of Osage's trucks. He had to be there.

He turned the rickety brass door handle, pushed the door. It squeaked open. "Theodore?" Wenzel shouted. "You home? It's Dan."

Nothing.

Wenzel walked through the living room, as spotless and neat as ever, through the dining room and the library crowded with myriad books. He checked the bedroom and the bathroom. No one. He finally found Osage in the kitchen.

Dead.

Theodore Osage had been shot in the back at close range. At the wooden kitchen table, the portly old man sat, slumped over the latest issue of *Bass Fisherman*. A pool of blood covered the magazine's pages, dripped onto the linoleum floor. Osage was dressed in overalls and a Pendleton shirt. His Sunday shirt, he'd once told Wenzel proudly. His eyes were open wide, filled not with rage or fear, but with peace. As if what he'd known all his life would happen had finally come to pass.

Wenzel bent over Osage, closed the man's eyes, sat down on the bench, and wept.

When his tears were spent, Wenzel shaded his eyes with one hand and recited Kaddish for his friend.

Yis-gad-dal v'yis-kad-dash sh'mey rab-bo...

Wenzel had become fond of Osage. In many ways, the older man had been like a child. Strong-headed, concerned with the little things in life, like his new truck and his red Pendleton shirt. He'd had his books and his fishing and his truck. Nothing else really mattered. He drank too much, but neither caused trouble nor went looking for it. He'd been kind, gentle.

And those bastards had murdered him. Wenzel got to his feet, stepped to the telephone that hung on the wall, dialed 9-1-1 with a trembling hand, then realized the line was dead. In his grief, he thought nothing of it and dialed 9-1-1 on his cell phone. It took over a minute for emergency services to answer.

"Theodore Osage's been murdered," he blurted out. "Yes, he's dead. Shot at close range. He was dead when I got here. Send someone right away. Twenty-two Rural Route One, Macon Grove." He hung up and regained his place beside Osage.

It was now completely dark outside. The fire in the hearth glowed red; Osage's last fire. Wenzel sat near his murdered friend and recited Kaddish over and over, his upper body gently davening forward and backward. He did not hear a car arrive, swung his head in surprise when two men crashed through the kitchen door.

The shorter man held an identification badge inches from Wenzel's face. "FBI. Stand up and place your hands behind your head. You're under arrest."

"Under arrest?" He stood, walked to the agents.

The shorter agent grabbed him by an arm, twisted it behind his back, flipped him around, slammed him against the formica counter, and patted him down.

"Dammit, that hurts!"

"Shut up!" The taller agent placed handcuffs around Wenzel's wrists and secured them tightly. Wenzel winced as the metal bit into his skin with each movement of his wrists.

"You have the right to remain silent. Anything you say can—"

"I'm a lawyer. I know my rights. What's the charge?"

"The murder of this man." The taller agent pointed at Osage's body.

"What? Are you crazy? I didn't kill him. He was dead when I got here."

"You can tell that to the court, Mr. Wenzel."

They pushed him roughly out the front door, down the creaky steps to a dark blue sedan.

As they shoved him into the rear seat, a blue and white Chevrolet Caprice Classic drove up the gravel driveway, skidded to a halt inches behind the dark sedan, lights flashing. The local sheriff jumped out from behind the driver's seat, ran over to the agents.

"What's going on here?" Sheriff Boone demanded. "Who the heck are you?"

The short agent flashed his badge. "FBI, Sheriff. We're arresting this man for the murder of Theodore Osage."

Boone observed the badge carefully, spat a wad of tobacco on the ground. "The heck you are, son."

"I don't think you understand, Sheriff. This man shot and killed the man in there." He jerked a finger over his shoulder. "He's under arrest."

Boone moved closer, potbelly straining against his shirt, brushing against the agent. "No. I don't think you understand." He waved his index finger under the agent's nose. "I don't give a rat's ass if this guy is the biggest mass murderer since Sherman. This here is my jurisdiction. You FBI boys have not one i-ota of authority here. Don't screw around with me, son. I may not have a huge police force, but I'm not some green country hick born yesterday. This murder was committed here in Macon Grove. Now I don't want any trouble with the FBI, but unless Judge Thompson moves this case to federal court, this guy stays right here in Macon Grove."

"Now list—"

"You got that?" Boone rested his right hand on a pearl-handled Colt .45 revolver, a family heirloom. He had grabbed the weapon in haste on the way out of his house. He never had to use it and wondered if it was even loaded.

The shorter agent turned red, gesticulated wildly. He looked about to rush Boone head-on when his partner restrained him.

"Fine, Sheriff, fine." The agent walked to the car and uncuffed Wenzel. Wenzel massaged his wrists. The agents got into the car. The taller one rolled down the window and looked up at Boone from the passenger seat. "I'm telling you right now, Sheriff. You're interfering with the FBI in a federal investigation. That's a federal offense."

"So I'll be arrested and finally be able to take a vacation." He delivered a wad of tobacco juice on the car's front tire to emphasize his point.

The shorter agent launched a curse against the sheriff's southern ancestry, and the sedan drove off in a cloud of dust.

"And cussin's not going to score you any points with Judge Thompson!" Boone ushered Wenzel into the back seat of his cruiser, radioed his deputy.

"What's going on around here, Sheriff? Why do they think I killed Osage? He was dead when I got here. I swear it. Just like I told 9-1-1. And why the hell is the FBI involved?" The words came out like a river undammed. "Theodore was my friend, Sheriff. Why would I kill him?" He wiped away tears.

"I believe you." Boone turned around and looked at him. He had checked up on Wenzel during the past week, satisfied himself Wenzel was an okay guy. "But tell me something. Were you really serious about what you said this afternoon? About the feds not wanting your boss to start a mine down here? About the feds interfering?"

Wenzel looked up at Boone and wiped his bloodshot eyes. "Absolutely. Why?"

"Well I don't know what kind of experience you've had with the FBI. But despite what Hollywood seems to think, the FBI doesn't just pop into a house in the middle of Arkansas farmland, arrest someone out of the blue, and try to take them to federal prison. I'm no Columbo, but I can tell you this. Those boys were as serious as I've ever seen the FBI. Those badges were real. But they sure as heck didn't follow standard FBI operating procedure."

"What are you saying, exactly?"

"I'd have to say that someone pretty darn powerful wants to stop your people from building that mine."

"They knew my name."

Boone looked at Wenzel quizzically. "What's that?"

"They knew my name, they called me 'Mr. Wenzel.' I'd never met them before."

Boone nodded. "So I'm right. It was you they were after. Not Theodore's killer."

"You think...you think this whole thing was a—"

"A frame."

18 APARTMENT

Normally, investigations involving missing Muscovites were handled by the overworked and underpaid Moscow Militia. The Pyashinev matter was far different. The director of Komdragmet's disappearance merited official scrutiny.

Orlov initially considered turning over the Pyashinev investigation to the Interior Ministry and its troops, the MVD. But doing so would have left out the secret organ's military counterpart, the GRU. True, the GRU had been reduced in stature and strength since its failed coup, but it was better to rehabilitate the wounded organization and earn its gratitude than to leave its leadership and ranks to suffer and incur its still-dangerous ire. Also, the MVD was responsible for internal matters, and Pyashinev's case had far too many international implications to be investigated by the Interior Ministry. Based on these political considerations, which for Orlov were far more instinctive than analytical, the responsibility for the investigation fell on GRU Colonel Kovanetz.

Kovanetz had not actively supported the GRU's attempted coup. He was thus spared from Orlov's purge of the GRU and the SVR/FSB—the former KGB. But Kovanetz was not satisfied merely with survival. He craved more power than the wounded GRU could grant him legally, and he had allied himself with a force he believed would soon be able to provide what he sought: Russkost.

Other than Pyashinev's offshore bank account, the helicopter crash in Mexico, and the cryptic handwritten note, there were few clues. Whereas this lack of clues might have closed the dossiers of more mundane investigations, the Pyashinev investigation was a matter of national security. It could not stop.

The entrance to Leonid Pyashinev's apartment was cordoned off with police tape. Since the disappearance of its resident one week earlier, only the GRU team had been permitted entry into the luxurious premises. It searched the apartment three times. Once upon Pyashinev's initial disappearance, to secure any documents of state importance. A second time upon the discovery of Pyashinev's flight from Russia in a military jet. A third time when it was discovered Pyashinev had been in the employ of Waterboer most recently to the tune of $5,000,000 and, hence, was not merely corrupt but a traitor.

All three searches of the apartment failed as dismally as those of the man's office and the GRU's interrogations of family, friends, and servants. But now Kovanetz had a new reason to search the apartment. He had received new orders. Not from Orlov. This time, the orders had come from his other boss. From Molotok. Molotok had received information that Pyashinev knew of a KGB diamond stockpile whose existence he had not disclosed to the Russian government and whose location he had not revealed to Waterboer. Molotok wanted it. Now that Pyashinev was dead, who better to find it than Kovanetz, who was heading up the investigation into Pyashinev's death? And Molotok paid well. If you succeeded, he let you live.

Kovanetz repeated the words on the note over and over in his head. *Rossiya, trieti sloi. Nie dopustit im wziat eto.* Russia, third layer. Must not let them get it.

Everyone leaves clues, Kovanetz knew. As one scholar had remarked, absence of evidence does not signify evidence of absence. So if there were no clues to the note in the reports, they had to be in the apartment. Somewhere in the posh apartment were facts that would allow him to decipher the cryptic phrase and lead him to the diamond stockpile.

Kovanetz returned the crisp salute of the young private who stood guard at the doorway. The vacant apartment was as cold as the snowy streets below its ornate windows. A cloud of frozen breath trailed behind him as he walked through the foyer into the living room. It did not take GRU training to deduce Pyashinev had enjoyed a source of income beyond his salary as a civil servant. Paneled in blue silk and carpeted with eighteenth-century rugs, the apartment was more reminiscent of a tsarist palace than a bureaucrat's residence. Polished rococo antiques of carved wood and gold leaf crowded even the smallest space. Crystal chandeliers hung from intricately moulded ceilings like immobile ice flakes. Photographs proudly displayed the former resident with members of the Russian and international elite, not the least of which was Waterboer's Piet Slythe. A glass case enclosed a superbly executed scale model of the *Potemkin*, the tsarist warship that witnessed the famous mutiny of imperial troops in 1905, later immortalized for Communist propaganda in Eisenstein's 1925 film.

Paintings of other warships, in placid waters or engaged in naval battle, lined nearly every wall between filigreed candelabras.

Careful to observe every detail, Kovanetz made his way to Pyashinev's office. He smiled at the subtle efficiency with which his team had sifted through the apartment. Except for the documents that had been removed from the wall safe, not a single sheet of paper was out of place, not a molecule of dust disturbed. He doubted that even Pyashinev would have realized a team of investigators had scrutinized each of his personal effects.

Pyashinev's home office was a formal affair. An imposing Louis XVI sculpted desk laden with paperwork sat in the center of the room under the watchful gaze of photographs of modern Russian warships between palms that stood guard in each corner of the room. A large emerald-cut diamond scintillated under a glass dome on an ornate coffee table. Kovanetz did not disturb any of the late director's effects. It was not necessary to soil his gloved hands. His team had already read, analyzed, and cataloged each and every scrap of information in the apartment. Kovanetz knew the answer to the hauntingly simple riddle would not be scrawled on a scrap of paper. He searched for something far more visible and, at the same time, more subtle. So he scanned each room with his slow gaze and repeated the words of Pyashinev's note in his mind.

Rossiya, trieti sloi. Nie dopustit im wziat eto. In the library, shelves of books seemed to hold up the frescoed ceiling like pillars. On a shimmering wood table, books on diamonds, publications on naval history and design. Nothing here. Only books. His team had cataloged Pyashinev's literary collection with a precision that would have put the most scrupulous librarian to shame.

Kovanetz proceeded through the bedrooms, the kitchen, the bathrooms, the gymnasium, the media room. Nothing. Ornate, but not unusual. Nothing on the premises seemed out of the ordinary. After nearly an hour of silent observation, Kovanetz accepted that the apartment was not speaking to him.

Kovanetz saluted the private and made his way back to GRU headquarters in his chauffeured Lada. He would make two reports. In writing for President Orlov. By phone to Molotok. The line between the two bosses was more than a political tightrope. Walking it, Kovanetz risked far more than political disgrace. Failure was not an option.

His problem was that, in his post as a military intelligence officer, Kovanetz was a man of action, not an analyst. He was accustomed to obtaining information, not interpreting it. Unlike a trained detective, Kovanetz was too focused, was looking too hard. He was unable to take a step back to see the obvious fact that a Moscow Militia detective would have spotted immediately.

19 AIDE

Main Justice Building
Washington, D.C.
8:07 A.M.

Carlton sipped java from his white DOJ mug and watched the weak winter sun through his office window. He yawned. For the second night in a row, he had not slept. Cold from lack of sleep, he let the strong black coffee coarse through his system. He rubbed his eyes, mentally waded through the facts for the nth time.

The devil may be in the details, he knew, but the truth was in the facts. Although his case and MacLean's difficulties seemed to be intertwined, at present the only common denominator was the law firm of Fox, Carlyle. Fox, Carlyle represented Murfreesboro Mining Corporation. Fox, Carlyle was trying to buy MacLean's land in Arkansas for an undisclosed client. Fox, Carlyle had formed the nonprofit environmental group threatening MacLean not to mine. And according to Pink, Fox, Carlyle represented Waterboer's interests in the U.S.

Waterboer had a vested interest in diamond mining. That explained its interest in any diamonds in Arkansas. Waterboer could not operate legally inside the United States. That explained why it would hire an unscrupulous, high-powered law firm such as Fox, Carlyle to do its bidding. And it might explain Fox, Carlyle's formation of a bogus environmental group to put pressure on MacLean. But it didn't explain why the government was involved. Not just one agency, but two. Perhaps three, if Carlton counted Pink at CIA, of whom he remained suspicious. Something more was lurking in the shadows.

The telephone interrupted his mental meanderings.

"Pat Carlton."

"Pat." The voice was rushed, grave. "It's Dan Wenzel."

Carlton looked at his watch. 8:10 A.M. "It's five in the morning for you, Dan. What the he—"

"Osage's been murdered. The farmer who sold MacLean the land."

"Murdered?"

"Shot point blank in the heart. Last night. Two FBI agents tried to arrest me after I discovered the body. The local sheriff refused to let the FBI assert jurisdiction, thank God. The autopsy proved that Osage was shot at the time I was making a speech."

"Why would the FBI be involved in this?"

"I don't know. I—"

Carlton sat up. "Hold on. I've got to check on something. I'll get back to you." Not just the National Trust and the Bureau of Land Management and maybe CIA. Now the FBI was involved. He found the number in his address book and dialed. Mazursky picked up on the third ring.

"David. It's Pat Carlton."

"Oh yes. From DOJ. How are you?" The Senate aide was clearly busy but made a distinct effort at cordiality.

"I'm glad you're in early. I have something urgent to go over with you. Can we meet? I don't really want to discuss it over the phone." Carlton heard his own paranoia, wrinkled his nose. "Just a few minutes, I promise."

Mazursky sat back into his chair, stared at the DOJ confirmation on his screen. Flakes from all over Arkansas, even other states, called Mazursky and the other LAs in the senator's office, droned on and on about government and other conspiracies involving the Trilateral Commission, the New World Order, Freemasonry, Scientology, the Vatican, and the Zionist Occupational Government. Those he regularly sent packing. But Mazursky, a keen legislative staffer, hoarded business cards the way others collected matchbooks or stamps. He had checked on Carlton. The guy had gone to UCLA undergrad, George Washington law. Merchants of Pain on K Street. Lieutenant in the Navy Reserves. Justice Department. Carlton was no flake. So although the call sounded like it could be a complete waste of time, Mazursky decided to take Carlton's paranoia at face value. "I can meet you, but on such short notice only for about ten minutes. Will that work?"

"That's all I need."

"I have a meeting in the Capitol in forty-five minutes. Can you swing by the office? In about thirty? We can talk while we walk."

Carlton raced down the hallway, a storm in cowboy boots. He spotted Erika at the end of the corridor, half-walking, half-jogging toward him.

When they met, she turned and ran alongside him. "I've got to talk to you."

He felt her observe his wrinkled shirt, disheveled hair.

"What happened to you? You look like hell."

"Good morning to you too. I can't talk now. I've got to get to the Hill."

Erika didn't let him off that easily. "It can't wait. I'll go with you."

Carlton stopped, placed his hands on her shoulders. "It was a mistake involving you in this. I should never have—"

"But you didn't. I involved my—"

"Erika." He looked at her in silence for a moment. She was fresh, radiant in a beige suit and white blouse. He stared at her lively green eyes, smelled her perfume. "It doesn't matter who involved whom. Trust me. You want to get as uninvolved with this thing as you can. It started out as interesting. Now it's dangerous. Whoever's behind this murdered one person, tried to frame another."

Erika stared at him hard, her friendly eyes and soft pout replaced with a tight-lipped scowl. "Are you done with the male chauvinist bullshit?"

"Erika, plea—"

"I found something, Pat."

"It doesn't matter. It's got to—" He paused. "Arkansas?"

She nodded.

He sighed. "Okay. Come on." He started jogging down the marble staircase. "You're going to regret this."

"I already do."

Carlton's muddy Cadillac tore up Pennsylvania Avenue toward the Capitol. Erika gripped the door handle and prayed for her life as Carlton weaved through traffic and described the incidents in Macon Grove.

Within five minutes, the Shark's tires squealed to a stop in front of the Hart Senate Office Building, a bulky white marble cube of an office building between Union Station and the Senate side of the Capitol.

Two uniformed security guards continued their Redskins Super Bowl prognostications as they casually verified the pair's DOJ identification tags. Carlton and Erika walked through a metal detector into the imposing atrium, where a jagged black steel sculpture rose five stories to meet the black steel plates of a Calder mobile suspended from the ceiling.

David Mazursky greeted them as they pushed their way past the round seal of the State of Arkansas on the plate glass doors of Senator Bigham's office. "I'm glad you made it. I was about to leave. Sorry we can't meet longer."

"Thanks for seeing me. This is Erika Wassenaar. Also at Justice."

"Nice to meet you. Let's walk."

The three took an elevator to the basement and walked to the Senate subway station through another set of guards, another metal detector, another ID check. Few people knew about the subway that linked the United States Senate with the Russell, Dirksen, and Hart Senate office buildings. Its design was a bizarre mix of Disneyland, ancient Rome, and cold war styles. The underground subway ferried legislators, staffers, and ID-toting lobbyists on a series of small open-air trams along a single track through granite-reinforced tunnels.

Carlton brought Mazursky up to date on events since the settlement, leaving nothing out, including Erika's disturbing information about Waterboer and its closure of the Arkansas mine in the 1920s. He finished as the tram stopped at the Capitol station. The three squeezed through the smallish door, past the guard, and walked to an escalator bank leading to the main floor of the Capitol.

Mazursky turned to Carlton. "I realize that this is more than you told me over the phone the other day, but it doesn't change what I told you. The Arkansas diamond story is one of the tallest folk tales in the state. People have been going on and on about it for years. Decades. But it's never been proven, Pat. Just a few months ago, three different geological surveys were performed in three areas near Murfreesboro."

"And?"

"Nothing."

"But what about the farmers in my case?" Carlton asked. "They were mining diamonds. Rather profitably, according to the figures I read."

"Of course there are some diamonds in Arkansas. There are simply no deposits sufficiently large that a company as enormous and at such risk in the U.S. as Waterboer would give a second glance to. The mine in your case was probably a fluke. It probably would have soon petered out. Your 1920s survey? Who knows if it's even real? Trust me. I've seen the most recent reports with my own eyes. There's not much down there."

Carlton said nothing. Erika nodded silently.

"I'm sorry I can't lend more legitimacy to your Waterboer theory. I know they're racist, monopolist bastards. I'd love to kick their butts. But this Arkansas diamond business is just another folk tale."

"The guy was murdered, David. Shot in the heart at close range. Fox, Carlyle represents the defendant in my case, the party who's trying to buy MacLean's land, the environmental group that threatened him, and Waterboer. You don't find that just a little suspicious?"

"Yes, I do. Everything you're saying is suspicious. No doubt about it. But you have no evidence that the murder and the attempted arrest were connected to the mining in any way. And just because Fox, Carlyle represents a party involved in your case and in MacLean's doesn't mean much either. Fox is a huge firm. They may represent Waterboer, but they also represent hospitals, charities, and companies that make apple pie. And after all, the cases do involve parcels that are practically right next to each other. The firm probably represents a client with interests in the general area." He glanced at his watch, looked at Carlton, obviously frustrated. "I'm sorry, but I've really got to go."

Carlton relented. "Okay, okay. Thanks for your time."

"Not at all. Sorry I couldn't be of more help. Call me if anything else turns up."

"We will."

"Nice to meet you, Erika."

Carlton and Erika shook hands with Mazursky before he stepped onto the escalator.

As they wound their way to the ground floor of the Capitol, Carlton shook his head. "I really thought he'd be able to help. Now I'm right back to square one."

"No, now *we're* back to square one."

"Sorry. *We.*"

"Except that we're not."

"What?"

"I told you I found something, remember?"

"And?"

"Since the U.S. Geological Survey wasn't forthcoming about old surveys showing diamond deposits in Arkansas, I called a dozen private geologists in Arkansas, large and small. None spoke to me, which told me that there was something to hide. One woman from California finally talked to me. Your Dan Wenzel put me in contact with her. She's the one who did the estimates for MacLean. She faxed me this after getting Wenzel's okay." She handed him a single folded piece of paper.

"A map? This looks like test borings on the MacLean property."

"Look at the numbers."

"Estimated deposits…Ten million carats?" He stared at Erika. "When were these borings taken?"

"Three weeks ago."

20 FROG

Henri Monet did not have the personality the Justice Department ordinarily strived to employ. At thirty-two, the French-American could barely string together three words of English without using French. He had a temper. He suffered from wild mood swings. He was a cultural chauvinist. He took two-hour lunches. He demanded six weeks of vacation a year. He smoked Gitanes cigarettes illegally in his office. But for all of his eccentricities, which Monet enthusiastically attributed to Gallic *savoir vivre*, the man possessed a talent great enough for the department to overlook his personality and give in to his demands.

Monet was a master at computer research.

Un maître.

Henri Monet's father, a *maquisard* in the French Resistance, was saved from the Gestapo by the American army advancing in Normandy in 1944. After the liberation of France, he emigrated to the United States. Reasoning that the French *lycées* created by Napoleon were so good, France was the only country to export its education, he insisted on sending young, American-born Henri to France for schooling before he continued his life in America. Despite Henri Monet's French education and cultural chauvinism, like many first generation Americans, Monet was a fierce American patriot and had many a French schoolyard scar to prove it.

"So what is it, Henri?" Carlton was aware of the man's touchiness when it came to his name and pronounced it in the French manner: "On-ree." He seated himself in a creaky wooden chair near the large oak desk that filled most of Monet's cramped underground cave. He had nearly left his office to pack his bags for Hawaii when Monet had rung. First Erika's discovery of the geological estimates, then Monet's call. When it rains, it pours.

"Monsieur Carlton," the thin man began through his thick French accent. He stared at Carlton in the dim light through round metal-rimmed eyeglasses, removed a thick Gitane cigarette from its blue package and lit it with a disposable Bic lighter. He inhaled deeply, pointed at Carlton with his cigarette, and exhaled loudly. "I have found nothing, Monsieur Carlton."

"What do you mean, nothing? You called me down here to tell me you found nothing?"

Monet screwed the cigarette between his yellowed teeth, lifted his palms upward, arched his eyebrows in exasperation. "Simply that, Monsieur Carlton." He removed the cigarette and tapped it on an ashtray stolen from the Tombs, one of Monet's Georgetown haunts. "There is nothing."

"Then why did you ask me to come down here? I don't have time for this, Henri." He lifted himself from his chair, made for the door.

Monet lifted his cigarette straight up. "*Un moment.* Just because I found nothing doesn't mean that I haven't found something."

Carlton stopped, turned. "In English, Henri."

"Pardon. I'm not making sense. I did not sleep last night."

"That makes two of us."

"As I said, I researched your *histoire* about the diamond mine in Arkansas and this man Waterboer who supposedly shut it down. I found nothing. And believe me, Monsieur Carlton. I looked." He wagged a finger in front of his face, theatrically contorted with deep concern. "And when I look, I look, *hein?* Of course, in the 1920s, there was little radio, no television. I assumed that I would find very little. But I found nothing at all. Particularly about a diamond mine in 1920. *Rien du tout.*

"I looked everywhere. National newspapers. Local newspapers. Books. Government records. Geological records. Land records. According to the records, this survey"—he picked up the photocopy of Osage's 1920 geological survey that Carlton had given him—"does not exist. It is not in the records."

Monet may have been eccentric, but he was a crack cyber-researcher. Carlton knew that Monet took his work as seriously as he did. If information was out there—any information—

Monet would have found it.

"But if the rumor about this mine is true, it would be strange not to find anything, no? And so it is strange. If the rumor is true. But sometimes you do not find what you are looking for." He paused. "Before starting a research project, first you construct a research strategy."

Carlton's exhaustion decreased his ability to decipher the words cloaked in French intonations.

"Your story has many parts, *n'est ce pas?* There is the diamonds part, the Arkansas part, the Waterboer part, the 1920s part, et cetera. It is only when I put all of these parts together that I found nothing. *Rien.* But after finding nothing, I decided to research each component separately. And this is why I stayed up *toute la nuit.*

"For each component, there is *beaucoup d'information.*" He shrugged. "You can imagine. About diamonds, for example. Hundreds of thousands of pages of articles and books and photos. The same with Arkansas, of course. Tons of *littérature.* Also with Waterboer. On this there is less, but still *énormement.* I couldn't possibly read all of it. So I broke each component down into smaller categories. I broke down diamonds into mining in America, for example. Less information, but still *énormement.* I broke down Waterboer. I broke it down into America and this man, Nicholas Waterboer. There was much less on this. When I looked at Waterboer and America, I found mostly cases from our *ministere*—the Justice Department. Cases that tried to hold Waterboer liable for violations of this monopoly law, how you say…"

"Antitrust."

"*C'est ça.* Antitrust." Monet mangled the word through a cloud of acrid smoke. "Then I looked up references to the name Nicholas Waterboer. Again, since he lived in the 1920s, apart from references in current history books and in the South African press, there was *très peu*—very little. In fact, there was only one item in American records. One." He let the statement dangle much like his cigarette, which had developed quite a long ash.

"But one must mine a long time before finding a diamond,

n'est ce pas?" He smiled with yellow teeth. The ash fell as he reached for a manila folder on his cluttered oak desk. "This is what I found." He tendered a document to Carlton.

Carlton looked at the paper intently. It was a high-quality computer printout of a grainy black and white photograph from a newspaper dated 1921. In it were six men dressed in the formal business attire of the early twentieth century, assembled around a display case. The man at the far right looked oddly familiar. A caption was scrawled under the photograph. "Dedication of the South African diamond exhibit at the New York Museum of Natural History. L to R: Jonathan Pierce Blakely. Gladstone Fricke. Nicholas Waterboer…"

"So that's what he looked like, the bastard." Carlton looked at the man with the wire-rimmed spectacles, white hair, and vivid eyes, continued to read the names in the caption. "…Jacob Storia. Abraham Morgenstein. Zed Galloway."

"What about these other people in the photo? Can you research them?"

"I already researched them. All night long. Blakely, Fricke, Storia, and Morgenstein were Waterboer's bankers. *Des gros sous.* Big money. Waterboer, of course, is Waterboer."

"And Galloway?"

"That is the most interesting one of all. Dr. Zed Galloway, geologist, worked for the United States Geological Survey. *Très interéssant.* So I tried to find out more on him from old USGS records." He exhaled loudly. "Nothing. As though he never existed."

"How did you find out he worked for the USGS?"

"Ah," Monet broke into a smile. "Even more *interéssant.* I looked up the publications in the Library of Congress. Every book published in the United States is in the Library of Congress. This is a French invention, you know. François Premier, the French king in 1537, required that a copy of every book published in France be given to the state, and—"

"That's fascinating, Henri, but I don't see—"

"Dr. Galloway was a geologist. He taught at Harvard and published several books. Mostly about diamonds. In 1920, he published his first book. A book on kimberlite pipes containing diamonds in Arkansas."

"In Arkansas?" Carlton could barely control himself. "And?"

"*Calmez vous*, Monsieur Carlton." Monet savored the suspense he weaved. "The interesting thing is that I could find all of Galloway's books except for this one. All of his other books are available in the Library of Congress. I called some of my colleagues in France at the *Ecole des Mines*, the School of Mines. They didn't have it on their shelves, but found a copy in their university computers and emailed it to me. It is Chinese to me, as you say."

"Greek."

"Perhaps, but the book has an introduction from the professor that I think you will find *très interéssant*." Monet leaned over his desk, removed a printout from the manila folder. "Please read the line I marked in yellow."

"Arkansas presents an intriguing geological matrix which combines both the intense concentration of kimberlite pipes and a topography that would facilitate mining activity. The yields are incalculable." Carlton looked up, stunned.

"Look at the credits."

Carlton glanced downward. At the end of the one page text was the name of Dr. Galloway, followed by the location where he wrote the book. Murfreesboro, Arkansas, 1920. "So it's true. There really was a diamond mine in the 1920s. It's not there anymore. Nicholas Waterboer was involved."

Again, Monet bowed his head. "And now it all makes sense. All of the references to the mine have been eliminated. Galloway probably wrote the book before he was involved with Waterboer. Before the mine was shut down, by which time it was too late to eliminate a book already published and sent to universities around the world. Whoever covered this up wasn't able to eliminate all of the copies sent to other countries. And, obviously, they had not foreseen computer research."

"But how could Waterboer accomplish that?"

"It is a *grosse entreprise*."

"Not that big. Not in the United States. Not in 1920. Waterboer couldn't have done this on its own in the U.S. back then or keep something like this hidden all of this time. Waterboer would have needed a lot of help. A heck of a lot more help than a New York law firm. Only one organization is big enough and long lasting enough to pull something like this off. Secretly."

Monet crushed out his Gitane, looked up at Carlton, and exhaled smoke. "*Le gouvernement*."

"Exactly. The question is, who in the government?"

The floor receptionist informed Carlton in her southern accent that Mazursky had left for the Senate floor five minutes earlier. Yes, she opined, he had probably taken the underground subway. It was snowing, after all.

Rumpled and badly in need of a shave and a fresh change of clothes, Carlton exited the underground Senate tram and dashed toward the escalator. The move aroused the suspicion of a beefy Capitol security guard. "Hey you! Come back here!" Getting no response, the guard started after him.

Carlton forced his way up the escalator stairs, past the horde of staffers, lobbyists, and pages each making his or her way to their respective legislative destinations. The security guard fought to catch up, but his beer gut made it difficult to squeeze past already irate escalator riders. "Stop him!"

At the top of the escalator, Carlton paused to scan the main Capitol floor. Almost everyone was dressed in cookie-cutter navy blue and gray. He spotted Mazursky in the distance, bounded toward him as the guard continued to lay chase.

"David!"

Mazursky spun around, obviously saw the rumpled Carlton running toward him, a frenzied guard fast behind him.

"Hey!" The portly guard finally managed to grab Carlton's arm with a meaty grip. "Just where do you think you're going, buddy?" He fought to catch his breath.

Also panting, Carlton reached inside his pocket, flashed his silver badge. "Department of Justice. Official business."

The guard released him. "Sorry, sir. You could've just flashed your ID. You gave me quite a scare. You never know who's a terrorist."

"For God's sake, Pat. What's going on? You're making a scene." Mazursky scanned the area, smiled nervously.

Carlton breathed deeply. "The recent geological surveys. The ones you told me about this morning. The ones you said didn't show any diamonds in Arkansas. Who did them?"

"What—"

"The surveys. Who did the work?"

"USGS, I think. Why?"

"The United States Geological Survey? They drafted the surveys?"

"Right."

"Look at this." He handed him MacLean's boring map, still panting. "Three weeks ago. Look at the estimated yield."

"I don't understand. The USGS surveys I read—"

"That's the key, David. The USGS. My computer guy spent the past twenty-four hours researching every record on the planet about diamonds and Arkansas."

"And?"

"He found zip."

"That's what I told you, remember?" Mazursky replied, confused and annoyed.

"No. He should have found *something*. There should have been something in the records. At least something saying that there were no diamonds. Or very few diamonds. And then he found this." He handed Mazursky the photo, the introduction to Galloway's book.

Mazursky scanned both. "So?"

"So he was part of the USGS. That's the connection, David. The federal government. That's the missing piece of the puzzle. The feds are the ones who started putting pressure on MacLean. They're the ones who wanted me to settle and not make this into a trial. They're the ones who tried to frame Wenzel. They're the ones who are shipping me out to Hawaii. Dollars to donuts the geological reports in your three recent USGS surveys are bogus.

"There are diamonds in Arkansas, David. This boring survey proves it. Tons of diamonds. And someone in the government is trying to keep that secret."

"I—"

"I should be institutionalized, right? So before you say it, I'll say it for you. I don't believe in conspiracy theories either. Just do one thing for me. Just one. Look into this. Please. From the federal government angle. Please."

"Do you realize how ridiculous this sounds? Especially coming from a DOJ lawyer. A federal government conspiracy? Come on, Pat. The next thing you'll tell me is that aliens killed JFK. Why on earth would the federal government keep Arkansas diamonds secret? It doesn't make any sense. Look, I'm sorry, but I just don't have the time for—"

"No," Carlton interrupted loudly, leaning forward. "You're wrong. You do have time for this. You've got all the time and all the interest in the world."

"Are you nuts?" Mazursky practically shouted. "Do you have any idea how busy I am? Give me one reason I should do this." He lifted an index finger into the air. "One."

"I'll give you two hundred million reasons. Next November. Senator Bigham, your boss, is going to make a run for the White House. You know it and I know it. And Bigham's from Arkansas. If Bigham can blow the cover off this thing; if he can show that the federal government conspired to keep millions, billions of dollars worth of diamonds from production, he'll get massive press, massive credit, and massive name recognition. On a non-partisan issue. If you blow the cover off of this for Bigham…"

In the global capital of power politics and political maneuvering, there was no need for Carlton to finish his sentence.

21 TAKING

Shaughnessy, McGuire & Wenzel, LLP
Century City, California
2:35 P.M.

Wenzel's venerable 1939 Lavazza espresso maker hissed with the excess pressure that bled from its old seals. Wenzel walked to his desk, miniature Illy espresso saucer and cup in hand. He sat in his black leather chair, sifted through the bundle of mail Gertrude had organized, opened, date-stamped, and laid out during a very long and very boring client lunch at the Grand Havana Room, his private cigar club in Beverly Hills.

Continuing Legal Education on the Bar materials. Charity appeals. Invitations to legal seminars. *California Bar Journal, Los Angeles County Bar Association Journal.* Newsletters. Mail from opposing counsel. Interoffice memos. Bills, bills, bills. Résumés, résumés, résumés. A letter from the dean of his law school. United States Department of Justice.

What had Carlton sent? The official-looking white envelope carried the DOJ seal. Below the seal and return address was typed "Environment and Natural Resources Division." Not Carlton's division. A green certified mail receipt was affixed to the envelope. Not having received any instructions from Wenzel to the contrary, Gertrude had signed off on it.

Wenzel opened the envelope with a miniature saber letter-opener, a gift from a brown-nosed summer associate. The summer associate was history, the letter-opener remained.

Inside the envelope was a letter on heavy bond letterhead watermarked with the seal of the United States Department of Justice and a check for a huge sum.

U.S. Department of Justice
Environment and Natural
Resources Division

Robert F. Kennedy Building
10th & Constitution, NW
Washington, D.C. 20530

VIA REGISTERED MAIL
RETURN RECEIPT REQUESTED

MacLean Arkansas, LLC
c/o Shaughnessy, McGuire & Wenzel, LLP
1800 Century Park East, 35th Floor
Los Angeles, CA 90067
Attn: Daniel J. Wenzel, Esq.

Re: Order of Immediate Possession/22 Rural Route 1,
    Macon Grove, Arkansas

Ladies and Gentlemen:

This Order of Immediate Possession (this "OIP") constitutes the formal exercise by the United States of America through the Department of Justice (the "Department") of its sovereign right of eminent domain under the Fifth Amendment to the United States Constitution over all right, title, and interest in and to that certain real property in the County of Pike, State of Arkansas, commonly known as 22 Rural Route 1, Macon Grove, Arkansas, more particularly described in Exhibit "A" attached hereto and hereby incorporated herein by this reference, all improvements thereon, and all easements, rights-of-way, privileges, licenses, tenements, and hereditaments thereunto appertaining, including, without limitation, all subsurface minerals (collectively, the "Property"), which right, title, and interest at present are vested in MacLean Arkansas, LLC (the "Titleholder") in fee simple by way of that certain Warranty Deed recorded as Instrument 238715 in Book Number 347 at Page 112 in the Official Records of the County of Pike, State of Arkansas.

Pursuant to the certified appraisal enclosed herein, the Department estimates the fair market value of the Property at Fifty Million Seven Hundred Thousand Five Hundred Twenty Two Dollars ($50,700,522.00), the sum of which is tendered to Titleholder in full by way of the check enclosed herein, less all monetary liens of record.

This OIP shall be recorded in the Official Records of the County of Pike, State of Arkansas. Possession of the Property shall transfer immediately to the Department upon the recording of this OIP, regardless of the depositing or cashing of the enclosed check.

The Department hereby grants Titleholder a temporary revocable license over the Property for a duration of twenty (20) calendar days (the "License Period") for the sole purpose of removing any and all chattels from the Property, which License Period shall commence immediately upon the recordation of this OIP. Pursuant to federal law and the above mentioned transfer of possession, any and all removal, boring or mining—exploratory or otherwise—of any subsurface elements whatsoever, including, without limitation, solid or liquid minerals, by Titleholder or its employees, contractors, or agents at any time hereafter shall constitute an actionable federal criminal offense.

In the event that you have any questions, please direct all inquiries to this office.

Very Truly Yours,
W. Frederic Quentin, Esq.
Deputy Director
Environment and Natural Resources Division

Wenzel read the letter again, then a third time, to make certain he had not failed to notice any important details. He dialed MacLean's private line.

"Hello," MacLean answered. Wenzel heard sprinklers in the background. Gardening, he concluded. After diamonds, roses were MacLean's latest obsession in his sacred quest for beauty.

"It's Dan. I'm afraid I have some more bad news."

"From our friend Carlton?"

"From DOJ, but unfortunately not from our friend Carlton. The federal government is exercising eminent domain over the Arkansas property."

"Eminent domain?"

"Under the Fifth Amendment, the federal government can take any private property it wants, as long as it does so for a public purpose and pays fair market value for it. DOJ's estimated the land to bc about $51 million. I'm sorry, Max. Any hope for the mine is history."

"All those stones? Gone? All those beautiful stones? Just like that? What if we oppose the taking? What if we argue the government hasn't paid us enough for the land? What if we attack the government's appraisal? Or argue it isn't for a—what did you say? A public purpose? They'll have to give us access to underground samples! We can prove there are diam—"

"Thought about that. It won't work. This isn't cut and paste, by-the-book real property litigation. Whoever is behind this has faked reports dating back to the 1920s, destroyed countless others, killed Osage, and nearly framed me. Do you honestly think that they're going to let us expose what's under that land in open court? And as for arguing it isn't for a public purpose, it's a good argument that's been working in the courts lately, but the feds will just build a public campground on the land or something similarly public. I'm sorry, Max."

"All those stones. Those beautiful stones. Lost." MacLean's voice dropped. It was not profit MacLean mourned. His enterprises generated more money than he could ever spend. It was the loss of beauty. MacLean loved the prospect of mining the tiny brilliant pebbles, having them cut, and pouring them in his hands.

Wenzel suspected MacLean had thought of them incessantly. Obsessively. Dreamed of them. Fondled them in his mind's eye. Now, with the short stroke of a cheap government ballpoint pen, the beauty was gone. "I know this is difficult for you, but as your lawyer and your friend, not to mention your business partner, I advise you to drop this thing, Max. Take the government's money and forget all about the diamonds. At $51 million, you made a killing on the property. Let it go."

"No," MacLean said coldly. "Listen to me carefully, Dan. I don't give a flying flip who these bastards are. They've taken my stones. Our stones. And like Carlton says, the federal government isn't doing this clean and fair because it needs the land. Someone else is behind this. Someone we haven't found yet. I may be out of the family business, but no one takes from me like a thief in the night. Now you get on the phone to Carlton and do what you need to do. I want to know who is responsible for this. I want to meet them face to face."

"Max, I—"

"Do it."

22 SPY

The sheet of paper was commonplace. Similar to millions of other pieces of cellulose shuffled daily between the white collars of corporations around the globe. Except for the fact this particular page was among others, which, when collated into the blue leather book, constituted a complete list of disbursements by Waterboer to foreign individuals, businesses, and government organs during the previous fiscal year.

Not the public list. That list was far shorter. Names and numbers on a public list had to be legal. This was a long list, complete to the last detail, highly classified as an internal document only. Waterboer adhered rather fanatically to its policy of non-disclosure. Its paranoid secrecy was born of legitimate concern. The disclosure of almost any entry in the ledger to an external source would spell financial distress and government prosecution, at best. At worst, it would shut down Waterboer Mines Limited.

Piet Lassiter, aka Piet Den Haar, was not a member of the Waterboer inner circle. The South African was employed as a computer technician. A technician who enjoyed snooping and otherwise placing his well-trained hands on documents that were none of his concern. It was not the place of Den Haar to browse through the internal list in Van Kaeke's office on the fifth story of the stone-faced concrete and steel office building on Main Street. Chief Accountant Van Kaeke had gone to the men's room down the mahogany-paneled hallway while Den Haar fiddled with the man's computer into which he had introduced a simple disabling virus an hour before via a standard, company-wide email.

Seeing no danger, he hunched over the desk and scanned the page. The amounts listed staggered him. He stopped at the fifteenth entry:

$5,000,000 L. Pyashinev/Bank of Vanuatu/117833714
These guys really do have everyone in their pocket. He continued.

$25,000,000 (250Kcts.) Russkost/Bank of Vanuatu/117837622

Russkost. The Russian nationalists. Further down, a third entry caught his eye.

$350,000 Delpin, J./Virginia/cash

Virginia? Too close to Washington. Too close for comfort. The entry below it was far more cryptic.

$20,000,000 Cleveland Metals, Inc./Bank of
Vanuatu/113567854

Cleveland Metals, Inc.? It sounded like an American corporation. *Twenty million dollars to a U.S. corporation through some obscure bank?* For a corporation prohibited from transacting business legally in the United States, the sum was enormous.

What was Cleveland Metals?

The notation was unclear but captured Den Haar's interest to such an extent that he failed to hear Van Kaeke's silent return. He would have been caught *in flagrante delicto* if not for the casual greeting of a secretary.

Den Haar knelt down near Van Kaeke's computer hard drive and continued fiddling.

Den Haar generally consumed a pint of beer after work at the local white collar pub across from the stone-faced Waterboer headquarters. Today, he skipped his daily ritual and instead proceeded past the bristling security devices of the corporate compound and into the warm summer sunset. Several blocks away, he drove his dusty red MG into another underground garage on Stockdale Street. The lot was home to the Olde English Garage, a cavern dedicated to the maintenance of the British automotive heritage and any motor vehicle with a paying owner.

The smell of the dimly lit garage lay somewhere between an abandoned gasoline station and a church. Dented hulks of vintage Jaguars, weathered Austin Healeys, and the odd patrician Bentley rusted and collected dust in quasi-darkness, monuments to the fading glory of hand-built automobiles. More contemporary models presented their undersides from the undignified elevation of hydraulic hoists. Light bulbs imprisoned by wire mesh hung from rows of moldy cement. A man in greasy blue coveralls banged gingerly at the muffler assembly of a British Racing Green Jaguar sedan, cursing it back into service.

Den Haar parked the MG next to a bright blue 1963 Mini Cooper. Without a word, he stepped from the MG and into the Mini. The pair of keys under the seat started the overpowered lawn mower engine. A minute later, he drove out of the underground garage.

The last slivers of orange sunlight illuminated the austere interior of the Mini as Den Haar put the glorified go-cart through its paces. Five miles later, he pulled over to the side of the road and took a tiny Motorola cellular telephone with a glass-faced fax attachment from the glove box, removed a pen-like instrument and switched the unit on. He scrawled a message in code on the glass with the inkless pen and composed a number on the telephone keypad. When the line answered, it paused as encryption devices matched. A green light blinked on. He pushed the "send fax" key and shut the unit off, replaced it in the glove compartment, and drove off.

Den Haar exhaled a sigh of relief. The already untraceable unit would receive a new chip when he returned the Mini to the garage tomorrow morning. The procedure was as unnecessary as the code he had used, Den Haar reasoned, because the message itself was scrambled by a cryptographic chip that used natural atmospheric non-repetitive algorithms as code inserted inside the glove compartment and unscrambled over nine thousand miles to the northwest. But his employer's policy dictated the use of code, so code he used.

Den Haar savored the smell of the purple jacaranda blossoms as he turned into an alley. Perhaps he'd call that girl. *What was her name?* Molly. *Yes, Molly.* The movies, perhaps. Maybe even dinner. She was very blonde and very—well, she was very feminine.

He fantasized about Molly's attributes as he walked up the creaking staircase to his second floor abode. Lust pounded in his veins. The sun faded beneath the horizon. Yellowish light from the old fixtures installed in the hallway ceiling forty years before supplanted the rose-colored afterglow of the dusk sky. He smiled languidly, thought of champagne, perfume, and soft flesh as he pushed open the door.

A strong hand suddenly clamped down on his right arm, yanked him inside the apartment with tremendous force. He gasped as the air was knocked out of his lungs. The door slammed shut and cast him into darkness. Someone had drawn the drapes. He could see nothing. Worse, he was unarmed. A debilitating wave of adrenaline drowned him. He thrashed at his invisible assailant blindly until a fist slammed into his jaw and knocked him to the ground. Before he could get back on his feet, a thick boot positioned itself firmly on his windpipe. He lay on the floor, immobilized.

A second man flicked the lights on, blinding him. He struggled to breathe against the pressure of the boot and the ooze of blood in his mouth. He blinked at the bright light, stared up the silencer and muzzle of an enormous IMI Desert Eagle handgun into the demonic eyes of a hulking thug in a rumpled beige suit.

Den Haar was familiar with the handgun. Manufactured by Israeli Military Industries, it could bore a hole through a person's chest from over one hundred yards. This one was an inch from his skull, and the psychotic glare from the thug's oddly mismatched eyes betrayed murderous intent.

In a single sweeping movement, the man lifted him from the floor with a single tree trunk-sized arm and pounded him against the wall. Strangely, he reflected his apartment was in shambles. Bookcases lay overturned on the hardwood floor, the contents of shelves and cupboards strewn on the floor in heaps. The wood dining table was flipped onto its back like a helpless insect.

The man with one blue and one black eye spoke in a calm, oily voice: "Good evening, Mr. Den Haar."

Den Haar twitched at the heavy Afrikaaner intonation. He could not see the man.

"But why mince words? Good evening, Mr. Lassiter." The hairs on Lassiter's neck prickled with fear. The man moved to face him.

"You've got the wrong man. Take what you want. My wallet is in my suit pocket. Just please don't hurt me."

The man's right eye twitched slightly. "Come now, Mr. Lassiter. Be reasonable. It isn't your wallet we want." He moved his face to within inches of Lassiter. "It's your life."

The Afrikaaner fired a single shot into Lassiter's chest. Lassiter lay still on the hardwood floor in his entryway. With studied calm and gloved hands, the Afrikaaner removed Lassiter's wallet from his suit pocket and liberated its cash. His companion moved the television and stereo equipment through the front door. It would look like a burglary gone wrong. The Afrikaaner swept the scene with a cold professional gaze, smiled before he shut the door with a gloved hand.

Lassiter gasped in pain. Already, feeling had disappeared from his arms. He could not reach the telephone a mere five feet distant. Anyway, it was probably disconnected. He felt his life ebbing away fast. Soon the pain ceased. Waves of calm washed over him. As darkness swirled about him, Lassiter began to pray.

Our Father. Who art in heaven. Hallowed be thy name...

23 MEETING

Erika walked into Carlton's office just as he answered the telephone.

"Pat Carlton." He motioned for her to come in and shut the door.

"It's Dave Mazursky."

The man was panting; his voice was rushed. "Hi, David. Did you find anyth—"

"I did. You were right. I mailed you something. Can we meet? I can't really talk on the phone."

"That's a switch, isn't it? You wanting to meet me." He chuckled.

"I'm serious."

"How about the Coast in ten minutes? That work for you?"

"I'm on my way."

Once again, Erika held onto the Shark's door handle for dear life and cringed in the passenger seat as Carlton accelerated up Pennsylvania Avenue, then onto Constitution Avenue toward Capitol Hill, Sinatra crooning through stereo speakers. The wheels slipped on slushy snow, nearly sending the massive Caddy fishtailing around the corner. The car slid on the ice, came to a halt inches from another car's bumper in front of the Tortilla Coast, directly across the street from the white brick Republican National Committee headquarters. Two blocks up, the resplendent Capitol dome glittered white. The light atop the dome was shining: Congress was in night session. Reminiscent of a postcard, the sight never ceased to mesmerize Carlton. Tonight, the view was veiled by his own foreboding.

Erika uncramped herself from her seat and stepped onto the sidewalk. "I think I need a drink."

"Still not used to the Shark?"

"I'd feel safer with Jaws, thank you."

The two rushed around the corner and into the Tortilla Coast, another one of Carlton's regular Hill haunts. They joined hordes of Hill people who trampled through the swinging doors to join fellow members of the legislative herd amid a fog of blue cigarette smoke at the House-side watering hole. "It's packed in here. Let's split up, see if we can find him."

Happy hour on the Hill was time to make up for grueling hours in cubbyholes poring over proposed legislation, vote counts, committee reports, and constituent mail delivered by the truckload. Carlton walked around the crowded room, searching for Mazursky. The worn rectangular oak bar was mobbed by the legislative crowd, unleashed from a long day's work on the Hill. The happily inebriated patrons seemed unaffected by the deafening noise or the presence of opposing party members. As Speaker Tip O'Neill once remarked, after five o'clock all people on the Hill are friends.

No sign of Mazursky.

"He's not in the restaurant section either," Erika said. They pushed through the crowd toward the bar. It was three rows deep with thirsty patrons. Erika was oblivious to the fact men stared at her. Carlton scowled at them, *back off*. He was surprised by the intensity of his possessiveness, though now he did not shy away from the emotion. He enjoyed the warmth of Erika's closeness, the fact she was with him. He thought about the impropriety of associating with a female subordinate outside of office hours, again at a bar. But this was an office matter, he rationalized, ever the lawyer. It's not as though it was a date.

One of the bartenders waved at him, grinned. "Hiya Tex." Like his trademark boots, his nickname had stuck. The bartender scowled at two annoying, snobbish government types who tried to impress others with their bureaucratic titles. "I'm sorry gentlemen. Those stools are reserved for these people." He smiled at their ire.

Carlton and Erika sat on the two stools while the two men slinked away. "You never cease to amaze me, Steve. So what's new?"

"Same old, same old, man. Usual suspects. Crappy weather. Crappy tips. I'm glad you're here. So who—"

"Has anyone asked for me tonight? I'm supposed to meet someone."

"No sir-ee, Bob. Who's your lovely date?" He eyed Erika with the polite yet obvious look that men adopt when trying hard not to stare at a beautiful woman.

Carlton again noticed his feeling of possessiveness. No. Jealousy. "Careful, Steve. Not a date. Erika is a coworker. Erika, Steve. Steve, Erika." Carlton watched Erika shake Steve's hand. Who was he kidding? He didn't like Erika just as a coworker. He liked Erika, period.

Get real, Carlton. She's out of your league. Women like her date hip actors and worldly investment bankers.

"Still, you make a lovely couple."

Erika blushed, the red in her cheeks accompanied by a girlish smile.

Carlton dodged the comment by scanning the crowd. "Still no sign of Mazursky. Where could he be?"

"So. The usual?" Steve asked.

Carlton was happy for the change in topic. "You bet. With—"

"Lots of ice and plenty of lime." They finished the sentence together. "And you, lady-not-on-a-date? What's your pleasure?"

She placed her elbows on the bar and held her head in her hands, grinned. "I think I'll have a glass of champagne. I love champagne."

"Very romantic," Steve said, spotting Carlton's glare. "Just kidding, just kidding." He smiled and turned to fix their drinks.

Despite the riot of noise in the bar, a tense silence enveloped Carlton and Erika. Absent Steve's comments, it would have been easy for him to continue the charade that he had no interest in her.

Erika smiled, smoothed a crease in her skirt, avoided eye contact. Carlton reached for an Upmann Corona, decided not to bother Erika with the smoke. "I wonder what Dave found. He really didn't seem to be buying our side of the story. Whatever he found, it must be big enough that he couldn't wait until tomorrow morning. So why isn't he here?"

"Maybe he got stuck at the office. Maybe he had second thoughts."

"He didn't sound like it. I'm getting antsy."

"Here's your booze." Steve placed their drinks on the bar top, held up a shot glass. "And here's mine. To you two, who aren't on a date."

Carlton and Erika sipped their drinks while Steve downed his shot.

"You allowed to drink on the job?"

"No way." He moved away to attend other thirsty patrons.

His favorite cocktail calmed him down. The anxiety quieted and he no longer felt so nervous with Erika. "So, coworker. I hate talking about me. Until Dave shows up, tell me more about you."

"I thought women were the ones who are supposed to ask about men and sound interested."

"It's the twenty-first century. And you're wrong. I am interested." He realized how that must have sounded. "You know, we're coworkers. I like to know the people I work with."

"You want the Proust version or the *Reader's Digest* version?" She was so beautiful, thought Carlton. Beautiful but not bimbo. Smart and educated, but funny and not cold careerist. And warm.

"Proust. Stream-of-consciousness, like in *Remembrance of Things Past*. Definitely more interesting than *Reader's Digest*."

She sipped her champagne. He knew Proust. "I'm already buzzed. I may not be coherent." *God please don't let me babble*.

"I don't mind." He motioned to Steve for another drink.

"Well. Here goes. Born in 1975. Dad and Mom are Dutch…"

Mazursky never showed.

PART II
CLARITY

"As the circle of light expands, so does
the circumference of darkness around it."

—*Albert Einstein*

24 REVELATION

Main Justice Building
Washington, D.C.
11:03 A.M.

Four consecutive days of insomnia had made Carlton more dependent on caffeine than ever before, something he hadn't thought possible. He reclined in his creaky office chair and sipped yet another mug of fresh joe from his DOJ mug. The courier from the travel office would soon deliver his airline ticket to Hawaii. He had no desire to go to Hawaii. But what else could he do? Although everything he had learned pointed to the sinister hand of Waterboer, he had no hard evidence. Even if he did, Waterboer itself was untouchable. And the federal government's role would be even more difficult to prove, let alone prosecute. And so he waited patiently.

He had left several messages on Mazursky's voicemail at Senator Bigham's office but had yet to receive a reply. He decided to read the *Post* to pass the time. He had been so involved with diamonds in Arkansas that he had neglected all other news for the past few days. Maybe it would get him back to the bigger picture of the real world. He leaned forward, scanned the headlines. One caught his eye.

SENATE AIDE FOUND DEAD IN SOUTHEAST

A burst of adrenaline jerked Carlton upright. He grabbed the paper from the desk.

SENATE AIDE FOUND DEAD IN SOUTHEAST

Noel Haney, Post Staff Writer

Washington, D.C.—A man was found dead at 5 A.M. on Wednesday morning in an alley off of South Capitol Street, in Southeast Washington. Police identified the victim as David Mazursky, 36, of McLean, Virginia.

Holy Mother of God.

Mr. Mazursky was Legislative Assistant to Senator Wade Bigham of Arkansas. Captain Raymond Jackson of the District of Columbia Police Department announced that "the victim died of multiple bullet wounds in the chest and limbs." Jackson listed no suspect or motive but said that the "shooting might be drug related."

They murdered him.

A senior White House official who asked to remain anonymous stated Mr. Mazursky was a long-time drug user.

Bullshit. Mazursky was no druggie.

Mazursky's wife Rachel, a doctor at the Bethesda Naval Hospital in Maryland, was outraged by the suggestion her husband used drugs. "I've been married to David for eleven years, and not once did I witness him taking any type of drug or see any signs or side effects of drug use. The accusation is an insult to David and our family."

Police said that they "have no prior knowledge of Mr. Mazursky's alleged drug use." But it does raise the question of what the McLean, Virginia, man was doing in a gang-ravaged part of Southeast Washington on the night of his murder. Police found two empty vials of crack cocaine in the victim's inside pocket, and stated that the victim's body was riddled by "bullets that came from an UZI submachine gun," the illegal weapon of choice among drug gangs.

Carlton shuddered, grasped the table to steady himself against his mounting dizziness. A ball of heat burned in his gut.

They murdered him. Those bastards murdered him.

He must have been intercepted and killed between the Hart Senate Office Building and the bar. That's only a few blocks. Whoever murdered him knew he would reveal something.

Someone knew he knew. But who? And what?

Carlton ran his right hand through his hair, gazed up at the ceiling, remembered Mazursky's words.

I mailed you something.

Mail. He hadn't received anything from Mazursky in today's mail. Mail from the Senate would have made it to his desk by now. But no, he reflected. If it was that sensitive, Mazursky would have sent it to his apartment. Would have gotten the address somehow. D.C. to Arlington, it would get there tomorrow probably. But he would have mailed it from the Senate. The Senate had direct pick up by the Postal Service. Today. It would get there today. And if they knew about the planned meeting between him and Mazursky, they'd probably know about the mail, too.

Carlton glanced at his watch—11:40. The postwoman on his street finished her rounds around noon.

He bolted from his chair. Jarvik shouted something about Hawaii as Carlton dashed past him.

The Shark tore out of the underground garage. The deep rumble of its massive 390 engine roared through the dark underground passages. The thick whitewall tires burned on cement as the massive Caddy flew over the top of the parking ramp and slammed onto the pavement in a hail of sparks. Carlton threw the tailfinned classic into convulsions as it slid precariously on the capital's slushy avenues half a mile from the White House.

He sped down Pennsylvania Avenue, fishtailed left on 15th Street, flew past the outer rim of the White House Ellipse. The Department of Commerce's red awnings and oversized forged steel torch lamps blurred past on his left before he flung the car right onto Constitution Avenue and slalomed wildly between cars that seemed immobile on the wide avenue. He glanced at the clock on the dashboard—11:51.

Ten minutes.

Whoever ordered Osage's and Mazursky's assassinations and Wenzel's frame up would have no compunction about breaking federal law by rifling through Carlton's mailbox. Along with the mail would disappear whatever it was Mazursky had discovered, and with that probably the key to the Murfreesboro Mining and MacLean cases.

Two deaths already.

Carlton fought off the chill of a cold sweat. Constitution Avenue gave way to I-66. At this hour, the eastbound highway was not yet limited to carpoolers. Carlton stomped on the accelerator until the Shark exceeded the posted speed limit by thirty miles per hour, Virginia troopers the last thing on his mind.

Six minutes.

Son of a bitch.

The run home on I-66 seemed to take forever. Finally, the Shark tore down the single lane of Washington Boulevard East of Glebe Road.

Four minutes.

Come on, come on.

The little hills of the residential neighborhood rolled by like soft waves. The Shark flew over the peak of the third hill.

Carlton gasped.

A long traffic jam had worked its way back from beyond the curve in the road ahead. Carlton hadn't seen it; couldn't have seen it. The last car in the queue was only four car lengths ahead.

He stomped on the large brake pedal and slammed the shifter into the lowest gear. The brake shoes dug into their drums. The engine whined.

Luckily, the asphalt had been cleared of snow. Still, the Shark hurtled toward the last car in line, only a few dozen feet away. Carlton clenched his jaw, braced for impact.

Only three car lengths. He couldn't move to the busy opposite lane.

The wheels locked.

Two car lengths.

One car length.

Carlton maneuvered the Shark to the right near a deep ditch and came to rest inches away from the car in a jackknife position. Carlton exhaled in relief, removed his cramped, sweaty fingers from the white plastic steering wheel. He straightened the Caddy, tried to maneuver around the queue. Cars continued to whizz by in the opposite lane. He slammed the shifter up into reverse. His tires screamed backwards into the nearest side-street, now blocked by cars that had accumulated behind the Shark.

He squinted ahead.

Three hundred feet in front of the traffic queue was the toy-like outline of a squat white Grumman United States Postal Service truck, with its blue and red stripes and fat tires. It was only a few houses from Carlton's street. He threw open the Caddy door and began a mad dash toward the mail truck. It waddled ahead tauntingly, one mailbox at a time.

The air was frozen. His lungs began to burn, then the muscles in his legs. He hated himself for smoking so many cigars, not exercising more regularly. But he kept running, focusing only on the mail truck. Two minutes later, his breath barely enough to supply oxygen to his lungs and legs and brain, Carlton reached the truck, panting madly. He steadied himself against the side of the truck. A head popped out of the driver's side and looked back at him.

He looked up at the attractive African-American postal worker, smiled, still gasping. "Marcie! God am I glad to see you." He placed his back against the truck, his lungs searing with pain.

"Mr. C?" She asked, obviously confused. She squinted to make certain the unshaven breathless man was in fact Pat Carlton.

"Thank God," he wheezed. "Thank God you remember me."

"Of course I remember you. What's the matter?"

"I can't explain right now. Can you please give me my mail?" He coughed.

Marcie squinted again. Technically, she was not allowed to deliver mail to anyone personally except in their homes or in their mailboxes, which were federal property. But Mr. C was nice. He always gave her a check and card at Christmas, twenty dollars this year. He was good people; a lawyer at the Justice Department. If you couldn't trust the Justice Department, who could you trust?

Besides, she had always had a thing for him. "Sure thing, Mr. C."

She disappeared inside the truck, emerged with a small bundle of mail. Carlton leafed through the envelopes nervously, still panting in the chill wind. Most of the envelopes were junk mail. Coupons. Special offers. Sweepstakes entries. Sales pitches. A letter from Cartier. And—

Aces!

A white business-sized envelope, its upper right hand corner displaying the scratchy signature of Senator Bigham. According to the Congressional franking privilege, it was guaranteed delivery anywhere in the United States without postage, free of cost to the member of Congress, although not to the taxpayer.

Carlton snatched the Senate envelope and the one from Cartier from the pile, shoved them into his pocket, handed the remaining letters to Marcie.

"I'm still pretty new in the Postal Service, but I've never seen anyone so happy to get mail before. What—"

He looked up at her. "Don't ask. Can you put these in my box?"

"Uh…sure thing, Mr. C."

"Thanks, Marcie. You're a doll."

Marcie beamed.

Carlton jogged back to the Shark, slowed to a brisk walk as his lungs and legs began to ache again. Cars behind the unattended Cadillac honked as the traffic jam inched forward. He jumped in, accelerated onto the grassy right shoulder. A flick of the power-steering wheel sent the Caddy swerving hard right around the next corner. He proceeded to his apartment building through side streets, slowly. He pulled around a dark corner, parked under the snow-laden outline of an elm tree, turned off the engine, and waited.

He found it strange to spy on his own apartment. A bit paranoid, like something out of 1940s film noir. But he wasn't paranoid. Two men had died. Whatever was in the envelope in his pocket was important enough for someone to kill twice. And despite popular opinion and tragic local news stories, it was rare for people to commit murder without a reason, no matter how mad the reason might be.

The engine ticked as it cooled in the glacial air.

Tree-lined Kenilworth Street was serene, as always. A dog barked at a cat. Cars on Washington Boulevard fought the log-jam a block away. Cartoons blared from the house across the street. Another neighbor poured antifreeze into the aged bow-els of his ancient AMC Gremlin.

Carlton focused on his brick apartment building. The elderly tenant on the third floor trudged from room to room, tea in hand, past florid drapes. Finally, Marcie's mail truck pulled up. She didn't see the Shark up the street and walked inside, deposited the mail into each tenant's respective mail slot, and moved to the next building. Several minutes later, another mail truck pulled up to the apartment house. A tall bearded man dressed in the blue-on-blue uniform of the Postal Service got out of the truck and walked into the lobby of Carlton's build-ing, carrying a mail bag over his shoulder. Carlton squinted, saw him open a box, sift through its contents. He returned to his truck and drove away.

Bureau of Land Management. National Trust for Historic Preservation. Federal Bureau of Investigation. United States Geological Survey. Maybe the Central Intelligence Agency. Now the Postal Service. The government connection was clear, although the reason for it remained a mystery.

Carlton calmly started the engine, proceeded down the next street, and drove to a car wash two miles away, one of those automatic contraptions where the driver sits in the car and watches the brushes and soap and water work from inside. His nephews back in California loved the things.

Carlton paid the gas station attendant and obtained a car wash token. He waited until the Shark's fins were fully engulfed by brushes, foam, and water before removing the folded envelope from his suit pocket. Out of breath and trem-bling slightly, he turned on the interior light, ripped the white envelope open, and nearly tore its contents in the process.

Mazursky died for this.

The envelope contained two sheets of paper. He read the first page:

Cleveland Metals Inc. $20,000,000. 113567854. Bank of

Vanuatu.

Cleveland Metals?

He had heard the name before. *Hadn't Josh at SEC mentioned….That was it.* Cleveland Metals owned Murfreesboro Mining Corporation.

The brushes stopped. Water poured over the Shark's soapy metal skin and washed away thick coats of accumulated grime. Drops of water leaked through the well-maintained but old convertible top. He ignored them and flipped to the next page.

It was a copy of a recent check written by an "L. Churchman" from the same Bank of Vanuatu account number to the order of "Little Rock Savings and Loan," in the amount of $1 million.

On top of the page were scrawled the words:

Scott Fress owns this bank

The loud blasts of air shot out from nozzles jolted Carlton backward in his seat. He stared at the two pages.

Scott Fress? Scott Fress was the White House chief of staff. If he owned the bank, L. Churchman had just paid the White House chief of staff $1 million. Nice round number. But who the hell was L. Churchman? Besides the fact Cleveland Metals owned Murfreesboro Mining Corporation, the information did not seem to have any direct bearing on Murfreesboro Mining, MacLean, or Arkansas diamonds.

The only thing he knew was the bank. In the 1980s, Switzerland was the secret offshore place to bank. In the 1990s, after the discovery of Swiss bank accounts belonging to drug lords and to Holocaust victims, the Caymans became the banking locus of choice. In the new millennium, little obscure banks in exotic places like Eastern Europe, Africa, and the South Pacific became all the rage, *le dernier cri*. Vanuatu Atoll was in the South Pacific, previously known as the New Hebrides when it was a British colony. It had "offshore" all over it. Whatever these transactions were, they were meant to be secret and as untraceable as possible.

The air nozzles died down with a whine and stopped.

Loud honks jerked Carlton's head up. He stared into the

rearview mirror. The impatient owners of dirty cars behind him wanted in. He replaced the papers in his suit pocket with one hand, shifted into drive with the other, and floored the clean Shark out of the car wash with a loud squeal.

Who is L. Churchman? Mazursky had died for this. The answer had to be here.

Driving back to the office, he realized the hirsute postal worker would keep looking through his mail every day until he found Mazursky's letter. He searched for his cell phone, realized he'd left it in the office. He searched for a pay phone, pulled into the local 7-11 parking lot. He fumbled in his pocket for change, found none. He ran into the small convenience store.

"No change, sir. You have to purchase something," the clerk informed him smugly in a heavy Middle Eastern accent. They changed workers so often at the store Carlton never got to know the employees.

"I just need to make one call. I buy stuff in here all the time."

"I'm sorry, sir. We do not make change. That is our policy."

It was too much for Carlton. "Your policy? Your policy?" He shoved his right hand into his suit pocket, removed his badge, held it an inch away from the man's face. "Well here's my policy. United States Department of Justice. Now make change before I inspect this place for federal violations."

The shocked clerk nervously converted Carlton's five-dollar bill into change.

"See? Policies can change." Carlton stormed out, dropped a quarter into the grimy pay phone. For the first time since morning, he realized how cold it was.

"Erika Wassenaar."

"It's Pat."

The voice at the other end was muted by the traffic.

"I said it's Pat. I'm at a pay phone. Listen. Yes. I saw the paper. Just listen. I can't talk. Drop whatever you've got…Forget that—just listen: I need you to get—listen carefully—I need you to get me a blank envelope from Senator Bigham's office. I don't know how. No, I can't explain. Just get it. Before five P.M. It's got to be before five. I'll find you before then. Then have Henri Monet search for information about

Cleveland Metals Inc. and man named L. Churchman. Got it?"

Carlton stood and stared at the pay phone in a stupor. He felt his heart pump. His head ached. Nausea struck. He trembled as the questions of the week converged with the new facts.

Scott Fress was in this. The government connection finally made sense. If the White House chief of staff was involved, it would be easy for him to rally several federal agencies, make honest, hardworking federal employees believe that Mazursky, Osage, and MacLean were criminals. It also meant Carlton wasn't fighting a private defendant or a single government agency. He was fighting the White House itself, which for some unknown reason was involved in Arkansas diamonds.

Back at DOJ, Carlton ran down the hallway past his office to the photocopying room. He leaned against the yellowed wall, panting and wheezing, ran his hand through his matted black hair and across his stubbled chin. The jog from the parking garage across Penn Avenue and up to his floor had beaded sweat on his forehead, soaked his already rumpled white shirt. He gulped air, shifted his weight from the wall to one of the two behemoth Xerox machines busy spewing photocopies at a crazed pace. It filled the small room with heat and noise.

A surprised short-haired clerk smiled at him.

"In a bit of a rush today, aren't you, Pat?"

Carlton jumped. "I didn't see you. Yeah, I am in a hurry. Mind if I make five or six quick copies?"

"No problem." She smiled. "You look like a truck just ran over you. Are you…are you okay?"

"Yeah, yeah. Just in a hurry. Thanks."

He removed the wrinkled papers from his pocket, made three sets of copies, turned to the clerk, thanked her again with a nod and smile, then trudged to his office down the dimly lit hall.

Harry Jarvik waited patiently behind Carlton's desk. "Out for an afternoon stroll, Carlton?"

"One moment, sir. I'll be right with you." *Shit!*

"Carlton, I—"

"Only take a second." *Great*. Now on top of this he had to

deal with Stalin. He dashed from the office down the hall and found Erika in her office. "Boy, am I glad to see you. Did you get it? The envelope?"

"Sure did. Right here." Erika beamed. "I guess the male receptionist in Bigham's office likes redheads."

Carlton took the top page from the sheaf of papers in his hand, the page with the information about the Waterboer transfer to Cleveland Metals, but not the one about Scott Fress, folded it inside the envelope, licked it shut, addressed it to his home, and handed it back to Erika. "That should throw them."

"What are you—"

"Don't ask questions. Don't stamp the envelope. Take the Metro to—forget it, take a cab to the Central Post Office next to Union Station. Drop the letter in a mailbox inside the post office. Before five o'clock. It's got to go out before five. Then go to the Tortilla Coast. I'll meet you there. Don't talk to anyone. Understand? No one. Not even DOJ people. Got it?"

She nodded yes.

"Okay."

Erika turned, started down the hallway.

"Wait!" Carlton grabbed her by the arm. "Take these and give them to Henri in the basement." He pointed to the floor. "Tell him what I told you and have him meet us at the Coast, too. Now go!"

Carlton walked back to his office to confront Stalin.

"I'm sorry, sir. I had to get something out pronto."

Jarvik eyed him owl-like through his horn-rimmed glasses. He wasn't buying. "I see. How professional."

He reclined in Carlton's chair. "But what I don't see is your absence. What are you still doing in D.C.? And what's all this material on diamonds I see on your desk? I told you to settle that silly case. Now that you've settled it, you're supposed to be on a plane to Hawaii. Why aren't you on that plane?"

"Sir, I—"

"Yes?"

"Sir, I—"

"I'm waiting, Carlton."

"I really wish you would send someone else to Hawaii, sir. I have several engagements in town, and besides, why isn't the local U.S. Attorney's office handling the case? Why me?"

It was a stupid excuse not to go to Hawaii, but it was all he could think up in his exhausted state. He knew, as always, that he'd find a great excuse later, once he no longer needed it.

He sensed clearly for the first time that something in Jarvik's manner was off. It made him uneasy about divulging any information about the Arkansas diamonds. Something about Jarvik didn't fit, didn't feel right. Like how he knew about the USGS survey.

"Why? You want to know why?"

"Sir, it's just that I—"

"Well, I'll tell you why. Because the U.S. Attorney's office in Hawaii doesn't have anyone with antitrust experience, that's why. The FBI has built up a great case, and they need an antitrust lawyer to litigate it. Is that good enough for you? And I don't have to explain my orders to you. I'm your damn boss!"

Listening to the words, Carlton suddenly realized what Jarvik had told him several days ago, and again just now. The FBI. He wanted Carlton to report to the FBI in Hawaii. The FBI had tried to arrest Dan Wenzel. And why couldn't he do Hawaii's legal work from here?

Carlton looked down. "I...guess that makes sense."

"Well, I'm so glad you concur, counselor. Now I want your pathetic white-shoe ass on a plane to Hawaii inside the next twenty-four hours. Do I make myself clear?"

"Sir, I—"

"Twenty-four hours, Carlton. Got it? Or you're out of a job. End of story."

Carlton continued to look at the floor, frustrated by his inability to concoct a viable excuse to prevent his forced exile. "Yes, sir," he mumbled.

"Good." Jarvik left, slammed the door.

Carlton knew he could pull out then and there. No one had threatened him yet. No one was aware he knew about Fress— not after Erika mailed the letter to him at home so the make-believe postal worker could find it. The only thing they would discover is that Mazursky had sent Carlton information about Cleveland Metals, which did not seem too important. But it was also clear if there had been two recent murders and so many federal agencies involved, the White House chief of staff at its center, something pretty damn secret was happening. Something that had apparently been covered up for more than eighty years. Both his sense of justice and his professional curiosity prevented him from leaving well enough alone. To hell with Stalin. He was going to blow this thing open.

He knew Jarvik's story about the U.S. Attorney's (USA) office in Honolulu not having any antitrust experience was unadulterated horse manure. The Hawaii USA's office had won an antitrust case just last month. It was a small case, but it had made it into the monthly internal department memorandum. Further proof that Jarvik didn't keep up with developments in his own section, yet another reason for suspicion. Carlton raked his exhausted mind for a solution. How could he get out of the Hawaii assignment? He needed a valid excuse to stay in Washington. A reason Jarvik would accept. It had to be something important.

Important or from high up.

Erika interrupted his thoughts as she walked into his office, stone serious.

"Lock the door." He walked to her. "Mazursky mailed me a letter before he was shot," he whispered. "Cleveland Metals is the link. They're making payments to a bank owned by Fress."

"Fress? Who's Fr—"

He placed a finger on his lips. "Scott Fress. The White House chief of staff," he whispered. "Look at this." He handed her copies of Mazursky's letter. "Cleveland Metals wire-transferred twenty million dollars to an account in the South Pacific. Some guy named L. Churchman made a million dollar payment to an S&L owned by Fress. Cleveland Metals owns Murfreesboro Mining."

Erika seemed unimpressed by the enormity of what he had just revealed. She just nodded. "That explains a lot, then."

Now Carlton was incredulous at her calm detachment.

"What?"

"I had Henri run the Lexis search you wanted on Cleveland Metals."

"And?"

"I'll spare you the corporate maze. Bottom line, Cleveland Metals is a legal U.S. subsidiary of Waterboer Mines Limited."

"Oh, shit."

"And that Churchman guy? He's a partner at Fox, Carlyle."

The phone rang.

"What now?" Carlton mumbled, holding his throbbing head in his hands.

"Hello?"

"It's Wenzel."

"Do you want to hear the latest from here first or do you want to start telling me what I'm sure is more bad news from your end?"

"You haven't heard, then. The Justice Department. Your own agency. It just condemned MacLean's property in Arkansas."

"What?"

"I checked around. Justice just condemned the Raymonds' farm too. The Orders for Immediate Possession have already been issued and recorded. The government now officially owns the properties."

Carlton responded with silence as he fought to pin down an elusive thought. "The guy who tried to buy the property. The guy at Fox, Carlyle?"

"Yeah?"

"What was his name?"

"Lester Churchman."

"And how much did he offer for the property?"

"Nineteen million."

Carlton shook his head. "That's it, then." Twenty million transferred to the account. One million transferred to Fress's bank. That left nineteen million. The price Waterboer offered to buy the land.

"That's what? What are you talking about?"

He was about to go through the entire series of events, but stopped. Two people had already been murdered, three if one counted Osage's father in 1932. Wenzel had nearly been framed, perhaps targeted for assassination as well. This information was killing people; Wenzel didn't need to be involved anymore. The government had purchased MacLean's land. Against MacLean's wishes, but it was technically legal.

Carlton knew he'd have to go this alone. Wenzel might have been a zealous lawyer for his client, but he wasn't a law enforcer. Carlton was. He had a responsibility to enforce laws. White collar crime and now, it appeared, violent crime as well. Right now, that meant keeping quiet. "Listen to me, Dan. They took the land and paid for it. Just let it go. Walk away."

"MacLean wants to—"

"I don't care what he wants. Just let it go. Walk away. Just exercise client control and convince your client. I'm not kidding." He hung up, slumped heavily into his chair, emotionally and physically drained. A paper jabbed him from inside his jacket. He reached inside and removed the hard white envelope from Cartier. He ripped it open, slid out a letter and a brochure.

Dear Monsieur Carlton,

It was a pleasure assisting you and the Department of Justice in your research. I have enclosed a brochure about diamonds for your information. Please call me if you have any questions whatsoever.

Sincerely,
Therese de la Pierre

Carlton looked at the accompanying pamphlet. Superposed on a photograph of a mound of sparkling diamonds was the phrase "What You Should Know About Diamonds" in black letters. Below were the words "Diamonds Are Beauty" and "Waterboer Mines Limited."

"Fucking animals. You're going to pay for this."

25 IMAGERY

Pink stared wearily at the Russian submarine clock on his wall, a reminder of the cold war and, for Pink, its romantic mystery. He had always wanted to be part of the CIA's clandestine service. But like the college youth of the late 1980s who anticipated the wealth of the Decade of Greed with baited breath, only to be disappointed by its rapid closure, the cold war was won when Pink entered the Agency. Rather than becoming a cold warrior, he had been relegated to analyzing the mess of post-Communist Russia. He still experienced the clandestine service, of course, but only from behind a desk in the Company's fortress across the Potomac from the capital of the cold war victor.

The telephone jolted him out of his late night stupor. "Pink."

"I didn't expect to find you in the office," a nervous voice replied.

"Who is this?" Pink demanded, waiting for the caller's information to flash on his computer screen.

"Pat Carlton."

"Again?"

"You were right about staying away from Waterboer. But I got sucked in anyway. I'm going to make this short. I've found information that frankly I wish I hadn't. They killed the Senate aide, Mazursky. They killed a farmer in Arkansas." The words streamed out without punctuation.

He was calling from a cellular telephone registered to Lieutenant Carlton, United States Navy Reserves, Pink noted. "Why would they do that? It doesn't make sense."

"Not without additional information, no. But I have that information. I don't expect you to take my word for it. Check it yourself."

"Okay."

"Take this down. A company called Cleveland Metals Inc. The account number 1-1-3-5-6-7-8-5-4 in the Bank of V-A-N-U-A-T-U. The Little Rock Savings and Loan in Arkansas. The law firm of Fox, Carlyle. The diamond deposits in Murfreesboro, Arkansas."

Pink finished writing on a memo pad. "I got it. What is it?"

"Waterboer is bribing Scott Fress to prevent billions of dollars of diamonds from being mined in Arkansas. The money trail leads from Cleveland Metals' account at the Bank of Vanuatu to the S&L. Verify it. And be careful. Like I said, they've already murdered two people."

"Those are enormous allegations."

"I know I sound like a nutcase. All I ask, as a Justice Department attorney and as a lieutenant in the Naval Reserves, is that you confirm the information. It was hard to get. As I said, two people already died for it. But it should be easy to confirm."

"I will."

"Thanks."

Pink stared at the receiver for several moments, smiled. To think that for a moment he had actually taken this guy seriously. *I must really be getting tired.* Scott Fress? The White House chief of staff? *Please.* He had real fish to fry.

He crumpled the sheet of notes and tossed it through the miniature basketball hoop in the corner of the office. It dropped into the trash can. He got up to pour himself a fresh lick of java before attacking his assignment for the tenth time.

Only a few more hours remained until he had to brief Forbes, and he had yet to make heads or tails of the data. The problem was clear: the data didn't make sense. He had combed through both official Russian government diamond production figures and the unofficial figures supplied by operatives inside the Russian Komdragmet agency, the SVR/FSB, and the mines themselves. No matter how he chopped up the figures, they didn't match.

"Again." He sighed, wondering what he was missing. He forced himself to churn through the facts yet another time. The only piece of information he hadn't analyzed was the satellite imagery of the fire at Mirny. But Jerry Delpin in DST had already reviewed the imagery. The senior analyst's report concluded the fire had been caused by a natural gas explosion. Not unusual in a region so cold that frozen pipes often burst like brittle glass. Delpin was an old hand at satellite imagery. If he said it was a natural gas fire, it was. Still, the satellite imagery was the only piece of data he hadn't reviewed. Might as well take a peek.

His back cracked loudly as he rose, stretched, then walked down several hallways to a brushed aluminum elevator. The sterile fluorescent lights overhead stung his bloodshot eyes. The elevator opened on the second floor. A thin security guard stood at attention next to an armored glass door.

"Evening, Tom."

"Evening, Roger." Another yawn as he inserted his digitally imprinted identification card into a slot next to the armored glass double doors that read IMAGERY in white letters. A light on the door shifted from red to green.

"Go ahead."

Pink waited for the first glass door to close, punched his personal security code onto a small keypad. The second door whirred upward. The technology at the Agency never ceased to amaze him. He thought of his law school classmates. They might get bigger paychecks, but their offices weren't this cool. Polished mahogany conference rooms were their world. Digitally encoded armored offices were his. For the most part, their patriotism and interest in the real world ended where high salaries and perks lavished by real estate development, securities law, or tort litigation began.

He continued down the hall to an unmarked door and knocked.

A portly, raven-haired woman in her late thirties opened the door. She stared at Pink, smacked her lips, chewed a wad of gum loudly. In contrast to Pink, she was very awake, on that strange high that comes from working the night shift.

"Hi, Elaine."

Elaine smiled for the first time that night. "Well, hello there, Mr. Bond."

Elaine Franklin's reputation was legendary in the DI and DST. Throughout the entire Agency, truth be told. People called her the Witch. Physically, Elaine was homely. Her hair was greasy, unkempt. She bore a permanent scowl, wore a white lab smock complete with pocket protector and food stains. Walked around in little squeaks of rubber-soled shoes. In contrast to her relationship with other members of the Analysis staff, Elaine got along with Tom swimmingly. Whereas others treated her with condescension, Pink treated her like the consummate professional she was. In turn, Elaine respected Pink. This, in addition to their mutual veneration of '60s spy movies, had led them to become friends.

Pink rubbed his eyes. They burned with dehydration. He would have given his right arm for a drop of Visine. "Listen, Elaine," he raised his hand, palm forward. "I know Jerry Delpin already ran the imagery on the Mirny fire, but I need to do it all over again."

"Delpin screwed the pooch?" Her dislike of Delpin was no secret.

"That's what I need to find out."

For anyone but Pink, Elaine would have been angered by having to perform the same job twice. "Let's try it again, then."

"You're a Godsend, Elaine." He gave her a wide grin.

"One of my many charms." She locked her office door and led the way down the hall to a room aglow with a Christmas tree of red and green LED lights, red digital numerical read-outs, and green liquid crystal displays. The collection of electronic equipment in the room had always fascinated Pink. Millions of dollars of the most sophisticated video equipment crammed into a room the size of a large elevator. Ventilators whirred silently in their continuous efforts to cool the massive machines, each one years ahead of the retail market, each one classified.

"If only we could market this stuff," said Pink. "Bye, bye Sony."

Silently, Elaine dialed up the Mirny selection on an ordinary-looking keyboard. It was connected to one of the Company's seven supercomputer servers, nicknamed the Seven

Dwarfs. A mechanical arm in an adjacent sterile room removed an encrypted high-definition digital cassette from a series of racks on the wall, inserted it silently into a playback mechanism. She played with the controls of her tape deck, which had about as much in common with a regular tape deck as a Cray supercomputer had with a Nintendo Game Boy. She turned on a rectangular video monitor. Its fifty thousand pixels of resolution came to life in a white haze. Pink waited patiently, gazed in wonder at the machinery around him. The tape player buzzed with a faint electronic hiss.

Elaine reached into her mouth, stretched her gum until it sagged. This drove most people nuts.

Pink found it amusing. "One day you're going to gum up the works."

She snorted. "Maybe then people will notice the importance of my work."

"I never questioned it."

"I know. Okay. Here it is." She punched a switch, extinguished the overhead halogen lights with a quick turn of a rheostat, and fiddled with the brightness and contrast sensors. "From the beginning?"

"If you don't mind," Pink replied.

"I don't mind. I've never seen it."

"What do you mean? You didn't watch it with Delpin?"

"Negative. He wanted to do it alone."

"Strange. But whatever, let's roll."

A digital clock at the bottom of the monitor displayed hours, minutes, seconds, and tenths of seconds. Tenths of seconds flickered forward with incredible speed and gave the impression of fast motion even though the image moved at slow speed. The monitor reproduced images in the infrared portion of the electromagnetic spectrum. As a result, the screen was not completely black. It glowed in colors that represented various intensities of heat. White was the hottest. Then came yellows, oranges, reds, greens, blues, and purples that finally blended into black. At present, the screen showed a few interspersed white dots encircled with green against an almost black background.

Pink turned to Elaine. "Barrack lights?"

"You're a natural, Tom."

"Can you freeze it, please? Turn up the lights a bit? I need to look at this map here."

He shuffled through Delpin's thin report, now crumpled, found a detailed map of the Mirny diamond processing center. He shifted back and forth from the map to the screen until he determined that the blotches of white and green were in fact night illumination lamps in the compound.

"Thanks. Please continue."

The digital clock came back to life. A pair of amoebalike purple shapes moved across the screen, each preceded by a dark green blob.

"What's that?" Pink exclaimed.

"Didn't Delpin mention it in his report?"

Pink shook his head. "What are they?"

"There are two of them. They're moving at the same speed, far too fast to be people. My guess would be airplanes."

"But there's no engine heat signature. Unless…What about those green blobs?" He pointed to the front of each fuzzy purple shape.

"Not hot enough to be engines. Pilots more likely."

"Pilots but no engines?"

"Gliders." They said in unison.

"Gliders? In the middle of the night? In Siberia? Over Russia's main diamond processing center?"

"Delpin screwed the pooch."

"Killed and buried Lassie is more like it." Pink scribbled furiously on the pages of Delpin's report. "Keep going."

They watched intently as the purple blobs moved across the screen directly over and past the Mirny processing center.

Suddenly, the screen exploded with white light.

Pink jerked his head back in surprise. "What the heck was that?"

"Looks like fire." They watched the screen for several moments before Elaine broke the silence. "But it's strange, you know."

"No kidding, strange."

"No. I mean, it doesn't have a specific geographic locus of origination."

"And in the Queen's English, that would mean…"

Elaine rewound the tape, advanced it frame by frame to the point immediately between darkness and the flash of light.

"See? The area"—she referenced the entire screen with a circular motion of her finger—"goes directly from black to white. Very cold to very hot. There's no progressive shift. The contrast is almost total."

"So?"

"So. A fire has to start somewhere, right? This," she pointed at the proto-white image that trembled on the screen, "looks like a simultaneous explosion throughout the entire compound."

"Gotcha. What would cause the entire compound to explode instantaneously in sub-zero temperature?"

"I have no idea. But it's definitely not your run-of-the-mill fire or gas explosion, that's for sure."

He scribbled again on the report. "Better move on."

Pink and Elaine stood in the cramped room for the next seven minutes and watched the satellite images in real time. The edges of the compound flickered as outer buildings burned and crumbled. The intensity of light did not waver. Over several minutes, it spread outward in a narrow strip toward the north. The progression of the strip continued in a straight northern line and ended several minutes later. After approximately one minute, a bright green glow appeared at the end of the strip and traveled east from the blaze, much faster than the strip had moved. Bright green blobs approached the southern end of the compound, stopped at the outer edge of the fire.

"Emergency vehicles, you think? Fire trucks? Ambulances?" Pink inquired.

Elaine squinted. "Probably," she finally agreed, her gaze riveted to the screen. "Except maybe for this one." She pointed at the blob that moved east, away from the compound.

"Not an emergency vehicle?"

"We didn't see it get there, did we? It just appeared and left. By itself, not a big problem. But all of the other emergency vehicles came from the opposite direction. Here." She pointed to the tip of the screen.

Pink screwed his lips tight and gazed at Elaine. "Why would emergency vehicles move away from the compound?"

"Exactly."

"People trying to escape?"

"Maybe. Maybe they found a jeep or something and took off."

"But it can't be. Company sources say no one escaped. The entire garrison died in the blaze. That's why they—and we—couldn't figure out how this thing happened. They didn't have anyone to interview after the fire."

"Well, someone was wrong then," Elaine said. "Someone did escape."

"Or," Pink said, "someone was right and no member of the garrison was left alive. Why wouldn't a soldier from the garrison want to tell his superiors about the fire? It doesn't make sense, right?"

"Right," Elaine assented.

"So that person wasn't a member of the garrison."

"I'd follow up on it for your report to Malcolm."

"I will." He stared at his watch. 3:15 A.M. "If I don't die of exhaustion first. Thanks for your help, Elaine."

26 LENA

Piet Slythe sat on the edge of his bed in the ornate Grand Palace suite of the newly completed Golden Ring Hotel. It had been built by the presidential office that oversaw the billions of dollars of government housing for high-ranking civil servants, diplomats, and foreign dignitaries. Not to mention Russian *mafiya* dons. The last thing Moscow needed was another five-star hotel. But the Kremlin real estate office knew it could steer international delegations there and make a killing. In U.S. dollars.

He had arrived a day early to adjust to local time so he could perform at his peak during his negotiations with the Russian president the following day.

Gilded bed posts supported a flowing baldachino. Swaths of white silk and gold brocade covered the walls. Slythe made his way to a marble bathroom with ornate golden faucets and mirrors, turned on the shower, and enjoyed the spray of hot water against his body. He smiled. Tomorrow he would bring Orlov to his knees.

Almost more so than during the cold war, Russia was in desperate need of hard currency. Despite Orlov's reforms, the ruble was still perilously low, the state coffers nearly empty due to Orlov's assiduous payment of Russia's foreign debt to boost the country's credit rating. Orlov needed every imaginable source of hard currency to replenish the government's coffers if he was to prevent communist and nationalist crazies like Molotok and his Russkost from taking over. Orlov had no leverage. Slythe and Waterboer held all the cards. Waterboer would dictate its price. His smile grew wider. Once again he would prevent outsiders from harming the Slythe family's diamond empire.

He stepped out of the shower, examined his svelte muscular body in the gilded mirror. He found himself quite attractive. Except for his gray hair, he could pass for a man fifteen years his junior. He toweled himself dry and walked through the bedroom to the ornate living room. He removed a large glass vial of cocaine from his attaché case.

Possession of the drug would earn Slythe ten to twenty years in a drab and merciless Moscow penitentiary—if he was convicted. But Waterboer Mines Limited and Slythe flew in circles far above the Rule of Law. Not for Slythe commercial air travel. Not for him the delays of baggage handling. Not for him the annoying customs queue. Not for him the taxi queue. Private hangar, customs a mere formality. Mercedes limousine with Moscow Militia escort. Presidential suite. Clearly no risk of criminal prosecution for something as personal as possession.

Slythe poured some cocaine onto a small glass plate, carved it into two lines with a platinum cutter. He held a matching platinum tube between his manicured fingers, leaned toward the plate, and snorted deeply. He held his head back and sniffed, eyes wide open.

"Can I have some?" asked woman with a pronounced Russian accent. She stood in the shadows, invisible.

Slythe was startled. "Who's there?" he demanded, searching the room. He saw her. "What are you doing here? How did you get in?"

"Man with strange eyes opened door." She spoke softly. "I am Lena. I was sent to room by…friend. To be sure you are happy with room." Slowly, the voice moved into the light. The woman was stunning, not more than twenty. A girl, really. She stared at Slythe, smiling with large doe-like brown eyes, her long lashes fluttering playfully. Her innocent face was accentuated by high cheekbones, giving her the look of a grown-up doll. An angular chin framed a set of full lips painted hot pink, held in a sultry pout.

Recovering from his shock, Slythe's stare moved down her body. She was dressed in a jet black bodysuit, seemingly sprayed on by a master airbrush artist, that left nothing to the imagination. Lena was tall, with long, graceful legs. Slythe followed their flowing lines lecherously from her high platform shoes to her small round rump. She stood on one leg, bent the other backward to prop herself up against the marble wall. The black jumpsuit was interrupted only by a gold chain that rested in an inviting diagonal on the soft curves of her hips.

She reached downward with long fingers and removed the bodysuit in a single movement. Firm breasts bounced and jutted slightly upward, capped with erect nipples. She was as slim as a model, her belly button pierced with a diamond belly button ring. She bit a long pink fingernail playfully. Slythe could barely tell whether she was a natural brunette.

"You like?" She turned around, tilted her head forward, flipped it backward, and turned only her head toward Slythe, smiling with a mischievous grin. Her long brown hair shimmered down her graceful back and stopped short of a small Imperial Russian double-headed eagle tattooed above her round backside. "*Da?*"

"I do. *Da.*" He sat down on the sofa, held out the platinum tube.

"*Da.*"

Lena had been using coke for two years, a big step up from her earlier days as an impoverished teenager in her depressed native town near Archangelsk in northern Russia. In those days she had sniffed gasoline.

She snorted deeply, amazed at the purity of the drug. "*Ochen harasho.*" She grinned, reached into Slythe's lap, removed his bath towel, and slid to her knees. Rich western businessmen were usually fat and ugly. This one could be a movie star. She looked up at him, smiled, for once not totally repulsed by performing her hired services.

She soon changed her mind.

Lester Churchman shifted restlessly under the thick covers of his bed. Not only was he responsible for his master's legal wranglings—more than a full-time job in itself—but his large body had a very low tolerance for jet lag. After several hours of unsuccessful attempts, he had barely managed to fall asleep when a woman's scream of terror howled down the hallway. He opened his eyes and sighed. It was 3:04 A.M. He'd never get any sleep if Slythe continued his games.

Lena regained consciousness around 5:00 A.M. Her body throbbed with pain. She turned, fought the urge to vomit, seeing the demon lying naked in bed next to her.

She shuddered. The things he had done. *Solkin sin.*

In all her experience as a prostitute since age fourteen, Lena never imagined that such things were possible. She vomited dryly into the toilet bowl before examining her wounds in the large mirror. The intense pain would go away, she knew. Her pimp had a good doctor to take care of his stable of sex slaves. What terrified her were the large purple bruises and red welts on her legs and face. The long bloody lacerations along the full length of her back she could hide, not the bruises on her face and forearms.

How long would it take for them to disappear, she wondered, rubbing her aching wounds tenderly. None of her customers would pay her looking like that, certainly not her *mafiya* clients from *Tsarskoye Oxota*—Tsar's Hunt—the restaurant where she met them.

Regaining her composure, she tried to hide the marks with makeup, fearing the militia would pick her up in the lobby. Heavy makeup masked enough for a quick getaway from the hotel. She wanted to run out the door, but she had not yet fulfilled her mission. She had wanted to give him the message last night, but he had not allowed her to speak. Only to scream. She stared up at the ceiling, fished inside her bag for a cigarette and a match. Her half-conscious mind strained to devise a solution to her problem as she tore the wrapper off of a fresh package of Marlboros. If she didn't deliver the message, Ulianov would be displeased. She didn't know what he'd do, but she was sure it would be worse than what Slythe had done. He might even kill her.

She shuddered again, opened a matchbook from Most, the Moscow nightclub of the moment, struck a match. As she took a long drag, an idea dawned on her. She quickly removed a pen from her bag, cupped the matchbook in the crook of her soft hand. Frantically, in a shaky hand, she scrawled the exact message Ulianov had given her on the inside of the matchbook cover.

If anyone is watching, they will think I left him my phone number.

She crushed out her unfinished cigarette, stood, placed the matchbook in Slythe's vest pocket, and turned back toward the bed.

She spat on Slythe, turned off the lights, and escaped through the doorway.

27 MESSENGER

Old Post Office Building
Washington, D.C.
11:41 A.M.

Washington, D.C., was no longer its merely unpleasant self. The city was now deadly. Carlton knew he had to get out of Dodge City. Osage and Mazursky were gone. If he stayed, he'd probably be next.

Wrapped down to his boots in a long black overcoat, he walked across the street from Main Justice to the food court in the Old Post Office Building, one block from the White House.

The sickly aroma of a dozen open restaurants inside the warm shopping center made him queasy. Lunchgoers were already queued like cattle near stalls that offered everything from falafels to hamburgers. Most were DOJ and FBI employees who longed to be out of their marble fortresses, if only for an hour.

Food was the last thing on his mind. The combination of stress, insomnia, and government coffee had made his nerves raw, his stomach sour. A travel office had recently opened on the ground floor of the shopping center. Carlton often lingered in front of its small window, where large color photographs depicted inviting tropical and snowy destinations. Today he was not going there to escape from government work. He was going there to escape from the government.

Carlton stepped onto the escalator. On the ground floor, he turned right, made his way toward the small travel office.

"Excuse me?" A man's voice sounded in Carlton's ear. He jerked around nervously to see who it was, bumped into a dark-haired man dressed in khaki pants, a thick sweater, suede shoes. An expensive Japanese camera was strapped around his neck, a fanny pack tied around his waist. Tourist.

The man stared at him from smiling blue eyes. "Excuse me, sir," the man repeated in a heavy cockney accent. "Could you tell me how to get to the White 'ouse? The missus wanted to shop around 'ere and we got lost."

Carlton smiled. If there was one thing he enjoyed, it was telling visitors how to get around his beloved capital. At least there were some normal people left in this world. "Sure thing." He gave the man directions.

"You Yanks are so friendly." The man grinned. "Much obliged."

"Don't mention it. Enjoy Washington."

Carlton resumed his walk toward the travel office. He nearly reached the small shop when he felt something in his pocket. Something he did not remember being there earlier. He reached into his pocket, removed a small manila envelope. The envelope was sealed, not addressed. He ripped open the flap, removed the contents: a key and a photograph of a mound of sparkling diamonds.

The ball of heat smoldered in his gut again.

Beneath the photograph were scrawled a few handwritten lines.

500 one-carat brilliant-cut D-colored SI diamonds. The real ones are in a vault at your bank. Use the enclosed key. We appreciate your cooperation. You have a lovely associate.

Carlton looked inside the envelope. He had missed something. Another photograph. A recent snapshot of Erika, it looked as if it had been taken with a high-powered zoom lens. His heart froze. An inscription under the photo read:

Erika Wassenaar (1975–?)

Holy Mother of God.

The British tourist—the man posing as a British tourist— must have placed it in his pocket. He turned, scanned the wide spaces of the shopping center. The man had disappeared.

Carlton bolted up the escalator, pushed his way past lunchgoers who hurled insults at him. By the time he reached the next floor, it was clear he would never find the man.

They were threatening Erika! In a flash of emotion, he realized not only how much he cared for her, but that he was no longer willing to hide it. The fact they were threatening her enraged him far more than the threat to his own life. He thought about scribbling an expletive over the photograph of the diamonds and looked at the mound of brilliant stones.

He did not know the value of the 500 D-colored SI diamonds purportedly in the bank vault, but after the discussion with de la Pierre at Cartier, he knew they would be upward of $5 million. More money than he would make in all his life. Tax free.

He could retire from law, buy a house, never have to work again. He would be safe, without fear of being followed or killed. It was tempting.

He wavered for only an instant.

If Waterboer and Fress and Churchman had performed the most minute amount of research on him, they would never have attempted the ploy. They would have realized it would insult him. Enrage him.

He ran back across the street to his office, wrote a reply on the back of the glossy photograph of the diamonds.

Offer rejected. May God have mercy on your souls.

He resealed the envelope, key and all, addressed it to Lester Churchman, Esq. at Fox, Carlyle, Ashton, Chase, Whitfield & Whyte in New York, and placed it in his outgoing mail tray.

He checked his messages a final time, hoping for a call from Pink.

No luck.

He walked to the door of his office, turned and stared at the cluttered desk, the stacks of books, the green banker's lamp, the grimy windows.

"So long." Maybe forever.

28 ALLIANCE

Molotok Dacha, Aldan River
Republic of Yakut-Sakha (formerly Yakutia), Siberia
Russian Federation
8:04 P.M.

An unrelenting glacial wind whipped through the arid Siberian taiga. Day after day, night after night it howled. Through the boreal forests, through the vast open deserts of ice, through the small villages of huts and traditional yurt dwellings. For thousands of years, it had followed the same winter path, mindless of obstacles. On such days, the brutal taiga offered nothing but wind and cold and loneliness.

In contrast to the sub-zero cold outside, steam rose from the hot water *banya* in Molotok's lavishly appointed dacha, hundreds of miles from the nearest human outpost. Molotok whipped his barrel torso with a leafy birch branch to stimulate circulation, inhaling the strong aroma of the leaves. He rested his immense frame on the ceramic ledge and removed a bottle of one hundred–proof Stolichnaya vodka from a large silver urn filled with ice and uncut diamonds. He took a long pull of the clear potato alcohol, wiped his thick mustache, and passed the bottle to Ulianov. "Yet another contribution of Holy Mother Russia to world civilization."

The fact that vodka originated in Poland and not Russia would have infuriated the rabid nationalist.

The superbly fit Ulianov grabbed the bottle from his master, took a short sip. "*Da*. Nothing like a good Russian *banya* and vodka to relax the muscles and build up a hearty appetite."

Molotok slapped a giant hand on Ulianov's back. He grabbed a handful of uncut diamonds from the Mirny mine, let them drop back into the silver urn, gazing at the translucent stones. "So much wealth in such small stones. So much power."

"*Da*."

"We owe much of it to you and your Volki. Compromising Pyashinev with Waterboer. The raid on Mirny. Assassinating

Marshal Ogarkov. *Ochen harasho*. Your use of fire instead of artillery was excellent. The satellites must have thought it was a natural gas fire. They will never suspect a raid." Molotok slapped Ulianov's back anew. "*Ochen harasho*."

"*Spaceba*."

He took the bottle from Ulianov and drained it. "But power is worthless unless it is used." His voice was hoarse. The result of too many loud speeches and Kosmos cigarettes. "How did the first shipment of diamonds go?"

"Just as planned, and the deployment of a new garrison proceeded perfectly. Hand-picked to ensure loyalty to Marshal Aleksakov, who was ordered to take Ogarkov's place after his untimely death." Ulianov smiled. "Aleksakov's men loaded the diamonds on one of our trucks before the artificial diamonds were loaded on the truck from Komdragmet. As always, the geologist from Komdragmet sampled some of the diamonds, and pronounced them genuine without a flinch."

"Why not? He's well paid. And the South African? Has he paid us?" He groaned.

"*Da*. Waterboer's man in Vladivostok approved the diamonds while we counted his money and left port with 250,000 carats. One hundred dollars per carat. $25 million." Ulianov looked at his Red Army watch, a souvenir from his many missions in Afghanistan. "The next shipment from Mirny is in one month. Another $25 million. At least we don't have to rely on the contract hits in the United States to run Russkost anymore."

"One hundred dollars per carat," Molotok whispered hoarsely. "So cheap! That South African bastard is raping Russia's natural resources."

"Patience, Molotok. Patience. We will raise the price later. When we control the entire region. The flow of money is sufficient for the moment. The Mirny mine produces 250,000 carats a month. That's $300 million a year. That's not a small—"

"We don't have a year," he snapped back, then calmed himself. "But the $30 million we already have is sufficient to purchase a first load of American rockets."

"Still, it is not enough to launch our campaign. We must find the missing diamond stockpile. Kovanetz better find it soon."

"Soon, my friend. Soon."

Ulianov nodded. He had served as a colonel in the elite Spetsnaz division and been a faithful Communist Party member since he was old enough to attend the *Octobrist* rallies for small children. In his forty-five years, his loyalty had never wavered. But it was a loyalty to the Soviet state, not to the Party. The collapse of communism had little effect on Ulianov. It was the dissolution of the Soviet Empire in 1991 that struck like a dagger to his soul. The wound had never healed. Rudderless, without a goal, the new masters of Russia had "retired" him. Placed him on "indefinite leave." To Ulianov, the breakup of the Soviet Empire was more than an historical cataclysm. It was a personal humiliation. But rather than lie down in defeat and dwell on past glories like so many others, Ulianov found a way to restore his passion from the ashes of its defeat.

Ironically, the lifelong Communist went into business. In the United States, his choice of trade would euphemistically have been described as a "family" enterprise. Similar to the hundreds of groups that leeched every imaginable Russian enterprise, public and private, Ulianov and a dozen of his Spetsnaz commandos became part of the new Russian *mafiya*. Not the big *mafiya*, the former Communist managers and directors—the *apparatchiki*—the oligarchs who still ran most of the economy and government, but the street *mafiya*. Ulianov wasn't strong enough to compete with the *apparatchiki*. Not in the beginning.

To the corrupt and underfinanced police, to the hordes of other small mafia groups, Ulianov's men became known as the *Volki*—the Wolves. The Volki's unofficial growth would have put most entrepreneurs to shame. Quick, efficient, deadly, the Volki made full use of the military version of the *vertushka* network of Russian supply quartermasters, inventory supervisors, longshoremen, motorpool directors, telephone managers, state bankers, hotel managers, pilots. The *vertushka* was ubiquitous and invisible. Properly used, it supported a veritable shadow government.

Unlike the tens of thousands of drunken, drug addicted, petty *mafiya* thugs who ran unofficial Russia without true legal identity, dependent only on the greedy whims of their former *apparatchik* bosses, the Volki operated as a disciplined, organized force. There was a studied, rational business plan to their operations. At first, it involved only armament and ordnance, the easiest commodities for army officers to obtain, transport, and sell, most often to the terrorist nations of Iran, Iraq, and Libya and the terrorists operating freely in so many other countries. Later, the operation diversified. The Volki began to sell almost everything stored in army depots. Then in other government depots. After several years, their operations grew to the level of the *apparatchiki* and included many more lucrative businesses. Extortion, bribery, smuggling, prostitution, narcotics. Banking, real estate, technology, media. The Volki smuggled Russian artifacts, precious metals, weapons, chemicals, and enriched rare earth minerals for nuclear weapons construction to the highest bidder, regardless of national or political provenance. China was their best customer by far, particularly for missile and nuclear technology. The Volki amassed funds received for hired "hits" on businessmen, bankers, politicians, and mafia dons throughout the world, particularly in the United States and other Western countries, where the old Sicilian mafia had mostly gone corporate and rarely dirtied their hands with such work.

After several years, Ulianov and his Volki had amassed sufficient wealth to set their sights on their true objective, the resurrection of Holy Mother Russia. But the Volki could not achieve their goal alone. Revolutions were accomplished by an elite group through force, but they needed a charismatic leader. The Volki needed a forceful ally with a popular following. Ulianov had long scrutinized the Russian political landscape for such an ally. In an ocean of corrupt jellyfish, he had encountered one particularly impressive shark. The nationalist who called himself "the Hammer" and imagined himself as the reincarnation of Josef Vissarionovich Stalin.

Cautiously and slowly, Ulianov developed a tenuous relationship with the rough, outspoken Molotok. It began as a single business venture. For two years, Ulianov and Molotok danced a cautious dance. Ulianov demonstrated his resourcefulness and honesty to Molotok. He had not stolen. Had not charged outrageous prices. Had not raised prices unexpectedly. Had not double-crossed. Those were the trademarks of the other childlike *mafiya* groups, which Ulianov avoided carefully. For his part, Molotok proved himself worthy of Ulianov's trust, not only through their business dealings—Molotok paid on time and never renegotiated—but through his fiery lust for Russian power and glory. As it was in the old days, Molotok said, under Peter the Great. Under Stalin.

Ulianov first waded cautiously, then was sucked in and engulfed in Molotok's fiery nationalist rhetoric. Rather than the reverse, it was Molotok who assimilated Ulianov into his organization. Where Ulianov had searched for an ally, he found a master.

"Now let us feast." Molotok lifted his massive frame from the bath and grabbed a thick towel from a cedar rack. Ulianov's disciplined muscular body followed. "Our guests should all be here by now."

He slapped Ulianov on the back once again. The first two slaps had left a red welt on the athletic former colonel. He did not complain and followed Molotok's hulking form into the dressing room. When they had dressed, Molotok led the way to a private reception room, richly decorated with oil paintings hung on polished pine above chairs covered with sable skins. The paintings depicted the construction of the Trans-Siberian railroad. The fire that roared in the corner provided the only light. As the two men entered the room, a figure in unmarked army fatigues stood from one of the chairs.

"Marshal Aleksakov," Ulianov said. As if still in official service to the rodina, he saluted the newly promoted marshal in command of the Eastern Ground Forces and the Mirny garrison. The wiry marshal returned the salute, smiled.

Molotok grasped the man's hand in his giant paw. "It was good of you to come, Marshal. Intelligent of you not to dress in uniform." He tapped his index finger against his hairy head.

"Thank you, Molotok. It is I who must thank you for your hospitality."

"Not at all, my friend. Not at all. We are allies." He gestured theatrically. "What is mine is yours."

"*Spaceba*."

"I wanted to congratulate you on a job well done, Marshal. Without you, Russkost would never have been able to exercise its control over the diamonds at Mirny to fund its campaign for the *rodina*."

Aleksakov was thankful his two hosts could not discern his beet-red blush from the compliments, a result of the man's willful, albeit unconscious, participation in Molotok's personality cult, which the Siberian bear developed tirelessly.

"The Mirny diamonds are the centerpiece of our campaign for Holy Mother Russia. I only wish I could show my gratitude more eloquently." Molotok's face broke into a well-practiced smile.

"Being at your side in the great campaign is gratitude enough, Molotok," Aleksakov said.

"*Spaceba, spaceba*." Molotok performed a quick bow, then turned to Ulianov, who had not yet relaxed from his military stance before the Marshal, a carryover from his life in the military. "Come, *tovarishi*. Let us meet our allies." Molotok led the small procession through a narrow corridor into the largest room in the dacha.

The room was walled by varnished Siberian pine. Thick wool rugs covered the floor in folkloric patterns of blue and red. Ermine, sable, and bear skins hung on the walls near triple-paned glass windows. In the center of the room sat a simple wood table over thirty feet long. A large stone hearth roared with burning fir logs. Above the table hung three chandeliers fashioned from the antlers of Siberian elk. The oily black wicks of fat cylindrical candles burned messily. Like the hearth, the candles were merely decorative. A large on-site generator provided power and heat for the isolated compound.

Ten men dressed in tailored suits stood silently in the spacious room. Like Marshal Aleksakov, the only other high-ranking military godfather had left his uniform behind. Some of the men were used to corporate boardrooms and banks. Another more familiar with the media. Others with railroads, warehouses, shipyards, and airports. Others with computers and energy production. These were the top ten *krestnii otets*:

the godfathers of the big Russian *mafiya*. Half were well-known business personalities seen on television and in the newspapers. The others were so powerful they were not known publicly at all. Each man kept as much distance from the others as possible. Their faces alone revealed similarity, creased with the perpetual anxiety and distrust caused by lifetimes of disreputable activities, the threat of discovery, imprisonment, death. The Russian people referred to them differently over time: *apparatchiki*, *kleptocrats*, *oligarchs*, *mafiya* godfathers. They had thrived under Yeltsin, suffered minor setbacks and a reshuffling under the SVR/FSB rule of Puzhnin, but fought a losing war against Orlov. They needed an ally.

Stares followed Molotok as he descended the wooden staircase in silence. He waited until Ulianov and Aleksakov entered the room before he greeted each of the men with a firm handshake, some earning a full bear hug.

"*Tovarishi*," he announced in a loud voice. "Welcome!"

Except for the military *krestnii otet*, the men disregarded the un-uniformed Aleksakov, whom they did not know, and focused on Molotok. Him they knew. Him they feared despite their own power. Him they trusted. They also concentrated on Ulianov. Most of them had engaged in some form of battle with him and his Volki during the past few years. All were mindful of the power Ulianov, his Volki, and their collective new master wielded. They had learned of Molotok from rumors, at first. Then through lucrative business dealings. Little by little, Molotok and Ulianov had scrupulously whittled down the list of *krestnii otet* candidates for their Russkost strike group. Most of the godfathers were unreliable. Others had been greedy. Others did not want to join Molotok or Ulianov, much less the two combined. Or to obey orders. As the saying went, there was little honor among thieves, which is what all of them were. They were simply too highly placed for the label to apply officially. So the list shrank from nearly two hundred to the ten men in the room.

Although allied with the godfathers in Molotok's plan, Ulianov and his Volki were a dramatic contrast to the godfathers. The Volki killed, extorted, bribed, and corrupted to finance an ideological movement, Russkost. To the godfathers who basically had no ideal other than wealth, sex, and Western comforts, the synergy of Molotok and Ulianov, Russkost and the Volki, was intimidating.

Molotok gazed at the face of each man in the room silently. "I know it was difficult for you to come here, all together. I assure you, you are quite safe. If you have not already done so, it is now time to put your disagreements and competition behind you." Molotok paused, stared at his audience. A familiar fire began to burn in his breast.

He pointed a finger at the small crowd. "You are already the most influential men in Russia. You have more influence than all the marshals. More influence than all the members of the Duma. Under communism, most of you ruled Russia as *apparatchiki*." He made a fist. "Today you have influence over everyday life in Russia as the people have come to know it. Over the media and finance. Over criminal activity. Over communications. Over energy and transportation. Over government agencies. Even over parts of the military. You could control Russia." He opened and closed his huge right fist. "But you have only influence. Not power. You can push and pressure people in power to do things, but you can't order them to do anything. Not officially. You don't have power because you are fragmented." He paused. "Why?"

The men's faces showed their displeasure at the insult. Particularly because it was true.

"Why?" Molotok leaned forward and squinted at each individual's face. "Because you no longer control the government as you did under communism. Sooner or later, Orlov's reformist government and the West will destroy your operations. How is it that you men who strike fear in the hearts of all Russia bow to the weak, corrupt, mindless bureaucracy?" He wanted to shout and rant and rave, but these were not people one could shout at, not even Molotok, the Hammer.

"Because you are disorganized. Each of you is organized. Yes. But you do not work as a team. And why not? And why not put the pieces of a machine together and have it accomplish something instead of just sucking the *rodina* and the *narod* dry?"

He paused and continued to stare at the godfathers. Finally, he grinned broadly. "Now it has ended. Because we have joined as one, as Russkost, to take back control. You are not here by accident. Each of you has been selected. Over time, each of you has been tested. Your organization, your leadership. We wanted others to join us. But they were weak. There is no room for weakness in Russkost.

"Although we have dealt with one another one by one, never before have we joined together at the same time and in the same place. I congratulate you for your courage to do so." He clapped with his large hands.

"Now that we are here all together, I can give you the outline of the entire plan, not merely the individual plans we discussed one by one. The course of action we will follow is simple. Russkost will pay you to amass an arsenal. For men like you, this will be child's play." He smiled. "Once the arsenal is complete, the men in your respective organizations will join our ranks: the Volki, the members of the armed forces loyal to Russkost, and the Russkost political party. Each of you already knows his own responsibility.

"The rebirth of Holy Mother Russia finally is possible because we are united. There will be no battles. No bloody revolution. The days of Lenin and Stalin are over. Bloodshed is unnecessary."

He lied, but the godfathers preferred to believe the lie rather than Russia's history. No one had ever taken control of Russia without bloodshed, apparent or hidden. The godfathers looked at one another. It had been difficult for Molotok to band them together. But Molotok had made sure none of the ten controlled similar business interests. Each of the godfathers was brilliant, tough as nails. Successful. But they lacked vision beyond their respective spheres of control. The famous man who controlled the media—few thought of him as a godfather, though he was—cared only about total control of the media. The godfather who controlled the gas industry cared nothing about arms sales. And so on. They were too busy keeping their monopolies over their respective industries and activities and fighting, corrupting, and influencing the government to think bolder thoughts. It had taken Molotok's boldness and political organization, Ulianov's discipline and Volki strike force to open their eyes to the vision of unity.

"With your control of energy, transportation, production, and banking, media, weapons, and troops, this revolution will be simple. We will grind production to a halt. We will stop food transportation. We will cut off gas supplies. Oil. Electricity. We will shut down the airports. The railroads. The fields. The media will broadcast an image of Orlov resigning and appointing our candidate as acting president. Once he takes office, we will be in control. The *narod* will beg us to put everything back in order. We will do what the *narod* asks. Then we will be in full control. Total control. Whatever power you now have will increase tenfold. What wealth you have, likewise.

"If the people are happy, who will dare stop us? The army? They are already on our side. They are tired of a weak Russia. They want strength and glory. The bureaucrats? They will finally be paid regularly. The *Amerikanskii?* They will want to avoid an international incident and poor diplomatic relations. Besides, this will not be an international matter. There will not be bloodshed as in Chechnya. This will only be an internal Russian matter. Neither the *Amerikanskii* nor the European Union will interfere. But control is only the beginning. After control will come the reason for control: the rebirth of the empire."

Molotok's hulking arms traced sweeping arcs. "We will rearm and revitalize our military. We will take over the enterprises controlled by the foreigners. We will reclaim our lost territories. We will…"

Molotok's list was long.

At CIA headquarters in Langley, Virginia, Pink was pleased by the interruption caused by the daily mail. He sifted through the small pile of letters and magazines, hopeful for something that would change his ideas for a few moments. Company policy dictated against receiving personal correspondence at the office, so Pink rarely received interesting mail at work. Mostly internal mail he had nicknamed "infernal" mail. *Bo-ring.* Then he saw something bright sticking out from the latest issue of *Washington Lawyer*. He pulled it out and smiled. It was a postcard of a nubile young woman wearing barely anything other than a tan. He turned it over.

Mr. Pink:
I knew this would get your attention.

PC

PC? Who's P—? Must be Pat Carlton. He was about to throw the card away, but decided to pin it up on his cork board instead. She could keep him company while he finished his project for Randall Forbes. Not really Company policy, but he had a private office, not a cubicle, so the postcard couldn't be seen by other workers. One had to be careful with such things in offices these days. He returned to the Russian diamond production figures in front of him, but the postcard had derailed his concentration. Why would Carlton send a postcard when he had agreed to check his information? Especially a postcard without any message. It didn't make sense. He took the card down, turned it over. There was nothing else written on it, but Pink noticed a small white tape that melted into the rest of the white card. He peeled it off and, sure enough, found the information Carlton had given him over the phone.

"What a psycho," he mumbled, pinning the card back onto the cork board. At least the photo was nice.

29 CONTRACT

The Kremlin
Moscow
11:12 A.M.

The gleaming black Zil limousine and its six-motorcycle escort whisked through the Kremlin gates under the watchful gaze of heavily armed guards. To Russians, the sleek Zil limousine represented Soviet automotive accomplishment. Few knew Franklin D. Roosevelt had forced the Packard Car Company to transfer its moulds, dies, and tools to the Soviet Union, where they made Zils that eventually evolved to their present form.

The motorcade stopped at the base of marble steps that led to the Great Palace of the Kremlin. The three passengers who emerged from the warm comfort of the Zil winced at the icy wind that sliced into them from the north. They were pleased to pass through the massive steel and wood doors atop the marble steps.

Vasily Orlov stood inside the ornate lobby. It was rare to greet non-governmental, foreign visitors at the entrance of the Kremlin, but Slythe was not just any foreign visitor. Russia needed the Waterboer contract badly.

"Welcome to Moscow, *tovarishi*. Mr. Slythe. We are honored by your presence." The white-haired Russian president extended a large hand in a warm gesture, his English nearly perfect, albeit heavily accented. Orlov's portly girth and large round face was in sharp contrast with the handsome South African's elegant angularity.

"It is I who am honored, Mr. President." Slythe took Orlov's hand, gave a perfunctory smile. "Thank you for your personal reception." *Sniff*.

Orlov introduced Novirsk and his other assistants.

"And if I might introduce my staff, Mr. President." Slythe turned and motioned to each in his party. "Lester Churchman, my counsel, whom I believe you have met on a previous occasion. My personal assistant, Ian Witsrand."

All exchanged handshakes and smiles. Ian Witsrand's eyes made Orlov shudder.

The Russian president led the way into the executive office, flanked by four agents of the eight thousand–member Presidential Guard, the Russian counterpart to the American Secret Service. Once their charge was inside his office, the guards sank into comfortable chairs outside, lit cigarettes.

Inside Orlov's office, Slythe was eager to conclude the business at hand. His smile was genuine, despite acute jet-lag, rendered more severe by his antics the previous night.

He gazed at the Russian president and assessed his opponent.

Orlov had been lucky. Capitalist democracy had seemed to replace dictatorial communism after the dissolution of the Soviet empire in 1991. But, as the world soon discovered, the transformation was only skin deep. Private property and a few political freedoms were established, but the painful economic reforms required to transform communism into capitalism, even socialism, were never made.

The lack of genuine economic and political reforms had made the massive infusion of foreign and international economic aid to Russia useless and ineffective. As one American adviser had commented, foreign aid to Russia had made a brief stop in Moscow before ending up in Cyprus, the Caymans, or Liechtenstein. Instead of privatizing the state-run economy fairly and evenhandedly, the former *apparatchiki* privatized the state-run economy by selling its crown jewels to themselves for a pittance, itself "loaned" to them by siphoning off money from state banks, international lenders, and humanitarian aid. A few grew wealthier even than the former tsarist aristocracy, while the great majority of the *narod* lingered in post-communist limbo, amidst massive unemployment, stunningly low and often unpaid wages, with no safety net. The more it changes, the more it stays the same. In fact nothing had changed. Since communism. Since the tsars.

In the late 1990s, the mounting economic crisis came to a head. Backroom oligarchs running the kleptocracy opposed economic reforms and appropriated international aid to such an extent that not even another massive IMF/World Bank bailout could prop up the anemic Russian currency. The ruble plummeted. Communists and nationalists were increasingly elected to the Duma. A global nail-biting political turmoil ensued, with only two apparent exits: a last-ditch effort at a genuine, unpopular, and wholesale reform of the government and economy, or the adoption of popular anti-Western, despair-driven policies advocated by the nationalist-communist coalition.

Instead, the deathly ill, but still wily Russian president chose a third alternative. Resignation. Not only resignation, but resignation prior to the end of his term combined with the appointment of a successor and a full pardon for any and all crimes committed while in office. His move was melodramatic, unexpected, bold, clever. It was Russian. And at first, it succeeded.

The president's anointed successor Yegor Puzhnin was not just another drab member of the Russian political apparatus. He was a former high-ranking KGB officer. Unlike the long succession of prime ministers chosen by the former Russian president, Puzhnin was disciplined and strong-willed. His KGB training and ties served him well in his first few months in power. He renewed the war against the mafia-supported Chechen rebels and won, galvanizing public opinion in his favor for winning a conflict the Russian people had suffered as their second Vietnam the first being the failed Soviet invasion of Afghanistan.

Puzhnin continued a dialogue with the West while looking to the East for new alliances with China and India and turning Central and Western Europe against the United States. To bolster his power within the elite, he began to repatriate into Russian coffers the billions in hard currency the KGB had exported to Western banks and corporations prior to the fall of the Soviet Union, including a massive diamond stockpile.

As Friedrich Engels would have predicted, the destruction came from within. This was the first time in history Russia was truly dominated by an ex-KGB officer. Not like Yuri Andropov and his aged Politburo, but by a young, energetic, and loyal former KGB member who waged a steady cold purge—a *pieredishka* of the rank and file, replacing the bureaucrats with members of the former KGB, renamed and somewhat split by the former president into the *Federalnyii Sluzhba Bezopasnosti* (Federal Security Service, or FSB) and the *Sluzhba Vnutrinii Razvedtki* (Internal Intelligence Service, or SVR). Soon the FSB dominated Russian politics. The inevitable infighting followed, along with institutionalized paranoia. Soon the military establishment was under attack by the FSB, for whatever reasons the ruling institution could find: espionage, corruption, any number of official sins. Opponents of the FSB-led government, such as the opposition parties and opposition media, were silenced, often by imprisonment or worse. Most of the oligarchs remained, now directed by the government, rather than vice-versa.

The forced ideology of communism and the greed-centered zeitgeist of the oligarchy became the terror-driven paranoia of the state secret organ.

Hit particularly hard was the *Glavnoe Razvetskaya Upravleniye*—the military Main Intelligence Directorate, or GRU. Seeing the GRU as a competitive force, the FSB leadership moved against its rival organ, resorting to nearly Stalinist arrests and other terrors. But these were not Stalinist times, and the GRU knew how to fight back. A splinter group of GRU officers, reading the Cyrillic writing on the Kremlin wall, decided it was time to reclaim Russia from the FSB. Not that they wanted freedom for the people, they wanted to reclaim power for themselves. Counting on their military family to back them up, the GRU group organized a coup by kidnapping the top ten Russian officials—among them the president. But the GRU officers miscalculated.

Knowing they would be exchanging one secret organ of repression for another, knowing real economic reforms were the only thing that would keep them well-cared for, the Russian military intervened by forcing elections and supporting a strong leader who would for the first time in Russian history impose real economic reforms.

Thus Vasily Orlov had been elected to power.

Untainted by scandal or corruption, the high-level, well-meaning government civil servant was the only rational choice. Orlov quickly proved himself to be an effective and careful reformer. He created a currency board and pegged the ruble to a reserve of mixed Western currencies including the U.S. dollar, the British pound, the German deutsche mark, and the French franc before the last two were replaced by the lackluster euro. He wisely avoided adding the Japanese yen to the reserve until Japan jumped into economic maturity and adopted its own sorely needed economic reforms. He pushed Russia closer to the European Union, knowing that membership in that body was one of the few hopes to prevent the economy from back-sliding. Tax collection from all citizens and corporations, wealthy or not, became a national priority, an annual reality, initially encouraged by countless military raids on corporate—and *mafiya*—accountancy offices. Most energy and raw materials monopolies were dismantled and state-owned enterprises privatized. The directors of all remaining state facilities were fired, cutting deeply into the FSB's power base. But Orlov had studied Niccolò Machiavelli's writings and knew to keep both the FSB and GRU very close, as enemies should be.

The shock therapy started to work. But for a country without a democratic history or sense of free market economics, the process was slow. Too slow and too painful for many. Soon, the good yet long-suffering Russian *narod* again started to complain about the economy. Foreign investment was slow to return. Job creation remained low. Paychecks were again late. After Orlov's reelection, accomplished with little help from the cautious military, the military began to suffer from shortages and a yet unrepaired infrastructure. Orlov was again on shaky political ground, faced with a nationalist-communist coalition, who some suspected included the *mafiya*, led by a mysterious man who called himself Molotok—the Hammer.

Slythe accepted a glass of tea proffered by Novirsk on a silver tray. What he really wanted was a snort of cocaine.

Orlov sipped his tea, lit a Davidoff cigarette. "Now, Mr. Slythe. I do not wish to waste your time. As you can see, Finance Minister Voroshilov and the directors of Komdragmet, the Federal Diamond Center, Almazy Rossii, and Almazy Rossii-Sakha did not join us. By my request. This conversation will be private." He looked up at Vladimir Novirsk, Lester

Churchman, and Ian Witsrand, indicating that Slythe should unleash his dogs.

"If you wish." Slythe turned to his aides, sniffed. "Please excuse us." They stepped outside.

"Mr. Pyashinev is not here, of course. But you already know that."

"Yes," Slythe said sadly. "An unfortunate accident, I understand. His expertise will be greatly missed." He meant every word. If Pyashinev had survived, Waterboer would now be in possession of the Russian diamond stockpile. He sniffed again.

Orlov began in perfect English. "Let us recap the current situation, if you will permit. Since 1985, Russia has had a contract with the great Waterboer Mines Limited company. Under the terms of this contract, which as we both know expires this month, Russia sells 90 percent of its rough diamonds to Waterboer, approximately nine million carats a year. In exchange for this, Waterboer pays Russia a little less than $1 billion a year. Although the Union of Soviet Socialist Republics was dissolved in 1991, the Russian Federation continued to honor the terms of the agreement without question."

Slythe nodded, wondering where Orlov was heading.

"I do not know how to say this diplomatically, Mr. Slythe, but you and I are beyond formalities and I am a simple man, so I will state it plainly. My predecessors were overly generous with Waterboer. The terms of the contract cannot continue."

Orlov paused, stood, and began to pace heavily but slowly through the room, cigarette firmly clenched in his fingers. Slythe craned his neck to follow the heavyset Russian.

"This is so for several reasons. First," Orlov enumerated on his left hand, "new Russian mines have come on line since 1990. Russia produces far more diamond roughs than in 1990. Second, Waterboer has undervalued the quality of Russian diamonds."

"Mr. President, I—"

"Please allow me to finish," Orlov snapped. "Russia realizes Waterboer loaned us $2 billion to modernize our diamond mining operations." He bowed slightly, touched his chest. "For this, Russia is grateful. I am grateful. But as you recall, the terms of that loan were quite strict. Russia turned over her entire diamond stockpile to your company in exchange for the loan. That single act removed Russia's ability to destabilize the international diamond market. And Russia's diamond stockpile was worth far more than $2 billion, but that is history, and I mention it only in passing."

"Russia agreed. Of its own accord."

"That is true. My predecessor accepted the terms. Just as Germany and Japan accepted the terms of surrender after World War II. What other choice did Russia have? Russia needed the hard currency to finance its astronomical defense projects of the cold war. But when Russia needed the money most, in 1991, after the cold war, to implement the reforms that would save Russia and finally transform it into a true world power," he jabbed a finger at Slythe, "Waterboer reduced its purchases by 40 percent, damaging us beyond measure. That 40 percent would have meant the success of our reforms, but again, Russia was powerless to break the agreement."

His pause left Slythe in a tense silence.

"Now, on top of all this, I learn Waterboer pays $400 per carat in some African countries as opposed to the $150 per carat it pays Russia." He lifted his hand to silence the South African. "Do not deny it!" he shouted. "The FSB is many things, but blind and inaccurate it is not."

He continued softly. "Do not misunderstand me. We are pleased that poor African nations are getting high prices for their precious natural resource from a company that enslaved black miners for decades. But the Russian people will not tolerate a low price for its diamonds. However, we are willing to continue selling our diamonds to Waterboer. Waterboer needs this. Russia needs this." He stopped pacing, regained his position behind his desk. "So what is to be done?" He stared into Slythe's eyes. "*Shto?*"

"Mr. President, you…you take me quite by surprise."

Orlov allowed the comment to reverberate in the ornate room. He lit another cigarette and expelled the smoke upward. "*Nyet.* I don't believe I do."

"I am shocked by your assessment of our relationship, Mr. President."

Orlov ignored the man's theatrical outrage, scrutinized his cigarette. "Shocked?"

"Yes. Quite shocked indeed. First, Mr. President, Waterboer Mines reduced its purchase in 1991 not out of a desire to harm the Russian state but because of the drop in the diamond market. A great drop, Mr. President. There simply was no way for Waterboer to purchase as many diamonds as before. You know this."

"Not so. Not only could Waterboer have continued its purchases. It was required to continue. It was part of the contract. A contract you signed personally, sir." Orlov wagged the cigarette between his index and middle fingers. "A contract Russia and the Russian people adhered to. To the letter."

"Mr. President, although I detest legalism, I will remind you the agreement also contained provisions for a change in purchase quantity. Waterboer also adhered to the contract," Slythe continued, regaining his confidence. He shifted in the eighteenth-century chair. "Second, Russia did not adhere to the contract, as you argue. The quantity of diamonds your government delivered to Waterboer was far less than Russia's thirty-million-carat stockpile. Roughly $4.5 billion at the time. Third, it is true Waterboer has, in very rare circumstances, paid $400 a carat. But that is immaterial. The purchase price for Russian diamonds was set by the contract terms at $150 a carat. It was not subject to change."

"As a base price, yes. A base price. But the price could increase if there was a change in quality of the diamonds produced. There was such a change."

It took a few seconds for the South African to recover from the President's statement. Slythe had overconfidently assumed Orlov had never read the agreement. "Mr. President, no analysis has shown an increase in Russian diamond quality."

"You mean your analyses. Pardon me for saying so, Mr. Slythe, but your team of analysts could make the Hope diamond look like dirty glass. I am discussing real analyses."

"Surely you don't suggest that—"

Orlov raised his bulk to full height and scowled. "I most certainly do! Enough games, Mr. Slythe! Do you really think Waterboer is so powerful it can keep corruption from the eyes of the Russian government? The old KGB noticed nothing. Probably because Waterboer paid them off. But after 1991, the SVR detected it."

Bluffing was Orlov's strong suit. In 1991, the SVR didn't have anywhere near the funds to perform such detective work. It could barely afford carbon paper and videotapes, much less diamond analysts. But Orlov knew he was right, particularly after what Kovanetz had told him about the payoff to Pyashinev. If Waterboer had corrupted Pyashinev, far more corrupt plundering of Russia's natural resources was occurring. He knew.

Slythe took the defensive. "I have no knowledge of such payoffs, Mr. President."

Orlov sat down, crushed out his cigarette and opened a manila folder filled with numeric information. "Would you like account numbers and wire transfer dates? Our dearly departed Mr. Pyashinev's South Pacific bank account, for instance?"

Genuine shock struck Slythe. For the first time in many years of negotiations, he began to sweat.

"Come, now. You really thought that we didn't know? That we wouldn't find out?" Orlov paused. The outline of an enlarged vein protruded from his temple. "The Russian people who it seems you consider poor, stupid, and backward will no longer tolerate Waterboer's rape of its diamond resource."

"But I—"

Orlov again bolted out of his chair. "No more lies! Lies about not paying off our officials! Lies about the Russian diamond stockpile! I personally reviewed the files. Every carat in our vaults was transferred to Waterboer. Do not lie to me. The Russian people will not be lied to!" He slammed his palm on the polished desktop.

Two presidential guards, busy watching and recording the meeting through hidden cameras, exchanged silent smiles. They liked what they saw. A true Russian who drank vodka like a Cossack and rebuffed attacks by Western multinational corporations with verbal cannon fire. Maybe voting for Russkost in the next election would be a mistake. Orlov was a good leader.

Slythe felt lost. Nothing was happening the way he had planned. The Russian was threatening him. Him. Piet Slythe. The Diamond Lord. He reassured himself with the knowledge the Russian had no leverage, no matter how right he was. But he would have to change his tactic. Lying to Orlov would not succeed. Lies were only powerful when seen as truths.

Orlov knew the truth. About everything except for the stockpile, it seemed. It was strange. Could it be Orlov didn't know the Russian diamond stockpile had been only partially transferred to Waterboer? If so, Pyashinev had done his job very well. A pleasing thought. If Orlov didn't know about the stockpile, he wouldn't look for it. It would make Molotok's search easier, increase Waterboer's chances of taking possession of the destabilizing stockpile.

Orlov sat back down, composed himself. He forced a smile. "Come, now, Mr. Slythe. Russia and Waterboer have had a relationship for decades. Poor during the last few years, but good health can return." He lit a third cigarette. "Since the 1960s, we've been selling diamonds to Waterboer. Let us not become enemies because of a few unfortunate mistakes. Regardless of what has occurred in the past, Russia is still very interested in a new contract with your company."

Slythe glanced up hopefully. "I propose a price of $175 a carat."

Orlov disregarded the proposal as though he had not heard it. "I propose Waterboer and Russia enter into a contract for three years. Russia will sell 50 percent of its diamond rough to Waterboer. The rest, Russia will keep and sell on the secondary market. Russia needs new jobs as well as hard currency. Why not those of diamond cutters and marketers? The price will be fixed at $200 per carat for the first year, to be reevaluated annually based on a neutrally supervised sampling of every mine in Russia. The diamonds we keep and sell on our own will be subject to purchase by Waterboer, of course. But on the secondary market."

Where the price is higher, Orlov did not have to add.

Slythe was stunned. In truth, the terms were not far off from present market prices, but they were unacceptable to Slythe.

More troublesome than the high price Orlov demanded was the sale of only half of the Russian diamond rough, allowing Russia to sell the other half at realistic prices in direct competition with Waterboer. The market price for diamonds would drop like a stone. In its 120 year history, Waterboer had never engaged in true competition with any other large-scale diamond producer. Its strength was based on monopoly.

"I'm afraid those terms are unacceptable, Mr. President."

"I see. Too much competition for your monopoly." Orlov smiled wickedly. "I understand. There is, of course, a second option."

Slythe leaned forward, eyebrows arched.

"Russia will sell every single carat mined to Waterboer, its entire diamond production—"

"Yes." Slythe could not contain his excitement. Sniff.

"At $300 a carat."

"Three hundred? Impossible. Waterboer would become insolvent within months."

"I doubt it." Orlov smiled, blew smoke through a mischievous smile.

"No, Mr. President, it's simply too much."

"Russia wants to be reasonable, of course. The last thing Russia wants is for Waterboer to perish. To whom would we sell our diamonds? But I disagree with your dire economic prediction. Waterboer would not suffer such a fate. True, $300 a carat is a high price, but only compared to the prices paid by Waterboer. Not the prices it charges. In that light, $300 is quite within the market price, a price that includes the added premium of control, Mr. Slythe. Control of the entire production of Russian diamonds would allow Waterboer to continue to raise the price of diamond roughs, as it has every single year for the last one hundred years, and to turn its attention to stemming the massive flow of diamonds on the open market from Canada and Australia and the civil war–torn countries of Africa."

Slythe shook his head. "I cannot agree to such a proposal."

"Of course, if you wish, Waterboer can operate without a new contract with Russia. We would have to find a new purchasing source for our diamonds. It would be difficult. But far more difficult for Waterboer. It would result in a loss of control of twelve million carats into the market each year. A loss of control I doubt Waterboer could afford." He stared. Silence.

"None of these options are viable." *Sniff.*

"There is, of course, a third option."

Slythe waited for it in stoic silence.

"You could be arrested."

Slythe was stunned. "Arrested? Are you mad? On what charge?"

"I'm not a lawyer, of course. But I would assume the charge would be the possession of illegal narcotics, assault, battery, and rape. Maybe attempted mur—"

"Rape?" He stood. "Are you insane? You dare accuse me?" He shouted, placing a hand on his chest. "Me?"

Orlov retained his calm. "You would be granted a full jury trial, of course. These are not the times of Stalin and Beria. We have juries in Russia now." Orlov smiled wickedly. "Perhaps you would like to view the evidence?"

He grabbed a file folder from his desktop, opened it. He leafed through its contents, selected a particularly nasty photograph of Slythe's chilling S&M session with Lena, showed it to Slythe. "This is my favorite."

Slythe gazed at the glossy black and white, shuddered. Not at the bloody image, but at the implications. His considerable public relations team had succeeded in creating an image of Slythe as a benevolent corporate patriarch. Photographs of him smiling sadistically over the bloody body of a Russian prostitute would destroy that façade in one blow. The thought made him so nauseated he had to sit down.

"It was a mistake reserving a room in a government-owned hotel. Russia hasn't completely changed. Particularly its intelligence organs. So many cameras. Of course, I'm certain Waterboer can afford better trained lawyers than the impoverished Russian state, but it would be a pity if these photos were to find their way to the international press, don't you agree? Cocaine and rape. A bit far from the 'Diamonds Are Beauty' campaign. Not a good marketing combination. The Western news organizations adore shocking stories. They would pay us handsomely for these photographs."

"Enough. I know when I'm beaten," his voice cracked. "I will sign the new contract."

"I'm so pleased."

"This is blackmail, you realize. This is not done of my free will. It's unenforcea—"

"Blackmail. Something with which Waterboer has no experience." Orlov's smile disappeared. "Please don't use that reasoning with me. It's insulting. I'm impervious, but I am reasonable. Which of the contract term options will Waterboer select? Fifty percent at $200 a carat or one hundred percent at $300?"

Slythe bowed his head in defeat. "Russia's entire diamond production at $300 a carat."

"*Da. Harasho.*" Orlov grinned. "I will destroy these negatives." He picked up another folder from his desk, removed a two-hundred-page document, pages alternately written in Cyrillic and Latin alphabets. Orlov's own legal team had stayed up several nights in a row preparing contracts for each of the president's alternatives. "Here is the contract. Have your lawyers review it. I suggest you make as few changes as possible. The contract is concluded between you and me, of course, but the Duma is touchy. It may want to start modifying its terms if you don't sign it soon. And Piet? Between you and me. The cocaine? Drop the habit. It will kill you."

Slythe returned to Sheremetyevo II airport, Churchman and Witsrand in tow, without uttering a single word. The others were too afraid to utter a word. The white Waterboer Boeing Business Jet waited patiently on the frozen tarmac, engines already hissing. Slythe fell into a leather chair in the cabin, puppy Kimberley cradled in his arms, and snorted cocaine from a small platinum receptacle. He stared upward and sniffed. Smiled.

Poor Orlov. So convinced he'd beaten the Slythe family and Waterboer. In truth, everything had gone in Waterboer's favor. Maybe not the final price. But everything else.

First, Waterboer had a new contract for all of the Russian diamond production and retained its monopoly. There wasn't really a true secondary diamond market, as Orlov knew. Waterboer generally controlled that market, as well. It was, however, good politics to let the world think there was some part of the diamond business Waterboer did not control.

Second, it was apparent from Orlov's statements and his reasoning he was unaware only part of the Russian diamond stockpile had been transferred to Waterboer before the counterrevolution of 1991. This left Molotok free to search for it without government competition.

Third, and perhaps best of all, not only did Slythe avoid a nasty public relations fiasco with the incriminating photographs—he still didn't believe that he could have been arrested—but the whore Lena had given him excellent news. He pulled out the matchbook she had left in his coat pocket. Inside the cover was scrawled a handwritten message:

GRU Colonel Kovanetz investigating Pyashinev, also looking for diamond stockpile for Molotok

Not only was Molotok searching for the diamond stockpile, he was being helped in his search by members of the Russian security organs themselves, Orlov's own people.

For the first time since his orgasmic infliction of pain the previous night, Slythe erupted with laugher.

30 WARNING

Washington, D.C.
2:35 P.M.

"Hello."

"Erika. It's Pat." Carlton pushed the tiny cellular telephone hard against his ear to hear her soft voice over the Cadillac's throaty engine.

"Where have you been? I checked your office and—"

"Listen to me."

"—and I—"

"*Erika!*" he shouted. "You have to listen."

"What?"

"I want you to catch the first flight back home."

"What?"

"They know about you." He stopped short of telling her they had threatened to kill her.

"They *who*? What are—"

"I'll explain later. Just do what I tell you. Don't pack anything. Don't call anyone. Just grab a cab and go to National Airport. Take your cell phone with you. I'll call you later. Do you understand?"

"But I—"

"Do you understand?"

"Yes."

"Do it now. Quiet. Fast. I'll call you later." He punched the END key.

31 DDI

CIA Headquarters
4:31 P.M.

Pink was about to knock on the carved mahogany door when it unlatched from within, with a heavy metallic sound. He had never met CIA Deputy Director of Intelligence (DDI) Randall Forbes, the man CIA staff referred to as Malcolm. Everyone in the Agency was afraid of Forbes—even the director, it was rumored—and Pink was no exception. He was sweating profusely. His throat and mouth were dry. He pulled the thick brass door handle forward.

"Come in, Pink," a voice announced from a wheelchair behind a carved oak desk.

Pink gazed at the opulent office, wondering how a civil servant, even a DDI, could afford such an office before remembering Forbes' wealth. He probably paid for it out of his own pocket. In his exhausted state, especially after Forbes had pushed their meeting back nearly eight hours, the thought had haunting echoes. *Maybe Fress and Forbes are working together.* If anyone could help Fress in the international arena, it was Forbes. *Maybe Forbes' money really comes from Waterboer and isn't family money after all.*

The office was spacious, with a large window and view on the green inner courtyard of the New Headquarters Building (NHB). Beyond the armored glass, the late afternoon sun shot rays of sunlight through clouds as in a Turner painting. The floor was covered with a deep pile, navy blue carpet that contrasted with the dark red painted walls. Small autographed photographs of the DDI with a constellation of presidents, members of Congress, and high-ranking military figures surrounded two gargantuan nineteenth-century American landscapes by Bierstadt, illuminated by halogen lights. Near the entrance of the office sat three heavy brown leather button chairs opposite a similarly upholstered sofa. In the center, a glossy oak coffee table reflected the flames from a white-painted brick hearth. Light emanated from brass candleholders on the wall and bankers' lamps on the desk.

The door bolted shut behind Pink automatically, giving him the sense of being imprisoned.

"Sit down." Forbes motioned to the sofa.

"Thank you, sir." Forbes wheeled himself to the coffee table next to Pink, who sat stiffly on the deceptively hard leather couch next to a velvet pillow that bore the pale blue and white shield of the DDI's alma mater. *Lux et Veritas*. Light and Truth. Yale.

Forbes was the tenth-generation descendant of a wealthy Episcopalian Connecticut family. But he was far more interested in affairs of state than in the daily buy-low, sell-high grind for which many of his fellow Yalies had opted. Those matters he relegated to the bourgeois bankers, as he termed them. Forbes suffered a paralyzing leg injury during his very young infantry service in the Korean War and had been in a wheelchair ever since. A graduate of Yale Law School, Forbes practiced law in Boston after his service in military intelligence. In the early 1960s, he was appointed ambassador to South Africa. There and then began his fascination with diamonds.

Unlike many East Coast WASPs at the time, Forbes loathed apartheid. The violent racism and intransigence of the former South African government pushed him to leave the diplomatic service. He returned to the United States and was elected to the House of Representatives from his native Connecticut district. An honorable politician, he served only two terms before leaving his seat to another. Another chief executive, not so coincidentally also a fellow member of Yale's undergraduate Skull and Bones Society, appointed him deputy director of Military Intelligence. Several years later, Forbes opted for a return to a dull and uneventful life as the *éminence grise* of his former law firm as an "of counsel." This too was short-lived.

He was soon dragged back into the fray of intelligence affairs by his appointment as assistant DDI of Central Intelligence. The appointment surprised him. He had no background or ties to the Company. But Forbes was a keen analyst and accepted the appointment out of duty, not desire. He grew to tolerate the position, then to enjoy it. He was then promoted to DDI. Never married, now he relished his job more than life itself. He had been awarded a Congressional Medal of Honor that remained secret for his neutralization of coordinated terrorist activities on January 1, 2000, in the world's ten largest cities.

Forbes' attire was a credit to his East Coast patrician family. His lean frame was clothed in a conservative white shirt, yellow Hermes tie, and bespoke blue pinstripe suit tailored by his longtime sartorial supplier on Savile Row.

Forbes assessed his subordinate with gunmetal gray eyes focused through gold framed eyeglasses under thinning silver hair that women found attractive. The artificially thin lenses corrected a myopia inflicted by endless hours of study. Although the man rarely smiled, he was sufficiently at ease with himself that his gaze came off as professional rather than cold.

Pink fidgeted in his seat, clasped his manila file folder.

Forbes pointed to the file folder. "Careful. You don't want to tear that." His accent was pure New England elite. "Listen here, Pink. I know you spent a god-awful time analyzing this. It's your first assignment for me personally. You're nervous, exhausted, sweaty, hungry. You're no longer thinking straight. You are uncomfortable speaking with me in the absence of Debbie Gold and because I'm in a wheelchair." He paused. "Stow all of that. All I want is solid analysis. Give me that, and I'll be happy."

"Yes, sir." Strangely, Pink felt more nervous.

"Good. Smoke if you got 'em." Forbes busied himself with a burl walnut pipe and a pouch of aromatic cherry tobacco. "You've analyzed the Mirny incident and the most recent trip to Moscow of everyone's favorite saint Piet Slythe." He lit the pipe with a cedar match and puffed until his head was enveloped in a cloud of fragrant blue smoke. He held the pipe between straight white teeth clenched firmly on the black stem, peered at Pink through the haze. "Tell me about it."

"Yes, sir. Where should I begin, sir?"

"Your conclusions first. I appreciate the respect, Pink. But drop the sirs. They grate."

"Yes, sir...er, yes. My conclusion is twofold. First, Slythe's visit to Moscow and the Mirny incident seem unrelated.

Second, it seems a Russian diamond stockpile still exists despite the apparent transfer of the entire Russian stockpile to Waterboer in 1990."

He paused. Forbes' gaze goaded him onward.

"But I believe there may be a third conclusion to be drawn from the data. I realize Jerry Delpin already made conclusions about the satellite imagery. But in my opinion, sir, the imagery from the Mirny fire contains quirks that require further study."

My opinion. The words struck Forbes. He was used to analysts inventing new ways of coating facts with weasel language to avoid responsibility for rotten conclusions. Finally here was an analyst who wasn't afraid of putting his ass on the line. "Interesting. On what do you base your conclusions?" More puffs.

"Well, as you know, in 1990 Waterboer loaned Russia $2 billion to modernize its diamond mining and processing operations. In payment, Waterboer got Russia's massive diamond stockpile. The loan was a sham, of course. By getting the stockpile, Waterboer neutralized its potential destabilizing force. For $2 billion, which worked out to a pretty good deal on a per-carat basis." He paused, sifted through his mental fog for what followed next.

"According to our intelligence reports, the stockpile was transferred from Moscow to London, then shipped to Waterboer vaults around the world. No problem up to this point. The crunch comes in calculating the actual number of carats transferred to Waterboer. According to our sources in Komdragmet, every single carat of the Russian stockpile was transferred to Waterboer in Moscow. About twenty million carats of gem-and industrial-quality stones. But the same sources that indicate the transfer of the twenty million carats give us figures that collectively indicate a total stockpile of thirty million carats."

"So ten million carats are unaccounted for?" Forbes stared at him through a cloud of smoke.

"That's what it looks like. Yes."

"Your conclusion is what certain Agency analysts came up with in 1990."

He knew? Pink's heart sank.

"So either the sources are wrong and the stockpile really totaled twenty million carats, or the sources are correct and ten million carats are unaccounted for."

"Correct. My first instinct was to discredit the sources. But to the best of my knowledge, no source was aware of the others, and each provided the same production and stockpile transfer figures. That leaves only one conclusion: the sources were all telling the truth, and ten million carats of Russian diamonds are unaccounted for. Since the sources were adamant internal that sales records, receipts, transports, warehouse logs, bank records, and so on reflected a total stockpile of only twenty million carats, intentional falsification of Russian governmental records is indicated."

"Your conclusion?"

"In my mind, sir, the only possibility is that someone at the highest level falsified records and was able to keep ten million carats of diamonds hidden from our sources at Komdragmet."

"How many dead presidents are we talking about?"

"If leaked on the international market slowly enough not to bloat supply and push the price south, at current prices, the ten million carats would be worth between one and three billion dollars."

"So it seems Ivan was less than candid." It was the former diplomat's way of saying the Russians had lied through their teeth. "Of course, it isn't a surprise." More puffs. "After all, many of these official numbers and records date back to the cold war. Given that industrial diamonds are relied upon heavily in computers and other defense systems, Ivan certainly had no incentive to tell the truth." He clamped down on the pipe.

"I agree. But there is something strange here. Very strange." Pink closed his eyes to translate his thought to words. "The sources who provided us with the figures—our people at Komdragmet—they believe the entire stockpile was thirty million carats. And at the same time, those very people believe the entire stockpile was turned over to Waterboer."

"So they never bothered to put two and two together?"

Pink shook his head. "No. That would be too simple."

Forbes shifted the pipe stem to the other side of his mouth. "How do you explain it, then?"

Pink stretched out his hands to make his case. "They know production is high. But they believe the stockpile is small—well, smaller, anyway. The logical assumption is that something made the people at Komdragmet believe the stockpile was smaller than it really was."

Forbes puffed. "Or someone."

"All three sources gave us the same information. They must all have believed the same thing."

"Colluded and fudged figures?" One of Forbes's eyebrows cocked skeptically.

"I don't think so. No," Pink nodded vigorously. "These people were too highly placed. And again, they had no knowledge of each other. I doubt they would risk exposure to get their stories straight and give false information. But why would someone go to such trouble to make the Agency or anyone else believe the stockpile is smaller than it really is? I mean, it's nice to know the facts, but why would anyone in Russia give a"—he caught himself before launching an expletive—"give a hoot about whether or not the CIA knows the size of the stockpile?"

"You're assuming the Agency was the target of the disinformation." Forbes stressed the last word, staring at the burning tobacco in his pipe.

"Isn't that logical?"

"It is." A pause. "Until you learn a fact I withheld." Forbes pointed the stem of his pipe toward Pink. "One of the Komdragmet sources was also an informant for Waterboer. Leonid Pyashinev." He puffed. "What of your third conclusion? About Mirny?"

Pink was too accustomed to Eastern European corruption to be surprised at the revelation. "The imagery reveals three quirks. First, someone seems to have flown over the facility with unpowered aircraft immediately before it exploded. Second, the facility exploded all at once rather than catching fire progressively. Third, someone not part of the garrison escaped from the fire."

Forbes sat up in his wheelchair, for the first time genuinely surprised. "And your conclusion?"

"Why would someone fly over Mirny with gliders instead of self-propelled aircraft? At night? In those temperatures? Improbable. Not a single soldier escaped the fire, as our people in the Russian General Staff informed us. If these things were not coincidental, they were intentional."

Forbes nodded silently.

"If they were intentional, someone engineered the explosion."

"That's a bit far-fetched, isn't it? Why would someone set fire to the Mirny complex and not destroy the processing structure?"

"The neutron bomb," Pink blurted out.

Forbes removed the pipe stem from his clenched teeth. "I beg your pardon?"

"The neutron bomb, sir. It was designed to kill people and leave structures intact."

"You lost me, Pink."

"The neutron bomb was designed to leave buildings intact so when the radiation disappeared, the physical infrastructure could be used after a war. At Mirny, the fire destroyed the wooden barracks, but left the cement processing center intact."

"You think whoever caused the explosion at Mirny did it to eliminate the soldiers and leave the center in working order?"

"Something like that."

"To continue your neutron bomb analogy—not a bad one, by the way—the purpose of the neutron bomb is to allow the victor to use the facilities."

"Right."

"So extrapolating your analogy, the purpose of the explosion at the Mirny processing center would be for those who engineered the explosion to continue processing diamonds."

"Yes."

"But in our scenario, we know that the new commander of the Eastern Ground Forces, Marshal Aleksakov, who replaced Ogarkov, sent in replacement soldiers, rebuilt the barracks, and is now operating Mirny as before. Why burn down an entire complex to eliminate soldiers when you know they'll be replaced a few days later?"

"We're assuming that."

"We're assuming what?"

"We're only assuming Mirny is operating as before. If the fire was intentional, it was to accomplish something. To change something. What has changed? The only thing that changed after the fire was the garrison. The soldiers. The processing center is still there. It's armored concrete, it didn't burn. The wooden barracks are being rebuilt. Whoever started the fire went to a lot of trouble to kill the soldiers and leave the rest intact."

The conclusion had been right in front of him the entire time, but it was so obvious Pink hadn't thought of it. "And to make sure that the satellites didn't detect anything. Of course."

"So let's assume someone went to great lengths to kill off the garrison," Forbes conceded. "Let's go further. Why change the garrison?"

Pink marshaled his thoughts. "The new garrison must be different in some way."

"Its individual members are all different," Forbes said, reloading his pipe.

"Do you think maybe…" Pink's voice trailed off. The idea was on the outer edge of his mind, just beyond its reach.

"Different loyalties than the members of the old garrison, perhaps? Their commanding officer is new. Marshal Aleksakov."

"That would make sense. But loyalty to whom? Waterboer?"

Forbes shook his head slightly. "Waterboer couldn't be paying off over a hundred soldiers. Anything so obvious would fly against the rule of conspiracy." He referred to the axiom that a secret propagates to the cube of the number of people who know about it. If only one person knows, he can keep a secret, but then it's not a conspiracy. If two people know, then at some point eight people will know, and so forth. Which was why popular ideas of secret conspiracies were not only far-fetched, but virtually impossible.

"What if Waterboer isn't paying off the entire garrison, only the new commanding officer?" Pink asked.

Forbes considered it for a moment. "There is only one fly in the ointment, or rather one inclusion in the diamond, if you'll pardon the expression." He stoked his pipe, lit it carefully. "Motive, Pink. What motive could Waterboer have to pay off the CO of a garrison protecting Mirny, if Mirny is still producing diamonds? The garrison has no role in the diamond production, only its protection."

Pink's theory imploded. He was crestfallen. "Right. If Waterboer had engineered the explosion, they would have made certain the center stopped producing diamonds." He looked through the window past Forbes' desk. His thoughts wandered, refocused. "But that doesn't kill the conclusion. If it's not Waterboer, it must be someone else. Someone did this."

"But who?"

Pink grinned. He was so used to looking for hidden information the obvious had never entered his mind. "Russia. The only group involved in Russian diamond production other than Waterboer is Russia. And today, Russia has many faces, many powers."

"Russia is paying off the CO?"

"Communists, nationalists, the mafia." Pink interrupted. "Whoever controls the Mirny diamonds can sell them. Waterboer, the secondary market. You name it. The question is: who controls Mirny?"

"It certainly fits. Orlov is pushing for a higher price for Russian diamonds. Whoever controls Mirny can sell diamonds to Waterboer at an artificially low price and still make a huge profit. Waterboer would jump at the opportunity. They already had Pyashinev on payroll. He fudged the numbers for Waterboer so Orlov's people wouldn't suspect a thing. And whoever controls the Mirny diamonds could conceivably fudge the payment balances as having been received by the Russian government."

Forbes paused and smiled for the first time during their meeting. "An excellent analysis, Pink. I would say correct, too, in light of information we received yesterday morning. Which is why I asked Gold to analyze this in the first place. Otherwise I would have left it up to our friends across the river at Justice."

Pink thought of the telephone call and postcard from Carlton.

With a quick flick of his wrist, Forbes managed to throw a folder on Pink's lap, facing straight. Pink opened it, stared at the rows and columns of black figures set against bright white paper. They faded in and out of focus because of his blurry vision. They seemed to be a chronological list of assets and debits for hundreds of items.

"An internal Waterboer balance sheet for the purchase of Russian diamonds during the past month," Forbes said. "None of it made any sense until your analysis. It's the last entry I'm interested in."

Pink looked at the last entry on the sheet, paused. "I'm not an accountant, but it looks like a purchase of two hundred fifty thousand carats at one hundred dollars a carat." Pink looked up from the folder. "The present contract is for $150 a carat, and we know from our sources in Orlov's office that the new contract is for $300 a carat."

"If 250,000 carats is roughly the amount processed at Mirny each month, and if Waterboer paid $100 a carat instead of $150 or $300, Waterboer must have purchased these diamonds from a source other than the Russian government."

"Maybe it's not the production from Mirny that's being sold. Maybe it's the missing diamond stockpile."

"The numbers are too close. 250,000 carats in a month. After what happened at Mirny? Too much of a coincidence to be a coincidence."

Pink bit his lip before asking the question he had wanted to ask since Debbie Gold had given him this assignment. "Please forgive me for asking, sir, but I don't understand why the Agency is involved. Diamond contract or not, this seems to be a domestic Russian problem. Why is the—"

"Why, indeed. There are many reasons. I'll give you three. First, there is almost never a thing as simple as a purely domestic Russian problem. Generally, extrapolated to its logical conclusion, a domestic Russian problem becomes an international problem. Second, the Company operative who supplied the information in your hand was murdered by Waterboer no less than twenty-four hours ago."

Pink stared at the document, the numbers having suddenly taken on grave importance. An agent died for them.

$5,000,000 L. Pyashinev
$25,000,000 (250Kcts.) Bank of Vanuatu/117837622

A word that preceded the name of the bank seemed to have been whited out.

"The third reason is because the South Pacific bank account on the sheet of paper in your hand was accessed two days ago to purchase ten stolen AGM-136 Tacit Rainbow units on the black market for $55 million. Are you familiar with the Rainbow?"

Pink shook his head.

"The Rainbow is an air- or ground-launched defense suppression missile with a forty-pound fragmentation warhead. It looks just like a cruise missile. Unlike the cruise, the Rainbow can linger in a target area for long periods of time. It's extremely accurate, and its prelaunch programming is virtually unjammable."

"Who—"

"The name on the account is a front for an organization you know well." He paused. "Russkost."

"Russkost? The Russian nationalists? Molotok? Those crazies are the ones behind this?" He paused. "If they're behind this, then—"

"Then someone is about to start a Russian civil war that'll make Chechnya look like a county fair."

Pink sat in stunned silence.

"That's why the Agency is involved."

"Then Russkost controls Mirny as a source of funding?"

"It appears that way from your analysis."

"But if they control Mirny through the new garrison commander and sell the diamonds to Waterboer through who-knows-what channels, they can buy weapons from anyone they want." He stood. "My God. They can bankroll—"

Forbes motioned him back into his seat. "No they can't. Don't you see? Mirny is their weak point. Their Achilles heel. The 250,000 carats a month coming out of Mirny aren't enough. Like the Chechens. They're armed, but not well enough—$25 million monthly, if the production from Mirny continues. It's enough for a real good shootout, but not enough to reach critical mass. The key isn't Mirny. The key is what you confirmed—that ten million carats are missing from the stockpile the Russian government sold to Waterboer.

"We have to assume Russkost doesn't control that yet, or they would already have sold it to Waterboer. If they do get their hands on the stockpile, Waterboer will pay Russkost whatever it demands to keep them from tanking diamond prices." He puffed on his pipe.

"So you see? The familiar dance continues, and the dance cards are full. Us against them. Except them isn't the Kremlin anymore. We're on Orlov's and Russia's side in this one. Them is Russkost and Waterboer." Forbes wheeled himself behind his desk, indicating that their meeting was over.

Pink continued looking at the document on his lap. An entry caught his attention.

$20,000,000 Cleveland Metals, Inc./Bank of
Vanuatu/113567854

There it was, black on white. The company Carlton told him about. And the Bank of Vanuatu. Was it the same account number? He tried to memorize it so he could verify.

Pink was about to tell Forbes about Carlton, but an inner voice stopped him. If Carlton was right and Fress was involved, there was no telling who else in the government could be involved. Carlton said they had already killed the Senate aide and a farmer. It sounded almost like a covert operation. Could the Agency be involved?

Pink walked out of Forbes' office calmly, then bolted to his office and tore Carlton's postcard from the wall.

113567854

The same account number.

"Son of a bitch. Son of a bitch!"

He rifled through the papers on his desk for Carlton's work and home numbers, called the work number first.

"Hi. This is Pat Carlton with the Department of Justice. You've reached my voicemail. To bypass this message hit pou—"

Pound. "Carlton, it's Pink. I checked your figures. Please call me. And you've got to disappear. Fast." He left his number, called Carlton's home.

"Hi it's Pat. I'm not home right now, so please—"

Pound. "Pat. It's Pink. I got all your stuff and you're right. Get the hell out. As fast as you can."

32 PATRIA

The Gulfstream V's twin BMW–Rolls Royce BR710 fanjets hissed while Todd Kerry ran through his preflight checklist in the all-glass Honeywell cockpit. A former Navy fighter pilot, Kerry now wore the white uniform of the *Patria*, the largest and fastest jet in the MacLean fleet. Thick clouds had cast a cold gloom over Los Angeles when Kerry received MacLean's urgent telephone call. Now those same clouds pelted rain mercilessly against the white hull and thirty-foot wings of the $40 million aircraft. Not that the weather conditions bothered him much. The *Patria* was certified for IFR, which allowed the aircraft to take off and land without visibility. The tardiness of his passenger bothered him far more than the weather.

Kerry busied himself with the instruments. He input wind speed, weight, and other information into the performance management computer, waited a few seconds for the program to synthesize the data into optimal rates of takeoff and climb. He began requesting preliminary taxiing instructions from the tower as soon as he saw MacLean's British Racing Green Bentley Arnage rush toward the jet, illuminated by the aircraft's wingtip projectors. The massive sedan slowed to a halt, disgorged two passengers, and sped away into the stormy night.

A large man dressed in black walked up the slick metal staircase to the door hatch. He was one of the Sicilian watchers MacLean had appointed to protect Dan Wenzel. The bodyguard gazed right and left in smooth movements, unaffected by the beating rain and buffeting gusts of wind. Wenzel followed him up the staircase, far more eager to get out of the rain. An attractive, strawberry blonde flight attendant dressed in a white *Patria* uniform helped them inside and sealed the oval door hatch behind them.

"Thanks, Nastassja." Wenzel caught a glimpse of pilot Kerry through the open cockpit door and waved.

The *Patria* began to taxi through the pools of rain on the concrete tarmac as Wenzel and the silent Sicilian made their way to the sumptuous main cabin. They strapped themselves into soft black leather seats. Wenzel removed the handset of a satellite telephone attached to the large armrest and dialed MacLean's private line.

"MacLean."

"It's Dan. I'm on my way."

"Good. Saunders will arrange your landing. Call me when you get there."

It seemed as though his client wanted to say more but stopped himself, careful not to disclose any unnecessary information over telephone and fax lines he was certain were bugged.

MacLean was fed up with the bullshit Washington hurled at him. The man was reasonable, but he would brook no further threats from the alphabet soup of federal agencies, culminating with Wenzel's near frame and the DOJ condemnation of his Arkansas property. He despised threats from parties unknown. A bottom-line man, he wanted bottom-line answers.

All he heard so far were threats from cowards afraid to show themselves. MacLean never turned away from a fight. He was used to them. And to the son of Giancarlo Innocenti, a fight with the federal government was just another fight.

It was no surprise to Wenzel when MacLean announced his intention to confront the powers-that-be directly. In person. But Wenzel's advice was as sound as ever. He convinced MacLean to let him go in his place. MacLean's absence would make any negotiations less dangerous, Wenzel argued. If the real powers behind this remained hidden, so should he. At first, MacLean categorically refused. Gradually, however, he came to realize the value of Wenzel's argument.

Wenzel would fly to Washington, unannounced. Unlike in Macon Grove, however, he was not taking any unnecessary risks. He would fly MacLean's jet instead of a commercial airline. He would be shadowed by the Sicilian. He would make contact with Colonel Saunders, a MacLean friend at Andrews Air Force Base in Maryland, who would give him a measure of local protection.

For his part, MacLean also took no chances. On Wenzel's counsel, he had not stepped foot outside Castel MacLean in two weeks and had replaced his hired security guards with soldiers supplied by the trusted family of Don Forza in Sicily, who Giancarlo Innocenti had mentored long ago. Direct from Sicily, the ten soldiers, including the one accompanying Wenzel to D.C., preferred the knife and garrotte to firearms, despite the Steyr sharpshooting rifles that hung from their shoulders. Silent and dressed in black from head to toe, they were devoted adherents to the Sicilian code of *omerta*. On the order of their don, each would die protecting the only son of Don Giancarlo Innocenti, each would remain mute if interrogated.

Kerry opened the throttles wide. The unmuzzled fanjets screamed to life. Their 29,500 pounds of thrust pinned Wenzel and the Sicilian into their seats, rocketed the G-V down the runway. Seconds later, the *Patria* pushed through the thick layer of rain clouds shrouding L.A. below. Stars blinked on one by one in the black sky through the oval portholes. The "No Smoking" sign winked off. Wenzel placed a cigarette between his lips. Nastassja lit it with a Zippo lighter held in white gloved fingers. Wenzel watched a billow of smoke rise to the ceiling, where it was sucked into the filtration system.

"Thank you." He exhaled.

"My pleasure, sir. Would you care for a cocktail before dinner?"

"Sure would. Scotch and soda. On the rocks, please."

"Yes, sir. If you would care to take a look at the menu." She handed him and the Sicilian silk-lined menus embossed with the navy blue insignia of the *Patria*.

He smiled. Knockout flight attendant, white gloves, cocktail, dinner menu. MacLean was incorrigible. Even in the midst of crisis, the man retained his devotion to the esthetic.

Kerry banked to port over Santa Monica Bay, executed a 180-degree turn east toward Maryland before accelerating to the G-V's maximum speed of Mach 0.9. He switched on the

PA system as the *Patria* continued its ascent to a rarefied altitude high above the congested airways of its commercial brethren.

"Good evening, Mr. Wenzel. Our ETA at Andrews is three hours and forty minutes. We'll be flying at fifty-one thousand feet, well above turbulence. Have a pleasant flight, sir."

Kerry clicked off and checked the altitude reading on the eight-inch Heads Up Display (HUD). The HUD flashed essential information directly onto the windshield, eliminating the need to look back and forth at the gauges. Had he glanced at the multicolored radar screen instead, he would have noticed a tiny dot that approached the *Patria* at vertiginous speed. Not that he could have done anything about it. As a fighter pilot, his instinct would have told him to evade, to launch countermeasures, and, as a last resort, to eject. But the *Patria* was not his old Navy Tomcat. It was unable to evade a missile, carried no chaff to confuse it, and had no ejector seat to deliver him from its impact.

When the proximity alarm wailed, there was nothing for Kerry to do but stare at the radar screen helplessly. And pray. Pray until the massive decompression from the surface-to-air missile's impact rendered him unconscious.

Unlike Wenzel, the Sicilian, and Nastassja in the main cabin, Kerry felt nothing when the *Patria*'s fuselage crashed, nose first, in the stormy swells of the Pacific Ocean in Santa Monica Bay.

33 ESCAPE

Carlton pulled into the parking area outside his apartment building. He was beyond exhaustion. Beyond confusion. He was operating on adrenaline and instinct.

Five minutes to collect his uniform and the bare essentials, maximum. After that, he would melt away into the scenery. Fade away into the cold gloom of winter. He walked from the Shark to the rear door of his squat brick apartment building through the half foot of snow accumulated during the evening's gentle yet steady snowfall. A storm of ideas, emotions, and instincts roiled in his mind.

He selected the key from his DOJ key chain. About to insert it into the lock, he stopped. Something was wrong. He turned around, braced himself, expecting someone—or something—to lunge out at him from the shadows of the parking area.

Nothing. Only the soundless fall of snowflakes from a black sky. He took a deep breath. His mind was screwing with him. It reminded him of his early childhood, when he would turn on his bedroom light and look under the bed to see the monsters that lurked beneath, only to find the space empty. Except now the monsters were real.

He remained still for some time, listening, gazing at the parking lot. If the past few days had taught him anything, it was to trust his instincts. Something was causing his fear.

He decided to ditch the rear door and enter the building from the front. He walked back to the Shark and opened the trunk. As an officer in the Navy Reserves, he could be called to duty at any time. For that reason, he kept certain items packed in the trunk of his car. He moved the cement blocks used to weigh down the car's rear on the icy winter roads, reached under the carpet partition. He pulled out a plastic case, unzipped it, and removed a black Glock 20 automatic handgun. The Austrian-made, polymer-frame, double-action weapon was considered by many experts as the pinnacle of handgun manufacture. Carlton placed a spare box magazine in his pocket, tossed the case back into the trunk, and slammed it shut. With rapid movements, second nature after six years of Navy training, he released the detachable box magazine from the butt, verified it contained a full load of fifteen 10mm Parabellum rounds, slammed the box back into place, and chambered a bullet. He held the weapon with his right hand on the grip, his left under the butt. He walked to the front of the building cautiously, hugging the cold brick wall to remain in its shadow, careful not to make any noise.

He stood still under the skeletal outline of an oak tree, and watched the front windows of the building. The windows of the apartment above were illuminated with flashes of blue-gray light from his neighbor's television. Sadie Kerwood was a woman in her nineties who exemplified the stamina and toughness of her generation by remaining independent, mobile, and sharp as a tack. Carlton helped her with her groceries. She often baked him cookies and kept a spare set of keys for him. In contrast to her illuminated window, Carlton's apartment windows were black.

The living room window was dark.

Strange.

Since childhood, Carlton had been a tropical fish aficionado. Despite his meager finances, he had managed to keep an aquarium through college and law school. Due to his wildly varying work schedule, he kept the aquarium light on a timer. It should still be on.

But it wasn't. The fluorescent bulb couldn't be burned out. Carlton had replaced it a month ago, and the bulbs lasted forever.

With a shiver, he recalled the man dressed in a Postal Service uniform who had checked his mailbox. He walked to the lobby door, pulled it open, walked up the half-flight of stairs to his front door, inserted his key, pushed himself against the side wall, and pushed the door open with his foot.

Darkness. Nothing else.

He reached inside and flicked on his living room light.

Nothing. Someone had cut the power.

Before he could retract his arm, a gloved hand grabbed his forearm like a vise, pulled him inside, and slammed the door, leaving the apartment in near total darkness. Carlton lunged for the door, but two hands grabbed his shoulders, a knee slammed into his groin.

He gasped in pain, doubled over on the floor, still clutching the Glock. He wanted to shoot, but it was too dark, the assailant invisible.

He heard his assailant's footsteps on the hardwood floor. Approaching. The thump of boots stopped. Carlton braced for the next blow. It came quickly. A swift kick in the head. Searing pain assaulted his every sense. The room became a vivid white of blotchy stars. He gasped more loudly than before. He had to get a clear shot somehow.

The assailant delivered his next blow, another swift kick. To the stomach, this time.

Despite the pain and gasps, he continued to grasp the Glock in his right hand. If only he could equalize the playing field so he could see—

A fourth blow. Again to the stomach. The assailant was toying with him before the kill. Carlton coughed, reached into his pocket and removed his DOJ Zippo before the assailant delivered his next blow. To the head this time. Stars flashed before Carlton's eyes. Pain throbbed in his head with every heartbeat. He gasped.

Almost by themselves, the fingers of his left hand opened his lighter. He heard the click, snapped the flint wheel. A bright butane flame appeared. He pushed the Zippo across the floor. Despite Carlton's blurry vision, the assailant was finally visible. The assailant hesitated briefly at the bright light that appeared in his night-vision goggles. It gave Carlton the precious second he needed. Still lying on his side, Carlton took aim at the blurry shape in the dim light and squeezed the Glock's trigger. Two 10mm Parabellum rounds tore into the man's neck before a third exploded his head. He was dead before his body crumpled onto the hardwood floor.

Carlton gasped for a few seconds before lifting himself to his feet, a slow and painful process. He staggered into the dark kitchen, turned on the tap, splashed his face and drank deeply.

He recovered the Zippo, clicked it shut. It was then that the shock hit him. He trembled uncontrollably, felt nausea well up inside him, and vomited on the hardwood floor of his living room.

Guns didn't scare Carlton. He was used to them. He had trained with guns for years, practiced regularly at a nearby shooting range. But he had never actually used a gun against another human being. Used a gun to kill another human being. He knew he had validly used self-defense, but his emotions didn't register the fact. He wanted to believe the assailant was a mercenary thug hired by Fress to kill him. But he knew that the person was probably an honest, dedicated soldier misguided by the chief of staff to eliminate a terrorist.

But now was not the time for remorse or fear, but for flight. He had to get out of there. Fast. He stumbled to his bedroom, stripped off his clothes, put on his Navy uniform. Then he heard the siren.

He picked up the Glock, ran back to the Shark, and slowly drove away from the snowy parking lot to one of the dark side streets. Seconds later, the police cruiser turned into his street from the main boulevard, roof lights flashing. Soon Carlton was speeding to Bolling Air Force Base, the nearest safe haven he could think of.

34 TRAITOR

GRU Headquarters
Moscow
2:53 A.M.

GRU Colonel Grigory Klimov was underpaid. Underpaid and decidedly discontented. For a man with his training, his education, and his intelligence, his pitiful GRU salary was intolerable. But Klimov was far too wily to rely solely on the state's meager salary. After all, Klimov possessed a very valuable commodity. As commander of the night watch at GRU headquarters, Klimov had access to information. Not just a little information. Reams of it. Truckloads of it. Although the cold war had been fought and lost and many classified documents declassified, many more remained and were as valuable as ever, more marketable now that more foreign powers had entered the fray.

Klimov did not discriminate. The highest bidder was always the winner, loyalty something that had to be purchased. If the *rodina* was stupid enough to pay brilliant men like him peanuts, it did not deserve his loyalty. One week it was the French *Service de Documentation Extérieure et Contre-Espionage*, or SDECE. The next, it was the Israeli Institute for Intelligence and Special Operations, also known as the Mossad. Or British Military Intelligence. Or the American Central Intelligence Agency. At one time, ironically, it was the KGB. As long as the currency was U.S. dollars or euros, from where it came mattered not.

To be sure, the GRU was far too experienced and far too distrustful of its underpaid employees to leave especially a senior officer like Klimov unwatched, and he knew it. He glanced at his digital watch, stepped out of the hangar-like file room into the hallway, and threw a pack of cheap Kosmos cigarettes on the desk of Private Semenov, the night guard.

"I'm going to visit Lenin," Klimov joked before going down the hall to the men's room, his way of telling Semenov he should not allow anyone entrance into the file room after he entered.

Semenov looked up from his Russian edition of *Playboy*. "*Da, tovarish* Colonel." As Klimov walked down the hall, Semenov dialed the number of Sergeant Anna Bucharovna, in charge of video and audio surveillance for the file room.

"Sergeant Bucharovna. Semenov here. Would you care for a cigarette break, Sergeant?"

"No thank you. I just took my break. Perhaps later."

"Very well. Have a productive watch."

Have a productive watch. The words alerted Bucharovna of Klimov's impending fishing expedition in the ocean of GRU files. Here, like nearly everywhere else in the Russian military apparatus, most of the underpaid soldiers were on the take. It was merely a matter of the right price. Klimov paid well.

Several minutes later, Klimov returned to the file room. The electronic door locked shut behind him. He walked to the tiny area where personnel with sufficiently high clearance could inspect files out of reach of the hidden video monitors. He glanced at his watch. It was 2:59 A.M..

Bucharovna waited until precisely 3:00 A.M., pressed the "Stop" button on the Sony videotape recorder in front of her, ejected the tape, and replaced it with a prerecorded videotape. Although she hit the "Record" switch, the one hour tape was unalterably prerecorded to show an empty file room. The only information that would be recorded on the tape was the date and time. From 3:00 to 4:00 A.M.

Klimov had one hour.

Inside the file room, Klimov waited until his watch read 3:05 A.M., to make sure Bucharovna had time to change the video-tape, then proceeded to a file cabinet marked with a cryptic code. Only he and the three other colonels who supervised the file room had a record of each steel cabinet and its contents. The armored cabinet in front of him contained the hefty GRU file of the late Leonid Pyashinev. Although the file had been opened when Pyashinev initially began his career at Komdragmet, it had recently been updated. Why, Klimov did not know. Nor did he care. The less he knew about the contents of files and the reasons for which his foreign clients sought them, the better. It would be that much more difficult for the prosecution to show a particular pattern of spying on any particular person, his lawyer friend at the Justice Ministry advised him.

Klimov opened the cabinet at the beginning of the row, eight cabinets down from the one that contained Pyashinev's file. The lock on each cabinet was linked to a computer that recorded the date and time at which each cabinet was opened and closed. Klimov had to establish a pattern of opening and closing each cabinet in the row for several minutes. To the person who reviewed the computer's record, it would appear as if Klimov were performing a regular inventory, an integral part of his duties. After all, the last thing the GRU needed was for a file to become misplaced. The GRU paid staff members to watch the surveillance videotapes at random. Luckily for Klimov, the GRU was so crippled by budget cuts it could no longer afford to reconcile the computer data of the cabinet doors with the videotapes. But why take a chance? Klimov might be a traitor, but he was a meticulous traitor.

For the next forty-five minutes, Klimov opened and closed the eight cabinets down from the one of interest, each for approximately five minutes, leaving him five minutes to rifle through Pyashinev's file.

Time moved forward in nerve-wracking silence.

At 3:50 A.M., two stories above the file room, Colonel Kovanetz appeared through the main doors of GRU Headquarters. Sergeant Bucharovna shot out of her seat, stood ramrod straight, and saluted the officer who had a chiseled face and lifeless green eyes.

Kovanetz returned the salute crisply. "Colonel Kovanetz, Sergeant. I'm going to consult a file."

Bucharovna's sweat glands kicked in. "You work very late, *tovarish* Colonel."

"Work for the *rodina* does not rest, Sergeant," Kovanetz replied tersely, without a hint of a smile.

"*Da*. Please sign in here, Colonel." She pointed to a registry and lifted a telephone receiver. "I will announce you to the file room."

"Private Semenov. This is Sergeant Bucharovna. Colonel Kovanetz is coming down to inspect a file."

Bucharovna replaced the receiver, again saluted crisply as Kovanetz replaced the pen on the registry and walked toward the bank of elevators behind her. He pushed the call button, tapped his foot nervously on the worn marble floor as he waited for the ancient elevator.

Klimov looked at his watch. 3:51 A.M. He closed the heavy cabinet, locked it, then finally unlocked the cabinet that contained Pyashinev's file. He searched through the thick wads of files, reached a file that read "Pyashinev, Leonid Ivanovicz." He removed the file and turned to the first of five pages Colonel Kovanetz had added during the past week. He pressed the chronograph, light, and date buttons of his digital watch in sequence, placed the face of the watch on the top of the first page. Slowly, he scanned each line of the page, each photograph.

The elevator door had barely opened when Kovanetz stepped inside and punched the basement button with his fist. The doors slid shut with a scraping noise. After a brief shudder, the old hydraulic elevator began its groaning descent to the basement.

Klimov turned the second page over, began to scan the third. The words were scribbled densely. He had to drag the watch over each sentence slowly to be sure that it recorded all of the information.

The elevator scraped open and disgorged its impatient passenger.

Private Semenov stood and saluted sharply. "Colonel Kovanetz. Sir!"

Again, Kovanetz returned the salute crisply. All he wanted was to read the list of Russian cities and foreign countries Pyashinev had visited during the past two years. Pyashinev's dying note was not much to go on. Perhaps the list of countries would give him a clue to where he might have hidden the diamond stockpile. It wasn't much, but it was worth a try. Counting sheep certainly wasn't helping.

"If you will please sign in, *tovarish* Colonel."

"I already signed in upstairs, private."

"*Da*. I realize that, *tovarish* Colonel." Semenov feigned embarrassment. "But regulations are regulations, and—"

"I know all about regulations, private." He hunched over and signed his name on a registry identical to the one guarded by Sergeant Bucharovna. Semenov's sweat glands were pulling double duty, and the steamy issue of *Playboy* safely tucked under his desk was not the cause.

Klimov finished scanning the third page and began to scan the fourth. Again, the page was dense with scribbles.

"There." Kovanetz replaced the pen on the registry. "Now open the door, private."

"Certainly. I will have to search you first, of course," Semenov heard himself say. His body became rigid as he prepared for Kovanetz's rage.

"You want to what?" Kovanetz demanded. "Search me? Are you out of your mind?" he shouted.

"Sir, I—"

"Search me for what? Do you know who I am, private? I'm a senior advisor to the president! Even the Kremlin guards don't search me!"

The colonel's jade green eyes chilled Semenov.

He looked down. "*Da*. I'm sorry, *tovarish* Colonel. Regulations are regulations, and—"

"Private!" The booming voice blew through Semenov's closely cropped hair like wind. "If you do not let me into that room immediately," he pointed behind Semenov, "you will have the luxury of cleaning radioactive latrines in Semipalatinsk."

Klimov finished scanning the fourth page and began work on the last page of Pyashinev's file, the page covered with a jungle of photographs and scribbles.

Shaking, Semenov removed a thick wad of keys from his desk, inserted one into a lock in the door, followed by another key into another lock.

"Private!" Kovanetz shouted in exasperation. "I'm losing my patience!"

"*Da*. The electronic lock is not functioning properly."

Klimov heard the rattle of the lock as he began to scan the last paragraph on the page. Something was wrong. Someone was coming in.

Private Semenov opened the third and last lock. "Colonel Klimov!" he bellowed. "Colonel Kovanetz is here to review a file!"

Klimov swiped the last line and dropped the watch into his pocket. He turned to face Kovanetz and the private. "Good morning, Colonel!" he said loudly, attempting to mask the sound of the cabinet as it closed shut.

"Colonel Klimov," Kovanetz cocked his head. "What are you doing in here?"

Klimov gave him an exasperated look. "Inventory, Colonel. Inventory. It never ends. I wish someone else would do this." Klimov locked the cabinet, then walked toward Kovanetz, carrying a clipboard he had with him to make his inventory look legit.

He saluted Kovanetz. As he did so, he glanced at the large clock on the wall. It read 3:59. The videotape would end in less than one minute.

"Pardon me, Colonel." Klimov leaned theatrically toward a hook on the wall behind Kovanetz, let the clipboard slip and fall to the floor. On its way down, it flicked the light switch down and extinguished the lights.

Klimov cursed. Kovanetz replied in kind. The terrified private remained silent. Klimov found the light switch, flipped it on. The fluorescent lights flickered on. He looked up at the clock—4:01.

A new, blank videotape was now recording. When viewed, it would begin when the lights were out. The viewer would assume Kovanetz had entered the file room when Semenov opened the door to allow light inside.

At 9:30 that morning, after a hearty, cholesterol-laden breakfast in the officers' mess, Klimov exited GRU Headquarters and drove to *Czas*, literally translated as "Time," a small watch store in his own neighborhood. He placed his Timex digital watch on the counter and asked the clerk for a new battery. Klimov browsed the small establishment. The clerk disappeared with the watch. When he returned, Klimov paid, replaced the watch on his wrist, and went home to sleep.

The source and the data were too sensitive to risk electronic transmission, even encrypted. The FSB/SVR's counterespionage capabilities were legendary. Before Klimov's head touched his eiderdown pillow, the microchip coded with the latest information from Pyashinev's file was inserted into an identical Timex, sealed into a package with other allegedly faulty timepieces, and picked up by the 10:30 A.M. Federal Express truck. When Klimov awoke seven hours later, the package had arrived in Paris and was on a newly reinstated supersonic Air France Concorde flight en route to Washington, D.C., locked inside a bulletproof case handcuffed to the wrist of a CIA courier. By the time Klimov began his next shift, the information in the microchip was being downloaded at a laboratory in Langley, Virginia.

35 LOGIC

CIA Headquarters
10:45 P.M.

DDI Forbes sat in his wheelchair behind piles of paperwork neatly stacked on his massive oak desk. He looked up as Pink entered.

"Good God, Pink. You look like hell in a handbasket. Rough day?"

"Yes, sir."

It had been. But not for the reason Forbes believed. In reality, Pink had spent the entire day wrestling with Carlton's information. He had still not heard back from the Justice Department lawyer, despite leaving him several additional voicemail messages.

The dead South African agent's intelligence report was all the independent evidence he had. And all the evidence implicated Scott Fress. Not some pencil-pushing, bean-counting, 10-to-4 bureaucrat, but Scott Hugh Fress III, Esq., the White House chief of staff. How many more in the federal government could Waterboer have corrupted along with him? The Justice Department. The FBI.

The CIA?

The suspicion went against everything Pink knew about the DDI. And so Pink's all night battle had raged, eating him alive. He had to tell Forbes. Regardless of the consequences. And so he did. Exhausted, Pink fell into a leather chair and came clean. He told Forbes everything. Carlton. The phone calls. The postcard. Confirmation of the account number. When he had finished, he exhaled deeply. The knot of stress in his stomach loosened.

"Why didn't you tell me when you first figured it out? Why keep it from me?"

"Sir…" Pink groped for words. "I had to verify the—"

"*Why?*"

"Forgive me, sir, but if Fress was…compromised…"

Forbes' eyes opened wide. "You didn't really think…"

Pink squirmed. "I'm sorry, sir."

Forbes squinted. His upper body began to shake uncontrollably. "You son of a bitch! Two paralyzed legs. Two Purple Hearts. A Congressional Medal of Honor. You bastard! How dare you think for a second I could be involved with that political shit Fress? And for what motive? For money? I could buy and sell Fress out of petty cash, dammit!"

Pink lowered his head. "I'm sorry, sir."

Forbes lit a fresh pipe. "Never—ever—even think such a thing." He took a deep breath, removed his pipe from between his teeth, paused for a long moment, and regained his patrician composure and WASP stiff upper-lip. "I think your analysis is correct about CIA as a whole, though. There has to be someone inside. Someone close. That leads to a much bigger problem. The reason you were unable to see me earlier this morning was because I had to give my weekly intelligence briefing to the president. We discussed a host of issues. Afghanistan, the Middle East, Pakistan, South Africa, China, Japan, North Korea." He waved. "The usual. Fress was there, of course. As always. I noticed he looked a bit more concerned than his usual self. But it was when we started discussing Russia generally, the diamond contract with Waterboer specifically, that Fress became unglued. Quite palpably unglued. He tried to hide it at first, but when I presented your findings, he turned white."

"My findings, sir?" Pink asked, shocked by the possibility Fress knew his name. It would be a death warrant.

"Not as gospel truth. Just as a theory. I didn't use your name. The last thing I need is to have my people killed or corrupted. No use in sticking one's neck out for the president only to have it chopped off. Anyhow, I hinted the Russian diamond stockpile delivered to Waterboer was only a part of the total stockpile, that the fire at Mirny was not an accident but a raid, that some group may have secretly taken over Mirny to sell its diamonds to Waterboer.

"Fress went mad. Stark raving mad. He contradicted everything I proposed. Asked how I could have such ignoramuses—

his word, not mine—working for me. He even called me names, the little shit. Then, quite suddenly, he cut the conversation short. Calmed down. Sat down. Even apologized." Forbes waved a hand. "But enough of that. We know what's what now." He paused.

"On the way back to Langley, I rehashed the briefing with Hiroshi Yamato, Debbie's counterpart in the East Asian section. I'd asked Hiro to come along to brief the president on the North Korean situation. He said something totally off the cuff that made me freeze. He said he'd had no idea the mafia was behind the Mirny raid."

Pink was riveted but somehow he had missed a step. "I'm afraid I don't follow, sir."

"You see, in the briefing with the president, when I suggested the Mirny fire might not have been an accidental fire at all but a raid by some nongovernmental group, one of Fress's enraged comments was I had no evidence of the army or the FSB or the mafia carrying out such an operation. The army and the FSB would be logical potential participants in a raid on Mirny. But the mafia? Why would Fress say that? Mirny is not a major diamond depository."

"That's exactly right. It's only a processing center."

"So why would the mafia take such a huge risk attacking a facility in the middle of the Siberian wasteland if there are just a few thousands carats for them to steal? You see my point? It's an old trick. Sooner or later, someone who tries too hard to cover something up forgets what he has said and lets something slip. That's why the police ask suspects to repeat their stories so many times."

Forbes touched the pipe stem to each finger of his left hand as he spoke. "So, the fire at Mirny was a raid. It was a raid by an organized group. After the raid, the army was sent to replace the garrison that perished in the fire. The—"

"That must be it, sir," Pink interrupted excitedly.

Forbes arched his eyebrows.

"I'm sorry to interrupt, sir. But the army. You said that after the raid, the garrison was replaced. But if the mafia didn't take over Mirny to steal diamonds, it must have had another reason for the raid. Which means the mafia and the army must have organized the raid together."

"Marshal Aleksakov?"

"One of the reports mentions he traveled to Siberia. Perhaps he met Molotok. Maybe about the purchase of the Tacit Rainbow missiles we discussed. Ogarkov was in charge of the Siberian forces, and he's killed right before the Mirny raid? Too much of a coincidence. Who would assassinate Ogarkov?"

"Could be a variety of groups, really."

"In terms of motive, yes. But who would actually pull the trigger?"

"A mafia hired gun."

"Exactly."

"So you think Aleksakov and Molotok are working with the mafia just to get diamonds? With that muscle group of his, the Volki?"

"And Waterboer. It's not so far-fetched. After all, the Russian mafia isn't like the American or Sicilian Cosa Nostra. The Russian godfathers, the *krestnii otets*, they're former *apparatchiki*. Former managers and directors of the old system. The collapse of communism changed nothing. They still control everything. Transportation. Communications. Food. Fuel. And that's just the legal stuff."

"It certainly would explain why Fress became so nervous. If he's being paid off by Waterboer and knows about its connection to Molotok's Russkost, he would try to steer U.S. foreign policy attention away from Russkost. Which is exactly what he did in the briefing. Q.E.D."

"How can a president as squeaky clean and sharp as Douglass appoint a chief of staff like Fress? It just doesn't make sense."

"Squeaky clean and sharp, yes. Politically shrewd, no. That's what made him so attractive to the voters, remember. Douglass was an Army general, then a preacher. He's knowledgeable, charismatic, and dead honest, rare for a politician. He has great strategic acumen, but for the big stuff, not the little stuff. He has neither love nor experience in day-to-day political dogfights. Fress did him a big favor during his campaign, tantamount to submitting a résumé, as Machiavelli did with the Borgias. Douglass was impressed and felt he owed Fress a debt of gratitude. So you see? It does make sense."

"Right." Pink shifted gears. "But if Russkost, Molotok, the Volki, the mafia—if they are going after diamonds, they're probably tied to Waterboer."

"And if they're tied to Waterboer, they're doing what Waterboer wants. And if they're doing what Waterboer wants, what they're really looking for is the stockpile. And if they had it…"

Pink finished the sentence: "They would sell it to Waterboer, take the money, and run. There wouldn't be a reason to attack Mirny, risk exposure. Which tells us that none of them knows where the stockpile is. Waterboer almost found out, but Pyashinev was killed first. And now, Waterboer still wants it, but neither they nor the mafia nor Russkost know where it is."

"They only have the information our GRU contact just sent us. Comrade Pyashinev's deathbed note, apparently." He handed Pink the information downloaded from Klimov's Timex.

Pink read it: *Rossiya, trieti sloi. Nie dopustit im wziat eto.* "'Russia, third layer. We can't let them get it'? What does it mean?"

"I don't know, but neither do they. The bottom line remains the same. We've got to find the stockpile. What Carlton unearthed is important, of course. Fress is a murderer and a traitor. He's got to go, and he will. But his ending up in the slammer making big ones into little ones, it won't stop Molotok and Russkost from unleashing some insane civil war with the money from selling the diamond stockpile to Waterboer." He exhaled a cloud of blue smoke. "Airing Fress's dirty laundry in the press will only make all of those parties nervous, the stockpile even more difficult to find."

Forbes allowed silence to fill the room, swiveled his wheelchair toward the window. Pink reclined in his chair, his mind racing around the problem of the missing diamond stockpile. "Still, there is a much bigger problem at work here, Pink."

"A bigger problem than not having any leads, sir? I can't—"

"You're pure, Pink." Forbes swiveled back toward Pink, smiled bitterly. "You see intelligence problems in terms of how to find what you're looking for before the other side does. Nothing wrong with that, of course. It's your job, after all. You do it well. But it's only half the job. The other half is my job."

"Sir?"

"Politics, Pink. Politics," he repeated. "It's not just that we have to find the stockpile before Molotok and Waterboer do. We've got to find it without them knowing we're even looking. Which means without Fress knowing we're looking. Fress is chief of staff. He controls the president. Not literally, but he controls his meetings and his schedule. He controls the president's stream of information. Fress may be a traitor and a first-class bastard, but he's sharp as a tack and he's a consummate politician. He has flunkies all over the federal landscape. FBI, Justice, even here." He leaned closer to Pink, lowered his voice. "Who do you think convinced the president to appoint the present DDO?" He referred to the deputy director of operations, the second arm of the Agency.

"You can't swing a dead politician in Washington without hitting one of Fress's cronies. Which means we have to rule out support from the White House and from any other federal agency, including the military. Even from this Agency. Forget the intelligence committees on the Hill. Congress leaks like a sieve." He breathed deeply. "It's simple, Pink. Nothing about Carlton or the Russian stockpile can find its way to Fress or any of his moles until this mess is over."

"Sir." The word came out as a crackle. "Is this what I think it is?"

Forbes nodded once. "It is, Tom. A black op. Totally covert. We're on our own. No White House. No Congress. No Court. No federal agencies. Not even this agency. What if the White House chief of staff has approached some of our clandestine service officers here at CIA with a special mission for the president, told them that it was to remain secret, even from me? It really can be only you and me. You because you brought me the information. Me because I'm ordering this mission." He paused to let it sink in.

"Now you understand what the media and other critics refuse to understand. Why some operations have to be totally covert. Totally black." He paused. "I'd love to have the president and Congress and everyone else sign off on this, be part of the team. But on this that can't happen." He stared hard at Pink.

Finally, Pink nodded.

Forbes lifted his index finger, pointed it at Pink.

"Sir?"

"You're the only one."

Pink's eyes grew. "Oh no, sir. I'm an analyst. I have absolutely no training for this sort of thing. You know that." He waved his copy of the cryptic Cyrillic words scrawled by Pyashinev moments before his death. "Not only do I have absolutely no idea what this means, I have absolutely no training for this."

Pink sifted through documents and photographs for a living. Now Forbes expected him to go out in the field. Alone. Not that Pink hadn't dreamed of it during those endless post–cold war nights, sitting at his desk before piles of satellite photographs and decoded transmissions. Was he simply afraid? The man who sat across from him in the wheelchair was a war hero. He had lost the use of both of his legs in combat. And Pink was afraid of going into the field to find information. He was ashamed, but the feeling of fear remained.

"I read your file. I know you're dying to do covert field work. All those manuals on your shelves. All those technothrillers and posters in your office. Remember the saying: Be careful what you wish for, you may just get it."

"Sir, with all due respect, wanting to do field work and knowing how to do field work are two different things."

Forbes looked up from his pipe, stared at him silently, the slight smile now gone. Pink heard himself breathe.

"Don't you think I know that? Do you really think I would trust this kind of work to some paper-shuffling weenie capable of nothing but desk assignments? I know you haven't been trained for this type of work, but it's not as though you were going to infiltrate a country's security organs, run agents, or kill people. This is analysis more than anything else. Analysis in the field. The most important thing in the field is the most important thing in analysis. It's all up here." He tapped his temple with his index finger. "Smarts. You've got 'em big."

Pink didn't know what to say, but he knew he had to say something. "But I've got no...I mean, going from a cryptic note to capturing a diamond stockpile is...especially alone."

"Alone? Why do you assume you're alone?"

Pink's face contorted in an expression of complete confusion. "Sir?"

"What makes you think you're alone?"

"Well you said it yourself, sir. This has to be a completely covert. Black."

"It does." Forbes smiled. "I said this has to be a covert op from the point of view of the Agency. Of the administration. Of the government. But an op isn't run only with government personnel. We're the only two in the government who know, but others, civilians, are already deeply involved."

"Civilians?"

"Your guy Carlton. He's already up to his ears in this mess." He shrugged. "You help him, he helps you."

"Sir, I don't know where he is. I don't even know if he's still alive."

Forbes lifted a thick manila folder from his desk, handed it to Pink. Inside were copies of all of Carlton's computer files on disk, all of the telephone numbers dialed to and from Carlton's home, cellular, and office telephones, up to and including the day before. Pink looked up at Forbes. "How...? Never mind."

"You're not alone. Insulated, yes. But definitely not alone. Carlton may be the only one who knows what he told you other than us, but he got help and information from others. They're assets. Resources. MacLean, for one. Do what you do as an analyst. Track them down and use them."

"Carlton may be wily and MacLean rich and connected. But there is only so much civilians can—"

"I realize that. But don't forget, these are Russian diamonds. We may want to prevent them from falling into Russkost's hands. But they still don't belong to us. As much as we'd like to keep them, that secret wouldn't last long. The diamonds belong to Russia. And Orlov's government has one heck of a motivation to recover them."

"And?"

"Which means that Orlov has one heck of a motivation to help us." He puffed on his pipe, looked at his watch, rolled himself to his desk, and hit the intercom.

"Yes sir?"

"Get Lavrenti Yagoda on the horn."

36 FLIGHT

Northbound
The Beltway (I-395)
Virginia
11:10 P.M.

Carlton raced toward Bolling Air Force Base, the nearest military installation. He kept one eye on the road, another on his cell phone keypad, which he punched furiously. Wenzel was nowhere to be found. He called information, and asked for MacLean's number. Unlisted. He dialed another number.

"Yes."

"Lieutenant Carlton for Lieutenant JG Whitecloud." Carlton slalomed through sparse traffic, waited for the duty chief. Faced with Fress, Waterboer, their allies inside the federal government and who knew where else, he felt like the proverbial David against Goliath. But at least David had a slingshot and stones. Right now Carlton had bupkus. There was one last asset he hadn't used, the U.S. Navy. But if Fress knew enough about Carlton to get to his apartment, they knew he was Navy. It was a compromised resource. He couldn't rely on it long-term. But he could use his contacts inside it.

"Whitecloud."

"Bob, it's Pat Carlton."

"Hi ya, Pat. What's—"

"I need the number, the private phone number, for Max MacLean. In L.A. Right away."

"What's it for?"

"I can't explain. Just please get it for me."

"Your word's good enough for me." He paused. "It's unlisted."

"Of course it's unlisted. Why would—"

"Relax, relax. I'm just yanking your chain." He gave him the number. Carlton knew they were probably tracing and listening to his cell phone calls, but he didn't have much of a choice.

"Thanks, man. I owe you one." He ended the transmission, punched in the number, almost clipping the front end of an irate Chevy Blazer with the Shark's tail fin as he continued roaring toward Bolling AFB.

"MacLean residence."

"Max MacLean, please."

"I'm sorry, sir, Mr. MacLean is not avail—"

"It's Pat Carlton. It's urgent. He'll want to speak with me."

"One moment, please."

MacLean came on the line almost immediately. "MacLean here. It's unfortunate we have to meet under such circumstances."

"Mr. MacLean, I was almost murdered in my apartment ten minutes ago. I called to tell you and Dan to disappear. If they're hunting me, they're hunting you."

"It's too late, Pat."

"What do you mean? Leave town."

"Dan is dead."

"Oh my God."

"My jet was taking him to Andrews. It crashed several hours ago. The Coast Guard is conducting a search, but I'm too much of a realist to think he's still alive."

"Nonetheless, you should get out now."

"And go where? I'm much safer at home. I have people guarding me."

"Well, that's your choice. I'm getting the hell out of Dodge. And I need your help."

"You have it." There was no hesitation. "But first I want to know whatever you know."

"You really don't."

"I do. Spit it out or you're on your own."

Carlton thought about the risks for an instant. Fress was already trying to kill him. How much worse could it get? "Very well. The White House chief of staff is being paid off by Waterboer to prevent diamond mining in Arkansas. The rest you know."

MacLean sucked in air. "That means that this won't just go away. It won't stop until one side wins. What do you need?"

"I need to disappear."

There was an awkward pause. "You're Navy, correct?"

"Yes." Wenzel did his research, that's for sure.

"Get to Andrews Air Force Base. See a man named Colonel Saunders. He was expecting Wenzel. I'll call him. He'll tell you what to do."

"But what if—"

"Just trust me."

"Thank you." He hung up, dialed Erika's cell phone number. If they had tried to kill him, had killed Wenzel, Erika was next.

"Hello?"

"It's Pat."

"I'm at National about to board. What the hell's—"

"Don't board! Whatever you do, don't board. Grab a cab. Go to the main gate of Andrews Air Force Base. I'll meet you there."

"Andrews? That's in Maryland. I'll rent a car."

"No. They'll trace you to it. They're probably listening, so it's already a race. Grab a cab. Do it now." He hit the "end" button, tossed the telephone on the seat next to him. Traffic was even lighter now. Practically no one was traveling D.C. to Maryland on the Beltway. He glanced at his speedometer— ninety-three. He slowed down. The last thing he needed was getting pulled over by state troopers. Andrews was in upper Maryland. It would have been easier to get from the opposite direction on the circular Beltway, but he could get to Maryland over the Woodrow Wilson Bridge and then go north. Maryland was a safer part of the ring than Washington.

The Woodrow Wilson bridge appeared ahead. Flashing red warning lights indicated the raising of the drawbridge above the juncture of the Potomac River and Chesapeake Bay. Carlton slowed to a crawl.

A car bumped him from behind. A burst of adrenaline shot through him. He had been too busy concentrating on the telephone and hadn't noticed the car, a navy blue Ford sedan. Government car. It rode less than a foot from his rear bumper. It was not slowing down in response to the drawbridge lights. It was accelerating!

Carlton stomped down the accelerator, revved the massive Cadillac V8 to life. The Ford missed his chrome bumper by inches, fell back, sped up to try again.

Only five hundred feet separated him from the part of the bridge that was beginning to rise into the air. On a motorcycle, he probably could have jumped the bridge. But he was in a Cadillac. A 1958, two-ton, chrome and steel Cadillac. This was not some cliché cop movie. Jumping the bridge was not an option.

The Ford rammed him this time, jolted the Caddy out of its lane. Then it shot forward and sidled up to the right of the Shark. Carlton slammed the gear shift down to second gear. The engine protested, but gunned the Caddy forward. But its '50s engineering was no match for the modern Ford.

Soon it was next to him again. Its tinted rear driver's side window slid down. Carlton's blood froze as a Heckler & Koch MP10 submachine gun appeared in the hands of a face-painted gunman. The 800-round per minute German weapon was less than six feet from Carlton's head.

He had nowhere to go. The Shark couldn't outrun the Ford. The drawbridge continued to tilt upward ahead. The opposite lanes were blocked by a solid concrete and metal wall. The Glock 20 on the passenger seat next to him was no match for the H&K submachine gun or the Ford's windows, which he suspected were bulletproof.

The gunman squinted.

Carlton stomped on the brakes. The Caddy's tires locked, burned rubber against the rough pavement. The Ford shot past Carlton as a flash of fire burst from the sub-machine gun. Firefly-like ricochets sparked against the wall next to him.

The Ford slowed to match Carlton's speed. But as the Shark continued to decelerate, wheels still locked, its rear end veered to the right. Its jackknife position afforded Carlton a straight line of sight to the Ford through his passenger window. He grabbed the Glock, fired four rounds toward the Ford, blowing out his own passenger window.

The Ford continued to approach, framed in Carlton's passenger window as the Caddy continued to skid.

The drawbridge was very close now. Carlton shifted into

first gear, pressed hard on the accelerator, corrected the Caddy's skid, and flew past the Ford a hundred feet away from the upturned drawbridge. He discharged five more rounds at the driver, who ducked unnecessarily as the bullets ricocheted off the Ford's armored glass windows. Unharmed, the driver accelerated and followed. Within fifty feet of the drawbridge, the needle on the Cadillac's speedometer reached fifty-two. Carlton shifted into second. Another burst of fire from the machine gun tore through the plastic rear window and exploded Carlton's windshield. He crunched low in his seat and momentarily shut his eyes to avoid being blinded by the shards of glass that whipped past him in the glacial air. The Ford was approaching fast, then matched speeds, then began to lose ground. One of his stray rounds had punctured one of the Ford's rear tires.

When Carlton smashed through the wooden drawbridge arm, the Shark was moving at over sixty. Luckily, the bridge operator had seen the chase and started to lower the bridge, but it didn't close in time for the Shark. In a roar, the two-ton block of chrome and steel rocketed up the half-raised drawbridge ramp and became airborne, fins and all.

Everything seemed to happen in slow motion. Carlton remembered his Navy training, kept his tongue inside his mouth to prevent it from being cut off in the jolt to follow.

The Cadillac smashed down the opposite metal ramp in a blizzard of sparks. Carlton was slammed deep into his seat. The Shark's underbelly groaned obscenely as its suspension tried to absorb the shock. He felt as though his head were dislodging from his shoulders. After several seconds of shock, he pressed down on the accelerator. The engine still worked! He put it in third gear and sped toward Northern Maryland, turned to see whether the Ford had followed suit.

It never even made it up the ramp.

Two for two.

He ejected the Glock's magazine, replaced it with a fresh one, and mouthed first a prayer of thanks, then a second prayer that 1950s American craftsmanship and Erika's cabbie would get them all the way to Andrews.

The Shark was tough, but there was only so much the 1958 Caddy could take. After the massive shock from the draw-bridge and the severe strain from the acceleration, the massive V8 engine sputtered and died. He pulled the car to the side of the road, tried the ignition. Again and again. There was still plenty of gas, he noted, but no oil. The engine was badly over-heated. His attempts at restarting the engine were met with grinding from the starter and a high-pitched whine from the radiator hose. He had both water and oil in the trunk. But from long experience, he knew that even refilling the radiator and the oil case would not revive the car.

"Dammit!"

He slammed the steering wheel with his palm, realizing at the same time how lucky he was to have made it this far. He could be lying in a pool of blood on the floor of his apartment, dead on the Beltway, submerged beneath the Potomac. He was alive. Stranded, but alive. And he intended to stay that way.

He holstered the Glock and stepped out of the car into the freezing darkness of the Maryland countryside. He would have to walk. The last sign had announced ten miles to Andrews AFB. That had been a ways back. He locked the car, turned up his collar, stuffed his hands deep into his uniform pockets, and started toward Andrews in the pitch black night.

Oddly, Fress's goons temporarily stopped worrying him. He had overcome them in his apartment and on the bridge. *Let 'em take their best shot*, he thought, his heart still rapidly pumping adrenaline through his veins.

What worried him was Erika. They must have followed her, just like they had followed him. They would not let her get to Andrews.

Maybe.

It was a maybe he would have to risk. He had no other options.

He moved on.

The brisk walk through the cold night air allowed him to think. Things had happened quickly. The note from Mazursky. The threat from Waterboer. The apartment. The instructions from MacLean. The shootout. The bridge. He had escaped, but to where? He knew what and where he was running from, but where was he running to? Saunders, MacLean had told him. Who the hell was Saunders?

Realizing he had more questions than answers, he tried to empty his mind, give it a rest.

Headlights appeared behind him, grew brighter. His shadow grew to grotesque proportions in front of him. A new jolt of fear nearly paralyzed him. He desperately wanted to run into the forest that lined the road, less than ten feet away. But he forced himself to continue walking at the same speed without looking back, hoping it would just pass.

The car slowed.

No.

Slower and slower. Louder and louder. Walking fast, Carlton turned back just as the car slowed to a crawl to match his gait. It was a Humvee, painted in green and black camouflage, although its camouflage wouldn't have helped much against the snowy forest. He shuddered with fear before remembering he was wearing his uniform. He stopped. So did the Humvee.

An African-American sergeant in fatigues stuck his head out of the window, saluted him. "Sir. That your car back there, sir?"

"Died on me on my way to the base," he said, returning the salute.

"Well, hop in, sir. We'll take you." Despite the internecine rivalry between the Air Force and Navy, to the sergeant any stranded American military man, even a Navy officer, was a brother in need.

"'Preciate it, Sergeant." He hoisted himself into the backseat above the massive tires. The Humvee roared back to life and sped through the snow.

The sergeant switched on the interior light, turned back toward Carlton. "Don't see many Navy personnel in these parts, sir," the sergeant said politely, meaning *Who the hell are you and what the hell are you doing here?* And why not? Carlton could be some nut in a rented Navy uniform.

"I'll bet." Carlton was about to flash his ID, decided it was too much of a risk. "Navy intel. We're everywhere and nowhere. At least that's what the recruiter told me." He chuckled, knowing he had to tell the sergeant something. "I've got a meeting with Colonel Saunders. Never would have made it on time if you hadn't come along. I appreciate it."

The mention of Saunders seemed to satisfy the sergeant. "We'll take you right to him, sir. Just sit back and enjoy the ride." With that, he killed the light and turned forward. Carlton had no idea who Saunders was, but the man's name had already helped him.

Ten minutes later, the Humvee stopped at the front gate of Andrews AFB, where the president's Boeing 747 and Sikorsky S-61—Air Force One and Marine One—were hangared.

"I'm here to see Colonel Saunders."

One of the two MPs verified Carlton's identification and waved the truck on without a word. The Humvee rumbled through the gates and passed by several barracks before it stopped in front of a large white brick building.

"You'll find Colonel Saunders inside, sir," the sergeant announced.

"Thanks for the lift, sergeant."

"Anytime, sir."

Carlton heard the Humvee drive off. A man walked out of the building. Illuminated from the back, he appeared only as a dark shadow. It didn't feel right. Maybe Fress's thugs had called ahead. But there was nowhere to run. Carlton kept walking. Only when he got to within a few feet of the man did he notice the bright blue Air Force uniform, the silver bird on his shoulder, his name tag. He exhaled with relief and saluted. "Lieutenant Carlton, sir."

Saunders returned the salute. "Follow me."

He led the way back into the building and up a stairway into a small, dark office. Myriad photographs of airplanes wallpapered the room. Saunders walked behind the desk, pointed at a vinyl chair. "Sit down, Lieutenant."

"Thank you, sir." Carlton sat on the edge of the chair.

Saunders sat at his desk, reclined. The African-American's dark face finally broke into a smile. "I believe we have a mutual friend…"

"MacLean."

He nodded once. "He tells me you need an airlift out of here. Last passenger DIA."

"That's right, sir. I—"

Saunders interrupted him with a raised hand, palm faced forward. "I don't want to know, Lieutenant. The less I know, the better. You understand?"

"Yes, sir." Who was this guy?

"A bird is coming in to get you. ETA is ten minutes."

"Thank you, sir. I'm also expecting an additional passenger. Name is Erika Wassenaar."

Saunders paused for a moment. "I'm afraid I don't know anything about that." Of course MacLean had not informed Saunders about Erika. How could he have? Saunders was a military man. MacLean had told him one passenger and one passenger he expected. Not two or three. One.

"I realize that, sir. But there will be another person."

"Where is this person?"

"She should be here shortly, sir."

Saunders reflected for a few seconds, picked up his telephone handset, and notified the front gate to let the woman in and bring her to his office. "The bird will be in and out. No time to wait for stragglers. She's got ten minutes. After that, she'll have to go commercial." He stood, announcing the end of the discussion. "I have something to attend to. There is coffee in the room next door. Help yourself. Remember. Ten minutes." He walked out of the room.

Carlton looked at his watch. *Come on, Erika.*

The ten minutes passed in a flash. Erika still had not arrived. Saunders returned to the office.

"Time to go."

"She hasn't arrived yet, sir."

"Obviously. But the time is up."

"Sir, I appreciate what you're doing, but it is imperative—"

"Imperative or not, Lieutenant, we're on a schedule here. Time to go."

Carlton stood, stared at Saunders. "What do you think this is, Colonel? A joy ride? You think I'm here because I want to avoid the crowds at Reagan Airport? I have no idea who you are, or what your relationship is with MacLean, sir. But in case he hasn't told you, here's who I am." He removed his DOJ identification, placed it an inch from Saunders eyes.

Saunders was now better informed, but still unimpressed.

Carlton didn't want to reveal any information, but he had to convince this man to wait for Erika. He was a friend of MacLean and hadn't killed him yet, so he probably wasn't one of Fress's people. But he probably didn't know all the information from Carlton's side. "DOJ does a lot of investigative work. Sometimes DOJ discovers illegal activities involving people in our government. Sometimes those people are at the very top. Some of the things DOJ finds, those people don't want revealed. Sometimes those people retaliate. Sometimes they simply eliminate those who have evidence. Those people have to run. Secretly."

He stared hard at Saunders, who was not about to be frightened by scare tactics from a DOJ lawyer, Navy or otherwise. "A farmer in Arkansas knew. He was murdered in his car. His son was shot in the heart in his kitchen. MacLean's lawyer knew. His plane crashed an hour ago. Senator Bigham's assistant, the one found riddled with bullets in Southeast D.C.? He knew. The person I'm expecting knows." He moved toward Saunders. "I know." He moved closer, whispered, "Would you like to know?"

Saunders backed away, just a hair. "You must be great in court. Okay. We'll wait."

They sat together in tense silence for nearly fifteen minutes before the telephone rang. "Saunders. There's what? I'll be right over. Of course don't let them in." He replaced the handset, bolted for the door. "Follow me."

"What's going on?" Carlton asked, following Saunders down the stairs, out of the building, and into an Air Force Humvee.

"Apparently the police want to arrest your friend. You know. The one who knows."

"Shit."

"That was my reaction." Saunders gunned the truck and stopped behind the entrance gate pillbox. Carlton spotted Erika, ran toward her.

He took her in his arms, held her for the first time, realized how much he had wanted to hold her, to be close to her. "Thank God you made it."

She tightened their embrace, but reality soon returned. He stared into her green eyes. Tears were streaming down her red cheeks. He wiped them off. "What's this about the cops?"

"I took a cab here just like you told me. As we pulled up to the gate two cop cars pulled up. They want to arrest me."

Carlton walked to the pillbox, where Saunders was engaged in heated conversation with two overweight Maryland troopers.

"She's under arrest, Colonel," the senior trooper insisted. "You've got to let us do our job and take her into custody."

"She can't be under arrest. She's on a federal military installation," Saunders replied coldly.

"Sir, she's a danger to—" The trooper's eyes went wide when he spotted Carlton. "Him too! They're both under arrest!"

Carlton walked to the gate, looked at the two angry troopers as though they were animals in a zoo. "What on earth for?"

"For murder!"

Carlton brushed it off. Was there anyone who wasn't part of this nightmare? "Do you have a warrant for our arrest?"

"We don't need a warrant!"

"Did you witness this so-called murder?"

"No, I—"

"Then you need a warrant. You'd better brush up on the law books." Carlton turned to Saunders.

The colonel looked conflicted. His training told him to follow procedure, which would have kept Carlton and Erika on base until the problem could be resolved through the proper channels. But these were two Justice Department lawyers. People who spent their days enforcing the law. And MacLean had never lied to him before. He followed his instinct.

The trooper kept shouting. "I don't need a warr—"

Saunders interrupted him with a raised hand. "Unless you have a warrant like the louie says, you'll have to go get one. For the moment, I suggest you leave."

"We will do no such thing! Those two are under arrest for the murder of a federal agent. This is a federal base."

"It is a federal base," Saunders said. Calmly, he turned to the MP private who stood by, listening to every word, wisely saying nothing. "Private, these men are disrupting a federal Air Force base," Saunders announced. "You will ask them to leave," he turned back to the troopers. "If they do not, you will take them into custody."

"You have no right to do that! They're under arrest for murder! We have a duty to—"

"Private, do your duty."

The youngish private stepped forward to the edge of the steel gate. "You heard the colonel. I'll say this once, gentlemen. You will leave immediately, or you will be taken into custody."

"Try me, sonny." The trooper unholstered his sidearm, turned to his partner. "Call for backup, Johnson." When he turned back to the MP, he felt the cold barrel of a Beretta .45 against his cranium.

"You will leave," the MP said flatly, cocking his weapon, "or you will be taken into custody."

"You two follow me," Saunders said, as he turned and walked away. Carlton and Erika followed him back to the Humvee and pulled themselves up into the tall vehicle. Saunders started its massive engine and roared away from the front gate, headed deep into the Air Force base.

Erika huddled against Carlton, shaking less from cold than from fear. The colonel negotiated a maze of streets on the base between efficiently plowed snowbanks on either side. She gazed through the truck's fogged windows to try to calm herself, to believe she was safe. No one seemed interested in the Humvee as it drove past seemingly interminable rows of aircraft hangars. Some dark, others brightly illuminated from inside, where ground crews worked on military aircraft of all shapes and sizes, many with engine cowlings gaping open to reveal the intricate guts of jet turbine machinery.

Soon the hangars disappeared. The cold winter night enveloped them for several minutes. They came to a series of tall lightposts that illuminated a half dozen aircraft on the tarmac. All but one aircraft were dark, covered with iced tarps tied down in precise military fashion. Saunders stopped behind the last aircraft in the row, an Augusta tilt-rotor jet-helo.

Carlton had never seen such an aircraft, although he had once flown in an Osprey, the aircraft's problematic military older brother, during a Navy Reserves exercise. He was surprised that the aircraft was civilian and not military, strange for an Air Force base. But then again, everything about their situation was strange. The $10 million Bell/Augusta 609 in front of them was a cross between a corporate jet and a helicopter. Its white fuselage was topped by a wing, each end of which held an engine tilted upward and crowned with an oversized three-blade propeller. The result looked more like an oversized toy than an airworthy form of transportation.

Carlton and Erika hopped down from the Humvee. She gasped at the cold and noise outside. The high-pitched whine of the engines was accompanied by deep chopping sounds as the huge propellers swept through the cold night air.

Saunders came up behind them and jabbed his thumb at a stairway below an oval opening in the fuselage.

Carlton nodded, stepped nearer to Saunders. "Thank you!" He saluted.

The colonel flashed a quick return salute and gave a thumbs-up before walking briskly back to the Humvee.

Carlton and Erika climbed the narrow metal stairs.

"Welcome aboard," a steward announced, somberly. "Mr. MacLean sends his best. If you'd be so kind as to take your seats, we'll be off." He punched a button beside the entrance, watched the mechanized staircase retract and fold behind the hatch, and sealed it carefully before checking Carlton's and Erika's seatbelts. Satisfied, he selected one of the four remaining glove-soft leather seats.

"Excuse me," Carlton said. "Where exactly are we going?"

The steward sat up, turned. "Atlantic City. We should be there inside half an hour."

Carlton and Erika exchanged curious glances.

Carlton was about to ask the steward if there was a telephone on board, but quickly realized what an incredibly bad idea that was. The thumping of the rotors increased in volume and speed. The white aircraft slowly lifted off of the icy tarmac.

When it reached an altitude of two hundred feet, its engines swiveled ninety degrees. Once the propellers were positioned like those of a traditional airplane, the aircraft began to move forward. The pilot accelerated, increased altitude. Ten minutes later, the hybrid flew in a northeasterly heading at an altitude of twenty thousand feet, close to its maximum speed of 317 miles per hour.

It took all of Carlton's discipline not to call MacLean and Pink on his cell phone. But using his cell phone was not an option either. Fress would triangulate their position and mount yet a fourth offensive. Carlton had escaped three times. He wasn't sure how many lives he had left. Although Erika had sensed danger and fear in Carlton's voice when he had called, she had no idea that events had turned so quickly and deeply for the worse. She gazed at him in shock.

Carlton didn't want her involved—hated the fact that he somehow had enabled Fress to target her. But she was here and she deserved to know. He told her everything. The only thing he left out was the direct threat to her life in the note from Fress's or Waterboer's courier. She cried, then toughened up.

They both remained silent, allowing their initial shock to pass and the dull throb of fear to replace it. Soon, the fact they were safe—for the moment, at least—flushed the adrenaline from their systems. Exhausted, Carlton closed his eyes and rested his head against the headrest.

Erika looked out the port window. Below them, soft silvery clouds glowed bright in the light of a nearly full moon. She turned away from the window, reclined in the warm leather seat, and watched Carlton, who slept as soundly as a child next to her. She allowed herself a smile, assessed Carlton longingly. The object of her affection was neither jock nor intellectual. It was clear from her discussions with him that he had not yet attained a level of satisfaction in his life that allowed him to be happy.

European-bred minds like Erika's generally assessed people by placing them in compartments. Education, profession, wealth, religion, nationality, family. But she found Carlton did not fit comfortably into any of her normal compartments. Something greater existed beyond the sum of his parts. A synergy that transcended his other characteristics. An overriding motivation. For success. Not in fame or fortune but in terms of a meaningful life. The meaning he craved was probably why he was going to such lengths to expose Fress and Waterboer. What else could it be, other than that he was honest?

She realized Carlton was fond of her, but shy. He wasn't sure how to treat her. Young colleague? Subordinate? Friend? Romantic interest? For her part, Erika could not deny her romantic thoughts. In a sense, Carlton's shyness made him more attractive. For all of her professional determination and obsession with career, for all her exterior toughness, she pined for the warmth of a deeply romantic relationship. Not with a man who merely fit the bill, like so many of her young lawyer friends who dated people after ticking off a required number of boxes on a checklist, but with a soul mate. A man sufficiently confident to allow her the freedom to succeed professionally and yet masculine enough to lead, not by force or financial coercion or emotional domination, but by love, experience, and example. A man complex enough to navigate the currents of professional and family life guided by simple, solid values. A man flexible enough to adjust to changing circumstances, inflexible in the face of challenge. And a man who would protect her. She wasn't sure Carlton was the one, but she hadn't found a fatal flaw in him as she had in so many others, often after a single date.

"I thought you were sleeping," Carlton said, without turning.

Erika averted her gaze, embarrassed. "Just thinking." She pulled her long legs onto her seat, hugged them close with her arms, placed her head on her knees.

Carlton turned, looked at her. Despite her exhaustion and the events of the past week, she radiated a beauty most women fell short of under optimum circumstances. She took a strand of long red hair in her right hand, toyed with it under her pointed nose.

"Thinking about?" he asked.

"About what drives you so hard."

He smiled. "Right now, pure terror."

She straightened in her chair. "What drives you so hard? Why are you doing all of this?"

He knew what she meant but didn't want to face all that right then. "It's not like I signed up for this. We're being chased by trained killers the chief of staff sicced on us. He's probably convinced them that we're terrorists or spies or God knows what. It's not like we have a choice."

"Not now you don't."

"When, then?"

"You could have accepted their bribe."

He hadn't thought about the bribe since he stuffed the note, photo of Erika, and the pile of diamonds back into the envelope. "I could never have accepted the bribe."

"I know that. That's one of the things that makes you who you are, that makes you rare."

"Would you have taken it?"

"Honestly, I don't know. I don't know if I would have been that strong."

"I think you would have done exactly what I did. Especially if someone's life depended on it." *Maybe if they hadn't threatened you I would have taken it.*

"You get pulled off a huge case, get stuck with a crummy one instead. When you win that, you keep digging because something's not right, even though your boss orders you not to. It could cost you your job, but you keep going. When you discover the enormity of what's behind it all, you keep going, even though two people have been murdered. It could cost you your life, but you keep pushing. You get offered a bribe bigger than the lottery. That'll set you up for life. But you keep going. Where does that strength come from?"

He knew she wouldn't let up until he opened up. "Faith."

"Faith?"

"Good and evil. Right and wrong."

"Are you religious?"

"Catholic. You?"

"Lutheran, but I never got into it. I studied the religions of the world in college. It was interesting. I see how religion brings charity and forgiveness. But it's also brought wars and repression. Just look at the Spanish Inquisition and the fundamentalist Islamic war against America."

"That's true. The way I figure it, religion turns into evil when intolerance enters the equation. Once you believe you're better than everyone else, that's when it becomes bad. Which is not to say you have to agree with everything, just respect other people's opinions, unless they harm others, of course."

"I've never been able to make the jump into religious faith. I guess it's just not logical to me."

"I don't think it's logical either. For me, faith and logic are on two different planes. You can't explain electricity with faith and you can't explain God with logic."

"But how do you explain the Holocaust? What about poor kids living in the street? People dying of hunger and disease? Old people with nowhere to live? What is God doing about that?"

"Plenty. I think God put us here to help those less fortunate, each in our own way with our own talents. To me, the question isn't 'What is God doing about it?' It's 'What am I doing about it?' But to each their own. That's just the way I think. But I can't stand people imposing their beliefs on others. I'm certainly not perfect and I'm certainly no saint." He looked at her, chuckled. "Do I sound like a loon? And what about you? Why are you doing all this? You could have bolted, too."

"No, you're definitely not a loon. Maybe a bit goody-goody." She laughed. "I'm kidding. If anything, it makes you much more—"

The PA interrupted her. "Folks, we're going to land in a few moments, so strap in please."

More what? he wondered.

37 SANCTUARY

Atlantic City Airport
Atlantic City, New Jersey
3:21 A.M.

As a commentator once noted, control of the gambling meccas in Las Vegas and Atlantic City had long ago passed from the families to a far more powerful group: the corporations. MacLean's father, Don Giancarlo Innocenti, had been one of the first Cosa Nostra family patriarchs to preach cleaning the gambling palaces' books and going legit. Many had followed his advice and succeeded. Most of those who had not were convicted or squeezed out.

Ironically, Max MacLean had gone back to Atlantic City, where his father had made a killing in the 1950s, and set up shop. Competition was fierce, and the corporate casino owners were a force with which to reckon, particularly when newcomers started from scratch along the Atlantic City seashore. However, as Don Innocenti's son, MacLean retained sufficient influence among the remaining families to make some space along the southeast New Jersey shore of fifty thousand inhabitants, especially because his operations were all legit. He built a casino resort that reflected the value he revered: beauty. The Star had grown from two hundred rooms in the early 1990s to more than one thousand rooms. Designed by Gerhard Heusch, a leading architect of the day, the Star was as graceful and simple as its surrounding competitors were gaudy and contrived. Instead of massing rooms and gambling halls on the ground level like the other casino owners, MacLean had built up. Although the edifice was already ten years old, it was the tallest and most breathtaking casino east of Vegas. So tall that the trademark brilliant orb at its forty-story summit could be seen by the two quiet men dressed in white shirts and black suits at the local airport. They waited patiently next to a shiny black Lincoln Town Car limo parked at the entrance of a private hangar. The slight bulges in their coat pockets were visible only to the most trained observer. The two men watched the Bell/Agusta jet-helo rotate its props horizontally, land, and taxi to the hangar.

One man got into the limo and drove the short distance to stop directly in front of the strange aircraft. The other jogged behind the limo to the aircraft, opened the hatch, drew a Glock from his breast holster, and hoisted himself inside. He quickly scanned the passenger cabin and found the steward, who nodded affirmatively. The man holstered his weapon and allowed Carlton and Erika a brief smile. He motioned with his hand. "Please follow me."

In almost any other town, the gleaming limousine would have attracted attention. In Atlantic City, it served as camouflage, particularly at night. It drove off as soon as their escort got in and closed the door. He sat opposite Carlton and Erika, facing rear traffic, handed Carlton an envelope. Inside, Carlton found a single faxed sheet.

Trust my people. Ask for what you need.
This isn't over yet. Good luck.

MM

Who was this Max MacLean that he risked so much to save their lives? Why was he doing it? Was it for justice or revenge, or did he simply refuse to lose? Carlton didn't know. He had never met MacLean, had only spoken to him once. Erika had researched him before Carlton contacted Wenzel. Perhaps it was MacLean's mafia background—discovered only after much digging—that pushed him to fight back against the government.

Whoever MacLean was, whatever his motives, his airlift out of Andrews had saved their lives. They had escaped. Erika once. Carlton three times. But they couldn't run forever. If they didn't run, where and how could they hide?

A tense fifteen minutes later, the limousine pulled into a dark, unmarked parking garage. Their escort got out, pointed to a drab door. He chose a key from a large bunch attached to his belt, opened it. Behind it was an open elevator door. He ushered Carlton and Erika inside, slipped another key into the keyhole, remained silent while the elevator ascended rapidly. It stopped on the top floor. Forty. The doors opened onto a dark corridor. Another guard also dressed in a black suit stood at the end of the hallway, near yet another door. He and their escort exchanged several rapid words in a Sicilian dialect, and the new guard opened the door wide.

"The presidential suite," their escort announced, "from the high-rollers' private entrance. Not every high roller wants to be seen. You'd be surprised who's addicted to gambling." He winked. "You'll be safe here for a few hours. If you need anything, knock and ask Tonino here. Don't use the phone lines. We have to assume they're tapped by now. Get some rest. I'll be back in a few hours." He bowed slightly, shut the door on his way out.

In a bit of a daze, Carlton turned to Erika. Her eyes. The narrow escapes. The fear. The exhaustion. The relief. Whatever the reason, he couldn't resist any longer. He took her in his arms and brought his lips to hers.

They held each other for what seemed like hours, pent-up emotions released in a flood of joy.

"Pat, I—" she whispered, tears streaming from her eyes.

He wiped them from her soft cheeks. "I know. Me too."

She began to cry again, brought her lips to his. He tasted the salt from her tears, pulled her body against his. It felt good, right. He felt emotions surge through his heart, his mind, and his body he hadn't felt—hadn't allowed himself to feel for a long time.

No, he thought. *It's more than what I've ever felt. More real. More complete.*

Finally, they released each other. He took her hand in his, and they toured the suite together.

"Just look at this place," she said, staring at the 1970s kitsch all about them.

"It looks like ABBA's been staying here," Carlton said.

The room stretched for what seemed like miles. Shag carpeting, lambswool throw rugs, chrome hanging lamps, orange sofas, and mirrors were surrounded by a 180-degree view of the neon-studded strip of ocean from floor-to-ceiling plate glass windows. A glass fountain, surrounded by a small forest of palms, gurgled at the center of the room.

"It's got everything you could want," he said.

She turned to him, smiled. "You're right. And what I want is a bath." She moved her mouth to his ear. "And I think you want one too," she whispered.

The bathroom was larger than most people's living rooms. It seemed carved from a giant block of green marble. In one corner stood a Swiss shower, surrounded by vertical and horizontal chrome jets. Next to it was a sunken tub large enough for a small navy. Erika inspected a battalion of multicolored bath salt jars, poured some into the tub, and turned on the faucet and whirlpool jets.

An enormous tropical salt water aquarium lined one entire wall. Bright blue, yellow, and red fish swam lazily amid thin streams of bubbles, white and pink corals, undulating sea anemones. Carlton stared at them, mesmerized like a small child. He felt himself relax.

He turned and watched Erika remove her dirty clothes. Her long legs gave way to slightly curved hips, and a small pert backside. Her graceful back arched upward and ended in straight shoulders. Her small breasts jutted forward. Red hair cascaded down her back, halfway down to her trim waist.

"I can't believe how beautiful you are." He walked to her, took her in his arms and kissed her. Her skin was warm. He continued kissing her while she removed his clothes. His wanting grew. Their kissing became more intense, more primal.

She led him into the foaming tub. "I hope we don't scare the fish."

They did.

Several hours later, a series of knocks sounded at the door. Carlton was awake, roused by a low but continuous buzz that rang in his ears.

Their escort appeared in the doorway. "Sorry to wake you, but it's time to go." He grinned. "They must have been following you pretty good. They shot the plane down a half hour out of Atlantic City." Carlton's eyes widened. "The pilot bailed out, but they probably didn't see him. It was pitch dark. By the time they make a search in the morning, you'll be safe."

"I don't know how to thank you. We—"

He raised his hand. "No need. But please hurry. We've got a car waiting."

"Where are we—"

"There's little time before dawn. I'll explain on the way. I brought you fresh clothes. I hope they fit." He placed two canvas bags at the entrance of the suite and left.

Carlton nudged Erika softly. She slept on her stomach, a faint smile on her lips. "Time to wake up." He moved her shimmering red hair to the side, and kissed the back of her neck.

"Mmm." She purred, getting to her knees and stretching like a cat. "Come back to bed." She reached over and tugged at Carlton, kissed him softly on the mouth.

"Honeymoon's over, baby. Need to leave. Better get dressed."

She smiled mischievously. "Over?"

"For now."

38 VENDETTA

Castel MacLean
Beverly Hills, California
10:36 A.M.

It took over a day for Dan Wenzel's death to hit MacLean completely. When it did, it shook him to the core. He had allowed Wenzel to fly to Washington. He blamed himself for the man's death. Wenzel had not only been MacLean's lawyer, business advisor, and confidant. He had been one of MacLean's best friends. Billionaires could not trust the friendship of most. MacLean's friendship with Wenzel was second only to his friendship and love for his wife.

And if they had killed Wenzel, he must be next.

MacLean had not managed to sleep for more than thirty minutes since the plane crash. He was the opposite of his usually well-groomed self. He had neither showered nor shaved. His hair was disheveled. His shirt was wrinkled and stained. His complexion was pale and drawn. Bags tugged at his bloodshot eyes. He sat on the black leather 1920s Corbusier sofa in his third-floor home office, door closed, blinds drawn, staring at the telephone in front of him.

Two bottles of Grey Goose vodka stood side by side on the glass cube MacLean used as a coffee table; one empty, the other half empty. He did not even bother to use one of his office bar's Baccarat crystal drams. He had started smoking again after finding one of Wenzel's packs of John Player Special cigarettes in the house. Pinpoint halogen light beams illuminated acrid blue cigarette smoke in the dark room.

One soldier was stationed outside MacLean's office door. Not one but two others followed Claire MacLean everywhere. Like MacLean, she did not leave the compound. She trusted MacLean implicitly but could not understand the sheer magnitude of the reality that was unfolding. The soldiers were there to protect her, she knew, but they scared her. The other soldiers were stationed at strategic points on the grounds. This was a government vendetta against MacLean, the trusted don had informed his soldiers. Although no place was truly safe, Castel MacLean was safest.

MacLean crushed out his cigarette, picked up the telephone receiver, and dialed the number he had located after contacting one of his local family contacts. The international code for Sicily he knew from memory. He knew it was bugged but was beyond caring.

"*Pronto*." A voice far away answered.

"*Buon giorno*. Don Forza, *per favore*."

"Please, who is calling?"

"Maximilliano MacLean."

"*Si signore. Subito, subito*. Right away. Hold please."

MacLean took a deep swallow from the bottle of vodka, the powerful clear liquid no longer ice cold as MacLean would generally have insisted. Today he couldn't even taste the difference. Yet after drinking steadily for two days, his mind was amazingly clear. The vodka burned going down.

"Don MacLean. I am so happy to hear you. I heard about the accident. I was so relieved to hear that you and Claire weren't on the plane."

"*Grazie*, Don Forza. And thank you for sending your *soldati*. All my money and still I can trust no one else to protect my family."

"It is my privilege."

Before MacLean's father had wound down his illegal activities, Don Innocenti had selected Tomasino Forza as his godson. Now a don in his own right, Forza had learned well. He had returned to Sicily with the sizable bequest Don Innocenti had devised to him in his will. After thirty years of continuing his mostly white-collar criminal activities in the Cosa Nostra, Forza had sufficiently enlarged his fortune to heed his mentor's teachings and similarly wound down his own illegal activities. Although Don Forza's operations were now entirely legal, they remained shady at best and dangerous at least. To protect himself and his family, he continued his vigilance against enemies within and without the Cosa Nostra and maintained his standing army of soldiers consummately loyal to him through the

Sicilian code of *omerta*. A contingent of these he immediately sent to protect his *padrino*'s son in America, whom he called Don MacLean out of honor and respect.

MacLean was in no mood for formalities, Sicilian or otherwise. And he was one of the few people who could not respect formalities and still remain respectful. He sighed, then paused briefly. "It was not an accident, Don Forza." He was about to tell Forza that a friend was on the plane, but stopped himself. In the Sicilian hierarchy, among the *uomini di rispetto*, other people came before friends. "My *consiglieri* was on the plane. That is why it crashed." *Consiglieri* was a Sicilian concept, the trusted family advisor, the counselor, often a lawyer, who advised on all things and who as a result knew of all things. A position of great respect within the *famiglia*.

"Your *consiglieri*. I did not know. I am sorry." Forza paused. The line crackled. "You say it was not an accident?"

"No."

"Who?"

"I know who, but they are untouchable," he said, referring to Piet Slythe and Waterboer rather than the White House chief of staff.

"No one is untouchable."

Despite the vodka, the words chilled MacLean. But that is why he had called. Still, he was afraid. He said nothing, let the Sicilian telephone line crackle.

"Maximilliano. Don Innocenti was my *padrino*. You are his son. You are in danger. *Comanda me*." Command me. "But the telephone…I do not hear it so good." *Don't implicate yourself over the telephone. Get me the information. You know how.*

"*Grazie*, Don Forza. *Grazie*."

39 YACHT

Atlantic Star
U.S. Registry Yacht
Atlantic City, New Jersey
4:50 A.M.

The Lincoln limousine drove onto docks that were dark and ominously still. The car slowed and stopped inside a warehouse filled with crates labeled MacLean Foods International Inc. in large stenciled letters. Carlton and Erika's escort opened the door, signaled for them to get out.

He led them across the giant warehouse, illuminated in pale yellow light from sodium lightbulbs trapped in metal grilles far overhead. Their footsteps echoed on the concrete floor, made the cavernous warehouse seem even larger, more forbidding. Soon the echoes from their footsteps were joined by another sound. A low-pitched, steady, powerful rumble. So low Erika felt it in her shivering body. The feeling also made her realize how hungry she was.

Trailing clouds of frozen breath, they emerged on the other side of the warehouse onto a wooden jetty. Moored to what seemed to be large steel mushrooms was the source of the rumbling sound, an enormous white boat. No activity was evident on or around the craft, but it blazed with light. The three emerged from the warehouse onto the jetty and were enveloped in a misty drizzle from the black sky. Erika wrapped herself tightly in the warm cashmere topcoat their escort had provided, huddled against Carlton.

"Mr. Carlton. Ms. Wassenaar. If you'll please board."

A tall man dressed in full uniform whites emblazoned with commander's bars met the two at the top of the gangplank. "Welcome aboard the *Atlantic Star.*" He saluted them. "I'm Commander Ramey. This is my executive officer, Mr. Krebski."

He saluted. "Sir. Ma'am."

"It's a pleasure to have you aboard, Mr. Carlton, Ms. Wassenaar."

"Uh…Thank you, Commander." Carlton gave the man's hand a heavy tug and eyeballed the men around them.

"There is a gentleman here to see you."

"Who's that?"

"If you'll follow me, sir. Ma'am." Commander Ramey turned to his XO. "Mr. Krebski, take us out."

He led them down a long hallway to a sitting room nearly as palatial as the *Star*'s presidential suite, though far more tastefully decorated. A man stood in the far corner of the room, his back toward them. Dressed in jeans, a T-shirt, a thick leather jacket, and sneakers, he gazed out to sea, apparently deep in thought.

"They're here, sir," Ramey announced, then turned to Carlton and Erika. "I'll see you later. Please make yourselves at home."

The man in the corner turned toward them. Carlton got the distinct impression they had just walked into a well-laid trap. But that didn't make sense. Maybe sleep deprivation and paranoia were getting the best of him. The African-American proceeded toward them without a word and extended his hand. "Tom Pink."

"Tom Pink?" It took a great deal of self-control for Carlton to refrain from launching himself at him. This was the man from Langley who refused to believe him, despite his repeated telephone calls and evidence.

"Glad to meet you, Pat. I'm glad you got my message."

Carlton squinted. "Your message? What message?"

"The message I left you last night. On your voicemails at home and in the office. Telling you to get out of D.C. Isn't that why you're—"

"The only thing in my apartment last night was a psychotic on steroids."

"That's what I called to warn you about."

"Yeah. Well you were a day late. Thomas. The name definitely fits. Doubting Thomas. So, now that you've researched for yourself, you finally believe what I told you in the first place a week ago?"

"As I said, that's why I called you."

"Well, better late than never." He pointed toward Erika. "This is Erika Wassenaar." They shook hands.

"I don't blame you for being sore. But you have to see it in context. I'm an analyst. I'm not used to getting real information from people outside the Agency."

"Even from a lawyer at DOJ and a Navy Reservist to boot?"

"You've got no idea how many fruitcakes call us with conspiracy theories. But once I confirmed your info, I acted as fast as I could."

Erika felt the tension, jumped in to defuse it. "How did you find us?"

"You forget who I work for, Ms. Wassenaar. It wasn't very difficult. I went through Mr. Carlton's computer files and the numbers he dialed. Got to MacLean quickly. A couple more calls later, here I am." He spread his arms wide. "But I'm not the only one looking out for you."

"Obviously."

"Thank God for Colonel Saunders, right?"

"Colonel Saunders? How did—"

"Company man. Like me. Don't worry. He doesn't know more than need-to-know. It also helps that he and MacLean go way back."

"I'm getting the feeling MacLean goes way back with just about everyone."

Carlton remained silent for a moment, still not entirely certain he could trust this man. The voicemails he referred to could have been intentionally placed as a way to establish trust. The assassin could have been a decoy. But the decoy was dead.

No. Pink had to be for real. Besides, it's not like he had many options right now. He'd just remain alert and watch Doubting Thomas carefully. Carlton's gaze drifted to the black marble bar at the far end of the room. "I don't know about you two, but I could sure use a belt. What's your pleasure?" He walked to the bar, scanned the forest of bottles lined against a mirror, poured himself a tall gin and tonic, with plenty of ice and lots of lime, and poured the others their chosen libations.

Following Carlton's cue, they hoisted their glasses. "To the invisible Max MacLean. For getting us out of this mess. For now, anyway."

They sat in a grouping of white velvet sofas and drank in silence, listening to the increased rumble of the engines, watching the docks getting smaller through the large bar window.

Carlton looked back at Pink. "So now that we're safe and

cozy, what's the plan? How are we going to arrest Fress?"

Pink winced. "I'm…afraid it's not that simple."

Carlton felt his heart sink into his gut. "Not that simple? But it is what you're here for, right?" Silence. "Why do I have a feeling I don't want to hear this?" Carlton walked back to the bar, made fresh drinks.

"You'd better sit down. A lot has happened."

Carlton and Erika sat, and during the next half hour, Pink outlined the Russian situation. Leonid Pyashinev, Molotok and Russkost, the Russian *mafiya* Volki, and the Russian diamond stockpile. They listened intently without interruption.

When Pink was finished, Carlton drained his second G&T, stood, frowned. "Let me see if I've got this straight. One, CIA won't let us arrest Fress because it can't risk this Molotok freak or Waterboer getting wind of what we know. Two, you want us—*us*—to help you find the location of the Russian diamond stockpile. Three, you want *us* to help you steal the stockpile from God-knows-what psychotic armed force is guarding it. All before Molotok and his wolves or whatever they're called get to it. Four, you have no idea where the stockpile is, except for some clues obviously so piss poor the CIA can't send an experienced team in to grab it. Five—we are already at five, right?—we won't have any government support because we can't let the information leak to Molotok and Waterboer through Congressional, White House, or Agency moles who work for Fress and Waterboer. No SEALs, no Rangers, no Delta Force, not even a group of angry interns with staplers. Six, both Molotok and Waterboer are also looking for the diamonds and are willing to do whatever it takes to get them. Oh, and I almost forgot—seven, we can't punt this over to the Russian government and let them deal with their own mess because we have no way of making sure that the person on that end won't be involved with Waterboer and transfer the diamonds just like Molotok. Is that about it, or am I missing anything here?"

Pink avoided Carlton's glowering stare, but couldn't blame the man. Pink himself hated the plan, Forbes' plan. Bad when Forbes first disclosed it, it sounded worse every time Pink heard it. Particularly from someone else. He shook his head. "That's about the size of it." He didn't have a choice, either.

"Well this just gets better and better. Why didn't you tell me? You knew I was already knee-deep into this nightmare. Why didn't you tell me?"

"Even if I had been able to reach you, which I wasn't despite many attempts, I couldn't tell you."

"Why the hell not?"

"First, we didn't know until we verified your information. Second, once we did, we didn't know if we could trust you. We just couldn't risk it. Third, all my phones were probably ta—"

"I don't understand," Erika said. "You couldn't risk what?"

"Putting you in even more danger than you were in. We wanted to protect you, and we couldn't risk the connection between Waterboer and Russia leaking." He placed his palms outward apologetically. "Not intentionally. Not even through you. But it could have leaked. CIA is almost as porous as the White House and Congress. You were already running from Fress. Imagine if Molotok and his psychos had also been chasing you. There's no way you'd have made it this far.

"Fress has moles all over the place, but he's got to be careful too. The Russians in this are different. They work out of Siberia. They pop in and out of the U.S., take people out the way you and I go to the supermarket. They don't have to be careful, just quick. And again, your knowing about this wouldn't have helped you in any way."

Carlton sank back into the couch. "So we have absolutely no choice. Someone asked for volunteers to step forward and everyone but Erika and I took a step back."

"Everyone but you, Erika, and me. It's not the way I'd plan it, okay, but—"

"Am I right?"

Pink sighed. "You are. But it's not because I or anyone at CIA is paranoid or masochistic, Pat. It's simply that until the Russian issues are resolved, you're not safe. Even if Fress is behind bars. If it makes you feel any better, I got stuck in the middle of this, too."

"No, it does *not* make me feel better. You're CIA. You volunteered for this crap. We're lawyers. Getting Fress yes, but hunting for a Russian diamond stockpile? It's a bit beyond us, don't you think?" He listened to his own words. He had never expected to say anything like it. For the past ten years he had wanted to stop sitting on the sidelines, to act, to be part of something that made a difference. Now he didn't want it. He didn't want it because he was afraid. He had acted tough by refusing Waterboer's high dollar offer, but now the consequences scared him. He felt like a coward and it disgusted him. He forced himself to shake it off.

"Okay, Tom. We're stuck in this. There's no use bitching about it. It's just the odds I don't like. If we go back to D.C., your people won't allow us to arrest Fress until the Russian issues are resolved. We'll be out in the open where Fress can find us. If we don't arrest Fress, we may as well save ammo and shoot ourselves now."

"Staying away from trouble is better than looking for it. You're assuming Fress'll find us. I'm not so sure. Regardless, the faster we find the stockpile, the faster we can get rid of Fress. The key is to find the Russian diamonds. Again, I'm sorry you're in this situation, but I'm—"

"Not as sorry as we are, Tom."

The *Atlantic Star* was one of two casino yachts reserved for the Star casino's high rollers. At the cost of $20 million each, many would think them a colossal waste. But MacLean knew different. The yachts were so popular, the highest of the high rollers regularly fought for the opportunity to take the *Atlantic Star* or *Caribbean Star* out for a week with thirty of their closest friends, all the while gambling away enough money to generate far more than the payments on each vessel.

Over two hundred feet long, the *Atlantic Star* was a monster of a ship. Despite her size, the ship's revolutionary honeycomb aluminum hull and superstructure were so light that, even at full weight, she displaced a mere three hundred tons, far less than ships half her size. Designed as an advanced technical prototype, the *Star* possessed the dual qualities of performance and luxury naval architects strived for but rarely attained. Powered by four twelve-cylinder Caterpillar engines, propelled by four quad-blade Lips propellers, and electrified by four Northern Lights generators, the *Star* could top forty knots, a speed unheard of in her class.

In contrast to her bulky brethren, the *Star* sported a teardrop design with nary a mast or rail to defeat its sleek profile. Instead of the tall superstructures of other luxury yachts, the *Star's* designers opted for width rather than height. The result was two decks rather than four, a shape that resembled a flying saucer more than a yacht.

Inside, the *Atlantic Star* remained true to MacLean's obsession with the aesthetic. Sandblasted glass, brushed aluminum, and baby blue leather. Requiring a minimum crew of only five, the yacht could sleep up to thirty passengers in fifteen staterooms, nourish them in gastronomic bliss in a palatial dining room with selections from a five-star kitchen and cellar, entertain them in a 360-degree bar, a state-of-the-art casino, movie theater, nightclub, and library, and exercise them in a full gymnasium complete with machine and weight room, racquetball court, jacuzzi, and retractable-roof pool.

After a hearty breakfast of bacon and eggs, yogurt, toast, coffee, and orange juice, Erika decided to catch a few more hours of sleep. Carlton and Pink sat silently at the large dining table with Commander Ramey. Pink pored over some of the CD-ROM files he had brought from Langley, rubbed his temples. Carlton savored an oily Fuente Opus X torpedo from the *Star's* humidor and gazed past the plate glass window that separated the dining room from the frothing black ocean a dozen feet below, observing the first red glow of dawn in the east.

"I realize this isn't a simple question, gentlemen, but where are we going?" Ramey asked, sipping a mug of coffee.

Carlton jabbed his thumb at Pink. "You'd better ask James Bond over here."

Pink finished reading his documents for the nth time, put on his eyeglasses, and looked up at the captain. "For the moment, and until we get more data, away from the coast and *east*. The farther we get away from D.C., the better."

Approximately one hundred and seventy-five miles southwest of Atlantic City, Scott Fress was wide awake. At a few minutes shy of 6:30 A.M., not even the most severe insomniacs were anywhere near their White House or Old Executive Office Building offices. But Scott Fress was up when the phone rang.

It wasn't a coincidence. The days of the White House chief of staff were often busier than those of his ward. Fress had to use the darkness of the early morning and late night to conduct the shadow operations that made him wealthy. He didn't sleep much.

That's what pills are for, he reasoned, popping a red oval pill into his mouth and chasing it with hot coffee as he reached for the receiver.

"Yes."

"It's Jones."

"Yes."

"We tracked the aircraft from Andrews to Atlantic City. It belonged to MacLean. We shot the plane down after it left Atlantic City."

"And?"

Silence.

"And," Fress repeated, remaining perfectly calm, not raising his voice.

"And they reappeared in Atlantic City, but then we lost them. I have no idea how. They—"

"I do. You're a *fucking moron*. But luckily there are a bunch of others to keep you company."

"Sir, we had them on the ground, and they…well they just vanished, sir."

"How did they vanish in Atlantic City?"

Pause. "I have no idea."

"It was MacLean's plane?"

"Yes sir. His company. MacLean Foods Interna—"

"What else does MacLean own in Atlantic City besides a plane?"

"A casino, for starters."

"So now you know where they are."

"But we don't—"

"Carlton is not the only who can be made to vanish."

"Sir, I—"

"Find them."

He replaced the receiver, stared at the bottle of pills, popped another one in his mouth. It was going to be a long day.

Czas
Moscow
11:06 A.M.

Originally created to spy both on the West and on the Russian people, the KGB's power had been neutralized by the close of the cold war until, like a hydra, the secret organ had regrown nearly out of control under Orlov's KGB-trained predecessor. Following the years of FSB/SVR government leadership until the failed GRU coup that eventually led to Orlov's election, the president had inflicted a mighty blow to the organization, both financially and governmentally. Its personnel was replaced, its budget sharply reduced, its role narrowed. So it was not an agent of the FSB but an officer of the GRU who led the mid-day raid on the small retail establishment that sold and repaired watches and clocks. The GRU had known for many months that sensitive information was being leaked to foreign powers. The United States, Germany, France, Great Britain, Israel. Only recently had the source of the leak been narrowed to the seemingly innocuous watch shop. The GRU investigations of bank transactions made it quite clear the little store did not live on timepieces alone.

The GRU team was overworked and had no time to waste on formalities. Two officers dressed in military uniforms entered the store with weapons drawn, handcuffed the two employees, then entered the back room. Watches and other timepieces lay on tables in various states of disassembly. They soon located and accessed a powerful IBM PC in a small cubbyhole behind the repair room.

"I have it, Major," announced the junior officer and resident GRU field hacker. "A list of customers."

"*Ochen harasho*, Lieutenant." Excellent. "Connect it up."

"*Da*."

The lieutenant removed a cellular telephone and modem from his belt pack, attached the modem to the port behind the computer, and hit an automatic dial key on the cellular. Twenty seconds later, the central GRU computer several miles away began a rapid-fire dialogue with the IBM PC. Within two minutes, it resulted in a list of state officials with access to sensitive information from the computer's customer list.

"Completed, Major."

"Let's take a look." The major scrolled the list down until he came across the name that he already suspected was there. He removed his own cellular telephone and dialed.

"Kovanetz," a voice on the other end answered tersely.

"Major Kasparov here, Colonel. It was as you suspected, sir."

"Klimov?"

"*Da*. Last transaction appears to be…two days ago."

"*Ochen harasho*, Major. Arrest him and begin the interrogation. I will meet you at your office."

"*Da, tovarish* Colonel."

Within a few hours, Major Kasparov had uncovered the latest information Klimov had sold to the American CIA. The entire Pyashinev file, including Pyashinev's note found at the site of the helicopter crash.

Rossiya, trieti sloi. Nie dopustit im wziat eto.

Russia, third layer. Must not let them get it.

41 CRUISE

Atlantic Star
Atlantic Ocean
502 miles east of Atlantic City
5:33 P.M.

At least a full decade ahead of the most advanced technology used in commerce, the National Security Agency's (NSA) electronic hardware, software, and superbly trained staff could listen to nearly any electromagnetic communication on Earth, including through keyword sampling and voiceprint recognition programs that scanned land, radio, and satellite lines—including cellular—and even communications in closed rooms through window vibrations caused by speech or computer keyboard strokes. Through the NSA, therefore, Scott Fress could locate nearly any person he pleased wherever they communicated. For this simple fact, despite the *Atlantic Star*'s sophisticated communications suite, no one aboard the oceangoing luxury yacht could risk communicating with anyone off the vessel, for fear of detection.

In addition to the communications blackout, Captain Ramey and his crew operated under the cover that MacLean's Star Casino had graciously provided the *Atlantic Star* to a high-roller Mexican businessman for a week to compensate for the man's unfortunate losing streak at the Star's baccarat tables.

But despite the electronic silence and clever cover, sooner or later the government's vast resources would allow the White House chief of staff to track and locate Carlton and Erika. It was unavoidable; only a matter of time.

Unless, Carlton reasoned, *Scott Fress abandoned his search*. But if nothing else, a lack of tenacity was not one of the chief of staff's shortcomings. The only way Scott Fress would abandon the search would be when he was sure that Carlton and Erika were dead. He paused. *When Fress is sure that we're dead*. Carlton stood and walked to the control room.

"How are you feeling, sir?" Ramey inquired.

"Fine. But I'd feel much better if you'd just call me Pat."

Ramey smiled. "Jack."

"Good. Do you think I could take a peek at your nav charts?"

"By all means, although I think you'd find the library more interesting," Ramey stated good-naturedly.

"Hey, I'm Navy. Nothing more interesting to me than reading charts, you know?"

"Yeah, well I'm ex-Navy and I know you're full of hot air, but you're welcome to 'em. They're in the room back there. All neat and organized."

"Thanks. And do you happen to have a current plot of planned trajectories for nearby vessels? Something current?"

"No, but I'll get you one." Ramey picked up the intercom. "XO to the bridge, XO to the bridge please."

"Aces, Jack. Thanks."

A half hour later, Carlton located a vessel with the trajectory he desired and convinced Ramey to make two communications, one to the vessel and one to MacLean. It was the most cryptic communication he could make, and MacLean might not understand a thing, but it would serve its purpose. That is, there was a small chance that it would serve its purpose. If they were lucky. Very lucky. Still, it was the only thing Carlton could think of. He let Erika know about the plan, but they decided to hold off on informing Pink.

After a walk around the deck, Carlton knocked on Pink's locked stateroom door. Pink appeared and squinted with bloodshot eyes into bright sunlight. His face was gaunt, his clothes slept in.

"Anything yet?"

"Very little."

"Hey, be positive. Very little is better than very nothing." Carlton followed Pink inside. He sniffed. "Whew! It's gamey in here."

"Smells better than your damn cigars. Anyhow, let me show you what we've got so far. Where is Erika?"

"In the library."

"Come on." Pink grabbed a folder and led Carlton to the ship's wood-paneled library, where Erika sat on one of the comfortable sofas with her legs folded under her, face buried in a book.

Located in the center of the vessel, the library lacked windows or other surfaces that could be tapped by the NSA. Carlton joined Erika on the sofa. Pink sat on a light green armchair opposite a red marble fireplace flickering with flames from real logs well-secured behind a protective glass partition and surrounded by two stories of books.

Pink cleared his throat. "As we discussed earlier, neither I nor the rest of the Russian analysts at CIA have any idea where the diamonds are. All we know is that a Russian stockpile exists. The Russian government doesn't even know it exists, much less where it is. Which means our people inside their government haven't been able to help us. We also discussed that the few clues we do have stink on ice, if you'll forgive the pun. The good part is that I managed to organize the clues we do have."

Pink handed Carlton a sheaf of papers. "Frankly, I don't think you'll make much of it. I sure haven't."

"You've been looking at that info for a long time. You're too close to it to be objective anymore. Have some faith in us non-CIA morons."

"I didn't mean—"

"Just yanking your chain, Tom." He flashed a smile and ran through the pages. "Okay. What are we looking at?"

"One of our agents inside Russian military intelligence, the GRU, got hold of the inventory they made of Leonid Pyashinev's apartment. Remember, until his disappearance several weeks ago, Pyashinev was the head of the Russian government diamond consortium Komdragmet. Even though officially the Russian government doesn't know about the diamond stockpile, Pyashinev would have known. He was in thick with the pre-Orlov, pre-Puzhnin, pre-Yeltsin KGB crowd that smuggled the diamonds out of Russia before the Soviet collapse in 1991. The GRU discovered Pyashinev had been working for Waterboer. The last place he was seen before he crashed was Murmansk."

"And the inventory?"

"Nothing. Zilch. That's the report you've got there, with a complete inventory of what they found in his apartment. Pyashinev's bio. A cryptic note, apparently written by

Pyashinev immediately before he died. I've been trying to understand it for a week."

"You're going to have to translate," said Erika.

"In English, it reads: 'Russia, third layer. Must not let them get it.'"

"Not much of a clue, is it?" Erika said.

"As I said, the information we have is pretty shabby."

"Still, if those were Pyashinev's last words, they must have some meaning. Maybe we can give you a fresh perspective, spot something an expert like you might overlook. No offense, of course. I don't want to step on—"

"No, no. You may as well. Give it a shot. It'll give me a chance to catch some sleep."

The four cups of coffee and half bottle of pills this day had made Fress progressively more terse. Terse and tense. He grabbed the telephone. "Yes."

"Colonel Lin from NSA, sir."

"Yes."

"Sir, we picked up a communication from Carlton."

"Where and what." It was an order rather than a question.

"Atlantic Ocean, sir. Approximately five hundred miles off the coast of Atlantic City. The communication was to MacLean in Los Angeles, via a ship's satellite phone. By using two satellites in tandem, our system was able to—"

"Spare me the egghead crap, Lin. These guys are killers. Just get me an encrypted transcript and their present coordinates."

Fress waited until the email notification icon appeared against his White House screen saver, opened the electronic envelope, and read the transcript. It made no sense, but the eggheads' computers had identified the voiceprint as Carlton's. He punched a familiar telephone number from memory.

"Jones here."

"I'm doing your job for you. Now get this information: Carlton left Atlantic City by boat. He's about 450 miles out to sea." He read off the coordinates. "This is your last chance. If you fuck it up this time, I'll—well, you know what it'll mean."

42 EXECUTIONER

Atlantic Star
Atlantic Ocean
632 miles east of Atlantic City
9:02 P.M.

Head of Fress's covert strike team, Jones had failed his master three times. Or rather, his men had failed. Which was the same thing, as far as Fress was concerned. Once in Carlton's apartment. A second time on the Wilson Bridge. A third in Atlantic City. This time he'd do the job himself.

Jones was a rogue dropout from a clandestine operations group so secret its members' identities did not exist, not even in the CIA, DIA, NSA, NRO, and other U.S. secret organ alphabet soup. He had no legal identity, but multiple clandestine identities. This afternoon, he slipped into his facsimile identity as a senior FBI pilot. As such, he routinely flew certain of the Bureau's aircraft in connection with its war on terrorism. The ease with which Jones took the Learjet for a simple test and recon mission was frightening.

At New York's LaGuardia FBI hangar, he simply walked up to the flight coordinator, showed his ID, and asked. He smiled, but not too much. Soon he was on an easterly heading in a Lear U-36A. The needle-nosed aircraft was a basic Lear 36 modified as an anti-shipping missile trainer. The only change Jones had to make was to switch the training missile with a live weapon. One of his men took care of that part of the op.

The full moon illuminated clear patches of the dark ocean below between breaks in the clouds. Three and a half hours later, he sifted through the contacts on his multicolored radar screen, focused on his target, a single green dot one hundred miles due east.

The *Atlantic Star*.

Just a few minutes.

Unlike its field counterparts, the training jet lacked a system for locking a target into the missile's brain. He would have to hold his fire until he had visual contact. He only had a single missile, but he did not consider that a problem.

He removed the safety catch from the control switch—the "pickle"—and waited to come into range.

Jones dropped the Lear below the clouds, lined up for the kill. He was close enough to see the *Star's* navigation lights and brightly illuminated superstructure. She was coming up fast. He lined up his heads-up-display with the boat, pressed hard on the pickle.

There was a shudder, a flash, then a bright white plume of smoke as the air-to-sea missile rocketed from under the Lear's fuselage toward the helpless pleasure vessel. The missile disappeared for several seconds, and Jones began to wonder whether he had missed when the *Atlantic Star* exploded in a giant fireball that illuminated the calm, black ocean for over five miles. Within minutes, the fire extinguished and the two sections of the vessel's sleek hull sank into the frigid waters of the Atlantic Ocean as if it had never existed.

43 FRIEND

Max MacLean seldom personally greeted guests to his palatial sandblasted glass and polished aluminum aerie atop Beverly Hills. But Abraham Cohen was family.

MacLean helped Cohen out of the rear seat of the Bentley in which Maxfield had collected the elderly man at his office on Rodeo Drive not more than two miles away. "I'm so happy you came."

"I'm always happy to see you, Maximillian," Cohen said, clutching MacLean's forearm, looking intently into his eyes. "I could have driven, you know. I do still drive. And why all this?" he waved at the two *soldati* who stood near the front of the marble steps, dressed in black from head to toe, compact Heckler & Koch MP10 submachineguns drawn, eyes alert.

"A lot has happened since we last spoke. Let's go inside, shall we?" MacLean ushered Cohen through the resplendent entryway and into the small elevator hidden behind an alcove.

Together they ascended to the second floor. MacLean led him into his office, blinds still drawn. "Please have a seat. Can I get you something? Tea? Coffee?"

Abraham sighed as he ensconced himself in the supple black leather of one of the Roche Bobois sofas. "Tea would be lovely, thank you. But it looks like you've been drinking something stronger." He picked up one of the empty bottles of Grey Goose from the squat glass block coffee table.

"I'm through with vodka for a while." MacLean rang Maxfield for tea, sat on the sofa opposite Cohen.

"What the hell is going on, Maximillian? I've never seen you like this. Scared. Paranoid. Hung over. What happened? Where is Claire?"

"She's under guard. Where it's safe."

"Under guard? By those goons you have out there?"

"Soldiers of a family loyal to my father."

"God rest his soul," Cohen whispered. "I'm sorry, Maximillian, but I don't understand. How bad can—"

"The people, the interests you warned me about. They killed Dan Wenzel."

"Daniel? Daniel is dead? Oh my God."

"It was my fault."

Cohen looked up, stared at MacLean, puzzled.

"I let him fly to Washington. I knew it was dangerous but he insisted on going. I could have….The plane he was on exploded."

"My God."

"I could have stopped him."

"Could have, would have. We do the best with what we have, Maximillian. So did you. No more, no less." Abraham sighed, far wearier than curious. "God writes straight with curved lines, Maximillian. If Daniel died, it was God's will, as difficult as it may be for us to accept."

"It doesn't make it any easier."

"No. It doesn't."

"Did you read about the Senate aide who was killed in Washington?"

"By the drug dealers?"

"Not drug dealers. The same people who killed Dan Wenzel. And an innocent farmer in Arkansas before that. And nearly killed two of my close associates."

"Why?"

"I decided to mine in Arkansas."

"I told you to—"

MacLean raised his palms. "I know you did. You were right, and I was wrong. But it happened, and it continues. That's why I had to ask you to come here. I'm a prisoner in my own house." Maxfield opened the door and entered with a silver tray heaped with tea and coffee service and homemade cookies and scones.

"Thank you. We'll take it from here."

"Yes, thank you very much Maxfield," Cohen said, giving in to his sweet tooth and retrieving a powdered sugar almond scone from the pile of pastries.

"Will there be anything else, sir?" asked Maxfield, eyeing

the two empty bottles of vodka.

"Please see to it we're left alone."

"Yes, sir. I shall, sir." He bowed slightly and removed the bottles of vodka. Maxfield was nothing if not a stickler for tidiness.

MacLean waited for him to shut the door before continuing. "I'm not going to give you any details. They wouldn't help you, and they would put you at greater risk."

"Who would harm me if I knew the details?"

MacLean stared at the elderly man for a moment before answering. "Waterboer."

Cohen nodded slowly, in reproach. "So it *is* Waterboer behind all this." He replaced the Limoges porcelain cup on the table. "I had suspected as much, but was never certain. Max, you've got to stop. Whatever it is, you've got to stop."

"It's too late. It's not just Waterboer now. The—" He stopped himself. "U.S. government agencies are involved. Foreign governments are involved. Political movements. This monster has a life of its own now."

Abraham responded to MacLean's agitated fear with total calm. "It often does and Waterboer invariably wins. Still, the monopoly is predictable. If you get out of the way, you don't get hurt. Waterboer doesn't look for vengeance or retribution the way some people do. They're far too organized and focused on the perpetuation of their diamond monopoly. Stop threatening the monopoly, and Waterboer will stop threatening you. It's that simple."

"Simple enough. But like I said, it's not just Waterboer anymore. Too many others are involved for it just to stop. It's got to burn itself out."

"More reason for you to stop."

MacLean stood. "No. Threats don't work well with me. If they had just come to me with a simple business deal: here is what we want, here is what we're willing to pay, here are some rare beautiful diamonds. That I could respect. After looking into their history and business practices, I would probably have agreed, provided the money offered was sufficient. After all, I've never been interested in competing with Waterboer in the sale of diamonds, in threatening their monopoly. I'm interested in beauty. Beauty and simple business."

"So? Make them an offer."

MacLean shook his head. "No. We're past that point. Things have gone much too far for offers. If Dan was still alive. If Claire and I weren't trapped in this palatial prison, hiding from the outside world. If my associates weren't being hunted. Maybe. But not now. It's too late now."

"Then what?" Cohen sighed loudly, obviously exasperated. "Maximillian. You're not being reasonable. I don't know if it's fear or sadness or remorse. Or booze. But you're being unreasonable." He leaned forward. "I advised you to abandon your Arkansas mine. You refused. You received threats. You refused to stop. Wenzel was murdered. Now I'm telling you you can't win against Waterboer, and you're still not listening."

MacLean stared at the floor, his head in his hands.

"Ah! It's no use! Why am I even here? You won't even listen to me!" Cohen stood and paced the shuttered office.

"I *am* listening, Abraham, but I won't back down."

Cohen stopped, turned. "Then why did ask me to come here? What do you *want*, Maximillian?"

MacLean lifted his unshaven face from his hands and gazed at Cohen's pale blue eyes. "I want you to tell me how to destroy Waterboer."

"Destroy Waterboer? *Destroy Waterboer*?" Cohen touched his temples, shook his head. "You're *meshuggene. Destroy Waterboer?* Waterboer survived wars, corporate insurrections, radical political regimes of all stripes, a multitude of restrictive legal structures. Not only survived but prospered."

"Just hear me out. Please."

Cohen sat on the edge of the sofa, shaking his head.

"At first I wanted to go against Piet Slythe personally. Hurt him. Hurt his friends. Hurt his family."

Cohen wagged a finger. "Don't become what your father worked so hard to protect you against."

"I was furious, reacting, not thinking. Hurting Slythe personally would only make things worse. And if Slythe were eliminated, someone else would take his place. Waterboer *is* the diamond trade. The Slythes are Waterboer. Hurt the diamond trade and you hurt Waterboer. Hurt Waterboer and you hurt Slythe."

"And?"

"I can't actually destroy Waterboer, I know that. But how can I damage the diamond trade to the extent I hurt Slythe? Big and *hard*. That's what I want to know."

"At least it's more realistic than wanting to destroy Waterboer."

"How do I do it, Abraham?"

Cohen poured himself a fresh cup of tea, added some sugar, and stirred the contents. He was a man who thought before speaking. Silence did not intimidate him. He remained silent long enough for MacLean to light, smoke, and crush out a cigarette.

"Many people have tried to destroy Waterboer in the past. All have failed. The key to Waterboer is that it's a monopoly. The company prevents competition, as you know, by all means available. But because it's a monopoly, it isn't equipped to compete. As able as it is to crush competition, it is also extremely susceptible to competition."

"I'm afraid I don't follow."

"Look at Ford. Ford makes cars. Some of its cars are very good. They compete well. People buy that model instead of a similar model made by another car company. But other models aren't as good. People buy the competition's models instead. What happens? Ford increases advertising, gives rebates, improves the model. Ford is prepared to compete. Waterboer isn't. If someone sells a more competitive diamond in high quantity, Waterboer isn't set up to compete."

"But Waterboer can't improve on its product. It sells diamonds. Unless it cuts them better or sells better quality stones, it can't improve its product."

"The only way for another company to compete with Waterboer is on price, not on product. But Waterboer can sell its diamonds so cheaply it would make any competing company unprofitable."

"But if it lowers the price on diamonds so much, wouldn't it have a difficult time raising prices after it had frozen out the competitor?"

"That's the weakness. It can never let any other company sell diamonds without some kind of price agreement. Demand would be severely impacted by a drop in price. That's Waterboer's Achilles Heel."

"You lost me again."

"If someone sold diamonds a little more cheaply than Waterboer, it would hurt Waterboer a little. If someone sold a massive amount of diamonds at dirt-cheap prices over a very short time, it would devastate Waterboer. It's Waterboer's greatest fear. That's why it controls and has always controlled production and the number of diamonds sold so fiercely."

"You're talking about dumping. Flooding the market with diamonds. I've heard that theory before. Hasn't that been tried?"

"It's been discussed many times, yes, but never actually attempted. Before anyone flooded the market, Waterboer made them an offer they couldn't refuse and bought the mine, or its production, or paid the mine owner not to produce. Or forced the government to ban the mine or repress its owners. Every new mine gets the same treatment."

"That's production. What about supply? Are there any stockpiles that could be dumped on the market? That would achieve the same result, wouldn't it?

"There are, and it would."

"Who has them?"

"Waterboer has the largest stockpiles, of course. Except for exceptionally large and flawless diamonds or colored diamonds, diamonds are quite common, so Waterboer sells only a fraction of its production. It can't shut production down because the mines' owners couldn't resist the urge to produce secretly. The rest it stockpiles. In many different locations, to prevent theft. No one knows where exactly."

"Who else has a stockpile? The United States?"

"Not really. The Department of Defense maintains a strategic diamond reserve for defense purposes. For optics, grinding bits, that sort of thing. And industrial diamonds can be manufactured synthetically now. So the stockpile is small, of industrial quality, not gem quality.

"Russia had a stockpile, but it sold it to Waterboer in 1990. Another example of Waterboer getting scared and paying high prices to prevent anyone from flooding the market. There are rumors Russia didn't sell its entire stockpile. That the KGB and other hard-liners saw the writing on the wall, realized they would soon be out of power, and hid the remaining stockpile. The same rumor also has it that the remaining stockpile contained large quantities of extremely valuable large, colored, and high-quality stones. Anyway, these are rumors only."

"Still, if the rumors persist, maybe—"

Cohen shook his head. "There are rumors about UFOs, but Washington hasn't been overrun by aliens with laser beams."

"Anyone else?"

"The Vatican is rumored to have a diamond stockpile. But the Vatican is so old and secretive that there are rumors about everything involving it. Besides, although the conventional belief is that the Vatican is swimming in riches, it's true about real estate and art only. But the Church is cash poor. Where would it get the kind of money to amass a diamond stockpile? And for what purpose?"

"Anyone else? Any other rumors?"

"Anyone else, no. Any other rumors, yes. King Solomon's Mines, the Lost City of Eldorado, Atlantis."

"Any Russian stockpile would be too difficult to tackle without U.S. government juice. The last time I tried to deal with the feds, Dan Wenzel was murdered and I lost a forty-million-dollar jet. Do you know anyone at the Vatican?" He placed his palms forward. "I know, I know. It's just a rumor. But assume for a moment there is a Vatican stockpile. Do you know anyone inside?"

"I know the cardinal in charge of the Vatican committee for dialogue between Jews and Catholics. I spoke before the committee after my testimony against the Swiss banks. We became friends. I asked him about the rumored stockpile. He laughed. Other than him, your connections in those circles are far better than mine."

"I know the Archbishop of Los Angeles. He's a member of the Curia. A powerful one at that. The 'Hollywood Cardinal,' the others call him. But anyone in the Church who would know about a stockpile would have to be much deeper inside. In Rome."

Cohen eyed him probingly. "You're not really thinking of going to Rome, are you?"

MacLean smiled. "Rome? I can't even leave the house to buy the paper. But I do know someone in Italy who—"

The telephone rang. Not the main house line that Maxfield answered, but the office line. Only those closest to MacLean or in the intelligence services had the number.

"Excuse me, Abraham." MacLean leaned toward the side table, picked up the green Bang & Olufsen receiver. "MacLean."

"Max. Channy." André "Channy" Chanzeransky was the general manager of MacLean's Star casino in Atlantic City, one of the few employees who could get away with calling MacLean by his first name. "I have horrible news."

"It seems to be following me these days. What is it?"

"The *Atlantic Star* just sank."

"It what?" MacLean shouted and stood. "What about the passengers and crew?"

"The Coast Guard just sent a rescue operation to the area, but it doesn't look good. The boat was six hundred miles off the coast. The waters are very cold."

"How did—"

"They don't know how it happened. She left yesterday night, taking some Mexican high rollers for a two day cruise. Her mayday signal didn't say what happened, just that she was sinking. I hired a private rescue team to join the official search. If there are any survivors, we'll find them."

"Keep me posted, Channy. Every hour on the hour."

"You bet. I'm sorry, Max."

MacLean replaced the receiver slowly and turned to Cohen, smiling. "Things are looking up."

"What is it?"

"One of my casino's yachts just sank in the Atlantic."

"Sank? You're happy because your yacht sank? You're completely *meshuggune*!"

"First the jet, now one of the boats. About $60 million lost in ten days. I bet the boys at Lloyd's have my face on a dart board."

44 TRANSFER

Atlantic Star Lifeboat
Atlantic Ocean
697 miles east of Atlantic City
12:45 A.M.

The plan had worked.

By the time the missile plowed into the *Atlantic Star*, the lifeboat was far away. Too far away for the lifeboat passengers to see the yacht sink, close enough to hear and see the fuel tank explode. The fireball illuminated the sky and sea for miles but did not last long. Four hours later, they were approximately a hundred miles away. Carlton could see the people in the lifeboat clearly in the light of the moon. To call the vessel a lifeboat did not do it justice. This was a twenty-foot enclosed motorboat with room for ten persons and full navigational lights and equipment. Commander Ramey was at the helm and kept the motorboat heading due east at a steady twenty-five knots. Carlton stood next to him, with Erika snuggling against him. Despite the fact they were shielded from the exterior elements, it was cold. To minimize the chances of being discovered, Ramey had turned on neither the running lights nor the emergency radio beacon.

"If I haven't thanked you enough, Jack, thank you."

"Don't thank me, Pat. Thank Mr. MacLean. He's the one who allowed this insanity."

Pink climbed on deck from the cabin below. "I can't figure it out. How the hell did they find us? We didn't communicate outside of normal boating channels, and they couldn't have just—"

Carlton turned to Pink. "Actually, we did."

"What do you mean?" Pink stared at him, on the thin edge between praise and reproach.

"Jack and I arranged it. I knew they'd keep following us. And between the FBI and the other agencies Fress was tracking us, it was only a matter of time before they found us. So I decided to make their kill as easy as possible: I contacted MacLean to thank him. As I figured, the FBI or NSA or whoever else was listening to MacLean's conversation heard the call. They must've tracked us down that way."

"But how will—"

"Before I called MacLean, Jack arranged for a pick-up with another of MacLean's ships, a cargo ship traveling from New York to Europe."

Pink stared at him in silence while the boat gently rocked in the Atlantic swells.

"Why didn't you tell me?" Pink demanded, more hurt than angry, gripping a rail for support.

"Like you did back at Langley, I had to make sure you were legit. If you were working with Fress, he wouldn't have killed you. So now we're safe because Fress thinks we're at the bottom of the sea and we know you're clean."

Pink turned to Erika. "You knew?"

"Sorry, Tom."

Pink turned back to Carlton. "I don't know whether to kiss you or punch you."

Carlton smiled. "Her I'll kiss. A handshake from you will do."

Several minutes later, Ramey pointed starboard. "Here she comes." He announced. "Right on time." Carlton could not see what the man was pointing at, then finally noticed faint running lights in the distance. The running lights grew steadily until the outline of a behemoth cargo ship grew clear. Using Morse code, Ramey flashed a small handheld spotlight at the vessel several times. After several tries, the vessel responded in kind. Ramey moved out of the vessel's path, followed on its port side as it slowed to a stop over the distance of nearly one mile. Bright lights illuminated the cargo ship's superstructure. Giant white letters spelled CLAIRE SAILING on its dark hull.

It was clear the *Claire*'s crew was highly experienced. Within five minutes, they had transferred all the passengers onto the cargo vessel and hoisted the lifeboat on deck. The *Claire*'s enormous dual screws started back up and began to push the cargo vessel forward on its original course, heading northeast.

Christened in New England twenty years earlier, the *Claire* was a thirty-thousand-ton vessel based in New York harbor. It plied the Atlantic, serving as a general transport ship from the United States to Europe for gastronomic delicacies wherever good deals could be found based on MacLean's agents' purchases.

The great majority of the *Claire* was devoted to cargo space, refrigerated and unrefrigerated, above deck and below deck. Despite its function as a cargo ship, MacLean believed that a happy crew made a good crew. The stern portion of the vessel contained the crew's quarters, cabins for occasional passengers, the galley, a dining room, a gymnasium, a small library, and a small theater room with satellite television and an extensive DVD collection. Instead of being shown directly to their cabins, Carlton, Erika, and Pink were ushered into a large wood-paneled dining room on the top floor dominated by a long, varnished wood dining table. A portly man in his sixties wearing a spinnaker-sized white apron stained from years of cooking greeted them enthusiastically.

"Ah, my dinner guests! Good evening. Please come in." He pumped each person's hand vigorously. "I am Paul DesJardins, ship's cook. I was told you were coming, but only two hours ago. I wasn't able to prepare anything very interesting, but I hope you will enjoy what I have prepared. Sit down, sit down. Please sit down.

"For dinner tonight, we have a lobster, crab, and tomato cream bisque, followed by cornish hens stuffed with lemon and rosemary accompanied by steamed baby vegetables with a vegetable broth reduction. After that a three-lettuce salad with…"

After the meal, Carlton lit a Padron 3000 maduro cigar with his DOJ Zippo lighter and turned to Pink.

"Well, I agree with your conclusion about your material on Pyashinev. A road map to the diamond stockpile it sure ain't. And it doesn't really tell us much else except the guy had one hell of an apartment." Carlton blew a large cloud of smoke upward. "Except his obsession with boats."

"His obsession with boats?" Pink cocked his head. "What do

you mean?"

"Yeah. Didn't you notice that? Maybe I'm focusing on it because I'm Navy, but the guy was nuts about boats." He waved the inventory of Pyashinev's apartment. "He had a whole library full of books on boats and a virtual art gallery of boat paintings and photos, and models all over his walls and tables."

"I didn't really focus on that, but okay, so he was obsessed with boats. What follows?"

"Well, it wasn't a sentimental obsession about life at sea. I mean, the bio doesn't say he was Russian navy or merchant marine. Still, he was crazy about boats. And—" Carlton half-lifted himself out of his chair. "Wait a minute. Read his note to me over again."

"Russia, third layer. Must not let them get it."

"I wonder if there is a boat called 'Russia.' Or—what's the word in Russian?"

"*Rossiya*."

"I'm sure a lot of Russian boats are named *Rossiya*, Pat. Just like there are a lot of boats named the America and the California."

"You think the *Rossiya* in Pyashinev's note was a boat?" asked Erika.

"Why not? Let's look at what we know." He touched off the fingers of his left hand. "One, Pyashinev had authority over the Russian diamond stockpile. Two, he wanted to keep the stockpile secret from the Orlov government. Three, since the Orlov government doesn't know about the stockpile, he did keep it a secret. Four…" He paused to clear his train of thought. "Four, he was a boat nut. Five, he left a cryptic note about not letting 'them' get the '*Rossiya*' right before he died." He continued with his right thumb. "Six, as sure as God made little green apples, like you said there must be boats named *Rossiya*. Seven, based on what you told us during the past two days and we've got here, there are no other clues. "It's not like we're choosing this clue and excluding others. After days of research, this is what we've got, right? And it looks as though it's all the GRV got, too."

"Yeah. But there's got to be a harborful of boats named *Rossiya*. What do you suggest, track them down on the high seas, board them with eye patches and cutlasses?"

"It's worth exploring. Besides, it's not like we have any other leads."

Pink rose to stretch his long legs. "Well there's only one way to find out from here."

Pink turned on his titanium Macintosh G4 and plugged in the *Claire's* telephone wire via a small encryption device.

"You're not going to call Langley on that thing are you?"

"Well, I'm not ordering books on Amazon."

"Tom, Fress has eyes and ears all over the place. That's how they found us on the *Star*. He'll trace—"

"No, he won't. The National Security Agency is powerful, but it's not omnipotent. I'm routing it through Saunders' system, then through the L.A. office. And it's encrypted. Forbes and I encrypted our systems before I left. We're the only ones with this encryption code. Highest level CIA code. Generated by random atmospheric patterns. See?" Pink lifted the telephone cord. Before connecting to the rear computer port, it passed through a small brushed aluminum box the size of Carlton's battered Zippo lighter, with which he was relighting his Padron maduro.

"Right."

Pink engaged the modem and waited as it dialed the CIA computer database number and automatically fed it the multiple identification codes and passwords required before the laptop screen showed the CIA computer system was ready. He typed his search command.

Naval vessels (military and civil!) and (Russia! and Union of Soviet Socialist Republics and USSR) and !Rossiya!

Over four hundred miles to the west in Northern Virginia, now armed with the command, the seven liquid nitrogen–cooled Cray supercomputers—the "Seven Dwarfs"—rifled through the Agency's massive electronic database. Seconds later, the screen showed the search had obtained forty pages of information. Pink hit the print command and disengaged the telephone connection just as the Hewlett Packard laser printer started producing a hardcopy of the research. "Here we go."

Pink collected the pages, bent over them, and began to read.

"Let me know what you find. I'll be on the bridge."

"I'll just follow the stench. Now stop infecting me with that cancer stick and let me read."

Pink waved away the billows of blue cigar smoke theatrically and began to pore over the pages, highlighting the important information with a yellow fluorescent marker.

A half hour later, Pink walked onto the bridge, handed the sheaf of papers to Carlton. "You were right."

Carlton read the highlighted sections. "It looks like there are twenty *Rossiyas*."

"Eighteen have sunk or been decommissioned."

"The other two?"

"One has been on duty with the Cuban navy since before Chernenko. The other is on active duty escorting cruise ships through Arctic ice floes out of Murmansk."

Carlton paused and stared at Pink for several seconds. "Murmansk? That's where Pyashinev—"

"Bingo."

"So, what next?"

"It's obvious, isn't it? We've got to get to Murmansk."

"Murmansk? In this boat?" Carlton reflected about it a moment. "It's a cargo boat. Not a bad cover."

"And Murmansk is a commercial port in addition to being a naval base."

"Murmansk it is, then. You do know this is insane, don't you?"

"Yep."

"But it's even more insane if we don't try, I suppose."

45 ORDER

The Order was founded in the early 1500s to provide intellectual and doctrinal shock troops to a Catholic Church unprepared to stem the spreading influence of the Protestant Reformation. Handpicked for their brilliance, talent, and devotion, its priest members were educated far beyond the level of other priests and unwaveringly obedient to the *pontifex maximus*—the pope. In addition to the vows of celibacy, poverty, and chastity that priests generally took prior to receiving Holy Orders, each member of the Order also took a vow of obedience to the pope. For the first two hundred years after its founding, the Order's leaders and members remained obedient, and a special relationship evolved between the papacy and the Order. In doing so, the Order played an important, if not pivotal, role in the education, politics, and science of nearly every power—and powerful figure—in Europe and America. The Order founded and ran schools, universities, research centers, observatories, libraries, and hospitals. Its priests taught, wrote, persuaded, advised.

But after two hundred years of total devotion to the papacy, in the 1700s, the Order began to turn against its master and closest ally. Imperceptibly at first, then rapidly. Subtly, then blatantly. To such an extent that the Order's leader, the Father General, the only cardinal in the Order, who wore a black cassock in imitation of the Order's sixteenth-century canonized founder, was often referred to as the "black pope." Many of the Order's priests did not stray, but those who did strayed far. In the late twentieth century, believing violent retribution was the solution to dictatorial oppression, members of the Order took up arms in support of liberation theology, the religious movement with an appealing name but based largely on communism. Certain members of the

Order went so far as to become high-ranking ministers in brutal communist regimes. Others embraced the human-centered New Age movement. Finally, they attacked the very basis and legitimacy of the papacy. Nothing short of blasphemy for a formerly obedient Catholic order.

The relationship between the papacy and the Order was now one of undeclared yet outright war. The battle continued nearly unchecked until it slammed into the doctrinal and intellectual fortress of the Polish Pontiff. Though the Order wielded tremendous power, so did John Paul II, the most traveled, most famous, and most beloved pope in recent history, backed by the historical power of two thousand years of uninterrupted papal reign. As a man who witnessed the inhuman evils of Nazism and communism in his Polish homeland, the pope equated the war against the Order with the Church's war against communism. He understood the intellectual bases of the war, joined the fight, and won decisive battles. Ranks were reorganized, undesirable programs terminated, unchecked influence curtailed, heretics silenced, doctrine corrected. There was, however, one facet of the Order the papacy failed to grind: finance. So finance was the aspect on which the Order's Father General—Cardinal Pedro Altiplano—focused.

A consummate player in the Roman Curia, Pedro Altiplano was a master of subterfuge and obfuscation. He had the same goal as the Order's leaders for the past two centuries, particularly after the Second Vatican Council of the 1960s: the destruction of the papacy. But by the time Altiplano acceded to the post of Father General, the Polish Pontiff had succeeded in closing nearly all avenues of battle open to the Order, except for finance. Years before he became Father General, Altiplano realized that, technically, over $1 billion flowed through the Order's coffers annually in the form of private donations to the Order's legion schools, universities, and hospitals. As head of the Order, Altiplano controlled those funds, but only theoretically. In practice, the funds were solicited, obtained, invested, and disbursed by individual principals, chancellors, and chief executive officers of those institutions. Altiplano's plan was simple: for the good of the Order, he directed all of the Order's funds channeled to a central depository and from there disbursed according to need only upon his consent. The plan had great PR value: take from the rich and give to the poor. Only a handful of the Order opposed his plan. In fact, what happened was quite different from the publicly lobbied plan. By taking personal control of the Order's global finances, Altiplano had possession of funds he could use to wage the Order's war against the papacy. He was sufficiently wise to recognize he could not win against the Polish Pontiff in a test of wills within the Vatican curia. But if he played his cards right, Altiplano believed he could influence key voting members of the College of Cardinals when it assembled in a Conclave to elect the Polish Pontiff's successor, the cardinal who would be elected to stand in the shoes of the fisherman and first pope, Peter.

He would use the successful formula of Washington special interests. He would promise to fund the pet projects of the key voting members of the College of Cardinals in exchange for their support of his chosen candidate: himself. Once elected pope, Altiplano would dismantle the papacy from within: by his own edicts.

But how would he transfer these funds to the key voting princes of the Church in an electronic day and age when flows of funds could be followed so easily? He would divert some of the funds in his newly acquired control into easily concealable, movable, salable goods.

Diamonds.

He quickly placed his plan into motion. Enormous sums of the new central depository funds controlled by Altiplano were siphoned off to secret offshore accounts. The monies were replaced by monies borrowed against the Order's gold-plated name at high rates of interest. Promissory notes were secretly executed and delivered. Obedient agents of the Order sworn to secrecy under penalty of excommunication by the Father General himself were dispatched to purchase diamonds outside the scrutiny of the Waterboer monopoly. Diamonds were deposited in one of Italy's best known banking institutions, whose chief financial officer's favorite nephew Altiplano allowed to become a priest of the Order despite his obsessive penchant for conquests of members of the opposite sex. Ledgers were falsified.

But Altiplano based his plan on flawed assumptions. One, that enough key voting cardinals would accept such a bribe to influence a papal conclave. Although many religious projects were in dire need of funds and the salaries of the princes of the Church were a pittance, these men had not become priests for pecuniary gain, and in most cases the great influence they wielded served as a counterweight to such low remuneration. Two, that the international flow of diamonds would not be discovered by the Institute for Works of Religion, also known as the Vatican Bank.

46 PREPARATIONS

Claire Sailing
Barents Sea
530 miles east of Kirkenes, Norway
2:11 P.M.

The *Claire* forged toward the icy port of Murmansk at twenty knots; nearly five hundred nautical miles a day. Most of that time was spent collecting information on the icebreaker *Rossiya*.

Together with the numbers and types of boats registered under the Russian name "Rossiya," Pink's computer downloaded search contained all available information in the CIA database on the ship, including schematics and press articles about the Russian nuclear icebreaker. Fortunately, the CIA had a great deal of information on the *Rossiya*. Carlton, Erika, and Pink pored through the information they had printed from Pink's laptop for hours. DesJardins kept them well-fueled with coffee brewed in his U.S. Navy tradition, black with a pinch of salt and so strong its good-natured brewer swore he once had made a metal spoon float in it. Carlton likened it to jet fuel. But it worked.

The first important information they discovered was the *Rossiya*'s regular route. If all proceeded as planned, the icebreaker would soon depart from Murmansk and power northwesterly, later clearing a safe passage in the thick ice near the North Pole for a Norwegian cruise liner.

After breaking for another of DesJardins' sumptuous lunches, Erika went to the stateroom to review some of the documents in quiet. Carlton and Pink expended their tensions and fears inventorying and assembling the equipment MacLean had provided to the *Claire* by helicopter long before the *Star* sank. They had worked for over six hours when Erika found them in one of the storage holds.

"I think I figured out where Pyashinev hid the diamonds," she announced.

They congregated in the dining room, where the documents were spread out. Commander Ramey joined them.

"I was reading some of the general information on icebreakers, but there was no mention of the *Rossiya* except a few cursory lines. Then I found this."

She heaved a thick sheaf of printed pages atop a chart and opened it to a dog-eared page. "This article was written in 1990, around the time the *Rossiya* was built and—"

Carlton stopped her with a raised hand, turned to Pink. "Wait a minute. Wasn't 1990 when Russia transferred its diamond stockpile to Waterboer?"

"Correct."

"Further likelihood the diamonds are aboard, then," Erika underscored. "But listen, that's not all. This says that the *Rossiya* was the first Russian icebreaker to have triple hulls."

"Triple hulls. Okay. So?" Pink wondered, not seeing any relevant connection.

"So, I think that's what the note means. 'Russia, third layer. Must not let them get it.' Pyashinev must have been referring to the hull's third layer."

"Makes sense," Pink agreed.

"Plus, remember Pyashinev was a boat nut," Carlton added. "So Pyashinev would have known about the new triple-hulled icebreaker in 1990."

"I hate playing devil's advocate," Pink said, "but aren't we grasping at straws here?"

"Grasping at straws is better than grasping at air," Erika responded, slightly frustrated.

"Maybe," Carlton admitted to Pink. "But I don't think so. One clue would be too little—the *Rossiya* being a boat, for example. But taken together, the name of the boat, the fact that its home port is Murmansk, where Pyashinev last stopped before his meeting with Waterboer, Pyashinev being a boat nut, the fact that the *Rossiya* was built in 1990, and the triple hull clue; too many clues to disregard the *Rossiya*."

"And if you had to hide that many diamonds, wouldn't triple hulls be a logical place?" Ramey ventured. "Remember, the diamonds would have to remain secret from everyone. The crew and all those performing inspections and maintenance." He opined, familiar with the intense maintenance naval vessels require.

"I suppose," Pink shrugged, still not convinced, but not having any other plausible conclusions.

"It's the best guess we've got. You'd make the U.S. Navy proud." Carlton kissed Erika on the cheek. She blushed immediately.

"Although..." Ramey's voice trailed as he thought.

"What's that?" Carlton asked.

"How long is she?"

"Five hundred feet."

"That's over a thousand feet of hulls to inspect," Ramey calculated, sucking in air. "Not to mention that the ship is over three or four stories tall. It's going to take a lot of looking."

Carlton winced. "Still, at least we know where to start."

"Assuming we find her," Ramey said. "From what you found, the *Rossiya* travels the area from Murmansk to Franz Josef Land. If she leaves Murmansk on schedule and keeps to her reported route, she'll be somewhere along here." He pointed to a two-hundred-mile region marked in red on the chart.

"That leaves a lot less for us to search than her entire twelve-hundred-mile route," Carlton said.

"Luckily more than half of that area is ice-locked," said Ramey. "She won't start icebreaking until the cruise ship arrives later in the day. They don't sail in those waters at night. If all goes according to plan, we should be in position in about fifteen hours."

"Which brings me to an important point." Carlton poured himself a cup of coffee. "We think we've figured out where the stockpile is hidden and where the *Rossiya* is at the moment. And we're almost there in person. But unless CIA plans to steal the diamonds once we get them—"

"If we get them," cautioned Pink.

"I don't see any reason not to ask for the Russian government's help. After all, it's their mess. But the problem is: who do we contact? Between Russkost and Waterboer, how do we know we'll be contacting someone who's clean? And even if we reach someone in their government who's clean, the information may leak. Then not only will we not prevent Waterboer from getting the diamonds, we'll be eliminated in the process."

"It depends on when Fress finds out," Pink responded. "If we communicate with the Russian government now and then contact Forbes or Saunders or whoever else right before the Russians send a team, there won't be enough time for Fress or Waterboer to send anyone.

"And I know who to call in their government that is most likely not involved with either Waterboer or Russkost."

"Who's that?"

"Yagoda. Lavrenti Yagoda. Heads up their military intelligence, the GRU. Forbes seems to trust him reasonably well. His name means 'blueberry' in Russian. Based on what I know of him, Yagoda has more to gain from Orlov and the current leadership than from Russkost. So he'll probably help us and retrieve the diamonds for Orlov rather than sell us out to Waterboer. Besides, he hates Russkost with a passion."

"Okay, then." He glanced at his watch. "Let's get the Blueberry out of bed."

47 GENERAL

His name was a cruel joke, thought Lavrenti Yagoda. A combination of the first name of Lavrenti Beria, Stalin's murderous head of the NKVD secret police, and the last name of Genrikh Yagoda, one of Beria's predecessors who carried out the first wave of Stalinist purges in the 1930s. Still, the stern man in his early sixties with close cropped gray hair was not unlucky. Yagoda had risen steadily through the ranks. Now a general, the head of the GRU had a hand in most military secrets and many non-military political ones as well. He drank little, worked hard, obtained results, and, despite turning a blind eye to several small-arms black marketeers to pay for the construction of his *dacha*, was uncorrupt. More than anything else, Yagoda was loyal. To his country and to his president.

He reflected on the telephone conversation he had just finished with the CIA deputy director of intelligence's point man on Russian diamond operations, Pink. For so long the secret Russian diamond stockpile had been somewhat of an urban legend among the intelligence services. Everyone had heard the rumor, but no one really believed it. Yagoda had serious doubts about its existence even after his initial conversation with Forbes several days ago. But now it appeared the diamond stockpile was not only real, but the Americans knew where it was and were sharing the information with his own government. The *Amerikanskii*, he reflected. The country may have been his political and military rival for a long time, but those who populated the upper levels of the DIA, CIA, and NSA he thought of as old friends. Still, the country across the Atlantic never ceased to amaze him. So rich that its intelligence services didn't even try to steal a diamond stockpile.

There was a loud knock at the door. "*Da!*" Yagoda answered.

A hard-looking man of forty appeared, breathing hard,

impeccably dressed in an olive green GRU uniform. The gold insignia on his shoulder bars identified him as a major. "Major Gerasimov reporting as ordered, *tovarish* general." He saluted crisply and replaced his arm by his side only after Yagoda saluted him in return.

"Yuri Nikolaievitch. Thank you for coming so quickly."

"I came as quickly as possible, *tovarish* general."

Yagoda pointed to a large map of the coast north of Murmansk. A red line drawn with a marker pen showed the *Rossiya*'s trajectory. "Your assessment?"

"Based on what you've told me, *tovarish* general, the mission could be accomplished with ten men, but twenty would be better. We could field the team with one of the submarines, but speed is more important than stealth. Helicopters would be fastest, but the *Rossiya* is too far even for our longest range helos. The only other solution is two high-speed patrol boats carrying ten men each, the *Kirov* and the *Omsk*. The boats are already here." He pointed at one of the naval bases in Murmansk. "I have already selected the men."

"I leave that to your judgment. How quickly can you secure the *Rossiya*?"

"Since this is a purely GRU operation, we can't use regular navy personnel. The men I need are far from Murmansk, unfortunately. We can all be assembled in Murmansk within ten hours. To make things faster, we will carry our own equipment. *Kirov* and *Omsk* will be fueled and ready. I've checked the present state of the ice floes. From the time of departure, ETA at the *Rossiya* should not be more than eight hours. So approximately eighteen hours from the time you give me the word, *tovarish* general. If the weather doesn't worsen."

"*Ochen harasho*. There is one more thing you must know before you go, Yuri Nikolaievitch. I am ordering you to secure the *Rossiya*, but I didn't tell you why."

"It is not my place to quest—"

Yagoda waved him off. "Are you aware of Leonid Pyashinev's disappearance?"

"*Da*, general. Colonel Kovanetz is investigating his case."

"*Da*. Pyashinev was in charge of the country's diamond production. He knew many things. One was the location of a diamond stockpile the former KGB and other *apparatchiki* hid before the collapse in 1991."

"I have heard of it, general. But I always thought it was a cold war rumor."

"Yes, so did I. But apparently it isn't. The American CIA tell us that the stockpile is on the *Rossiya*. All of our information tells us that they are correct."

Gerasimov's eyes grew wider. "The CIA?"

"Several of their agents will be on board when you arrive. I don't have the time to explain the details or the reasons why, but you are not to allow any harm to come to them. Guard the diamonds, but guard the Americans as well. Do you understand? In this matter, they are allies."

"They will be safe, *tovarish* general."

"*Ochen harasho*. Communicate with me as soon as you have secured the *Rossiya* and confirmed her cargo. I don't need to tell you how important this mission is to both of our careers, Major."

"*Da, tovarish* general. *Spaceba, tovarish* general." Gerasimov saluted, turned on his heel, and exited. He quickly descended the cold stone steps to the front of the massive building and walked to his car. Large snowflakes fell silently from the black sky. He started his drab Army Lada 4x4 and headed toward the military portion of Sheremetyevo II airport.

Halfway between headquarters and the airport, he realized he had forgotten to ask the size of the diamond stockpile. His team was not directed to move the diamonds, but circumstances might require it. He had to be prepared for every contingency. He dialed Yagoda's office, then canceled the call. *He probably doesn't know. He didn't even know the stockpile existed until recently.* Gerasimov dialed another number instead. *The colonel will know. After all, he's in charge of the Pyashinev investigation. He's probably got the most information about the stockpile.*

"Kovanetz."

"Colonel Kovanetz. This is Major Gerasimov."

"*Da.*"

"Forgive me for calling you so late, *tovarish* colonel, but I need some information that I think you may have."

"Information about what?"

"About the Pyashinev diamond stockpile."

48   TRAINING

Volki Base
131 miles north of St. Petersburg
(formerly Leningrad)
Karelia, Russia
12:35 A.M.

Wrapped in a double-breasted olive green military parka and a fur hat, Ulianov listened to the snow as it crunched under his knee-high leather boots. He stared ahead at the forest of birch trees illuminated by brilliant field lamps, covered in recently fallen snow, stopped and fished a Kosmos cigarette out of a crumpled pack, and lit it with an aluminum lighter. The scratched metal and faded red enamel star reminded him of the past, when he and his fellow Spetsnaz soldiers assured the protection of Holy Mother Russia.

Russia was far from holy now, and more like a grandmother. But that would change soon. Until then, he and his Volki would have to wait. He fixed his gaze back on the birch forest, listened to the wind that wound like a sigh through the frozen forest. "So cold, so quiet," he muttered under his breath, exhaling smoke that crystallized into ice in the glacial air.

He and his Volki had moved from their base near Molotok's Siberian *dacha* to a closed airfield. Before the fall of the Soviet Union, one of the *krestnii otets* allied to Molotok and Russkost had been in charge of government warehouses. The new government had ejected him from his government post in 1992, but was unable to strip him of his power. Now he used his power to ensure that the Volki had a home here, among air hangars and warehouses converted into barracks. The base was sufficiently deep in the countryside not to attract attention, but its airfield allowed rapid transportation to St. Petersburg, Moscow, and Western Europe via helicopters and jet transports. Obtaining those aircraft had been the assignment of another pro-Russkost *krestnii otet*, who had caused them to vanish mysteriously from military air bases throughout Russia.

Ulianov was restless. His Volki would launch a series of operations against Russia's infrastructure and government over the next several weeks. The different planned operations didn't bother him. Those were all fixed operations. His men knew their objectives, from and to where they were going, and how they would escape. It was securing and transferring the diamond stockpile that bothered him. It was impossible for him to plan such an operation because he had no idea where the stockpile was or how it was protected, if at all. He had drafted several possible plans, providing different entry and exit strategies for each. Air, water, land. One involved stealing three Royal Navy jets from the Keflavik NATO air base. The already superbly trained Volki rehearsed each of the scenarios again and again, until they could perform their tasks half-asleep. But before any of the strikes against Russian infrastructure and the government could be put into action, his Volki had to locate, take possession, and transfer the diamonds to Waterboer. Absent those events, Russkost and the Volki would have insufficient funds to complete their strike. So the former *Spetsnaz* officer waited. To bleed away the frustration and restlessness, he worked his Volki hard, preparing, rehearsing, improving their plans, pushing, prodding, and coaxing improved performance.

A Lada 4x4 in snow camouflage roared above a small hill and slid to a halt near Ulianov. The driver saluted.

"*Tovarish* Colonel. You have an urgent telephone call, sir."

"Who is it?"

"He said his name was Kovanetz."

"Let's go." Ulianov hopped in. "*Skorie!*" Fast.

The driver gunned the 4x4 toward the headquarters building. Ulianov jumped out before the vehicle stopped and ran into the communications room. A lieutenant handed him a telephone handset.

"Ulianov."

"It's Kovanetz."

"I know that. What's the news? Are you encrypted?"

"No. It doesn't matter. I know where it is."

"*Ochen harasho!* Where?"

"I'm encrypting it now. I'll fax it in a few minutes. You'll have to move fast. You don't have much time."

"How much?"

"Not more than eighteen hours."

Captain Andrei Akronsef was enamored with the sea, and like many of his fellow countrymen, he possessed an equal affinity for the cold. It was natural for the tall, soft-spoken man of forty with thoughtful eyes to combine his two loves and find peace in his country's small fleet of icebreakers.

Akronsef loved the *Rossiya* nearly as much as the frozen sea that surrounded her. He walked outside the warm cabin and greeted members of his seventy-person crew, admiring the ship's bright red superstructure. The boat's design never ceased to amaze him. Icebreakers had improved dramatically since the first nuclear icebreaker *Lenin* began to patrol these same waters over thirty years ago. Powered by twin pressurized-water nuclear fission reactors, the *Rossiya*'s generators produced over 75,000 horsepower, more than enough to churn the frozen sea with its massive screw and propel the five-hundred-foot vessel through the open sea at twenty knots, through ice at three knots. Its twenty-inch-thick, cast-iron bow and seven-foot-steel "ice-knife" casing could slice through the average eleven feet of Arctic ice like so much warm butter.

Once the *Rossiya* departed from Murmansk, it navigated past the crowded shipping lanes that led in and out of the major port, and headed northwest toward the North Pole. They would not rendezvous with the Norwegian cruise ship until tomorrow, when they reached the ice packs. Akronsef scanned the gauges and blinking lights on the control panels. Satisfied with the status of the ship, he turned to his first officer. "You have the helm, Teodor Alexandrovich."

"Getting there is easy," Ulianov informed Molotok over the encrypted telephone line from the Mil Mi-8 helicopter. "We'll be there after the Americans but probably before the GRU. It's moving the diamonds that will be difficult."

"Waterboer will meet us wherever we tell them to. Use the *Pushkin*. It's coming back from Zemlya Franca Iosifa, isn't it?

No one will see it," stated Molotok, referring to the aging Delta-III class Russian navy submarine the Volki had purchased as scrap through one of their contacts less than one year ago and kept hidden well north of the Arctic Circle.

"The Americans and British are preparing for naval war games in the GIUK gap," replied Ulianov, referring to the Greenland–Iceland–United Kingdom gap through which all naval traffic from Russia's Northern ports must pass on its way to the North Atlantic. "It will be guarded even more than usual. There is no chance for the *Pushkin* to get through. It's too noisy. No. Wherever the drop-off is, it has to be away from there."

"Why not deliver the diamonds directly to Waterboer in England?"

"How?"

"What's the range of the jets we're stealing during their war games?"

"*Ochen harasho*, Molotok! That's brilliant. And it fits into the *Pushkin* strategy. We'll have them rendezvous with the *Pushkin* and fly directly to Waterboer in England. Their range isn't sufficient from Iceland, but the jets in the NATO exercise will refuel in mid-air along the way. It will be a challenge for them to transport the diamonds. We're still not sure how large the stockpile is, but I'll figure something out." Although Ulianov's leader wasn't a military man and drank too much, Molotok did have sporadic flashes of tactical insight.

"I'll contact the South African bloodsucker and find out where the pilots should meet his people."

"Only a few more hours, Molotok."

"The most dangerous ones."

49 DON

Rafaele Mazzara generally relished the roiling noise and dust of Palermo's business center. But on sweltering days like today, he welcomed the opportunity to leave his painstakingly restored office in the Banco Napolitana Lucchese and venture to the seaside, where soft breezes from the Tyrrhenian Sea cooled the coastline. The gentle wind pushed away the smog and dust. It left the heavy sunshine free to pound down from a cloudless azure sky.

Mazzara's metallic navy blue BMW 328 growled along the winding roads of the Sicilian countryside to the main entrance of the five-star Villa Igea Grand Hotel. The chauffeur walked to the rear passenger door, held it open for his boss.

As Mazzara walked up the massive stone steps into the ornate lobby, he spotted the men who pretended not to watch him. Two were positioned at the top of the hotel steps, others in the lobby and gardens of oleander and jasmine. Mazzara did not need directions to find the man who had summoned him. He was clearly indicated by a quartet of men standing around a lone table under the lazy shade of a large African palm. Despite the heat, Mazzara shivered as he saw the man at their center.

"Don Arcangelo," he said quietly, not wanting to attract attention. He smiled from fear, not delight.

A square-shouldered man with coarse skin, a pronounced aquiline nose, and unforgiving eyes stared at Mazzara. Mazzara felt himself being appraised as if for the first time by the man who controlled most of the agriculture, real estate, construction, and gambling in southern Italy and Sicily, not to mention drugs, prostitution, and immigrant slavery. Mazzara perspired uncomfortably.

"There is no need to whisper, *dottore*." Don Arcangelo smiled. "We are among friends here." He motioned toward the gardens with a flourish, then to a chair. "Please, *dottore*. Sit down." He swiveled toward a waiter who wisely stood several yards away. "Alfredo! Bring some Regaleali for the *dottore*. And cold, eh?" He wagged an index finger, then turned to Mazzara. "Thank you for coming, Rafaele."

Mazzara bowed his head slightly, his smile frozen. "It is my pleasure, Don Arcangelo."

"How are things progressing? Is your new office to your taste?"

"*Si, si. Grazie, grazie*, Don Arcangelo." He squeezed his fingers into a pinch. "Absolutely stunning. You are too kind, Don Arcangelo."

The don shrugged. "Friends must help each other, no?"

"*Certo, certo*, Don Arcangelo." Of course.

"But now that we are on the topic of friends helping one another, please tell me where we stand."

Mazzara reached for his attaché case nervously. A hairy hand shot out from behind him and immobilized his wrist. He winced at the excruciating pain.

"Enzo!" Arcangelo shouted. "*Pazzo!* What are you doing? Are you crazy? Don't you know who this is?" The hand immediately loosed its grip. "This is *il dottore* Mazzara. The director of the Banco Napolitana Lucchese. Eh?" He waved his hand gracefully as if conducting a subtle orchestra piece. "*Piano, piano.*" Arcangelo nodded apologetically at Mazzara. "Please forgive him. He gets carried away sometimes."

Mazzara caught his breath and massaged his hand. "Loyalty is important, Don Arcangelo. I am pleased that you are so well protected."

Arcangelo smiled.

"All I wanted to do was to show you the figures here." He pointed to the attaché case.

He waved him off. "No, no Rafaele. It is too nice an afternoon to spoil with charts. I trust you. Just tell me."

"As you wish, Don Arcangelo." He stopped while the waiter set a chilled glass of Regaleali on the table. Water beaded on the wine glass. Mazzara sipped a tiny amount. "Excellent. Thank you."

Arcangelo bowed his head.

"Things are going very well. Exactly as you planned. The money from each of your transactions was deposited into each account in the exact amount and at the exact time specified in each of the government restoration contracts. Only one more deposit remains to be made. That will occur next week."

"*Perfecto*. As always, your attention to detail is admirable." Mazzara beamed. "*Grazie*, Don Arcangelo."

"Tell me, Rafaele. You are nervous. What is troubling you?"

"I…Please forgive me, Don Arcangelo." He swallowed hard. "But you could have asked me this over the telephone. I…"

The don smiled. "You are an intelligent man. Don't worry. There is nothing wrong." Relief washed through Mazzara. Arcangelo could feel it. He enjoyed playing with men's minds in this way. Kindness created loyalty, but fear kept people from abandoning it. The ability to shift from kindness to fear and back was at the center of his power. "I needed to see you in person because I have a request."

"Of course, Don Arcangelo. Anything."

"I'm a little nervous about Orlando Leonida. Our mayor started small. By putting a few of my men in jail, here and there. For small offenses at first. Then for larger things. That is normal. I have to give him some victories, after all, to make him and the government look good. Frankly, he's doing me a service. Prison is a necessary education for my men. Like university for you professionals. There are things you simply cannot learn on the outside." He winked. "But lately, Leonida hasn't taken any action. *Niente*. I was amazed he didn't move to stop a small transaction we made last week, one I practically handed to his informer on a silver platter." He shook his head.

"Something isn't right. I think Leonida is planning something big. I don't know what it is, but this nose," he pointed to it, "never lies."

"What do you want me to do, Don Arcangelo? *Comanda me*."

"I want you to move the accounts from Palermo to Banco Napolitana Lucchese headquarters in Rome."

"Are you certain, Don Arcangelo?" His blood froze as soon as the words had left his mouth. It did not do to question the don.

Luckily for Mazzara, the don was in one of his pleasant moods. He nodded. "Yes. Immediately."

"As Don Arcangelo wishes. I will do it immediately." Mazzara got to his feet. The don waved him back down.

"Rafaele. What kind of a Sicilian are you? Finish your wine. Enjoy the afternoon. Look at this glorious sunshine." He spread his arms. "You can do it later today. Let us talk about more enjoyable things. How are your lovely wife and children?"

50 OPERATION

Claire Sailing
Barents Sea
421 miles northeast of Murmansk
6:32 A.M.

Despite the Arctic temperatures, Commander Ramey was sweating profusely. He wiped his brow and looked beyond the *Claire Sailing*'s darkened bow at the running lights of the Russian icebreaker. "All stop," he ordered.

Krebski reversed the screw, immobilized the ship. "All stop, sir."

"Very well." Ramey turned to Carlton and Erika. "It's a little past dawn. We'll stop here and let the *Rossiya* come to us. Otherwise our heading away from Murmansk will attract attention."

Later in the day, the two Russian navy patrol boats carrying Major Gerasimov's GRU advance team—the *Kirov* and the *Omsk*—sliced through the glacial water of the Barents Sea toward the *Rossiya* at fifty knots.

"*Skorie, skorie!*" Faster, faster.

"This is as fast as we can push them, major!" The lieutenant at the helm of the lead patrol boat *Kirov* informed his CO, major Gerasimov. "They'll overheat if we try to go any faster."

Gerasimov recalculated their ETA a fourth time. Three hundred nautical miles. Another six hours. The Americans will be there in three. Hopefully the diamonds and the Americans will survive until we get there. Again he thought of contacting Akronsef, the *Rossiya*'s captain, and again he nixed the idea. There was no telling what the man's reaction would be to Americans boarding a Russian nuclear icebreaker. And Yagoda had been crystal clear: no harm must come to the Americans.

That evening on the *Claire Sailing*, Carlton woke from a short nap. It was eerily quiet. He walked through the cold hallway and poured two cups of coffee from the galley, then walked up to Pink's stateroom. He knocked and entered. Pink was snoring deeply, slumped over his desk. Carlton shook his shoulder.

Pink jerked up, startled. "What? What is it? What?"

"Time to make the call."

Pink glanced at his watch. "Right."

"Here," said Carlton, handing him a cup of coffee.

"Thanks." He took a sip. "Aaah. Nectar of the gods." He pressed a random key on his laptop, woke it from sleep mode, and entered his password.

July 4, 1776.

"Encryption and voice filters are on. For what good that'll do. Calling the Company computers is one thing, but speaking with Forbes—that's way more simple for NSA to track down."

An electronic fuzz sounded over the speaker, soon replaced by the sound of a ringer on the other end.

"Randall Forbes."

"Mr. Forbes. Pat Carlton and Tom Pink," announced Carlton, relishing the shock he was certain jolted through Forbes' body.

"Pat Car— You're *alive*? Where are you?"

"Never mind. Just please listen caref—"

"You're encrypted, but you're not secure."

"We realize that, sir," Pink replied.

"Then what are you—"

"Just please listen," Carlton announced. "I'll speak for myself because I can't speak for Pink here. But it was your idea to send us on this suicide mission, not mine. And now that I'm here, thinking that we found what we're looking for, we've got no way out. None. We're up shit creek without a paddle. Do you understand?"

There was a slight pause. "What do you have in mind?"

"I'll leave that to you. The Russians are sending a team out to meet us, so I think it would be appropriate to have some good old American flag-waving going on to show the Russian team that we're not expendable. Anyway, you obviously have a terrific imagination. I'm certain you'll think of something. Pink told me that you're a man of your word. Do we have your word?"

"You do."

"Are you triangulating our coordinates?"

"I am."

"Good." Carlton terminated the connection.

"That was a little harsh, don't you think?" Pink asked.

"Actually, I don't think it was harsh enough."

"Yes."

"Sir, it's Colonel Lin at NSA." The man spoke normally, as though he was speaking to his military superior. Behind him hung a sign that read: DON'T SPILL THE BEANS, PARDNER, THE STAKES ARE TOO HIGH. NO CLASSIFIED TALK.

"Yes."

"Sir, we just intercepted a communication between Carlton and Forbes at CIA."

Fress shot out of his seat. "He's alive? Where is he?"

"We'll be getting exact satellite coordin—"

"Approximately, Lin."

"Barents Sea. Around Murmansk. Again, the signal came through a maritime communications satellite."

"He's on a ship?" *But the ship was destroyed.*

"Affirmative, sir."

Carlton's not that stupid. He's got to know his communications are compromised. "Could he be running the line through other lines to throw us off?"

"Negative, sir. It would be transparent to us."

"Get me the coordinates as soon as you get them."

"Mr. Slythe is in conference. Who may I say is cal—"

"*Eta* Molotok. We must talk immediately!" Molotok roared. His accent was nearly impossible to understand, even if the vodka had not caused him to slur his words so much.

"One moment, sir."

Silence. Then a jovial voice. "Molotok. How are things going over there?" *Sniff.*

"We think we have the diamonds. Where can we deliver them in England with jets?"

Slythe reflected for a moment. "Aberdeen. In Scotland. We

have a deal with an airport there. Many of our transports that can't get into London go into Aberdeen."

"*Da*. Aberdeen. Be prepared. We will arrive there in one day."

"How will we—?" Slythe was speaking into a dead line.

That night, Captain Akronsef climbed the steel staircase to the elevated control room and removed his fur-lined parka. "What's on the scope, Teodor Alexandrovich? Any contacts?" he asked his first officer.

"A U.S.-registry cargo ship from New York bound for Murmansk, *Capitan*. The *Claire Sailing*. Gennady Iosevitch contacted her while you were outside. She's coming in close for the night. The captain said he'd feel safer braving the Arctic night near us. Those Americans! So afraid of the ice. We told him to pull alongside and make themselves at home. Nothing like Russian hospitality, eh? Also the patrol boat *Alexandr Nevsky* six-two kilometers to the Southeast, out of Murmansk. Another two, the *Kirov* and the *Omsk*, 2-4-8 kilometers, same course and heading." The first officer shrugged. "All general patrolling duties, it appears."

"Very well. Is all secure?"

"*Da, Capitan*."

"It is night. Drop the anchors," Akronsef ordered. At the press of a red button on the electronic console, both of the vessel's massive anchors simultaneously fell away from the hawesoles on either side of the bow and crashed into the glacial water. The *Rossiya* was near the southern limit of the winter ice pack. The cruise ship would not arrive until the next day. Breaking a passage through the ice fields toward the North Pole at this hour in this season would be a waste of time. The ice would close up before the cruise ship's arrival seven hours later.

"Anchors are down, *Capitan*. The ship is secure."

"Very well, Teodor Alexandrovich. You have the helm."

Erika shivered as much from fear as from the Arctic cold. The mile between the *Claire Sailing* and the *Rossiya* did not seem like much on the radar scope in the warm confines of the cargo ship, but on the ten-foot launch it seemed farther than the moon. Especially because the seven-person launch moved so slowly through the frigid waters in the dark. Seven of them were on board. Captain Ramey remained aboard the *Claire*. The four other crew members of the nearly fully automated cargo vessel—all ex-Navy—volunteered to join Carlton, Erika, and Pink. Erika had fought her way onto the team despite Carlton's concern for her safety. He piped down after she jabbed him hard in the stomach. Each person aboard was enveloped in a black aluminized parka with matching pants and a fur-lined cap. Engineer Chen carried a backpack containing gas tanks and an acetylene torch. First Officer Krebski's backpack contained a flexible neck camera. Not wanting to risk the ire of any *Rossiya* crew member and knowing the Russian GRU was sending a team to the *Rossiya*, none were armed.

Aboard the *Rossiya*, Second Officer Ilya Ilyushin was supposed to begin his watch on the bridge. Unlike other vessels, unless there was an icebreaking task at hand, the *Rossiya* generally shut down at night, so there was little for him to do. As the officers and crew consumed their well-earned dinner below, Ilyushin stared out at the lonely dark sea that spread before him beyond the triple-paned glass. He loved the sea but detested boredom. And to the young first officer, there was nothing more boring than watching a radar scope and monitoring infrequent radio chatter on an icebreaker at anchor in desolate waters.

We're anchored for the night. It's not as though we're sailing, he thought. *Besides, I can hear the radio from the bathroom.* Having sufficiently convinced himself, he walked to a desk at the rear of the bridge, picked up the sports section of the latest edition of *Pravda* that he had downloaded from its website, and headed for the bathroom.

Maybe those no-good hooligans finally won a game.

Thousands of stars scintillated in the black polar sky, free from light pollution. In complete darkness, except for the dim running lights of the *Rossiya*, Carlton piloted the craft slowly, without the aid of navigation lights, a task he had performed many times as skipper of his Navy PT boat on the Chesapeake Bay. He had to concentrate on the immediate task at hand in order not to think about how ridiculous this operation was. *How could Forbes expect us to perform a covert mission like this with no training and no information?*

The *Rossiya's* night lights cast eerie shadows on the icebreaker's hulking superstructure. Except for a row of ten portholes in the middle of the ship, all of the vessel's windows were dark.

Maybe everyone's asleep, Carlton thought wishfully. The darkness was a mixed blessing. It increased their chances of coming in undetected, but also made it nearly impossible to navigate. He decreased engine speed to a barely audible rumble and guided the launch toward the rear of the boat. The CIA database schematic documents showed that a ladder was built into the stern. Of course, those were just design documents and—

There it is.

He cut the engines and coasted toward the rounded stern.

Where the hell is Yagoda's team?

The *Rossiya* was not a military ship, so other than the *Rossiya's* nuclear reactor, there was little to guard. For that reason, the stern door was probably unlocked, Carlton hoped. He came to the door and twisted the latch. The door came open. He smiled.

"*Harasho*, Constantina Natalyevna. *Ochen harasho,*" Captain Akronsef repeated, congratulating his plump chef. Where she found wild hare and plums, he would never know. Nor would he ask. Mystery added to the pleasure of his and his officers' meals. He knew where the money for the food came from, of course. Some bigwig official in Moscow by the name of Pyashinev. Akronsef had not checked up on the man, although he was rumored to have been involved in the diamond trade. He did not want to get involved and, frankly, he could not have cared less. A particularly straight arrow, Akronsef had refused the bribes Pyashinev had offered to pay for him and his cronies to cruise around the Arctic once in a blue moon. And other special favors. Akronsef did it for free. Akronsef was far too intelligent to ignore the requests of a high-level official. So instead of personal bribes, he accepted funds for his crew's well-being. As a result, the *Rossiya* boasted state-of-the-art televisions and DVD players on which the crew watched the latest Russian and American movies, a computer with Internet access, a library stacked high with the latest Western and Russian magazines, and a larder that would have made a French *cordon bleu* chef turn green with envy.

Akronsef reclined at the table. All of his officers had gone to sleep. He swirled Georgian red wine in his glass and listened to the silence. He loved the silence of the Arctic. He gulped the last mouthful of wine and replaced the glass on the table top.

Suddenly, his ears pricked up.

What was that?

He instinctively cocked his head, thinking he had heard another noise.

Like a scrape, he thought. *Wasn't it? It couldn't have been caused by the wine glass.* He remained half standing, half sitting, bent over the table, straining to hear another sound. The cherubic face of his chef peeked out from behind the kitchen door, smiled.

"Some cognac?" She winked.

"It's you." Akronsef sighed with relief and stood. "*Nyet, nyet. Spaceba.* I had better retire for the evening. I'm beginning to hear things."

Chen lit the acetylene torch with a loud pop.

Pink raised a finger to his lips in the shadows, but Chen did not see him. From behind protective goggles, he concentrated on the bright blue flame that slowly bit into the icebreaker's innermost hull plate. Seven pairs of eyes darted nervously around the cramped confines of the *Rossiya's* lower deck, searching the shadows for crew members from topside.

"Where is Yagoda's team?" Murmured Pink.

They started near their point of entry at the stern, on the middle deck of the ship. They had concluded that the diamonds would not be located toward the bow, as that part of the boat was subject to too much maintenance work. Same with the stern, which was regularly disturbed to repair the engines. The diamonds also would probably not be located below the water line.

Luckily, the metal had little resistance to high temperatures. Within two minutes, Chen cut three quarters of a one-foot-diameter hole in the inner hull. "Come on, come on," he mouthed, blinking from the sweat that streamed down his brow. "Okay." He pushed the plate inside the circle of melted steel, bent it inward.

Pink removed the camera from Krebski's backpack, extended its illuminated flexible neck into the opening. He gazed at the night vision screen, rotated the neck by remote control. "Zilch. Let's try a little further up. I hope Yagoda's team gets here fast. This might take all night."

"Coming up on the *Rossiya, Capitan,*" First Officer Fedorov announced on the *Alexandr Nevsky's* bridge. "Strange that she hasn't contacted us."

"She's just ignoring us. We told her we were just patrolling the area. She doesn't want us to get in her hair."

PART III
CUT

"Nothing's as precious as a hole in the ground."
—*Midnight Oil, "Blue Sky Mine"*

51 PRESIDENT

Oval Office
The White House
Washington, D.C.
9:17 A.M.

John Douglass was the first African-American elected to the highest office in the land. He scowled at Randall Forbes from his impressive height, hands firmly clasped to the edge of JFK's former oak desk as if it were one of the pulpits from which the former Army general had preached after retiring from a distinguished military career.

"How could you do this without consulting me? And how could you send civilians in there without support in the first place? No SEALs, no backup? Have you lost your *mind*?"

"Mr. President, I—"

The president silenced him with his hand. "First things first. What's the closest asset we have out there?"

"The *Seawolf*, Mr. President. She's part of the carrier battle group that will conduct joint operations with the Royal Navy next week. Right now she's patrolling Novaya Zemlya, where Russia tests its—"

"I know where Novaya is," the president snapped. He punched his intercom. "Get Chuck in here *right now*."

Inside a minute, a Navy commander walked into the Oval Office, ramrod straight in his black uniform, and saluted the president. "Sir!" It was clear that the commander-in-chief was royally pissed off.

"The *Seawolf* near Novaya Zemlya. Get it to those coordinates yesterday," he ordered, pointing to Forbes, who handed the commander a piece of paper. "She's to extract a team of Americans on either an American cargo ship named the *Claire Sailing* or a Russian icebreaker called the *Rossiya*. Move!" Douglass sat while the commander retreated from the Oval Office.

"I can't believe you did this without my authorization."

Forbes was walking a political tightrope. He did not inform the president of Scott Fress's treason. He did not doubt the president's innocence in Scott Fress's criminal relationship with Waterboer, but informing the president of his chief of staff's misdeeds, especially this president who relied so heavily on his close aides, was akin to informing Scott Fress himself. Forbes did not relish keeping information from the man, but this was a question of priority. Fress was still unaware he was under suspicion, and his bribe-taking was not what Forbes was here to expose. That was a domestic matter, not the international conflagration he was trying to prevent. It could be handled later. For now, he couldn't afford tipping off the chief of staff. That would mean tipping off Waterboer, which would in turn tip off Russkost and derail his carefully laid plans.

"Mr. President, the government is a sieve. You know that only too well." He didn't admit his own agency was part of that sieve. "That's precisely why I made the operation totally covert. Like you did in Iraq when you were a general, sir," he said, for the benefit of the digital recorders that usually recorded all of the president's meetings. "Heaven knows how many informers Waterboer has in the federal government. You can just imagine the disaster if Waterboer and Molotok learned of the operation or the location of the Russian diamond stockpile."

"But why let civilians run the operation? They're brave, I'll give 'em that. Balls of brass brave." He cupped both hands. "They'll get a battery of medals if this pans out, I can promise you that." The commander-in-chief was a big believer in medals. "But why didn't you get field agents to run this? Except for the Naval Reservist, those people are all civilians. And your man Pink is an analyst. You could at least have sent in a few field officers. You had the authority to do that, even without my approval."

"Sir, Pink is an expert on Waterboer's relationship with Russia, and neither field officers nor SEALs would have improved our chances of *finding* the diamond stockpile. It was too risky to get President Orlov involved. The Kremlin is as much a sieve as Washington." He carefully avoided mentioning the White House. "But I did inform the Russian government by contacting Yagoda before running the op. The head of the GRU, somewhat one of my counterparts. So there was no possibility of a diplomatic incident. As soon as my team believed they had found the diamonds, they called in the GRU. So a military team would not have helped. In fact, it probably would have made things worse. But we can't assume that the GRU people are loyal. Russkost and Waterboer probably have assets in there just like Pyashinev in their diamond industry. So the only way to make sure the GRU is straight on this is to show the flag."

Despite the president's tall height, the black leather executive swivel chair made him appear smaller yet somehow more impressive. He smoothed his graying hair. "What's done is done. And contacting Yagoda was the right thing to do. As far as our national interests are concerned, the Russian diamond stockpile must go to the Russian government. It can only help improve our relationship with Orlov if we return the diamonds to the Russians."

"The Russian government."

"Point well taken, Randy. And just to make sure there's no misunderstanding, I'm going to call Orlov. He'll have a cow if he hears about the *Seawolf* surfacing outside the Polijarnii sub pens without advance notice about our help with the diamond stockpile."

Pink pushed the camera neck into another opening the team had made in the *Rossiya*'s inner hull. He stared at the small screen and rotated the neck. "Nothing. Dammit. This could take forever."

"You got a date?" Carlton asked.

Chen hoisted the torch, indicating *let's move up*.

"I'm going to patrol the corridors," Erika volunteered.

"Careful with that flashlight," Carlton cautioned. He heard her grumble something under her breath. "And where the hell is Yagoda's team, anyway?"

First Officer Fedorov of the patrol boat *Nevsky* pointed to the *Rossiya*'s running lights. "There she is, *Capitan*."

"*Harasho*," responded Ulianov. "Slow and circle her once."

"*Da, Capitan.*"

"*Capitan*, the GRU boats will be in range in a few minutes," the navigator announced.

"Get the torpedoes ready. We'll target them when we finish circling."

"*Da, Capitan.*"

It took five minutes to circle the massive red icebreaker. Ulianov noted that the Americans had already boarded the icebreaker when the *Nevsky* passed the *Claire*'s launch tied at the stern. Two men checked the *Nevsky*'s torpedo tubes, one on each side of the vessel. "Torpedoes ready, *Capitan*."

"Targets in range and programmed, *Capitan*."

"Fire one and two."

The torpedoes made a hissing noise as they launched out of the rear tubes and a splash as they entered the glacial waters.

"Torpedoes launched, *Capitan*."

"Targets at five kilometers."

Approaching by stealth without active radar, the *Kirov* and *Omsk* GRU boats were unaware of the *Nevsky*'s presence and continued speeding toward the *Rossiya* at fifty knots. The torpedoes sped toward the *Kirov* and *Omsk* at over fifty knots in the opposite direction, making their relative speed over one hundred knots. Even if Major Gerasimov had one of his men listen to passive sonar, the combined sounds of their powerful engines, of their high-speed propeller blades, and of their hulls cutting into the frigid waters would have drowned out the Volki torpedo engines. As a result, neither Gerasimov nor any of his twenty handpicked troops had any idea what caused the *Kirov* and the *Omsk* to explode, seconds apart. Most of the men were killed instantly. The remainder were badly burned and floated helplessly in the black water, so cold that it numbed their pain before taking their lives in the service of their country.

Carlton stood clear of Chen's torch. Its brilliant flame was leaving spots in his vision. It was amazing that none of the *Rossiya*'s crew had discovered their presence. But again, this was not a military craft. Except for the nuclear plant engines, the crew would not be in a high state of readiness. The boat was clearly asleep. The flame illuminated faces that expressed fear and apprehension.

"Dammit," Pink cursed, turning back from the third opening in the hull. "Still *nada*. Okay. Let's move up."

As they walked toward the bow, a face suddenly appeared out of the shadows and nearly gave Carlton a coronary before he realized it was Erika. She bore a look of excitement. "You'd better come take a look at this."

Second Officer Ilyushin saluted crisply. "To what do we owe this pleasure, *Capitan*?" he asked the athletic blond captain of the *Alexandr Nevsky* as he boarded the *Rossiya* amidships. He could feel the weight of the man's glacial scowl, below the red hammer and sickle on his fur hat. He didn't think anyone still wore the Communist symbol.

A column of heavily armed Russian Navy commandos massed behind the patrol boat captain. *All wearing hammers and sickles. Maybe he should call Murmansk to double check these guys. Then again, Russian military uniforms were in disarray these days.*

"Terrorists, Lieutenant," the captain announced flatly. "We couldn't warn you over the radio. Our transmission might have been compromised."

"Terrorists? Is that what we heard in the distance a few minutes ago?" Ilyushin demanded, frightened.

"Precisely, Lieutenant. Now if you will please lead the way."

"Of course, of course." Ilyushin led the way up the exterior staircase to the bridge. "But what would terrorists want with us? The *Rossiya* is not a military vessel."

"But she is a *nuclear* icebreaker, Lieutenant. This ship burns uranium. I hope I don't have to remind you what uranium and its by-products can be used for."

They entered the warm confines of the bridge. "Get some tea for the captain, Vasily," Ilyushin ordered his saluting first mate. He turned back to the captain. "What do you need from me?"

"Your cooperation, Lieutenant, for a few hours."

"Of course, Captain. You have it."

"*Harasho*. First, I will need you to maintain complete radio silence. One of my men will sit at your communications center until the situation is resolved." Without looking back, he pointed to the radio room. "Kokoshin!"

A stern-looking lieutenant stepped out from the small group of men behind the captain, installed himself at the communications console, strapped on the headset, and began tapping on the electronics keyboard.

"Second, I will need someone to guide me and my men through your ship."

"Immediately." He hesitated. "Should I wake the captain?"

"*Nyet*. The less commotion, the better."

"Of course. My first mate will guide you. Vasily!"

"I was walking by here when I noticed this." Erika stopped and pointed to a section of the hull. "Look."

Carlton shined his flashlight on the red steel. "Welding marks." Carlton turned to Chen. "What do you think?"

The engineer squinted and felt the hard bubbles of steel on a two-foot-square section of the hull, ten inches above the floor. His flashlight, attached to a headband like a surgeon's, shone brightly on the red paint. "Whoever welded this did it a long time ago. See the paint?"

Carlton moved his head closer. Several coats of paint flaked at the solder marks. He nodded. "Might as well give it a shot."

Chen crouched down, increased his flame.

52 SEAWOLF

USS Seawolf (SSN-21)
Seawolf-Class United States Nuclear Attack Submarine
Barents Sea
232 miles northeast of Murmansk
7:01 P.M.

The Seawolf-class of United States nuclear attack submarines was the culmination of over two hundred years of American submarine design dating back to David Bushnell's Revolutionary War *Turtle*. Designed to supplant the aging Los Angeles–class attack subs, the Seawolf-class was an improvement in nearly every performance category. At 326 feet long and forty-two feet wide, the namesake of the class was a behemoth that displaced 9,150 tons of water submerged. She boasted a classified submerged top speed in excess of fifty knots, a test depth of two thousand feet, greater comforts for her 140-man crew, and a deadly arsenal of fifty-two Mark 50 advanced capability (ADCAP) torpedoes, twelve Javelin cruise missiles, Harpoon anti-ship missiles, and a battery of decoys and mines. Its General Electric S6W pressurized water nuclear reactor was over twenty times more efficient than the latest, state-of-the-art commercial reactors. In short, the Seawolf-class was the largest, fastest, quietest, and deadliest class of submarines ever constructed.

Manufactured by General Dynamics' Electric Boat Division in Groton, Connecticut, at a cost of over $2 billion per vessel, the post–cold war administration had forced the Navy to pare down its initial order of twenty-nine to only three units.

The *Seawolf*'s captain, Commander Donald Grant Hendricks Jr., was physically unimposing. At forty-six years of age, the man was fit, but of average height and slight build. The stress of command had salted his dark brown hair with touches of silver at the temples. A graduate of the United States Naval Academy, he had married twice, once to the Navy and a second time to the submarine service—the "Silent Service." The

Seawolf was his second submarine command, a reward for his flawless performance as the captain of a Los Angeles–class sub. Although his demeanor was stern and he rarely laughed, Hendricks was revered by his crew as much for his lack of fear as for his fairness and concern. Standing in the command center dressed in his on-board khaki uniform, reviewing naval charts on the electronic display table, drinking from a mug of Navy bug juice, Commander Hendricks seemed more comfortable than in a lawn chair by a pool in summer, yet he exuded a palpable sense of confidence and command necessary to every successful submarine mission.

A bell rang in the communications room aft of the attack center, signifying that the Very Low Frequency (VLF) radio antenna trailing off the aft corner of the submarine had received a transmission from the Navy's massive underwater communications facility in Michigan. Because VLF transmissions were slow, approximately the speed of teletype, they were most often used to order the submarine to surface and receive a rapid communication from either an Ultra High Frequency (UHF) or Navy satellite signal. The sailor on watch called his officer, an 0-2 lieutenant, junior grade, who in turn called Commander Hendricks.

"Sir, VLF signals incoming FLASH priority transmission."

Dammit, Hendricks cursed silently, never voicing his irritation at orders in front of his bubbleheads, as submariners were sometimes known. Although the namesake of the Seawolf-class was the quietest submarine ever to leave the Groton submarine yards, this was only true when submerged. Any part of the boat that peeked out of the waves, even for a second, immediately left it open to detection by satellites. In the Silent Service, even the most remote possibility of detection implied danger. Particularly when a U.S. nuclear attack submarine was in and around Russian waters near the country's officially abandoned but still used nuclear testing range. They were supposed to be totally silent until they were away from Russian waters and back in the GIUK gap.

If we're receiving a satellite transmission out here, it's got to be damn important. "Acknowledged. Mr. Wathne, take us to antenna depth," he ordered his executive officer (XO), Lieutenant Commander Jack Wathne.

"Antenna depth. Aye, sir." The XO communicated the instruction to the diving officer and the chief of the watch, who respectively controlled depth and direction. The *Seawolf* rose close enough to the surface to poke its communication laser through the glacial waves and track the Navy's Submarine Satellite Information Exchange (SSIX). The message was then "sucked off" the satellite on the sub's directional S-band radio, and the *Seawolf* immediately dove back down to five hundred feet. The signal was fed into the sub's encryption system, decoded, printed, and delivered to the captain.

"Thanks, Jackson."

Z73446
FR: COMSUBLANT
TO: CO USS SEAWOLF
URGENT PROCEED LAT 74°03'00"N LON 41°31'01"W
XFLTRATE US CITIZ CLAIRE SAILING
DIRECT ORDER USCINC REPORT ASAP
AWAIT FURTHER UHF
END TRANS

"What the—" *Direct order USCINC? CINC* designated the commander-in-chief. The president of the United States. *Holy*—Hendricks handed the strip of paper to his XO. "Nav, plot the fastest course to 41-31-01 West, 74-03-00 North. Forward flank. This is by order of the president. Let's move it, people!"

"Forward flank. Aye, sir."

First mate Vasily Damov led the way down the exterior staircase and into the lower portion of the *Rossiya* and stopped. "Where does the captain wish to go?" he asked, pleased at the chance to help the Russian Navy. His father, a captain in the Soviet Navy, had regaled young Damov with tales of the glorious Soviet Navy at the time other nations trembled at Russia's military might.

"I want to inspect every square centimeter of the interior. Not the living areas or the engine room. Only the areas where terrorists could plant a bomb or hide without being spotted."

"I understand, *Capitan*. Follow me."

"This one's a real mother. Must have been reinforced," Chen said after ten minutes of cutting. He had cut three sides of the square section, was working on the fourth. "Almost there."

The air seemed as thick as the metal plate. Carlton wiped sweat from his brow, fought the urge to pull off the heavy Arctic parka that was nearly asphyxiating him.

"Done." Chen turned down the flame as Carlton and Pink grabbed the plate on either side.

Carlton grunted with the effort. "Man, this thing is heavy."

They placed the heavy plate to the side, against the inner hull. Pink directed the camera neck into the cavity. After a foot, it refused to go any further. Pink glanced at the monitor. The screen showed thick rubberized bags stacked one on top of the other inside the hull. "Bingo!"

Carlton grabbed one of the bags. It was incredibly heavy. He lifted it out of the cavity and onto the floor. Its top was closed with a tight knot. "Houdini couldn't have untied this thing." Krebski handed him his knife. The sharp blade easily sliced off the top of the heavy gauge nylon bag. Carlton shined his beam inside.

He stared at the contents, dumbfounded.

"My God," he finally whispered. Staring back at him were stones of such brilliance they made him wish he had brought his sunglasses. He dug into the bag, removed a handful of diamonds. All were cut and faceted. All were over one carat, many of them two to five he guessed, some even larger. It did not take Therese de la Pierre or any other diamond expert to conclude they were gem-quality diamonds. One was a blue diamond nearly as large as a golf ball, brilliant cut into a 58-facet stone that sparkled with such brilliance it seemed to glow from inside. He held it up to his beam, stared at it, mesmerized.

Pink exhaled a sigh of relief. "I can't believe it."

"Neither can I," a loud voice echoed from the shadows

behind them. The four turned in unison as overhead lamps turned on and bathed the long corridor in bright white light.

Carlton, Erika, Pink, and the crew stared in stunned terror at the barrels of a dozen Kalashnikov AK47 submachine guns leveled at them. Carlton tucked the blue diamond into his parka's cuff.

"Hands behind your head," Ulianov ordered in perfect English.

"I must thank you for deciphering Pyashinev's puzzling message. A boat named *Rossiya* and its third layer. Who would have thought it would be so simple? Of course, it *would* take an American to think of something so childishly simple." The smile disappeared. "Follow my man, single file."

"So you're working with Waterboer," Carlton said without emotion, accepting his fate, but looking for a way out.

"Why do you say that?" Ulianov shot back.

"Who else would pay you for these diamonds?"

Ulianov laughed dryly. "You Americans. Always believing everything Hollywood feeds you. We have no interest in Waterboer. Our only goal is to make sure Russia's diamonds stay safe inside Holy Mother Russia. Where they belong."

Holy Mother Russia? Hammers and sickles on the hats? Whoever these guys were, Russian Navy they weren't. Probably not Yagoda's GRU team either.

"Then how did you know where we were?"

"It was simple, Mr. Carlton. But I won't bore you with the details," Ulianov said, pointing toward the *Nevsky*. "*Spaceba*. Across the gangplank."

More angry than afraid, Carlton stepped onto the metal deck of the *Alexandr Nevsky*, followed by the others. He wasn't surprised that his encrypted call to Forbes was monitored. Fress would hear it, relay the information to Waterboer, and Waterboer would give their Russian contacts orders to track them down and recover the diamond stockpile that they were unable to find. So Waterboer-backed Russian mafia nationalists popping up hardly surprised him. What really pissed him off was that neither Yagoda's nor Forbes' rescue teams had arrived.

"You should be more careful when communicating."

"What are you going to do with us?" Erika demanded.

"What do you think? We are taking you back to your boat. Our mission is accomplished. We have the diamonds. You don't."

"You mean you're not going to…"

The dry chuckle returned.

"Kill you? It doesn't matter that you know we have the diamonds. In fact, I'm pleased you do." He turned to one of his men. "Take them to their boat and destroy their communications suite. Where one American soldier is, a thousand others are nearby. We can't risk them calling for reinforcements."

"Have a safe trip," he shouted at them from the railing of the *Rossiya*.

"They didn't…they couldn't just let us go," Erika announced, trembling back on board the *Claire*.

Pink pored over the fried jumble of molten electronics the Volki grenade had created in the communications room. Some wires still sparked.

"Let's not sit around, waiting to find out. Jack, get us the *hell* out of here," Carlton ordered Ramey.

Ramey was already starting the *Claire*'s massive engines. "You don't need to twist my arm." He jammed the throttles as far forward as they would move in their steel grooves. "Chen, Krebski, get below and check the engines for any weird stuff they may have left behind. Be careful."

"Aye."

"How's it look, Tom?" Carlton inquired.

Pink shook his head. "Nothing doing."

"You sure?"

"That radio doesn't need a repairman. It needs a priest. And the portable's too small to have any effect."

"At least the ship's still working. What did you make of those guys?"

"Not regular Russian Navy or GRU, that's for sure."

"Captain, where is the nearest—"

He was interrupted by a violent shudder, followed immediately by a second.

Ramey shouted as the lights cut in and out. He hit the engineering room intercom button. "Chen, what's going on? Chen? Chen! Come in!"

The ship began to list to port, slightly at first, then heavily. "Krebski! Report! DesJardins! Come in!"

The intercom crackled. "We've been torpedoed." Krebski's voice was muffled. "Amidships and stern. We're taking on water fa—"

Two more massive shudders knocked everyone on the bridge to the deck. Ramey recovered first, only to see flames roar up from the bow. "Krebski? Dammit, the line is dead."

DesJardins climbed the staircase on to the bridge. "Krebski says the hull ruptured in four places, Captain." He panted heavily. "She'll be under inside ten minutes."

"We'll either burn or drown. We've got to get off."

Ramey cursed. Another blow knocked him forward toward the communications console. Carlton yanked him backward an instant before his head slammed into the steel console. This time, the explosion came from the boat itself.

"You're right. We've got no choice." Ramey turned to the PA. "Abandon ship. Everybody, abandon ship."

The PA system reverberated against the metallic hull, then the lights went out. "There goes the power. Come on. Let's go."

The backup lights winked on and glowed an eerie red.

They groped their way through the tilted hallways and surreally angled outer decks. Erika and DesJardins donned parkas with difficulty while clinging to the railing. As they crept up the tilted deck, Pink stared in horror at the lifeboat cradles ahead. All four were empty, loose wires hanging uselessly from the metal arms. The Volki were thorough.

"All of the others are dead," DesJardins said. The vessel was large but its crew members were few.

"Any other lifeboats?" Pink shouted to Ramey over a surge of flames. The deck twisted abruptly as the *Claire Sailing*'s bow lifted out of the water, her stern now entirely submerged in the icy water.

"The inflatables in the supply room," Ramey, pointed back inside the vessel. The roaring flames advanced quickly, their heat burning the group's faces.

Carlton disappeared into the dark confines of the rapidly sinking hull.

"Pat, no!" Erika shouted. "Don't!" She made for the door, but Pink held her back, pushing a life jacket into her arms.

Carlton returned two long minutes later, clutching a single large backpack. "One better be enough because it's all I found." He yanked the rip cord and watched as the black rubber raft automatically inflated.

A wave of water burst into the main cabin, the force of the water knocking the raft out of Carlton's hand. The *Claire* abruptly rolled to port in response. The resulting air pocket exploded the glass windows outward, sending shards of glass flying at the five survivors.

"Jump before it's too far," ordered Ramey. One at a time, Erika, Pink, Carlton, DesJardins, then finally Ramey jumped into the raft. Ramey turned back, watching in frustrated rage as the vessel under his care sank unceremoniously under the glacial water.

Soon the flames consumed the burning fuel floating on the water. The frigid darkness enveloped them, with only a sparkle of stars above for light.

53 CONTACT

USS Seawolf
Barents Sea
381 miles northeast of Murmansk
11:14 P.M.

The USS *Seawolf* nuclear attack submarine was more silent than any other man-made submersible. The vessel's highly classified ability to decrease noise was so effective that its two fifty-two-thousand-shaft-horsepower turbines radiated only about as much energy as a child's night light. The uranium's fission turned water into steam, which turned the generator blades and produced electricity. Air scrubbers removed carbon dioxide from the submarine's internal atmosphere and bled it into the surrounding water aft of the fairwater while nitrogen/oxygen generators produced breathable air. A fresh-water plant produced ten thousand gallons of water daily. As a result, the *Seawolf* could remain submerged far longer than its typical six-month cruises; its underwater journeys limited only by the vessel's large but finite food supply. It enabled the *Seawolf* to submerge off the coast of its home port of Groton, Connecticut, and pop up in almost any sea on the globe unde-tected. But this presumed that the sub was not traveling at its top speed of over fifty knots, as it now was. At such speed, even the best-designed propeller blades made noise. Called cavitation, the sound resulted from high-pressure water crush-ing pockets of tiny vapor bubbles on the screw blades created by the rapidly moving gigantic single screw. Loud noise made the sub detectable. Detectability signified danger. Danger trig-gered intensified vigilance.

Sonar technician Jorge de la Torre Gonzales closed his eyes and cocked his head, concentrating hard. Nicknamed "Ears" by his fellow crew members, Gonzales had an uncanny talent for detecting even the faintest signals before the *Seawolf's* power-ful General Electric BSY-2—"Busy-Two"—submarine combat system. Ears thought he heard something. A faint noise amid the fuzz coming through his headphones. He looked at the Busy-Two's "waterfall" screen which monitored frequencies vertically.

Nothing.

The sound reappeared. Longer, this time. Ears adjusted the acoustical controls to isolate the sound, then lifted his right index finger. The signal was now continuous. Continuous and repetitive. *Far too repetitive to be biological. Definitely mechanical*, Ears concluded. He looked up at the screen again. *Bingo*. There it was. Faint, but there. A solid vertical line on the waterfall. "Sir, I have a contact," he announced to the sonar watch supervisor. "Bearing northwest."

"Acknowledged." The sonar watch supervisor hit the intercom button. "Conn, sonar. New contact designated Sierra Twenty-One bearing northwest." "Sierra" identified a new sonar contact. Each contact was assigned a new number. This new contact was the twenty-first since the *Seawolf* began its patrol. It was a large number of contacts for a patrol that had started only one week ago, but for the fact that they were in the busy GIUK gap before war games.

"Can you identify?" asked the XO.

"Analyzing now, sir." The sonar supervisor craned his neck. "What's it sound like, Ears?"

It would have been much easier for the sonar technician to identify Sierra 21's signature had the *Seawolf* been running silent. But its high speed caused so much cavitation that it drowned out most of the new contact's faint signal. "It's far, but it's moving like a bat out of hell. Cavitating all over the place. Sounds like a…sounds like a"—*it can't be*, Ears reflected—"like a Delta Three, sir."

"That can't be right. The Delta Threes were all scrapped."

"That's what I thought, sir. Checking with Busy-Two now, sir." Ears fed the sonar signature into the computer. The BSY-2 was rarely wrong. The distributed-processor-architecture system linked massive UYK computers through more than one million lines of Defense Department computer code and a data bus that integrated sonar, weapons, and fire control into a single unit. Within seconds, the waterfall displayed Sierra 21's most probable ID: a Russian Delta Three–class sub.

"Sir, Busy Two confirms Sierra as Delta Three *Kal'mar*–class. States 8-4 percent probability that it's the…" Ears hesitated. *That's got to be wrong too.*

"The what?"

"The *Pushkin*, sir."

"Now I know it can't be right. The *Pushkin* was sold for scrap over a year ago. *Stars & Stripes* even ran an article on it."

Ears closed his eyes and cocked his head again. "Sir! New contact bearing northwest."

"Designate new contact Sierra Twenty-Two bearing northwest."

"It's faint, sir. Very faint. I'd be able to hear it better if we weren't cavitating all over the place. But it sounds like…like crumples from explosions. Topside." Ears checked the BSY-2 waterfall display back and forth. "Three of them. Whatever's happening to Sierra Twenty-Two, it ain't pretty." He pressed his earphones hard against his ears. "Metal twisting. Underwater implosions. Sierra Twenty-Two's sinking, sir."

The sonar supervisor squinted. "Range?"

"Range is approximately 4-0 nautical miles. She's awfully close to Sierra Twenty-One, sir."

The sonar supervisor hit the intercom. "Conn, sonar. Unknown surface vessel sinking range 4-0 nautical miles. Should we render assistance, sir?"

The XO was about to reply but the captain cut him off. "Sierra Twenty-Two is close to our target. For all we know, she may even be our target. Until then, steady as she goes. What about Sierra Twenty-One? Any more data?"

The sonar supervisor turned to Ears.

"Heading 2-0-1. Depth 7–0–0 feet. Speed 2-4 knots, sir. Approximate range 3-0 nautical miles."

"Twenty-four knots for a Delta Three? That's its maximum speed. At least it's heading away from us." He punched the intercom again. "Conn, sonar. Busy-Two identifies Sierra Twenty-One as Russian Delta Three–class *Pushkin*. Course heading 2-0-1, speed 2-4 nautical miles. Range approximately 3-0 knots. Probability 8-4."

The XO turned to Hendricks. "Sir, the *Pushkin* was supposed to have been decommissioned."

The captain shook his head. "Correct, but this is no time for history, Mr. Wathne. Monitor it and keep moving. It's probably heard us too, I know. But it's moving away from us. Unless that changes, we maintain course and speed. Besides, Delta Threes have a top speed of only twenty-four knots. We can outrun her. We'll see about survivors after we've picked up our people." He hated when his orders conflicted with his seaman's instincts. Out there in the freezing cold an entire crew could be struggling in life rafts or worse yet, in the icy water. But there was nothing he could do. His orders were clear. And they came from the commander-in-chief himself. He could only hope that his target and Sierra 22 were one and the same so he could save the survivors.

"Steady as she goes. Aye, sir," XO Wathne acknowledged uncomfortably. Like any other submariner, he felt vulnerable whenever his sub generated so much noise, particularly when it was in another country's territorial waters. And especially when they were Russian territorial waters. His mind continued to analyze the situation. He stared at the chart on the plotting table, trying to understand the Russian sub's probable destination. There wasn't one for over a thousand miles. *So what's a decommissioned Delta III class sub doing heading nowhere at flank speed?* The notion was particularly troublesome in light of the fact that the *Pushkin* was a boomer—a missile sub— with vertical launch tubes designed to contain sixteen SS-N-18 long range ballistic nuclear missiles.

54 DECEPTION

Rossiya
Barents Sea
11:32 P.M.

"But I don't understand," muttered First Mate Vasily Damov, trying hard not to be insubordinate to an officer of the navy he so admired. "Why are you taking the diamonds off the ship? Shouldn't we inform Moscow and bring them into the proper authorities?"

"No," Ulianov shot back. "The proper authorities, as you refer to them, are corrupt. They're selling Holy Mother Russia out to the West. To those *Amerikanskii* you saw trying to steal them earlier."

"But I...I'm sorry, sir. I don't understand."

"You don't have to." Ulianov removed his silenced Makarov pistol from his shoulder holster and fired a round directly into Damov's skull.

Without a trace of emotion, he replaced the handgun into its holster and boarded the gangplank to the *Alexandr Nevsky*. "Go. Go! Cast off!" he shouted at his pilot.

As the *Alexandr Nevsky* gained speed, Ulianov entered the bridge and looked at his first officer. "What's our ETA to the *Pushkin*?"

"One hour, twenty-two minutes."

"*Harasho*. Do it now."

Less than a second later, the air was filled with a deep rumble as the explosives in the engine room of the *Rossiya* were detonated by remote control. Another rumble erupted, this time from amidships. Another from the bow, the final one from the stern.

The triple-hulled icebreaker was designed to withstand heavy shock from the exterior of the ship, but not from within. In less than fifteen minutes, the fire engine red icebreaker disappeared under the Barents Sea.

"*Da?*"

"Molotok?"

"*Da, da. Ulianov, shto et—*"

"Victory."

"You have it?"

"We have the—" As powerful as the Volki and their *krestnii otet* allies might be, Moscow still had ears. "*Da*. We have it."

"*Harasho! Ochen harasho!*"

"You should see them. They are nothing like I imagined. Pyashinev did well, the traitor. The best quality. The very best of Siberia. Like fire. Fit for the Tsar's court. And so many of them. It's like a fairy tale."

"You have done well."

"But it's not over. Now we must get this to its destination."

"Be careful."

"We have practiced the plan long and hard. All of the men are in place. Unless you wish otherwise, I will give the order to start."

"*Da*. I will contact the other side. Be careful, my friend. I don't have to remind you how much rests on your shoulders." To the Siberian bear and his ideologue soldier, this was not a stale cliché but a vibrant hope and caution.

Piet Slythe despised being awakened in the middle of the night. As far as he was concerned, almost anything could wait until the morning. Yet here was Ian, waking him, nearly shaking him out of bed. "Bloody hell, man. What is it? Do you know what time—"

"It's the Russian. Molotok."

"And?"

"He's on the telephone. He won't speak to anyone else." Ian offered his master a cordless telephone.

"Bloody bolshevik boor." Slythe sat up, took the phone. "Slythe here." *Sniff*.

"*Eta* Molotok."

"Yes, and I assume you have a bloody good reason to get me out of bed at this hour."

"*Da*. We found it. Found it and taken it."

Slythe shot out of bed. "Finally! Smashing, sir. Smashing!"

"*Da*. We are taking it to planned destination. Be ready, *da*?"

"My people will be there. For God's sake be careful."

Slythe hung up and turned to Ian.

"The Russian has the stockpile. He's on his way to Aberdeen. Tell our people to stand ready. No cockups."

55 LIFEBOAT

Claire Sailing Lifeboat
Barents Sea
420 miles northeast of Murmansk
12:09 A.M.

The shipwrecked survivors shivered in the pitch darkness and glacial cold of the open Arctic Sea, scouring the horizon and sky for some sign of rescue craft. Nothing. Once was enough for a lifetime. This was their second time in one week. But the first time was planned, and that lifeboat was motorized and protected from the elements. The *Claire's* real lifeboats were destroyed. The lifeboat they were in was no more than a glorified rubber life raft, with no engine, no heat, no light, no water, and no food. At least they were safe. For the moment.

The moment did not last long.

Freezing raindrops the size of grapes began to pelt the survivors. The rain drowned out all other sound, reduced visibility to nil. In the black night, none of them noticed an enormous shape rise behind them, no more than thirty feet away. Like a monster from the deep, it continued upward until it towered fifty feet above the overloaded rubber boat. If they could have seen it, they would immediately have noticed large white letters on its skin that read "SSN 21."

56 UNTOUCHABLE

Palace of Justice
Uffizio di Guarda di Finanza
Rome, Italy
10:03 A.M.

As mayor of the global Cosa Nostra capital, Orlando Leonida worked regularly with the Italian Ministry of Justice and its financial law enforcement arm, the *Guarda di Finanza* (GDF). But Leonida's level of work with the Ministry was unusual. Often, his predecessors had willingly exchanged their reputations and honor for a pittance from the Cosa Nostra masters. Mayor Leonida had stood firm in the face of offers of large sums of money and threats to his job, his life, and his family. Like the U.S. Treasury Department's Elliot Ness in the 1920s, Orlando Leonida was beyond threats and bribery. Untouchable. Even the 1992 assassination of the heroic anti-mafia Sicilian judge Giovanni Falcone, by a bomb of such power its blast had registered on seismographs throughout Europe, failed to sway Leonida.

Finally, through campaign after campaign, Leonida's tenacity was having its intended effect. The tide was turning. The patience not only of Sicilians but of all Italians had been exhausted. After decades of cynical shrugs, Italians finally realized the vicious killings, corruption, and criminal business activities of the Cosa Nostra were sapping the lifeblood not only of other countries but of their beloved *Italia* as well. Bleeding away Italy's economy, Italy's glorious patrimony, and most importantly, Italy's future—her children. Schoolhouses were infected with heroin, cocaine, ecstasy, and a host of other deadly narcotics available at prices artificially lower than anywhere else in the world. Enough was enough.

Basta!

Mayor Leonida became not only popular, he became a star. Never alone, a soldier of the Italian Armed Forces—sworn enemies of the Cosa Nostra—armed with a Beretta submachine gun stood guard in his room even when he slept. In the bathroom when he urinated. Leonida never left his apartment without a bulletproof vest under his flawlessly cut three-button suits. Bomb-detecting German shepherds always swept his path, even indoors. It was a high price to pay, but for Leonida it was worth it.

The bright sunshine masked the bitter Roman winter cold on this particular morning. Escorted by his handpicked retinue of armed soldiers and German shepherds, Mayor Leonida marched through the ornate hallways of the *Guarda di Finanza* and into the director's office.

Director Vittorio Umberto knew a personal visit from his colleague could mean only one thing. Umberto was one of the few other members of government unafraid to do what was right. Another untouchable, although it was easier for him in Rome, away from Sicily. He welcomed his colleague with a sincere smile, open arms. "*Buon giorno,* Orlando."

"*Buon giorno, buon giorno.*"

The men embraced in a warm hug. Leonida refused Umberto's offer of a comfortable velour chair and dismissed all but one of his soldiers. He removed a manila file from his attaché case, placed it on the director's parchment desktop, and opened it with a flourish.

"*Ché cosa?* What is this?" Umberto asked.

Leonida grinned. "This," he pointed to the open file, "is what we have worked on for the past six months. A list of five bank accounts in the Rome office of the Banco Napolitana Lucchese belonging to Arcangelo. It's finally time to bring him in."

Umberto glanced at the file and looked up at Leonida with with frustration. "Orlando. You know I want to bring him in, but just because Arcangelo has bank accounts doesn't—"

"This is different, Vittorio. Look closely. Notice these are not just bank accounts. These are bank accounts opened to receive funds from five government contracts for the restoration of monuments never begun. So far, nothing new."

Massive government disbursements over the years for the restoration of monuments in Palermo alone were enough to build *palazzos* from Sicily to China. Almost none of the monuments were touched with so much as a paintbrush. The funds went into the coffers of construction companies owned by the mafia, the monuments indefinitely closed with signs that read "*e chiuso per il restauro.*"

"But this is different. We obtained copies of the original government restoration contracts. They're in the file. The difference is that although the deposits in the five accounts are equal to the amounts of the contracts, the government agency hasn't made payments to Arcangelo's companies yet."

Umberto's eyes opened wide.

"See what I mean?" Leonida sat then and lit a cigarette.

"*Santa Lucia,*" Umberto whispered.

Leonida blew a contrail of smoke toward the ceiling. "Not only did the government not make the payments, but the amounts in those five accounts are identical to the payoffs on five corporate shakedowns and kidnappings Arcangelo recently pulled off in different parts of Italy. We know this from the electronic surveillance that the Americans helped us establish." He took a deep drag from his cigarette.

"I never would have noticed this level of detail, except I was watching for something strange. And finally Arcangelo made a mistake." He exhaled, removed a piece of tobacco that had lodged between his straight white teeth. "He moved the money from the Palermo branch to Rome."

Director Umberto still could not believe his ears and eyes. "These amounts are…" He looked at Leonida, down at the file, back up at Leonida. "There must be—"

"Roughly 100 million euros."

"Are you telling me the Banco Napolitana Lucchese—"

"Laundered 100 million euros of kidnapping money for Arcangelo. *Si.* That is *exactly* what I am saying." He blew a cloud of smoke upward. "And I'm not just saying it. Those documents prove it. And under the Piola Torre law, your *Guarda* can—"

"You don't need to remind me." Umberto stabbed at a button on his telephone.

"*Pronto,*" a woman's voice answered.

"Please come in here immediately."

Twenty seconds later, a smartly dressed woman stepped into the office through a side door. Trailing a wisp of fragrance, her graciousness and beauty fooled few people in the *Guarda di Finanza*. As Umberto's right hand, Simona Calfio was responsible for the day-to-day management of the *Guarda's* field operations. The Woman of Steel, the GDF staff called her. She bowed slightly toward Leonida before standing at attention near Umberto.

"Simona," Umberto began. He glanced at the antique clock on his desk. "We are finally moving against Arcangelo. By two o'clock this afternoon, I want the main branch of Banco Napolitana Lucchese closed. Closed, sealed, and guarded around the clock. I want every ledger, every computer disk, every vault, every scrap of paper locked down. I want that place guarded and sealed so tightly not even the plants can breathe."

"*Si, direttore.*" Calfio turned and walked out of the office.

He looked at Leonida. "I think you may have done it, Orlando. *Santa Lucia*, I think you finally did it!"

"Don't be too confident. I wouldn't stop praying if I were you."

By the time Mayor Leonida left Director Umberto's office ten minutes later, five unmarked armored Fiat vans containing forty armed officers in special tactics gear, computer technicians, accountants, engineers, and communications experts of the *Guarda di Finanza* rushed through the congested streets of the Eternal City toward the headquarters of the Banco Napolitana Lucchese.

57 HUNT

USS Seawolf
Barents Sea
400 miles northeast of Murmansk
12:42 A.M.

Carlton sat up on his cot in the *Seawolf's* infirmary. "What do you mean you haven't looked?" He nearly shouted at Commander Hendricks. "I told you. Those diamonds are a matter of national security."

"Come, now, Mr. Carlton. Just relax. You've just come out of shock."

Commander Hendricks had spent his entire career surrounded by military personnel. He was not accustomed to dealing with civilians. Particularly civilians attempting to discuss what they believed were national security issues. *As if he would know a national security issue if it bit him on the rear end.* Hendricks had followed orders, rescued the castaways, and reported back. Listening to civilians was not part of those orders.

"Just relax, son. I'm sure it'll be found sooner or later."

Carlton stared into his eyes. "You're not taking me seriously, are you? You're not taking any of this seriously."

The intercom crackled. "Commander. VLF transmission informing us of FLASH transmission."

Again? "Acknowledged. Take us to antenna depth. I'm on my way." He turned to Carlton. "Get some rest."

Russian nationalists. Diamond monopoly. Where did these people come from? He grabbed the strip of paper from the communications officer as he strode toward the control room.

Z73446
FR: COMSUBLANT
TO: CO USS SEAWOLF
URGENT LOCATE AND PROCEED TO RUS ICEBKR
ROSSIYA

AIRLFT ONLY JR PD AND EW
PC USNR 0-3 ACTV DUTY
PC AND TP TO ADVISE
XTRM COURTESY
END TRANS

Navy rank 0-3 designated Carlton as a lieutenant. "Great. I've just pissed off one of our own," Hendricks muttered. "And he was right about the icebreaker. Dammit."

He turned to Wathne. "XO. Find me the Russian icebreaker *Rossiya*, then plot a course to her. Do it fast." He swallowed hard. "I've got some apologizing to do."

Erika and Carlton had held each other close as they waited for the Norwegian Search and Rescue seaplane to take her, Ramey, and DesJardins to safety. Despite his exhaustion, Carlton had been unable to sleep for more than a few minutes at a time. He tossed and turned on the submarine cot, wondering where Forbes would hide Erika, whether he could keep her safe from Fress and his thugs until Forbes put him in the slammer. Finally accepting he wouldn't sleep, Carlton took a regulation thirty-second shower and shaved.

The crew located a lieutenant's uniform that fit him reasonably well. Pink, who managed to catnap for a bit, was issued a uniform stripped of Navy insignia. Feeling reasonably human again, they devoured steaks and baked potatoes in the officer's wardroom while filling Hendricks in on the issues facing them. They washed the whole thing down with coffee, the real fuel aboard the sub, known in the Navy as "bug juice."

"What do you mean it's not there?" Carlton demanded, referring to the *Rossiya*.

"It's not there," repeated Hendricks sitting on a chair facing backwards, his arms on its backrest. "We tried everything from active sonar to surface radar. There's nothing there.

"Have you tried satellite imagery?" Pink asked.

Pink was an enigma to Hendricks. Unlike with Carlton, the transmission had not divulged Pink's institutional affiliation. Yet it was clear that the calm man was no ordinary civilian.

Ordinary citizens weren't rescued by Navy subs in foreign waters and given extreme courtesy, as ordered by the transmission. Now the man was asking about satellite imagery. Probably DIA or CIA, he suspected. Hendricks cautiously did as he was ordered. "We're getting that in right now, Mr. Pink. We can go take a look once you're done."

"Well," Carlton took a last swig of his bug juice and rose from his chair, "*tempis fugit*, as we say at Justice. Lead the way, Commander."

A young ensign pointed to a chart under the glass of one of the two plotting tables in the control room. "Here, here, and here are the last reported positions of the *Claire Sailing*, the Russian patrol boat, and the *Rossiya*."

Each spot was marked with a different colored dot on the glass.

"Satellite imagery of the past twenty hours confirms the *Rossiya* disappeared at the same time our sonar picked up Sierra 20, the signature of the fourth sinking ship."

"The fourth? I thought only two vessels sank." Carlton squinted.

"Negative, sir," answered the ensign. "There were four. The first two were small ships moving fast from Murmansk to the *Rossiya*."

Carlton looked at Pink. "That was probably Yagoda's GRU team."

"It would certainly explain why they never showed up to the party."

"We picked up two other sinking ships after that, about ten miles and half an hour apart," Hendricks continued. "The first was most likely your ship, the *Claire*, the second the *Rossiya*." He nodded to the ensign.

"They sank the *Rossiya*?" Carlton exclaimed. "Then what's left?"

"Sir, the imagery reveals the last surviving vessel, the Russian patrol boat, is the *Alexandr Nevsky*," the ensign continued. "It was officially decommissioned and sold over six months ago by the Russian Navy."

"Decommissioned and sold? That tends to prove my theory that Molotok's thugs torpedoed the *Claire Sailing*," Carlton said.

"What about the patrol boat, the *Nevsky*? Is it still around?"

"No sir. The imagery shows it proceeded due west immediately after the *Rossiya* sank."

"Which means that—" Carlton closed his eyes in concentration. "They brought us from the *Rossiya* back to the *Claire*, then they went back to the *Rossiya*," he said, tracing the movements in the air with his hand, "torpedoed the *Claire*, took the diamonds from the *Rossiya*, scuttled the *Rossiya*, and went—west you said?"

"Yes, sir."

"Went west in the Russian patrol boat, the *Nevsky*."

"Looks like that's what happened," Hendricks affirmed, turning to the young ensign. "Where is the *Nevsky* now?"

"It dropped off screen three hours ago, sir." He moved toward the plotting table. "Here." He pointed to a spot between the Norwegian and Barents Seas, roughly five hundred miles from Hammerfest, Norway, in the North Cape region.

"Dropped off the screen? You mean it went out of range?"

"Negative, sir. It just disappeared."

"It probably sank," Hendricks concluded. "We just didn't hear it. Maybe because of the convergence zone of hot and cold water up top."

"Disappeared?" Pink asked. "What is this, the Murmansk Triangle?"

Carlton straightened his back, which cracked loudly. "These guys are after the diamonds, right? We're not following people or boats. We're following diamonds. They didn't *know* the diamonds were on the icebreaker. They followed us until we led them to the *Rossiya*, then located the diamonds on board. Right?"

Pink nodded.

"So forget about us on the *Claire Sailing* for a moment. They took the diamonds from the *Rossiya* then eighty-sixed her. They took the *Nevsky* and disappeared north of Norway's North Cape. Tell me, Ensign, did the patrol boat disappear as it was sailing or did it stop first, then disappear?"

"Well, I…" The lieutenant paused, thought it over. "It remained stationary for several hours before disappearing, sir."

Carlton grinned. "There's the key."

"I'm afraid you've lost me," Hendricks admitted.

"We're not chasing people or boats, sir. We're chasing *diamonds*. If the *Nevsky* stopped before it disappeared or sank—"

"The diamonds were transferred from the *Nevsky* before it sank," Hendricks finished.

"Right. Did any vessels make contact with the *Nevsky* before it disappeared?"

He shook his head. "Negative, sir."

"If it transferred the diamonds before sinking, it must have made contact with something."

"Helo?" Pink asked.

"Negative. Too far away from the mainland," Hendricks said. "I don't know of any helo that could make that round trip even stripped down to a gas tank with rotor blades. A thousand miles. Plus time to load. No way."

"You said the *Nevsky* was decommissioned?" Carlton asked.

"That's right." Hendricks swiveled and hit the intercom. "Sonar, conn. Give me course and heading for Sierra Twenty-One."

"Yes, sir." The sonar watch supervisor pulled up Sierra Twenty-One on the BSY-2. "Course heading at time of contact 2-0-1, speed 2-4 knots. Position was roughly 7-7 degrees latitude, 2-8 degrees longitude."

Hendricks turned back to the chart. "Seventy-seven degrees latitude is here. Twenty-eight degrees longitude. Here." He marked the position on the chart with an erasable grease pencil. "His heading was 201. That's this way." He moved the ruler and extrapolated Sierra Twenty-One's trajectory with the grease pencil. He looked back up at the confused faces around him, smiling. "I can tell you what made contact with the *Nevsky*, gentlemen. It was a Russian Delta Three–class nuclear submarine. The *Pushkin*. The *Nevsky's* decommissioning gave it away. You see, the *Pushkin* was also decommissioned by the Russian Navy."

Carlton wiped the sweat from his brow, shook his head. "This is getting worse and worse and worse. Are you telling me that the Russian diamond stockpile is aboard a nuclear submarine manned by Molotok's thugs?"

Hendricks nodded. "Mr. Wathne, inform COMSUBLANT we've tracked down the *Rossiya*'s cargo to Sierra Twenty-One. Get me all available information including recent SOSUS readings on Sierra Twenty-One." He referred to the United States Navy's $15 billion Sound Surveillance System network of passive sonar underwater listening devices linked by thirty thousand miles of underwater wiring installed during the cold war for NATO. "And set a new course heading 3-1-0. Flank speed." He turned to the others. "Don't worry. The *Pushkin* can do twenty-four, twenty-five knots tops. We can do—well, we can do far better than that. Wherever she is, we'll track her down."

Carlton stared into his coffee mug. "Hopefully, before it gets to where it's going first."

But twenty hours into the *Seawolf*'s mad rush, the *Pushkin* went dead silent, though no particular sound presaged the silence. Just loud flank speed one minute, dead silence the next.

"Well it didn't just disappear," Hendricks nearly shouted at Ears and his colleagues over the intercom in the sonar room. "Go dead," he commanded, hoping that stopping their engines would enable the *Seawolf* to detect the *Pushkin*.

"All stop. Aye, sir."

Although the *Seawolf*'s single screw immediately ceased churning, it took several minutes for the 9,150-ton submarine to stop. Freed from the noise pollution generated by the *Seawolf*'s propeller blades, the sonar technicians were able to detect a far wider range of acoustic signals. Human ears and electronic-signal-processing units strained to distinguish the *Pushkin*'s acoustic signature from the myriad new audible sounds.

The *Seawolf* possessed an impressive arsenal of sonar detection equipment that allowed its sonar crew to hear almost any vessel within fifty miles, no matter how silent. Unless a vessel was stopped. A BQS24 spherical bow array, a conformal low frequency array, a TB-16D medium range low frequency array, a TB-29 thin-line towed array, and a WLR-9 acoustic intercept active sonar receiver. Despite the sub's state-of-the-art sonar surveillance equipment, all that the sonar crew detected were USN and Royal Navy surface vessels preparing to engage in maneuvers in the far North Sea, and cargo vessels in the Barents Sea. The *Pushkin* remained undetected. Not even a "hole in the water," which was an acoustical area in the water empty of background acoustical signals.

"Sir, what are the possible explanations for the loss of signal?" asked Carlton.

"God only knows. It could be a whole bunch of things. Underwater warm and cold convergence layers, power failure, stopping dead to see if anyone's around."

"What about surfacing? Could the *Pushkin* have surfaced?"

Hendricks shook his head. "No surfacing sounds. When a sub surfaces, it makes a ton of noise. The *Pushkin* was at seven hundred feet, moving about twenty-four knots. Surfacing from that depth requires expelling water from ballast tanks, which makes noise. The decrease in water pressure makes the hull expand, which makes it groan and pop. We didn't hear any of those sounds, which would have been as loud, if not louder, than the screw noise."

"What if it surfaced slowly? Really slowly. Would the ballast and hull popping sounds have been as loud?"

"Far less, but still there. I doubt we would have missed it. What are you getting at?"

"From what you stated, unless the *Pushkin*'s got some amazing new silencing technology, which is doubtful since the sub was scrapped, as you pointed out, then it's stopped either on the surface or underwater, right?"

"It could be running. It's not necessarily stopped. But I see your point. It's only—" he paused to calculate—"four hours away if it's running, two hours away if it's immobile."

"This is time-sensitive, Commander. If the *Pushkin* is able to get the stockpile to Waterboer, as sure as God made little green apples you'll be facing fifty more fully armed *Pushkin*s out there within a matter of weeks. Or worse."

Carlton anticipated fierce resistance to his attempt to dictate Hendricks' course. Instead, there was only silence, while Hendricks contrasted his two options.

"Okay," he said finally. "You're the advisors. It's a bit strange, but I suppose these are strange circumstances. Instead of locating the *Pushkin* first, then intercepting, we'll take the risk that it's moving and intercept her at her last known position." Hendricks turned to his XO.

"Mr. Wathne. Forward flank. Continue original course heading and update COMSUBLANT."

"Forward flank. Same course heading. Aye, sir."

58 SEARCH

USS Seawolf
Arctic Circle Boundary
Norwegian Sea
675 miles northwest of Mo i Rana, Norway
3:05 P.M.

With nothing to do but wait, Carlton decided to do the only logical thing he could: sleep. He walked clumsily through narrow hallways to the crew sleeping area where a bunk had been assigned to him and Pink. Using the submarine procedure of "hot-bunking," the two were supposed to use the bunks alternately every six-hour shift, into which U.S. Navy subs' twenty-four-hour days were divided. Currently, it was Pink's turn. A loud snore emanated from behind the drape.

He shook Pink insistently. "Come on, Sleeping Beauty. Wakey, wakey."

Practically before Pink realized what was happening, Carlton had taken his place in the bunk and drawn the drape closed. But as soon as his head touched the pillow, Carlton knew he wouldn't be able to sleep. Erika. Waterboer. Fress. Forbes. Mazursky. MacLean. Wenzel. Osage. They all blended in a general buzz of anxiety too disturbing to cover with the blessed calm of sleep.

He prayed, tossed and turned, but could not exorcise his demons. He peered at his watch. Forty minutes, still wide awake.

He drew back the drape, went to the head, grabbed a cup of Navy joe from a tray, and walked to the control room. Pink stood behind the helmsman and planesman, arms crossed. "What's going on?"

"Still *nada*." Pink uncrossed his arms and pointed at him angrily. "You had no right waking me up like that. I was dreaming about this incredible woman that I—"

"If it's true love, she'll be there when you get back." Carlton grinned. "Anyway—"

"Sierra Twenty-One reacquired!" The intercom shrieked.

"Bearing southwest."

"Heading, range, and speed?" demanded Hendricks.

"Heading is…0-4-7. Range is 3-point-0 nautical miles. Speed 1-0 knots. Sir, she's headed directly for us!"

Carlton froze.

"Depth?"

"5-0-4 feet, sir."

"Continue course and speed. Give me distance and depth every ten seconds."

"Aye, sir."

"Why would it head directly for us?" Carlton asked.

"She heard us coming," Hendricks said. "She knows she can't hide and can't outrun us. Her only hope is to surrender or…"

"Or?"

He squinted. "Or take us down."

Carlton admired Hendricks, his Navy colleague. In a tin can surrounded by thousands of pounds of pressure, heading straight for a rogue Russian sub near the arctic, the man was cool as a cucumber. The expression of total concentration on the wiry man's face made it clear he'd take this to the very end.

"Plot firing solution," Hendricks ordered to the fire control technician. His voice was calm, steady.

"Aye, sir. Stacking the dots now." The technician referred to the mechanism by which a target's course, range, and speed were matched with time.

Hendricks detached a microphone from the wall, punched a button. "Torpedo room," a voice answered.

"This is the captain. Give me fifties in tubes 1-2-3-4."

"Aye, sir. Fifties in tubes 1-2-3-4."

Hendricks replaced the mike. "Range?"

"Target is 2-point-5 nautical miles, speed 1-0 knots, sir."

"Ready to shoot when loaded, sir," Fire Control announced.

At the *Seawolf*'s bow, two torpedomen began the arduous task of moving a 1,500-pound Gould Mark 50 torpedo into four of the sub's eight twenty-six-inch torpedo tubes. The wire-guided torpedoes could home into targets up to twenty-seven miles away. With practiced, calm, flowing movements, they moved the Mark 50s from their storage racks onto loading trays. Each of the tubes was inspected for any leftover torpedo wire and dispenser. Satisfied that the tubes were clean, the torpedomen loaded one torpedo—nicknamed a "fish"—into each tube with the help of a loading ram. They attached the "A cable" to the rear of each torpedo, which would transmit data from the launched fish directly to Fire Control in the command center. Finally, they attached a guidance wire to each weapon to enable the Fire Control technician to "swim" each fish directly to its target after launch. Finished, they sealed each of the four tube hatches. As his subordinate attached the "warshot loaded" signs to each loaded tube door, the chief torpedoman hit the intercom button. "Conn, torpedo room. Tubes 1-2-3-4 loaded, sir."

Upstairs and aft, the display for each torpedo tube winked on. Four red lights labeled "loaded" indicated that all four tubes contained a Mark 50. The Fire Control technician inspected the display. "Fire Control verifies tubes 1-2-3-4 loaded, sir."

"Range to target 2-point-3 nautical miles."

"Continue speed and course. Warm weapons," Hendricks directed, adding orders for torpedo speed and seeker-head mode.

"Torpedoes warm, sir," Fire Control responded seconds later.

Mesmerized and nearly trembling with adrenaline, Carlton watched the drivers sweat. The crew had faced such exercises in training countless times. But unlike their captain, they had never been so close to the real thing. A screw-up now wouldn't end in a black mark on their records that would ruin their careers. It would end in a watery grave. The planesman and helmsman squeezed their airplane-like controls hard to prevent themselves from shaking.

Hendricks balanced himself against the seat behind the weapons control panel with both arms, staring at the display in front of him. "Your theory was right on the money, Carlton. Congratulations."

"I had facts you didn't, that's all." Carlton reflected on whether it was appropriate to ask questions at such a time, decided to ask. "What do we do now?" The words came out of his parched throat as a series of croaks. He held on tight to his mug and realized that his hand was bone-white.

"We wait. She can hear us. We can hear her. The dance

begins. Who will shoot first?" He grinned, his eyes cold as the polar cap.

Silence reigned except for the calm tone of the sonar technician regularly reading off the range between the two submarines. It decreased at an alarming rate.

"Point-five knots. No change in course or speed."

Hendricks straightened himself. "Make the tubes ready in all respects," he ordered, uttering the traditional words used by the Silent Service since before World War II.

The Fire Control technician flooded each of the four tubes. The high pressure water that rushed into each tube created an enormous amount of noise, which quickly made its way to the *Pushkin*'s passive sonar. "Sir, tubes are flooded."

"Range point-three nautical miles."

"Continue course and heading."

"Range point-two nautical miles."

"Open outer doors 1-2-3-4," Hendricks ordered. "Has she flooded her tubes?"

"Negative, sir."

"Outer doors 1-2-3-4 open, sir."

"Firing point procedures," Hendricks announced, notifying the men in the control room all actions precedent to firing were now complete.

"Range five hundred feet. Speed and course unchanged. Sir, she's flooding her tubes!"

"Ping her!" Hendricks ordered. "Ping the *crap* out of her!"

The sonar technician activated the *Seawolf*'s spherical echo-ranging bow sonar. Calling it a "ping" was euphemistically akin to calling a sabertooth tiger "kitty." With 75,000 watts of radiated power, the wave of sonar energy that rushed through the icy water would fry the ears off of the *Pushkin*'s sonar technician unless his headphones had an automatic noise-sensitive shut-off system.

Ping!

The ping's technical purpose was to measure the distance between two subs. But Hendricks already knew the distance to the *Pushkin*, and the *Pushkin* knew the *Seawolf* knew. Hendricks was using the echo-ranging sonar, to deliver a clear message. *I've got my tubes flooded and my outer doors open and I haven't changed course yet. I'm going to shoot, you bastard.* That's what the "ping" really meant.

"Again!"

Ping!

"Again, again, again."

Ping! Ping! Ping!

Hendricks closed his eyes, inhaled deeply. "Match bearings and shoot number one."

Fire Control punched a button. The floor rumbled slightly. "Torpedo one away!"

The fish sped toward the Russian sub at one hundred knots, its own speed of fifty knots plus the *Seawolf*'s speed of fifty knots.

"Reload tube one!"

"Screw rotations slowing down, sir," the sonar technician announced. "She's stopped her screw, sir!"

"Full reverse! Guide the fish into her screw!"

The Fire Control technician counteracted the instructions previously fed into the Mark 50's brain and swam the fish into the *Pushkin*'s massive screw. The sub's drive had reversed, but the submarine continued to move forward. At the business end of the ten-mile wire trailed by the torpedo, the guidance control mechanism altered the torpedo's course to the enormous propeller blades. Seconds later, the *Seawolf* shuddered as the Mark 50 slammed into the *Pushkin*'s screw. "What happened?" Carlton finally asked, gripping a console hard.

"All stop! We've just immobilized her. She blinked first. If she wanted to attack, she would have opened her outer doors and changed course to respond to our attack. She stopped instead." Following the rules of engagement to which he adhered religiously, Hendricks would not sink a ship at surrender, which was apparently where the *Pushkin* now lay.

"So what happens now?" Carlton asked, wiping his brow.

"We wait to see what she does. She's at a total disadvantage. She's immobilized and hasn't opened her torpedo doors. If she does, we send her to the bottom with another three torpedoes." He flashed a wicked grin. "She's not going anywhere."

59 CAPTURE

Ears listened carefully to the *Pushkin* on his headphones. The sounds transmitted efficiently through the cold water bore the unmistakable signature of hull expansion and compressed air rushing into ballast tanks. "Conn, sonar. Hull popping," he announced. "She's surfacing, sir."

"Take us to thirty feet, Mr. Wathne," Hendricks ordered. "Give me depth readings. Tell Pulaski to prep a boarding party."

"Blow main ballast tank one," Wathne ordered the diving officer. He lifted the handset and pressed the button connecting him to the chief of the boat.

"Pulaski here."

"Chief, I want all the SEALs ready to board the *Pushkin*. We have to assume she'll put up a fight."

"Aye, sir. I'm on it."

Almost immediately, the *Seawolf* achieved positive buoyancy and floated toward the surface. The diving officer read off their depth at regular intervals. The silence in the control room was replaced with loud groans as the *Seawolf*'s hull expanded in the shallow water.

"Thirty feet," the diving officer announced. "Holding at thirty feet, sir."

"Up scope one," Hendricks ordered. He pressed his eyes against the Type 18 search periscope's eyepiece as its mast unsheathed from the fairwater. He rotated the scope toward the *Pushkin*. Despite a strong wind, the sea was unnaturally calm. The dark shape of the *Pushkin*'s fairwater appeared through the optics, followed by the top third of its hull. All the way aft, he could see the mangled remains of the *Pushkin*'s screw.

He waited until three officers established a bridge watch on the *Pushkin*'s fairwater, then began to tap instructions in Morse code. The message was transmitted via a flashing white light on top of the *Seawolf*'s periscope, the only part of the *Seawolf* above surface.

Rogue submarine *Pushkin*. This is USS *Seawolf*. Surrender at once. All personnel exit the submarine and stand on the hull unarmed. Once you comply, you will be boarded. Any person found inside the submarine will be shot. Repeat. Any person found inside will be shot. Acknowledge.

The officers of the *Pushkin* had no choice but to comply. Their tacit acknowledgment came quickly via flashes from the Russian sub's navigation light and a makeshift white flag hoisted on a small mast. Her crew disgorged from the fore and aft escape hatches.

"Boarding party ready, sir," Chief Pulaski announced.

Hendricks waited until the exodus aboard the *Pushkin* ceased, then turned to Wathne.

"Surface, Mr. Wathne," he ordered, struggling into a thick black parka with the help of a sailor.

Compressed air forced the remaining seawater out of the *Seawolf*'s ballast tanks. Within thirty seconds, the ominous jet-black hull of the *Seawolf* broke through the surface of the Norwegian Sea, seemingly unaffected by the low frozen swells.

"XO, you have the conn."

"I have the conn, sir."

Carlton turned to Hendricks as the captain grabbed a rung on the ladder that led to the fairwater hatch. "Commander."

Hendricks stopped, turned. "What is it?"

"Sir, Mr. Pink and I respectfully request permission to join the boarding party."

Hendricks stared at Carlton for several seconds as he gauged the pros and cons of granting them permission, concluding that there were no two persons on his sub more qualified to take part in a search of the Russian sub. After all, it was for their mission that the *Seawolf* was boarding the sub in the first place. He still did not know Pink's identity, but he did know he was the only man on board who spoke fluent Russian. "It's your funeral," he said, then turned to Wathne. "XO, have someone take these gentlemen to the boarding party." He turned back toward Carlton. "Better suit up, gentlemen. It's colder than a witch's tit up there." He squinted. "Kick ass and take names."

The *Seawolf*'s boarding party was made up of Chief Pulaski, Carlton, Pink, and six Navy Sea Air Land Special Forces commandos (SEALs). SEALs generally did not travel on U.S. submarines unless they were on special assignment. Fortunately for the *Seawolf*, a team of eight SEALs had been assigned to the sub as part of an intense five-day ice survival training course, which the Special Forces commandos would have completed but for the change in the *Seawolf*'s orders.

The bows of the *Seawolf*'s two black rubberized Zodiacs created trails of foam as they plowed through the frigid gray water toward the *Pushkin*. Hendricks watched their progress through binoculars high atop the *Seawolf*'s fairwater. Two SEAL snipers each on either side of him covered the boarding party. Motionless, they scanned the *Pushkin*'s personnel carefully through Leupold ULTRA M3 scopes atop Robar SR60D rifles, ready to take any of the sailors down at the slightest aggressive move. Unlike the days of World War II when submarines were equipped with cannon atop their decks, the *Seawolf* carried no such armament. Nonetheless, the situation was eminently clear: surrender or die.

As chief of the boat, Tadeusz "Tad" Pulaski was the senior enlisted man aboard. A bear of a man, the direct descendant of Polish General Casimir Pulaski who fought alongside George Washington in the Revolutionary War, he had seen more than his fair share of combat. He sat at the bow of the lead Zodiac, his gaze moving among Carlton and Pink, who carried customized 45ACP Colt revolvers, and the three remaining SEALs, each armed with 5.56mm Steyr AUG semiautomatic machine guns and MK2 combat knives. Bulletproof vests protected them from enemy fire. Seatec horse collar vests and DUI dry suits protected against immersion in the freezing water. Satisfied, Pulaski turned forward to the nearly black hull of the *Pushkin*, now only twenty yards away, turned back to the other SEAL driver and signaled for the three other SEALs to split off.

The two Zodiacs immediately changed course. Pulaski and the first team with Carlton and Pink headed to the front of the sub. The second team headed aft. The Zodiacs reached the *Pushkin* simultaneously. Though the Russian crew did not put up a fight, neither did it lift a finger to help the boarding party climb aboard. Still under the protective gaze of their sniper brethren, the six SEALs clambered up the hull of the *Pushkin* with practiced ease as though it was a department store escalator, then helped Carlton and Pink up.

Pulaski watched as the SEALs frisked the *Pushkin's* crew for weapons. What he saw bothered him. First, only thirty men stood on the deck of the *Pushkin*, a third of its regular crew. Second, although the men donned the uniforms of the Russian Navy, not a single one was under thirty. Most of the crew should have been in their late teens and early twenties. Third, the eyes of the men who stood silently on the hull revealed none of the surprise, fear, or hatred he would expect of military men in their predicament, rather a smoldering acceptance of failure. Pulaski sensed the threat was far more dangerous than he'd anticipated. He braced himself for some form of resistance. A faked nuclear reactor emergency. An attempt to scuttle the ship. For now, there was only cold silence.

"Okay, sir. They're all clean," a SEAL reported.

Pulaski silently motioned for the men to hold their positions and stand guard.

Careful not to interfere with the man's duties, Carlton waited for Pulaski to finish before he approached. "How does it look?" he finally asked.

"I don't like it, sir," Pulaski answered. "Not one bit. There's something screwy going on here." He spat, then listed his misgivings as he scratched his chin with the snout of his Colt. "No sir. I don't like it one bit." He motioned to two of the SEALs. "Let's go!"

While four SEALs covered the thirty *Pushkin* crew members, two other SEALs, Pulaski, Carlton, and Pink climbed the sunken handholds to the top of the fairwater. Although it was customary protocol for surrendering officers to salute their victors, the two senior officers atop the fairwater failed to move a muscle or utter a sound. They merely stood and stared at Pulaski, Carlton, Pink, and the two SEALs who held them at gunpoint from both sides of the fairwater.

"Chief Pulaski, United States Navy. We are taking possession of your vessel for acts of international terrorism against an unarmed American cargo ship, an unarmed Russian icebreaker, and two Russian Navy patrol boats," he announced, Pink providing translation to the senior officer, a man in his late thirties with a chiseled face and deep blue eyes who wore a fur hat with a red hammer and sickle.

Carlton immediately recognized him as the man who had torpedoed the *Claire Sailing* and left them to die in the Barents Sea. He waited for Pink to finish his translation.

"The United States Navy destroyer *Martin Luther King Jr.* will remove you and your crew inside three hours and hold you until the Russian Navy arrives," Pulaski continued. There was no chance of the crew escaping. The *Pushkin* was immobilized and Pulaski would put its communications out of commission. "Are there any more of your crew below deck, Captain?"

"*Nyet.*"

"You are certain, Captain? Any person found below deck will be summarily shot. I will give you one more chance to evacuate your crew."

The Russian's stoic face finally creased into a condescending smirk. Carlton eyed the man carefully. It was the first time he had taken a long, hard look at him. Not only was he clearly the man who had captured them on the *Rossiya*, but there was something else about the man that made Carlton think hard. He knew that smile. But from where?

Pulaski motioned for the Russian captain to proceed down the hatch, accompanied by the two SEALs. Carlton and Pink waited for Pulaski's signal, then followed him down.

The Russian captain had apparently complied with Hendricks's orders. The control room was empty. Bathed in red light from the emergency illumination system, the only sound in the cramped room was the heavy breathing of the five Americans, weapons at the ready. Pulaski switched the lights from red to white. He informed the two SEALs of the large cargo of diamonds believed to be on board and ordered them to search the ship. They separated, began a complete search of the boat. Pulaski scanned the control boards with an expert eye. "Torpedo tubes are empty. VLS is empty."

"VLS?" Carlton inquired.

"Vertical Launch System," Pulaski explained. "Delta-class subs have aft external tubes that contain vertical launch missiles."

"I thought this was an attack sub."

"Attack subs also carry missiles, just fewer than boomers." Pulaski referred to missile submarines. He pointed to the control board. "This boat is empty. Which makes sense. This sub is used to transport a diamond cargo. It doesn't need missiles, and less weight means greater speed."

Carlton nodded. Pink sat at the communications station, read the Cyrillic stamped below knobs and switches. Within two minutes, Pulaski managed to establish contact with the *Seawolf* on the Russian radio.

"All secure, sir," Pulaski announced. "No, sir. We haven't discovered anything yet. We're conducting a search right now. We'll contact you as soon as we discover anything."

As Pulaski replaced the handset, a rush of air swept by him, accompanied by a yell of raw anger as Carlton plowed his head into the Russian captain's stomach, slamming him against the aluminum periscope. The Russian's fur cap fell to the ground, revealing closely cropped blond hair. Staring straight into the man's blue eyes, Carlton shoved the muzzle of his Colt against the man's temple.

Pulaski instinctively drew his weapon, pointed them at the two men. "For God's sakes, Carlton. What the hell are you—"

"It's him." Carlton ground out behind clenched teeth. "The guy who gave me the package in D.C." He grabbed Ulianov's hair and jerked his head backward into the metal pillar with such force that it made a dent. "The bastard who threatened Erika."

"Calm yourself, Lieutenant," Pulaski ordered.

"*Amerikanskii*," Ulianov sneered, his face creased with the same condescending smirk he had flashed minutes before atop the fairwater. "Why can't you mind your own—"

"Why?" Carlton shouted. "Why can't we mind our own

business? Because every time the world becomes a better place, anachronisms like you fuck it up!"

Carlton kept tempo with his words by slamming the man's head repeatedly into the metal pillar. He raged with an anger he had never felt before. All of his pains and fears and frustrations and shames melted into a burning hatred concentrated on the Russian he pinned to the metal bulkhead. He felt his finger cock the handgun and push its barrel hard against the man's temple. So hard that the skin near the muzzle became white, then began to bleed. Pink and Pulaski stood frozen, afraid that any attempt to separate Carlton from Molotok's henchman would push him over the edge.

"I can kill you right here," Carlton whispered.

"*Da.*"

"I can blow your fucking head off."

"Then do it," Ulianov mocked.

"You would pull the trigger?"

Ulianov squinted at Carlton, grinned condescendingly. "I would kill you. Just like I would kill that cheap *nekulturny* slut of yours."

Carlton felt his body convulse with anger. His right hand tightened around the Colt's grip and jammed the muzzle harder against the man's bleeding temple. The Russian licked his own blood, smiled perversely.

"Well I'm not like you," Carlton whispered. "We live according to the rule of law. That's why your pitiful communist masters failed." A loud click resounded in the deathly still control room as Carlton's finger uncocked the Colt. "You'll be tried in a court of law. By your own people."

"*Yob tvoyu mat.*" Fuck your mother. Ulianov shoved him backward. His eyes filled with surprise and agony as Carlton launched his booted right foot between the man's legs. Ulianov pitched forward, bent in half. Carlton followed through with a nasty uppercut that sent the Russian to the ground, flat on his back.

"Don't press your luck," Carlton advised as he replaced the Colt in his side holster. He looked at the SEAL ensign who had just returned from his search of the forward end of the sub and jabbed his thumb upward. "Ensign. Take out the trash."

"Sir! Yes, sir!"

"What do you mean, 'nothing'?" Carlton asked the SEAL team leader once they were back on board the *Seawolf*, submerged at five hundred feet.

"There's nothing, sir. We checked everywhere. Storage lockers. Torpedo tubes. VLS tubes. Escape trunks. Crew quarters. Kitchen. Rec room. We even checked the trash room and bilge. Just a few diamonds on the floor." He handed them to Carlton. "Nothing else. We stripped this tub. There's no diamond stockpile on this vessel, sir."

"It doesn't make any sense," Carlton muttered to himself. He observed the cut diamonds in his hand, holding them to the light. They glowed. "The diamonds were definitely there."

"They're not there anymore, sir."

Carlton paced, then turned to Pulaski and Pink. "*Rossiya*'s last contact before she sank was with *Nevsky*. The team from the *Nevsky* transferred from the *Rossiya* to the *Pushkin*, then sank the *Nevsky*. There weren't any sonar contacts near the *Pushkin* while we were chasing her. So where the hell are the diamonds?"

"They could have tossed them over the side so we wouldn't get them," proposed Pink. "They could just retrieve them later."

"No way. They wouldn't have gone through all of this just to dump their ticket to power. They've got to get the diamonds to Waterboer."

"They could have marked the area with a sonobuoy for retrieval later," Pulaski suggested. "Or with some other form of marker."

"No. They couldn't risk anyone else seeing it."

Back aboard the *Seawolf*, Carlton gazed at Pink. "So what is it you want to check, exactly?"

"For one thing, if they did sink the diamonds, we can interdict access to the swath of ocean between here and the *Rossiya*'s resting place. The destroyer coming to pick up the *Pushkin*'s crew should be able to do that when it gets here.

Until then, the *Seawolf*'s passive sonar will monitor that area. Can we do that, Commander?" He turned to Hendricks, who nodded affirmatively.

"Fine." Carlton's tone made it clear that he thought the plan was anything but fine. Something didn't sit right with him. "That's assuming they did throw the diamonds overboard. But what was it you had to come back here to check?"

"From my limited understanding of submarines—please correct me if I'm wrong, Commander—the only way the *Pushkin* could have tossed the diamonds overboard is either by surfacing or by jettisoning the diamonds through the torpedo tubes."

"Affirmative."

"But our sonar didn't detect any such noise, did it?"

"No. But come look at this."

Ears led them to the BSY-2 sonar room and pointed at the screen. "Right here." He stopped the fast-forward replay of the passive sonar search during the *Seawolf*'s chase of the *Pushkin* and pointed to the left of the screen. The vertical white line that had been there a second before disappeared. He continued the fast forward mode. The white line reappeared several seconds later. "Looks like Ivan went dead for about ten minutes."

"Went dead, yes. But still no torpedo tube or surfacing sounds. It probably went dead just to listen," Hendricks said.

"To listen?" Carlton asked.

"When submarines move fast, they generate a lot of noise," answered Hendricks. "So it's hard for the sub to hear other subs with its passive sonar. Every once in a while, a sub moving fast stops its screw and listens for sonar contacts to see if it's being followed. Sometimes it clears its baffles by circling 360 degrees. This white line shows the sonar signature generated by the *Pushkin*."

Ears turned toward Hendricks. "I don't think she went dead to listen, sir." He grabbed a sonar printout. "I studied the SOSUS scan. See this?" He pointed to a short faint line that disappeared, reappeared, then disappeared for good. "Even though it's pretty far away from the nearest SOSUS detector, it looks like ballast noise."

"But ballast noise would be in this frequency over here, wouldn't it?" Hendricks pointed to the other side of the page.

"You're right, sir. But my theory is that this SOSUS buoy's brain was damaged by a storm or a biological or something. The contact is in the wrong frequency, but it's an identical signature to ballast noise. I'm convinced it's ballast noise, sir."

"I've learned not to disagree with your instinct, Ears. But that's still not hard evidence."

"How about this, sir? It matches up perfectly with the time periods." He reversed the BSY-2 display, moved it forward slowly. "Contact lost here." He pointed to the page. "Surfacing ballast signature here." Back to the BSY-2. "Contact reacquired here." Back to the page. "Submersion ballast signature here. See? No sonar evidence whatsoever of torpedo tube doors opening or flooding or jettisoning."

Hendricks sucked in air as he evaluated the fact. He remained silent for several minutes, squinting at the BSY-2 display. "Okay, Ears. You win. Good work, son."

He stood up straight, led Carlton and Pink back to the control room, pausing to grab a coffee mug emblazoned with the *Seawolf*'s insignia: a snarling wolf with a shark's tail.

"So the *Pushkin* surfaced and threw the diamonds overboard here." Carlton pointed to the position on a plotting table map where the *Pushkin* had surfaced. "All we need to do is search that area with everything we've got." He straightened.

"The destroyer *Martin Luther King Jr.* coming to pick up the *Pushkin* crew will initiate those procedures," responded Hendricks.

"But what if the *Pushkin* didn't sink the diamonds?" Carlton wondered.

"What do you mean? They're not in the sub and we know it didn't fire them through its tubes."

"They're not in the sub, but according to Ears, the sub did surface. What if it transferred the diamonds off the sub to a boat?"

"No." Hendricks pointed to the sonar report. "That's the whole problem. Sonar shows no boats or subs anywhere in the *Pushkin*'s path since it met up with the *Nevsky*. The only sonar contact in the vicinity was a group of whales a hundred miles to the south of *Pushkin*'s path. I don't want to brag, but our sonar is the best on the planet. If there was a sub or a surface vessel, we would have heard it."

"What about an aircraft?"

"Impossible. We've been through that argument before, before we knew about the *Pushkin*. We're seven hundred miles away from land. A helicopter could travel a couple of hundred miles, three hundred tops. Definitely not seven hundred. And that's only one way."

"What about a float plane?" asked Carlton.

"Sonar would have picked it up. If not our own, then SOSUS. I agree with Pink. They must have dropped the diamonds over the side. There's no other logical explanation. And that's only one way."

"They were picked up by air," Carlton offered.

Hendricks looked up at the ceiling. "I thought we buried that theory twice already." Obviously irritated, he started to rise, sat back down. "Look. Ears told us there was no sonar contact with a float plane. The *Pushkin* was always too far from land for a helicopter to do the job."

"I understand all that, Commander. But it's also the only explanation. Remember, once you've eliminated the impossible, whatever's left is possible, no matter how strange. And we've only eliminated float planes and helicopters as possible air-based transport. Those are only two types of aircraft."

"What are you suggesting? A hot air balloon?"

"A Harrier."

"A Harrier?"

Carlton motioned with his palm. "Vertical take off and land—"

"I am familiar with Harriers, Carlton. A Harrier couldn't have done the job. They can hover. But do you know how small a Harrier is? Where would they put the diamonds? Their range is only about twenty-five hundred miles. Wherever they came from would have to be pretty close to fly in, hover, and fly back. And there were no reports of unidentified Harriers in the area."

"One Harrier couldn't have done it." Carlton paused. "But a group of Harriers could have."

"They could have refueled mid-air," Pink said. "That would double their range to five thousand miles."

"Even if several Harriers came in and hovered or landed. And even if they were able to refuel in mid-air, how would the crew have gotten that many diamonds aboard?"

"Pods," Carlton said in a muted voice. "The Harriers could have come in unarmed then fitted with pods."

Hendricks continued to nod. "I've never heard of Harriers being fitted with pods while hovering. Still, assuming that it could be done, where would the *Pushkin* have kept the pods? The *Pushkin* is an attack sub. Every single item on board has to be brought through the hatches, including the torpedoes. I don't know if you've ever observed torpedoes being loaded into a submarine, but it takes hours, steady seas, special equipment. Even if they could have gotten the pods on board, they'd be too big for the torpedo room, even the tubes."

"When we entered the *Pushkin*, the chief mentioned something about the—what did he call them? The missile tubes?"

"The VLS tubes?"

"That's it. They were empty, right?"

"If that's what the chief said, that's what it is."

"So it's possible, isn't it?"

"Let me get this straight," Hendricks held up his hands. "You want me to believe that a decommissioned Russian attack sub operated by Russian nationalists made contact with a Russian patrol boat, sank it, submerged, resurfaced, transferred millions of carats of diamonds from the *Pushkin* in pods from the VLS tubes onto multiple hovering Harrier fighters that refueled in mid-air, and submerged again—all without the *Ronald Reagan* carrier battle group running exercises in the GIUK gap being aware of either Harrier jets or an airborne tanker?"

"That's about it, yeah." Carlton nodded.

"Well, I think you're nuts. There is no—" A loud chime interrupted him.

"Wathne, Captain. Sorry to bother you, sir, but VLF orders us to pick up a UHF transmission."

"Very well, XO. Go to scope depth, pick it up, then take us back down to five hundred. The weather's bad enough as it is."

Institute for Works of Religion
aka The Vatican Bank
Vatican City State
10:05 A.M.

"My God." Hundreds of millions. The head of the Order. Its Father General, Cardinal Altiplano, had stolen hundreds of millions of dollars. From universities and hospitals and missions. For over ten years. "How could I have let it happen?"

"You did not know, Eminence."

"Of course I didn't know, but I should have known. I should have known. Can you imagine the proportions of this scandal? It's...it's gigantic. It will make the Banco Ambrosiano scandal look like Ferragosto." The cardinal referred to the Feast of the Ascension of Mary, which in Italy was a national holiday. "*Santa Maria!* Just look at this horror!" He pointed to the reams of financial documents uncovered in the deceased Father General Altiplano's private files.

"We must have faith, Eminence."

"Faith. Yes." He exhaled deeply. "But so much money. So much money. Taken from children, the poor, the elderly, and the sick. And for what? For Altiplano's ambition to become pope. Can you imagine what will happen when this nightmare is discovered?"

"If it is discovered, Eminence. *If.*"

"But it will. And technically it was in our care. It will be discovered missing. Five hundred million dollars. May God have mercy on our souls."

"But the money has not disappeared, Eminence. It has only been... transformed. From intangible to tangible assets."

"That is easy to say. Here. In private. The Church already has such severe financial problems. What if the Banco Napolitana Lucchese fails? Declares bankruptcy? Its assets. Its loans. Its books and vaults. They will be scrutinized. It will cause a scandal. An enormous scandal. The Lord detests scandal, Lucca."

"Eminence. From the evidence we have, only Altiplano's most trusted agents made the purchases in Angola. Small purchases only. None over $50,000. Angola was in a state of civil war, everything confused and crazed, Eminence. There are no records."

"Lucca, Lucca. My trusted friend. God bless your silver tongue, but I am afraid that for all of the authority I wield as a prince of the Church, I am still only a simple peasant priest. I am terrified of scandal. Particularly such an enormous scandal as this. Not for me or you. We did nothing wrong. But I am afraid for the Church."

"The Church has regularly faced scandal for two thousand years. The devil tempts. Sometimes he succeeds. We must remember that evil and the jaws of death will never prevail over the Holy Church."

"In the end, yes. But what about now? How will the world react? Hundreds of years of hospitals and universities curing the sick and educating those hungry for knowledge, now in question. In doubt. Only an enormous amount of faith can overcome such a storm."

"Let us pray for faith, then, Eminence."

The prince of the Church, Cardinal Priest in the title of Saint Matthew, president of the Commission of the Institute for Works of Religion, and former peasant priest, together with his secretary, knelt on the polished inlaid hardwood floor before a seventeenth-century rosewood and silver crucifix that hung on the *fleur de lis* silk brocade wall. They performed the sign of the cross with reverence.

"*In nomine Patris et Filius et Spiritu Sanctus,*" the cardinal recited solemnly.

"*Amen,*" responded the Monsignor.

"*Oremus,*" the cardinal announced then bowed his head. "*Pater noster,*" he began. Our Father.

The Monsignor joined him. "*Qui est in caelis, sanctificetur nomen tuum...*" Who art in heaven. Hallowed be thy name.

61 CARRIERS

HMS Invincible
Royal Navy Nuclear Aircraft Carrier
Norwegian Sea
501 miles south of Longyerben, Spitzbergen
6:02 P.M.

Royal Navy Lieutenant Sandra Walters had called out three times to the missing RAF Hercules air tanker—nicknamed "Bernice" by the RAF—and the three RAF Sea Harriers that had just refueled from her in mid-air. Without response. But Lieutenant Walters was tenacious. She would try until she received an answer.

"Bernice. This is *Invincible*. Come in Bernice," she repeated. It had disappeared from her radar screen immediately after refueling the three Harriers on a training mission. The Harriers had departed the Keflavik NATO Air Base in Iceland and were supposed to refuel in mid-air, then return to Iceland. Not only did the Bernice disappear from the radar screen shortly after the Harriers had refueled, but the Harriers had also disappeared. And Lieutenant Walters' counterpart in Iceland couldn't locate any of them either.

"We have lost you from radar. Come in." She quickly switched frequencies. "Squadron Leader Leyland. Pilot Officers Carruthers and Fox. This is *Invincible*. Come in. Have lost you from radar. Come in, over." She repeated the entreaties a fourth time before summoning her CO, Commander Todd Shollen. "Sir, Bernice disappeared from our screen. So did the three training Sea Harriers en route from Keflavik. They just disappeared, sir. No radio contact. No mayday signal. No SAR beacon. Keflavik doesn't have anything either, sir."

Shollen saw the confusion in her eyes. Walters was not a novice. If Bernice and the three Sea Harriers were in the air, she would have spotted them on the screen or raised them by radio. Shollen picked up the handset. An airplane as large and slow as a Hercules tanker doesn't just disappear from radar.

Neither do training Harriers led by an experienced pilot such as Squadron Leader Leyland. It couldn't be an electronic glitch. The *Invincible*'s radar was fully operative. All of the other birds in range continued to register as green blips. Shollen winced, hoping for the best, sensing the worst. But regulations were regulations, and he followed them to the letter. "Keep trying." He punched the button marked AWCINC—Air Wing Commander-in-Chief.

"Hennessey." The voice made it clear that the interruption had better be important.

"Communications, sir. Commander Shollen." He paused. "Sir, we have a situation."

Within ten seconds, the wail of the Search and Rescue siren sounded above the flight deck. Two minutes later, a pair of Sea Harriers outfitted with special SAR equipment accelerated down and up the carrier's special ramps reserved for Harriers and rocketed on full afterburners toward the last reported position of the four missing aircraft.

Nearly one thousand miles to the south of HMS *Invincible*, the USS *Ronald Reagan* carrier battle group, designated CVBG-12, was steaming north to conduct joint NATO exercises with the *Invincible*, the French Navy's newest carrier, *Charles de Gaulle*, and their support vessels during the following week. The carrier battle group is the most persuasive tool of American foreign policy. While most people consider it merely as a group of warships, in reality it is a flexible, mobile, and sovereign American platform able to project a variety of offensive air and sea weapons systems on simultaneous, multiple and nearly indefinite missions in faraway regions. As such, carrier battle groups not only keep foreign threats far from America's borders, but concomitantly impose total military control over particular coastal regions.

Whereas most modern navies, such as those of Great Britain and France, maintained two aircraft carrier groups, the U.S. Navy maintained twelve carrier battle groups (CVBGs)— eleven on active patrol at any given time with one in drydock for maintenance—out of its total 350 surface ships and seventy-five submarines. As such, the United States Navy wielded a power unimagined by most civilians and feared by her enemies.

Centered around the post-*Nimitz*-class USS *Ronald Reagan CVN-76*, the $20 billion, one-month-old replacement of the USS *Kitty Hawk*, CVBG-12 was composed of two *Ticonderoga*-class Aegis-guided missile cruisers, one *Arleigh Burke*–class Aegis destroyer, one *Spruance*-class destroyer, two *Oliver Hazard Perry*–class guided-missile frigates, one *Sacramento*-class combat support vessel, one *Los Angeles*–class attack submarine, and Commander Hendricks' *Seawolf*-class attack submarine; a total of eight surface vessels and two submarines.

USN CVBG-12 Commander-in-Chief Rear Admiral Jack Yorbis was sipping a mug of coffee from the *Reagan*'s state-of-the-art bridge as he spoke to Royal Navy Admiral Hennessey. "Cyril. It's Jack. Listen, one of our Hawkeyes just received positive radar confirmation of three RAF Sea Harriers bearing southwest 110 nautical miles west of Lofoten, Norway. You fellas change the flight pattern?"

"Negative, Admiral. Southwest you say? They're supposed to be headed northeast, back to Keflavik in Iceland."

"Well southwest is where they're headed. They're flying like bats out of hell, 730 knots, two hundred feet above the chop. Looks like they're headed to London, although it's a bit early to be sure."

Based on Commander Shollen's report, Admiral Cyril Hennessey understood the gravity of the situation. He cleared his throat. "Admiral Yorbis, Her Majesty's Navy requests the United States Navy's cooperation in tracking down what may be rogue RAF fighter aircraft."

Yorbis approved of the man's difficult decision. "It is the U.S. Navy's pleasure to do so, Admiral. We'll intercept and coordinate with your people. I'll get back to you." He turned to his executive officer. "Turn us into the wind, XO." Aircraft carriers always turned into the wind during air operations to achieve greater airspeed for aircraft taking off. He hit the intercom and described the situation to the air boss on the Primary Flight Control deck, one flight up from the *Reagan*'s bridge.

The air boss listened, affirmed Yorbis's orders, locked his handset in place, and turned to his deputy, casually known as the "mini" boss. "Get a Seahawk and a Viking up A-S-A-P." Before any fighters could be launched, a U.S. Navy carrier generally sent up a Seahawk helicopter to conduct a search-and-rescue operation in the event of a mishap and a Viking refueling aircraft to top off long-range fighters' tanks shortly after launch. "Then scramble four Hornets. Intercept three rogue RAF Harriers. Coordinates to follow. Now."

Wathne ripped the message from the printer and handed it to Hendricks. Hendricks read it and passed it on to Carlton. "Maybe my use of the word 'nuts' was too harsh."

```
Z73446
FR: CINC CVW USS RONALD REAGAN
TO: CO USS SEAWOLF
3 RAF HARRIERS POS LAT E9°30'02" LON N68°15'20"
BRNG 216 SPD 690 ALT 211'
PART OF RAF TRAIN REFL TNKR LOST AFT CNTCT
HMS INVINCIBLE STATES HARRIERS REFUS RADIO
CNTCT
UNSCHD BRNG POSBL BANDITS
SCRAMBLED ETA 1903
XTRM CAUTN
AWAIT FURTHER UHF
END TRANS
```

Carlton glanced from the message to the chart console and back several times before handing the piece of paper to Pink. "Well, at least now we've got our proof."

62 HORNETS

USS Ronald Reagan (CVN-76)
United States Navy Nuclear Aircraft Carrier
6:12 P.M.

The *Ronald Reagan*'s 4.5-acre platform was home to seventy-five aircraft, not counting its deadly missiles. Thirty-six F/A-18E Super Hornet fighters, seventeen F-14D Tomcat fighters, four E-2C Hawkeye surveillance aircraft, six S-3B Viking anti-submarine/in-flight refueling aircraft, four EA-6B Prowler electronic warfare aircraft, two ES-3B Shadow communications intelligence/in-flight refueling aircraft, four SH-60F Seahawk antisubmarine helicopters, and two HH-60G Seahawk combat search-and-rescue helicopters.

The F/A-18E Super Hornet reigned as undisputed lord and master within the deep and wide panoply of American naval fighters. Designed by McDonnell Douglas—"Mac Dac"—before the company was merged into Boeing Military Aircraft, the Super Hornet was a necessary upgrade of the often-criticized F/A-18C Hornet. It combined stealth, speed, and electronic brainpower in an attack/air superiority/precision strike/enemy air defense suppression fighter so lethal that enemy missile ground crews quaked in their boots at the knowledge of the winged demon's approach, and enemy pilots often retreated with full afterburners from the mere possibility of an engagement.

The Super Hornet's first-ever fully integrated liquid-cooled avionics suite ran over one million lines of computer code at seven hundred million operations per second, roughly equal to the combined power of four Cray supercomputers. Mated to a full-color glass multi-function display (MFD) instead of traditional and confusing analog gauges, fitted with a holographic heads up display (HUD) system and a helmet-mounted weapons targeting sight, the vicious bird of prey's quad-redundant fly-by-wire flight control system allowed acceleration, pitch, yaw, and roll rates at a sustained nine times Earth gravity (9 Gs), limited only by the human endurance of its pressure-suited single pilot. The Super Hornet's landing gear and airframe were strengthened. Its ratio of fuel weight to total weight was significantly increased. Able to generate 22,000 pounds of thrust each, its twin General Electric F414-GE-400 engines could push the attack fighter through the envelope at still-classified vertiginous speeds. An ALE-50 towed decoy system protected the aircraft from enemy missiles. Its Hughes Electronics Forward-Looking Infrared (FLIR) targeting system was made to detect targets in infrared rather than visible light, thus granting the Super Hornet the best targeting system of any fighter in production. Although no self-respecting naval aviator would use it voluntarily, a "Mode-1" system could land the fighter on its own even on the often deadly swaying deck of an aircraft carrier. The bonus was that the Super Hornet's $58 million price tag was far more politically acceptable than its Air Force cousin F-22A Raptor's price of $214 million.

In sum, it was American.

It was the best.

The handler in charge of each aircraft's position on the flight deck ordered the deck crew to move four Super Hornets into position. The aircraft had been fueled with 19,000 pounds of kerosene by the purple shirt "grapes" and armed with ten AIM-9X Sidewinder Air-to-Air Missiles (AAM) by the red shirt weapons crews. Lieutenant Commander Milo Stevan (callsign "Smoke") and Lieutenants Peter Rieble (callsign "Senator"), Todd Samo (callsign "Elvis"), and Tanya Venice (callsign "Venus") exited the squadron ready room and climbed into the cockpits. The green shirt mechanics instructed the pilots to start their engines. As the canopies locked shut, the mechs gave each aircraft another check, careful to avoid the jet engine intakes that could—and sometimes did—suck deck crew members into aircrafts' bowels. With one of the hundred hand signals each deck crew member knew from memory, the mechs warned their colleagues of impending jet exhaust. The seawater-cooled Jet Blast Deflectors (JBDs) were raised aft of the engines. The pilots moved the Super Hornets under their own power across the slick metal deck and halted at the business end of three of the

Reagan's four C13 Mod. 1 catapults. The catapult crew secured each aircraft's front wheel into a catapult with a towbar and attached a holdback behind the nose gear. The mechs gave each Super Hornet a final once-over. Finally, the pilots received the order to go to full power. The weight of the aircraft was posted on a chalkboard. When all agreed on the numbers, the pilot saluted the catapult officer in the below-deck catapult "pod" and held on tight. Several seconds later, the launch officer signaled the "cat" officer—himself a former naval aviator—who hit the release button. The steam accumulated from the *Reagan*'s boilers accelerated the catapults one hundred yards forward and rocketed each Super Hornet from standstill to 150 knots in under two seconds. Now airborne, Smoke, Senator, Elvis, and Venus pointed their needle noses nearly due east. As a precaution, two Prowler aircraft were launched soon after the Hornets to jam possible enemy radar and communications.

"Interceptor. Interceptor, this is Strike," the air boss announced. "Bogeys are range 6-1-0 nautical miles. Course 2-1-6. Speed 6-0-2 knots." The term "bogey" designated aircraft whose allegiance was unknown or uncertain. "Bandit" designated an enemy aircraft. The rules of engagement (ROE) were vastly different for each of the two designations.

"Roger, Strike," Smoke acknowledged while his TRW navigation system calculated an optimal intercept course. "We're five-by-five. Climbing to fifty thousand. 6-1-0 nautical miles for bogey."

Hendricks stared at Carlton, not a little annoyed. "Carlton, just because there are fighters near the *Pushkin* that fit your theory doesn't prove your theory right. It may, however, be proof enough to order an interception, which the *Reagan* has done."

Carlton ran his hand through his hair, breathed deeply. "I realize that, sir. But look at the totality of the circumstances. The fighters match the only ones that could do such a job."

"The Harrier is one of the most common RAF jets, Carlton. The North Sea is full of 'em. Next."

"The message said 'possible bandits.' Why would the *Reagan* say that if—"

"Possible bandits, Carlton. Possible. Very different from confirmed bandits. For all we know, the English royal family could have taken the Harriers for a spin. We just don't know. Next."

He turned to the chart console and pointed to the *Pushkin*'s estimated path from the *Nevsky* to where *Seawolf* had intercepted it. "May I see the message?" He grabbed the piece of paper, read out the Harriers' coordinates, traced their estimated route from Keflavik, Iceland. "There, sir," he pointed at the chart. "The Harriers intersected the *Pushkin*'s course right about here."

Hendricks leaned over, nodded. "That's about where it would have been, yes." He looked back up at Carlton. "But it's still not enough proof to shoot them down." He sighed. "Do you realize the diplomatic incident it would cause if an American ship shot down three fighters belonging to one our allies? Not only one of our allies but Great Britain, the only ally the U.S. has been able to count on, time and time again? Flown by inexperienced trainees?

"Look. I think your theory is dead-on. Everything points to the Harriers. Their course. The *Pushkin*'s course. The fact they've been tagged as possible bandits. It's just not enough proof to recommend eliminating them. Besides, even if they do have the Russian diamonds on board, they're not threatening anyone with deadly force, are they?"

"Will you allow me to inform the battle group commander of this possibility?"

Hendricks stared at Carlton for several seconds. "That I'll do. Someone get the louie a pad to write on."

"Here, sir." An eager young ensign handed him a memo pad.

Carlton and Pink composed a brief message to Forbes. The *Seawolf* came to antenna depth, burst the transmission up to the Navy satellite, disappeared under the surface, and waited for Pink's boss to digest the information and relay it to whomever he thought would use it best under the circumstances. The CVW commander or even the CVN commander would not react to the political nature of the message as effectively as after it filtered to them through the intermediary of a military superior briefed by DDI Forbes.

Two thousand miles away, Forbes reached the same conclusion as Commander Hendricks. No deadly force threatened. No positive proof. No action. *Maintain position and observe* was the short message back to Pink on the *Seawolf*.

"Strike, this is Interceptor. Bearing 0-9-4. Request information on bogeys. Over." Smoke stared at the instrument readouts glowing on the glass cockpit's heads-up-display from behind the MBU-12/P oxygen mask that fed him an electronically regulated mixture of pressurized oxygen and nitrogen. As ordered, he and his three colleagues had refrained from performing an active radar search of the RAF bogeys for fear of detection.

"Interceptor this is Strike. Range is 1-0-2 nautical miles to bogey. Bogey has not altered course bearing of 2-1-6." The voice from over six hundred miles away sounded as clear as if it had been a foot from Smoke's ear. "Do not attempt radio contact until you have visual. Repeat. Maintain radio silence until visual. Over."

"That's a rog, Strike." A veteran of Operation Desert Storm, Smoke was not one to become nervous under stress. Still, it was strange. During the $1 million worth of training he had received from the Navy, he had been instructed to intercept enemy aircraft, engage enemy aircraft in air combat maneuvering, and destroy enemy aircraft with every weapon available in the American Navy fighter arsenal. He had even been trained to provide assistance in SAR operations. But never in his fifteen-year career as a naval aviator had Smoke ever been asked to intercept an allied fighter group. Particularly an allied training fighter group that refused to reply and radically altered course without approval of its carrier air wing CINC.

Strange, he repeated to himself. Something didn't sit right in his gut.

He pondered the orders. As lead, he was tasked with all on-site tactical decisions. If Strike did not want him to initiate radio contact until the Harriers were within visual range, it also meant that he was to remain undetected until the last minute. Which meant that he and his wingmen would have to come in from behind the RAF fighters, now racing in the general direction of

England. He made the required calculations, relayed them to his wingmen. "Elvis, Senator, Venus, this is Lead. Decrease speed to 5-0-0 knots. Adjust course to 1-1-0. Ready to initiate LPI search on my mark."

"Roger, Lead," replied Elvis.

"That's a rog," affirmed Senator.

"Roger, Ready to initiate LPI," acknowledged Venus.

Up to now, the four Super Hornets had refrained from using their active radar and instead relied on the *Reagan's* radar fix of the three RAF jets. That was about to change. Strike had ordered him not to engage in radio contact until visual ID. But that didn't mean he couldn't use his active radar.

The Super Hornets were equipped with the APG-77, the most advanced radar system ever developed. Whereas traditional radar used arrays of sensors fixed on a mechanical aiming mechanism that swept 120 degrees every fourteen seconds, the APG-77 used 1,500 independent non-mechanical modules that swept the same volume of space with simultaneous multiple beams in the blink of an eye. The true power of the APG-77, however, lay in its ability to perform low probability of intercept (LPI) searches. Because each of the modules acted independently, the radar system used low energy pulses to search a broad range of frequencies rather than a few set frequencies. The result was that a target was unable to read the pulses as an active search. In addition, the Super Hornet was crafted from carbon, thermoplastics, titanium, aluminum, steel, and other classified materials, then coated with radar-absorbing materials to achieve a radar cross section nearly one hundred times smaller than that of the fighter on enemy scopes. The combined effect was that Smoke, Senator, Elvis, and Venus could detect their targets, launch their Sidewinder AAM missiles, and destroy the rogue Harriers without their targets ever detecting anything more threatening than a large seabird hundreds of miles away.

Ten minutes later, Smoke gave the order. "This is Lead. Initiate LPI search."

63 INTERCEPTION

RAF Sea Harriers
298 miles due west of Mo-i-Rana, Norway
7:27 P.M.

The three Sea Harrier pilots cringed with pain as the high-pitched whine of their radar alarms exploded inside their helmets.

"Royal Air Force Sea Harriers. This is United States Navy Lieutenant Commander Stevan. Identify yourselves," Smoke announced in his best command voice.

The lead Harrier pilot dialed into the frequency, nearly cursed in Russian, stopped himself just in time. "Good God, mate! Where did you Yanks come from?" he replied with genuine surprise in a British accent. The last thing he had anticipated was American Navy fighters. Super Hornets, no less. His first impulse was to adopt evasive maneuvers, but he forced himself to continue on course. He wouldn't have a snowflake's chance in hell of outmaneuvering or outrunning the American fighters eight hundred feet below on his six. He cursed himself for no longer hugging the waves.

"From thin air," Smoke replied dryly. "I repeat. Identify yourselves immediately." At his altitude of two hundred feet, he could barely make out the outlines of the three Harriers through the fist-sized drops of rain that pelted his glass canopy in a wicked crosswind.

"Squadron Leader Leyland. Royal Air Force. With Pilot Officers Carruthers and Fox. For God's sake, Lieutenant Commander, take us off radar lock! You're scaring my trainees half to death!"

The alarms ceased. The radar lock was tactically unnecessary. The APG-77 radar would allow the AAM missiles to reach their targets without radar-lock. It had been performed entirely for demonstrative effect. "Thanks."

"HMS *Invincible* demands the reasons for your course change and radio silence."

"We've been trying to reach the *Invincible* for the past two hours. Our tanker exploded immediately after our refuel. I don't know what happened. The explosion must have generated an electromagnetic pulse of some sort. Our long-range communications capability was burned off. We can't communicate with anything farther than five thousand yards."

"That doesn't explain your course change, sir."

"Keflavik never properly de-iced us. Ice started collecting on the airframes immediately after refuel. No way for us to continue our original course north into the Arctic Circle. We dropped low. It's the only place warm enough for us not to accumulate ice. We're hoping to make London. Will you please contact *Invincible* and relay this to her? Would you also alert Aberdeen and inform them of our situation?"

"Affirmative, sir. We will escort you."

"That's very kind, but unnecessary. We merely—"

"Orders are orders, major."

Smoke mulled over the man's explanations.

First was the technical improbability of a simultaneous malfunction of long-range communications computers on three jets and the virtual impossibility of Keflavik overlooking a de-icing procedure on three aircraft that was as second nature as breathing to the air crews of the air base near the Arctic Circle.

Second, Squadron Leader Leyland's voice was far too calm, his explanations too pat. Almost canned. The pilot identifications did match up. True, the accents were British. The aircraft had not made any attempt to evade Smoke and his wingmen. Still, his instinct didn't allow him to believe a word of it. Why didn't the Harriers try to land at Tromso, Narvik, Bodo or Moi-Rana in Norway? Those cities were a mere hop from where the Hercules tanker had exploded, and even though they lacked air bases, Harriers could land vertically, without the benefit of a runway. If Squadron Leader Leyland had been concerned about ice buildups, he would have landed there. Or anywhere else on land. Besides, ice buildup itself would have started immediately upon their departure from Keflavik, not when they refueled. They would have turned back at once.

Still, as bad as they were, the explanations were explanations. Smoke was the investigator, not the judge. He switched to his external fuel tanks, prepared for the long flight to Aberdeen.

64 CONTACT

Castel MacLean
Beverly Hills, California
11:23 A.M.

MacLean blew a cloud of smoke before placing his Montecristo 3 Habana in a square glass ashtray and attending to the telephone's high pitched trill. "MacLean."

"*Buon giorno*, Maximilliano."

"Don Forza. Good morning. Rather good evening for you."

"You are well?"

"Yes, thank you. Don Forza, I must ask your forgiveness for canceling our…our arrangement about the South African as I did. At the last minute. It was disrespectful."

"*Per piacere*. There is no need to apologize. Besides, I knew that reason would prevail. One must never act out of hatred. It blurs one's judgment."

"You are a wise man." MacLean took a sip of coffee from a handpainted Christian LaCroix espresso cup. Uncertain why the Sicilian was calling, he simply remained silent as his father had taught him.

"*Grazie*. And I have good sources of information. Which is the reason for my call. I have a name for you."

"A name?" MacLean retrieved a pad of personalized Cartier message cards and a Parker Hemingway fountain pen from a small gunmetal case on his sandblasted glass desk.

"I understand you want to know the name of someone in the Church who knows about certain assets."

"Ah, yes."

"I am informed that one man is intimately aware of those assets. His name is Giovanni Benedetti."

MacLean wrote the name on one of the cards. The ink was red. He hoped it wasn't a bad omen. "And who is this gentleman?"

"Giovanni Cardinal Benedetti is the director of the Institute for Works of Religion."

"I'm afraid I haven't heard of that organization."

"Most people haven't. It's generally known as the Vatican Bank."

65 DESTRUCTION

NATO Air Base
Keflavik, Iceland
8:06 P.M.

U.S. Air Force Major Elmers was bent over daily reports when the telephone rang. "Elmers here."

"Sergeant Winston, sir. From maintenance. Forgive me for calling you directly without going through channels, sir. But it's an emergency." The sergeant was separated from the major by three full grades of rank. Regulations would have required the communication to go from Winston to her lieutenant to the captain and only then to Major Elmers.

"What kind of emergency?" He suspected that it was a surprise birthday party ploy. Each year on his birthday, the men and women under his command racked their brains for an increasingly original hook to get Elmers to come running to some plausible but fictitious emergency during the day, only to discover streamers and balloons and cheers.

"Well I...sir, you'd better come here yourself, sir."

"If it's that important, Sergeant, I will." He smiled. "Where are you?"

"The morgue, sir."

"The morgue. Very well. I'm on my way." The morgue? They definitely outdid themselves this year.

He drove his Humvee from the commander's apartment block on base to a large concrete building that housed the base hospital, rehab facility, and morgue. Sergeant Winston stood at the front of the building, saluted him as he approached in the freezing wind. The confused and fearful expression on her face caused him to think that she had one of the best poker faces he had ever seen.

"Lead the way, sergeant."

He followed her through the central corridor, past a private who saluted him tensely, and into the small morgue.

No streamers. No balloons. No cheers. What he saw surprised him far more than any secret birthday party.

The bodies of three men lay on stretchers.

Naked.

Elmers crouched beside the body closest to him and winced. "My God."

"Do you recognize these men, sir?" asked the head doctor, pulling double duty as coroner.

He pointed to each body. "Squadron Leader Leyland. Pilot Officer Carruthers. Pilot Officer Fox. Royal Air Force. What happened?"

"Please note it, Lieutenant." The doctor ordered his assistant before turning back to Elmers. "Hypothermia, sir. They're frozen solid. They were found in one of the dumpsters behind the officers' showers."

"Dumpsters? How did three naked pilots freeze in the dumpsters?"

"They must have been drugged. The autopsy should tell us how and...pardon me, Major. Did you say Royal Air Force?"

"That's right. They were part of an RAF training operation with a Royal Navy carrier this afternoon—" He remembered one of the daily logs. "Wait a minute. They left this afternoon at around 1400 hours."

"Sir, they're still he—"

"Not them. Their planes. Their Harriers left this afternoon."

"But Major. That doesn't make sense. How could their planes leave if their pilots are still—"

"I need your phone. Right now."

"Dead? They're dead?" repeated Admiral Hennessey. "But they completed their mid-air ref—*good God*." He turned to the young ensign next to him. "Get me Jack Yorbis on the *Reagan*. Immediately." He turned back to the handset. "Thank you for the information, Major. I'll get back to you."

The ensign handed him a handset. "Admiral Yorbis, sir."

"Jack? Cyril here. One of your majors at Keflavik just informed me our three Harrier pilots were found dead a few minutes ago."

"Dead? Then who the hell is—"

"Precisely."

"But now it all fits. Our scope shows the Harriers from Keflavik continuing on the same course and speed. Looks like they're headed for London. And the way it's looking, I don't think they're planning on having tea and cucumber sandwiches at the Savoy."

London. "Your interceptors?"

"Already intercepted."

"We have to assume the worst. I'm afraid her Majesty's Navy must impose on her American brothers further."

"What do you have in mind?"

"Force the bandit Harriers down. God only knows who is flying those planes or what they're flying to England for."

"I agree. Anywhere in particular?"

Admiral Hennessey traced the Harriers' course on the map in front of him. "The RAF base at Aberdeen, Scotland, would do. Right on their course."

"You got it, Cyril. I'll call you as soon as I have any information."

"Thank you, Jack. Aberdeen will do. But wherever they're forced down, they must be forced down. We can't let them anywhere deeper in England."

"I was in the Pentagon on 9-11, Cyril. You don't need to convince me."

Rear Admiral Yorbis slammed the bulky handset into its overhead receptacle. "Get me the Air Boss on the horn. Now. And send a message to the *Seawolf*. UHF urgent."

One minute later, Smoke, Senator, Elvis, and Venus received and acknowledged their new orders and armed their weapons. Within five minutes, the *Seawolf* poked an electronic ear through the surface of the glacial North Atlantic to receive the *Reagan*'s latest satellite transmission burst.

Carlton was beyond frustration, but his anger was not directed toward Hendricks. In fact, Hendricks genuinely appeared to share Carlton's belief that the Harriers were the true targets. But the calm, wise, experienced, and frustrating commander was right. The U.S. Navy could not simply blow RAF Harriers out of the sky, even as bandits. The communication from the *Reagan* was that the interceptors would force the Harriers down, not destroy them. They wouldn't do that without a greater reason. But without visual proof, how could he demonstrate the three RAF Harriers were carrying the diamond stockpile? He continued to dredge his exhausted mind.

Partly by instinct, partly by default, he fell back on his thinking as a jurist. Logic. The way he built cases against defendants back at Justice, now about a million miles and a lifetime away. But that was what he was, after all, wasn't it? A lawyer. He needed evidence to convince Hendricks. Not just to convince Hendricks but to give him a legitimate reason to act on that conviction. Like a jury. If he could pile on little pieces of evidence, they ultimately would grow beyond the sum of their parts. That was what he had to do with these Harriers. Take every piece of evidence and string all of them together until the damning evidence became incontrovertible. But he was so tired. List. He had to make a list. He looked around the plotting table for a pen and paper, hunched over the plotting table and began to list each piece of evidence against the Harriers.

When he finished, he looked up at Hendricks, who was apparently deep in thought. "Okay, Commander. You want evidence. I'll tell you what I want. I want to speak to the lead naval aviator who's up there escorting the Harriers."

"This is Lieutenant Commander Stevan. What do you need, Lieutenant?" Smoke demanded from his cockpit while he watched the Harrier's wings glow in the dim orange night of the setting sun.

"I need some information about the Harriers," Carlton replied.

Smoke would have hesitated to answer absent Admiral Yorbis's statement that Carlton had clearance. He gave Carlton a detailed report of the RAF Harriers.

"Are they armed?"

"Standard cannon. No missiles."

"What about tanks? Are they carrying tanks or pods under their wings?"

"About as many pods as they can carry. I count…four pods each. Which is pretty strange if all they were doing was training."

A grin creased Carlton's stubbled chin. *Go Navy*. "Thanks,

Smoke. Safe flying, Lieutenant Commander." He removed the headset and handed it back to the communications officer.

"It's enough proof for me, all right," Hendricks agreed with Carlton. "The problem is you're going to have to convince the CVW C-in-C. Even if I had the authority to shoot those bastards down on my own, our weapons don't have the necessary range. The only way you're going to splash those birds is to have the *Reagan*'s interceptors do it. They're there already. Problem is the Harriers still haven't threatened deadly force, and standard Navy operating procedure outside of a combat zone is not to fire unless fired upon. Even if they are bandits like the *Reagan* now says."

"Right. It's no use trying to convince the *Reagan*. Even if they had the political situation digested, which I don't even think we do and we've been on this since the beginning, they're not going to order a kill unless they're under orders to do it." Carlton looked at Pink. "What do you think, Tom? Forbes?"

"We can try."

"He have that kind of pull?"

"He can't order the CVW commander to splash the Harriers, that's for sure. He might be able to order a black op out of Aberdeen Air Force Base. That's nearby," he said, looking at the chart.

"That would only screw things up," Hendricks said. "You'd have a set of black op fighters with one mission heading for Harriers intercepted by Navy fighters with a different mission. Plus a black op is black because it's secret. There are way too many parties watching this to perform even a usual black op. The Brits. The French. The Russians. Who knows who else. Too conf—"

"I agree," said Carlton. "But I was thinking about something much more simple. Forbes will have to convince the president."

"The president?" replied Pink. "How is—"

"Carlton's right," Hendricks agreed. "CINC ordered us to pick you up in the first place."

"So he's definitely in the loop. Now all we need to do is to convince Forbes to convince him."

"Easier said than done."

"The good part is that Douglass won't waffle," said Hendricks. "He may be president and he may have been a minister, but he was a general for fifteen years. He'll make his decision quickly."

"Which means he may decide against it quickly, too."

"We'll have to see. Mr. Wathne, take us to antenna depth."

"Antenna depth. Aye, sir."

"I will not do it. You should know better than that as a Russian analyst. Give me Carlton."

"Yes, sir." Pink handed the handset to Carlton. "Good luck."

"He's your boss. You have to obey him. I don't." He grabbed the handset. "Carlton here."

"Have you lost your mind, Carlton? Are you really suggesting I wheel myself into the Oval Office to convince the president to shoot down three RAF Harriers?"

"I would think Tom made the suggestion quite clear, sir."

"It's unacceptable."

"It's not only acceptable, sir. It's imperative. We know these are bandit Harriers. The registration on those jets may read RAF, but the pilots flying them are former Spetsnaz working for Russkost's Volki. In any case, the dead RAF pilots in Keflavik prove this is at least a deadly situation. Whoever is flying those planes sure as heck isn't RAF. The Royal Navy agrees with the analysis and asked the Navy to intercept and escort them. And there's no other logical explanation. The Harriers have storage pods under their wings, and their course clearly intersected the *Pushkin*'s course. And as Tom informed you before, we know that the diamonds were transferred onto the *Pushkin* before the *Nevsky* sank. We have to splash the Harriers. Immediately."

"Are you finished with your tirade?" Forbes waited several seconds. "Good. The reason we can't shoot those planes down is precisely because they're carrying the diamonds. Those diamonds don't belong to us or Waterboer, they belong to Russia. The last thing we need in our relationship with Russia is to destroy a billion dollars worth of their property."

"Sir, didn't we just go through your suicide mission to find the Russian stockpile for the sole purpose of preventing Russkost from selling it to Waterboer and financing their civil war?"

"Finding the diamonds, yes. Destroying them, no."

"Sir, the purpose of finding the diamonds was to make sure Russkost wouldn't get them and sell them to Waterboer."

"Exactly."

"What do you think is going to happen once those planes land?"

"They'll be taken over by the British authorities."

"Exactly. Which means the diamonds be handed over to Waterboer within a matter of hours."

Silence. "I don't follow."

"Sir, the Brits don't have the monopoly laws we have. Waterboer operates largely out of London. The Brits have no problem with Waterboer's monopoly of the diamond market. That Waterboer operates out of London means they're connected, protected. You think Waterboer has U.S. government people in its pocket? Think about how many Brits they have when their main distribution point is in London. Just wait to see how many MPs will clamor against the U.S. for the stockpile to be returned to Waterboer. And most ironic of all is that the British government may legally be forced to hand the stockpile back."

"How?"

"The entire Russian stockpile was supposed to have been exchanged by Russia to Waterboer. The deal was for the entire stockpile. The *apparatchiki* may have pulled the wool over Waterboer's eyes and convinced them at the time the stockpile they transferred was the entire Russian stockpile, but now Waterboer knows that wasn't the case. They'll argue the Russians fraudulently hid the remaining stockpile, that the diamonds legally belong to Waterboer. And when Waterboer gets the diamonds, it'll finance Russkost because Russkost has control of the Mirny mines and will sell them Russian diamonds for far less than the Orlov government or just stop producing them."

Forbes paused for a few moments. Carlton could hear him smoking a pipe. "I hadn't thought about that. I agree. But Waterboer wins either way. If we don't destroy the stockpile, Waterboer gets the diamonds and removes a destabilizing stockpile from the potential market-place. If we destroy the stockpile, we remove the destabilizing stockpile for them. Destroying the diamonds helps Waterboer."

"I realize that, sir. But under the circumstances, it's the lesser of all other evils, considering what Tom has told me about Russkost. And—"

"Enough, Carlton. You've convinced me. I'll get back to you."

It took longer for Forbes to drive from Langley to the White House than for President Douglass to make his decision.

"Interceptor. Interceptor, this is Strike. Destroy all three bandit Harriers. I repeat. Destroy all bandit Harriers. You are weapons-free." The order was related by Admiral Yorbis, but it came straight from the Boss himself.

"Roger, Strike. Okay. You heard the man. Let's go get 'em boys and girls."

Smoke moved his finger expertly along his joystick. The Super Hornet targeting mechanism and ordnance were amazing. He could target an enemy aircraft directly by looking at it through his helmet. And since the AIM-9X missile could destroy an aircraft at a straight 90-degree angle, he could look at an aircraft directly beside him and launch a missile straight into it. However, his present situation was a far more traditional dogfight. He selected "TWS Dogfight" then "slave." Dead steady, his finger hovered over the pickle switch, then pushed down on it hard. He felt a rumble under his seat seconds before a plume of white smoke streamed out past his cockpit from the tail of an AIM-9X Sidewinder air-to-air missile. It tore through the sky and slammed into the unsuspecting lead Harrier as he broke hard left. The two remaining bandits immediately took evasive action, one breaking hard left, the other nearly straight up.

"Venus and Elvis take bandit one going ballistic. Senator, follow me in. I'm taking bandit two."

"I'm on your wing, Smoke," Senator obeyed.

"Venus copies."

"Right behind you, Venus," Elvis added, yanking back hard on his stick, sending his Super Hornet straight up into the dark blue upper atmosphere.

Smoke concentrated hard on his bore centerline targeting system. "Okay, Senator. I've got him locked." He punched the pickle switch. "Mark!"

The Harrier broke hard right and released chaff. The missile exploded, but it destroyed only an aluminum chaff countermeasure. Shaken but undamaged, the Harrier barrel-rolled and rocketed past Senator not more than five hundred yards to starboard.

"Target still alive! Target still alive!" Senator shouted. "I've got the angle, Smoke."

"Go to it," Smoke approved. "I'm off."

Senator broke off and reversed course. Within ten seconds of suffering over four G's of acceleration, he switched to "bore," lined the rogue Harrier on his boresight, and fired. He felt the familiar rumble and watched the canopy of the rogue Harrier fly off and the pilot eject seconds before the missile tore through and exploded his aircraft's rear nozzle.

"Good shot, Senator! Good shot!"

Venus and Elvis continued to follow the last Harrier. Already a hundred miles away from Smoke and Senator, they outnumbered the bandit Harrier two to one. Venus and Elvis each had launched an AIM-9X at the bandit, but the pilot—whoever he or she was—was good. The pilot had launched chaff countermeasures and broken hard, once to port, a second to starboard exactly at the appropriate time. The missiles detonated against the chaff. The Harrier used the precious seconds of uncertainty to maneuver around and below the two Navy Super Hornets. Loaded down with the diamond pods and without missiles, the pilot was armed only with two thirty millimeter cannons. He fired them at Venus and Elvis, who broke hard left and vertically, respectively, so that one would be able to re-engage the Harrier no matter which Super Hornet the Harrier pursued. Elvis' evasive maneuver came too late. Flames erupted from the starboard engine. "I'm hit! I'm shutting engine two down!" Seconds later, the flames and smoke sputtered out as Elvis shut off the fuel flow to the engine. He compensated by increasing power to the port engine.

By the time Elvis reengaged, Venus had reacquired the bandit Harrier, which had performed a 90-degree climb. With icy precision from years of hard training, culminating at Miramar's Top Gun in California before the base was closed and the elite fighter school moved to Fallon, Nevada, she selected the "bore" option, lined the Harrier on her boresight, anticipated the bandit's vertical evasive maneuver, and thumbed down on her pickle. The plume of white smoke traced away from her nosecone and arced to port as the AIM-9X tracked its prey with its single-minded electronic eyes and brain. Seconds later, it slammed into the Harrier's port engine and sent the third and last bandit spinning on a crazed clockwise yaw to its watery grave twenty thousand feet below.

"And they say women can't fly. You okay, Elvis?"

"I'm doing my bit to save the world's oil supply by flying on one engine. Other than that, no problem."

"There's no fuel left to make it back to the *Reagan*. We'll have to refuel at Aberdeen."

"Roger that, Venus." They joined up, navigated back to Smoke and Senator's position, and together flew to Aberdeen, shutting off their afterburners to conserve fuel.

"Strike. Strike, this is Interceptor. We are three-for-oh. Bandits are destroyed. We're heading for Aberdeen to refuel before coming home. Over."

"Interceptor, this is Strike. Good job, people. See you on deck. Over and out."

The pods attached to the Harriers' wings broke open under the intense shock of each aircraft's collision into the water and released their sparkling cargo. During their slow descent nearly eight thousand feet below the icy swells of the North Sea, a billion dollars' worth of diamonds carpeted a wide area of the sea bed. Underwater, the clear stones were nearly invisible. Over the next few days, strong underwater currents would spread the gems over a vast area.

Formed by intense volcanic heat and pressure, pushed toward the surface of the Earth, cooled and hardened into pure carbon, exploded, mined, and sorted, cut by Komdragmet diamond cutters, secreted away by the KGB, rediscovered, and stolen, the Russian diamonds had returned to nature.

PART IV
CARATS

"I will give you diamonds by the shower."

—*Frankie Goes To Hollywood, "Welcome to the Pleasure Dome"*

66 HOMECOMING

USS Seawolf
Entrance of U.S. Navy Submarine Base
Groton, Connecticut
9:14 A.M.

"I don't know what to say," grumbled Carlton, groggy from lack of sleep. "Except thank you...for everything."

"I'm just glad you all made it," replied MacLean. "If only my boats had been so lucky. What happened to you after the *Claire* sank?"

"Believe me, you don't want to know. Most of it's classified, anyway. I can tell you one thing, though. The United States and Russia are a heck of a lot safer because of what we were able to do with your help. Unfortunately, Waterboer became stronger, too."

"I suppose I have to take your word for it. As far as Waterboer, though, I think I found a chink in that armor."

"The flaw in the diamond?"

"I can't explain over an unsecure line."

"Please don't. What's involved?"

"I left the details with Colonel Saunders. He'll contact you."

The ball of ice returned to Carlton's gut. "Why do I not like the sound of this?"

"It won't be anywhere as difficult as what you've already been through, I imagine. We just need to get some information. From what I think is a friendly source. I can't go, Carlton. I'm trapped here. You can refuse, but it may be our last chance to hurt Waterboer hard, or at least the last one I know of."

"I'll wait to hear from Saunders. But remember, I know where you live."

"So does the White House chief of staff."

The smell of fresh marine air assaulted Carlton's senses as he stepped out of the *Seawolf's* manhole and onto the anaechoic, sound-proofed tiles of its forward deck. The crew enjoyed this moment at the end of each cruise. With the privilege and honor of wearing the United States Navy's twin dolphins on their uniform came the requirement of total silence concerning their cruises. The return from a cruise allowed a large part of the crew to stand on the forward deck and watch their families as the submarine entered the Groton, Connecticut, submarine base. It was an emotional moment for men who did not see their families for periods that often lasted six months.

Forbes had Erika, DesJardins, and Ramey under wraps, so Carlton had no one waiting for him. He enjoyed the crisp sea air on the *Seawolf*'s deck. It was far warmer than the last time he had been topside, when he had boarded the *Pushkin* near the Arctic Circle. Despite his exhaustion, he enjoyed basking in the pale light of the winter sun, hearing whoops from welcoming vessels and seagulls. Pink would have enjoyed being topside but had decided to remain out of public view until after his impending meeting with Randall Forbes.

Several minutes later, XO Wathne escorted Carlton off the *Seawolf* and onto terra firma for the first time in over two weeks. Carlton saluted crisply, then pumped the man's beefy hand. "Thanks, sir."

"You betcha, Lieutenant. If you ever want to switch from PT boats to subs, I'll be glad to sign you up for training."

He smiled, turned, and walked straight into someone. "Excuse me." He looked up and saw the smiling face of an African-American man dressed in a light blue Air Force uniform.

"You lost, son?"

"Colonel Saunders? What are you doing here?"

"You Navy pukes ever learn about saluting?"

"Yes, sir." Carlton saluted. "Sorry, sir."

Saunders saluted in return, grinned.

"Where is Erika and when can I see her, sir? MacLean said that you—"

Saunders placed an index finger over his lips. "Come with me." He turned to a young private who stood in his shadow. "Private, take the lieutenant's bag."

"Yes, sir."

Carlton followed Saunders into a waiting Humvee. They

drove in silence for five minutes. The private stopped in front a tired-looking brick building. Saunders led Carlton to the officers' locker room, handed him a garment bag. "Shower, shave, and change into these." He looked at his watch. "You've got ten minutes."

Carlton emerged as tired as he had entered but refreshed, comfortably draped in a black cashmere Loro Piana overcoat, a navy blue three-button Brioni suit, pale blue Charvet shirt, solid blue Tino Cosma tie, and spit-shined Prada square-toed lace ups. Never before in his life had he worn such expensive clothes. Any remaining doubt about the person responsible for the suit of clothes disappeared as soon as he opened a velvet box containing diamond cufflinks.

MacLean.

For the first time he understood why the wealthy spent so much on designer clothes. They felt great, soft, and tailor-fit based on measurements MacLean's people had somehow managed to obtain. The clothes were a welcome relief from the borrowed *Seawolf* uniform. Still, he felt self-conscious. "These clothes aren't for people like me. Why couldn't you have brought me one of my Brooks Brothers suits?"

"Because they're part of police evidence, along with everything else in your apartment."

"Figures. Where is Erika?"

"Safe."

"I want to see her."

"You will. But first you and I are going to take a helicopter ride."

"To?"

"Dulles Airport."

"Dulles? Who are we meeting?"

"Not meeting, flying. And not we, you."

"Where?"

"Rome."

"Rome? Rome, Italy? As in Sinatra's coins and fountain?"

"As in Vatican City. Relax. You'll love Rome. Art. Food." He turned and stared at Carlton. "Cardinals. Plus you're traveling first class and your luggage is already checked on board. We can discuss things on the way to Dulles."

67 BANKER

Vatican Bank
Vatican City State
Rome, Italy
10:17 A.M.

A uniformed member of the Vigilanza police force snapped a crisp salute as the black Mercedes S600 drove past the Porta Sant'Anna. The automobile bore Vatican plates, always preceded by the letters "SCV"—*Santa Civitas Vaticani*. A contingent of bright orange and blue-garbed Swiss Guards stood ramrod straight as the car proceeded past their barracks then past the papal apartments whose resident the Guard had protected for nearly five hundred years. The Mercedes stopped in front of the door of a three-story, tile-roofed building across from the Apostolic Palace. A valet clad in white tie and tails expertly negotiated the frozen steps between two statue-like Vigilanza policemen and opened the rear door with a white-gloved hand.

"Welcome to the Vatican, Signore Carlton," he announced in heavily accented English. "If you will please follow me."

Carlton shivered as he stepped from the warm car into the frigid cold and followed the valet, who led him through sculpted doors into an ornate hall with gilded baroque accents.

"You are expected. If you will be good enough to wait, I will announce your presence." The valet left with a curt bow and disappeared up a sweeping staircase.

Carlton paced the hall and did what was so natural in the Vatican. He prayed.

The diminutive geographic size of the Vatican City State was a sharp contrast to the immense power wielded by its sole institution: the Roman Catholic Church. The ancient history, the priceless art and architecture, the arcane traditions and hierarchy of the Vatican had a special ability to place even the most blasé of international diplomats a touch on edge. For Catholics and others as well, the spiritual and moral authority of the

Vatican far exceeded its temporal secular power.

The closest Carlton had ever come to Church authority was at his confirmation at age thirteen in the cathedral of San Diego, California, before the local bishop. He was recalling the event—it seemed so far away now—when a tall man dressed in a long black cassock with red buttons and a white priest's collar walked down the steps. He wore thin wire spectacles on the tip of a pointed nose, had a receding, prematurely graying hairline.

"Signore Carlton." The man smiled the disarming smile of a diplomat. His intonation was melodious, far less accented than the valet's. "Welcome to the Banco Vaticano. I am Monsignore Felici, secretary to his eminence." He offered his hand to Carlton, who shook it vigorously.

"Thank you, Monsignor."

"If you will please follow me, his eminence will see you now."

"Thank you, Monsignor."

Felici led him up the marble staircase bordered with sculpted wooden handrails that shone in the light of an Austrian crystal chandelier that seemed to float in mid-air. They proceeded down a long hallway with a curved frescoed ceiling, through an anteroom furnished with red velvet sofas, and came to a halt at a set of gilded doors.

Felici gave a perfunctory knock before swinging the double doors open to reveal a vast office. Veteran visitor of the Capitol and federal agency headquarters though he was, Carlton had never set eyes on anything so magnificent. Only a white IBM computer prevented Carlton from believing he had stepped into a seventeenth-century time warp. Roughly the size and height of an indoor basketball court, the office was constructed of polished inlaid wood floors, walls that displayed the Renaissance magnificence of Raphael, Titian, and Botticelli in carved, gilded frames, and curved ceilings adorned with frescoes in pale hues of blue, red, and yellow. Battalions of sculpted sword-wielding angels stared down from each corner of the ceiling, protecting their earthly wards below. Leaded windows, complete with wavy imperfections that evidenced their advanced age, amplified the weak rays of the winter sun. They shone on a massive seventeenth-century silver and rosewood crucifix affixed to a red silk brocade wall at the base of which sat a red velour kneeler. The splendor of the chamber was matched only by its relative emptiness. At the center of the room sat two chairs and a lone carved-wood and gold Louis XVI desk heavy enough to stop a medieval barbarian on horseback.

A portly figure clad in scarlet and white robes wearing a red *zucchetto* on his head rose from behind the desk and walked toward him. "Patrick Carlton." The white-haired man nodded with studied calm. "Welcome to the Vatican, signore. Welcome to the Banco Vaticano. I am Giovanni Cardinal Benedetti."

As a Catholic, Carlton's first instinct was to kneel and kiss the man's ring. He stopped himself, reflecting that he was here in an official capacity and that in this instance—as opposed to a personal meeting—such reverence would be inappropriate. *Americans bow to no one*, he reflected. *Only to God*. He shook the man's hand instead. "Eminence," he pronounced reverently, unable to restrain a slight bow. Despite the size of the room, there was no echo. Carlton suspected that it had been soundproofed.

"Please, Mr. Carlton. You've had a long journey. Let us sit. Some coffee, perhaps?" His words were unhurried without being slow. He gestured to the red velour seats, glanced toward Felici, who waited patiently by the doors. Without waiting for Carlton's reply, he ordered coffee. "*Due espressi per favore*, Lucca."

"*Si, Eminenza*." The efficient monsignor bowed and left, closing the doors behind him.

Both men sat, Carlton on the edge of his seat, Benedetti reclining comfortably. Carlton observed the prince of the Church fingering a heavy gold crucifix suspended around his thick neck. The man's large size did not seem to hamper his movements. It seemed as though the man's bulk was due to hard toil during his young years followed by long years without physical exertion, rather than an overindulgence in rich Italian fare. His face seemed oversized in contrast to the wisps of closely cropped gray-white hair on his round head. The beginning of a double chin. A pronounced aquiline nose. Had Carlton met the man in another place without his Church vestments, he would have guessed him to be a retired winemaker or farmer rather than an eligible successor to the throne of Saint Peter. The feature that struck Carlton most strongly was Benedetti's eyes. Unlike the photographs he had seen of members of the Roman Curia, whose eyes often reflected political cunning or arrogance, Benedetti's brown eyes were watchful, yet warm and unassuming, modest. They looked like eyes that would rather watch the soccer matches of children than the political maneuverings of an arcane financial institution.

Carlton had thought long and hard about how best to broach the topic of diamonds with the cardinal. He knew from his voracious reading of history and politics that the only way to get to the point with a member of the Roman Curia was to do the exact opposite and play the ancient diplomatic art of *Romanita*. In other words, to hide the ball. But Carlton was an American lawyer, simple and to the point, not used to playing hide the ball. For him, hiding the ball was synonymous with wasting time.

In fact, the problem was not so much one of approach as one of information. Any meeting between representatives of two foreign powers was a subtle dance between the selective sharing and withholding of information. The quandary lay in that, officially, there had been no U.S. involvement with the Russian diamond stockpile. Officially, Carlton had never boarded the *Rossiya*. Officially, Carlton had not been aboard the *Seawolf*. Officially, it had never chased the *Pushkin* under the Norwegian Sea and forced her to surface. Officially, there had never been—and the U.S. Navy had never destroyed—bandit Sea Harriers carrying the missing Russian diamond stockpile off the Shetland Islands.

How, then, could he broach the subject of South African diamonds casually?

He was busy trying to figure it out when Benedetti, apparently sensing his unease, graciously made the opening move. With characteristic Vatican diplomacy, Benedetti gave Carlton information he already knew, but which also revealed that the Church also knew the information.

"The Church is aware of your recent exploits, Mr. Carlton. It is a great honor for me to meet you. Not only because you were recommended so highly by Mr. MacLean, a great patron of the

Church, but because of your recent...activities against the Russian fascists."

Carlton was stunned. He did not attempt to hide the fact. "How did—?"

Benedetti smiled. "An institution as old as the Church does not survive on prayer alone. Your great nation has been involved in diplomacy for 225 years. The Church has been at it for two thousand." He smiled. "Do not worry. I know how to keep secrets. Now. I am at your disposal. How can the Vatican Bank be of service?"

Carlton faced not only an obscure Roman bureaucracy, but an incredibly efficient information-gathering body. He remembered the role the Polish pontiff and the Solidarity priests had played in obtaining information in the 1980s. Using the information and the priest network as a sword, combined with the Reagan Administration's help, the pope had ignited the Polish fire that later exploded Eastern Europe's Soviet shackles. Carlton could never hide the ball well enough to play the game of *Romanita* against a Vatican veteran. He went for broke instead. After all, he knew that Benedetti knew. It was merely a question of making the man comfortable enough to give him more information. Information Carlton did not have.

"Thank you, Eminence. As you know, I'm not a diplomat. So in keeping with my American heritage, I'll be direct and to the point. I'm here because your name surfaced in connection with a diamond stockpile, possibly held by the Vatican."

Benedetti's eyes opened wide with surprise. "A Vatican diamond stockpile?"

Carlton hedged his bets. "Yes, Eminence. Of course, I have no idea whether this stockpile actually exists. All I have is rumor, innuendo. However, rumors rarely develop without at least a kernel of truth."

"How did my name become connected with this?"

He hedged his bets further. "Merely because you are the director of the Vatican Bank and would be the best official to know about all movements of money within the Vatican. Whether officially authorized or not," he added, for safety.

"I see." Benedetti paused, tapped the fingers of each hand

against the others. "Well, let me begin by setting certain things straight. The Vatican Bank has no involvement with diamonds." Carlton observed Benedetti quietly. The cardinal chose his words carefully. "The Church is rich in history, Mr. Carlton. In real estate. In art. But like an old aristocrat, it is poor in cash. Most people do not believe it, of course." He chuckled. "The Vatican is so old and secretive that people think it sits on mountains of cash, gold bars and diamonds hidden away in secret vaults. Unfortunately, the sad truth is that the Vatican can barely meet expenses. Only in recent years did the Vatican Bank attain a surplus. Quite small at that. So you see, the idea of the Vatican buying diamonds is quite impossible. We don't have the funds. Besides, what would the Vatican do with diamonds? As I'm certain you know, there is no investment reason to buy diamonds, unless you're a diamond dealer. They decrease in price, and, unlike many banks, the Vatican Bank has strict moral guidelines. It could never associate itself with an organization as wretched as Waterboer." He paused. "Still, this does not mean the Vatican cannot help you. After what you have done, it is clear that your intuitions are aimed in the right direction. Tell me, how long will you be in Rome, Mr. Carlton?"

Carlton stared hard but stopped short of being disrespectful. "As long as it takes, Your Eminence."

"Very well. With your permission, I will look into this matter more carefully. Perhaps it is someone or some group associated with the Vatican you are after. I will make discreet inquiries in appropriate places. Perhaps they will yield something."

"I would very much appreciate that, Eminence."

"After what you have done, I consider it an honor to help you."

"Thank you, Your Eminence."

"In the meantime, you should get some rest. Forgive me for saying so, but you look as though you need it."

Benedetti listened to the recording of his conversation with Carlton for a third time, reclined. "What do you think?"

"I don't know, *Eminenza*." Seated in one of the two visitor's chairs in front of Benedetti's antique desk, Monsignor Felici shook his head. "I just don't know. His explanation is logical. He wants to continue investigating Waterboer after his victory against Russkost. He doesn't have to, but it has become a crusade for him. Uncovering facts will not be enough.

"Still, I don't think this is personal. Carlton is a member of the United States Navy, a prosecutor with the American Justice Ministry. But in Rome, he has no jurisdiction. Although I believe he is sufficiently determined to take action on his own, he is outside his element. He would require support. MacLean is backing him financially, that is certain. But someone must be backing him politically. His employers at the Navy and in the Justice Ministry apparently aren't. No one in the American government has declared Carlton their representative. However, I cannot imagine he is doing this alone, as a rogue."

Felici stared at the desk in silence and looked up at his boss. "CIA?"

Benedetti nodded. "It is the most logical answer. The CIA must have made the original push in going against Russkost. Who else could have put together the North Sea operation? The American Navy would not have acted on its own. And we know the president only became involved late in the game."

The cardinal sighed, running his fingers along the sides of the gold crucifix around his neck. "Now that he is here, he has no option but to dig. I can't blame him. In his shoes, I would dig also. But a few digs in the right direction...Well, you know what that could mean. Now that the Banco Napolitana Lucchese's books and vaults are sealed, it will be nearly impossible to avoid scandal." He paused for a long time, looked up at the younger cleric. "The Americans have an interesting saying. They say if life offers you lemons, you should make lemonade." Felici looked puzzled. "Carlton scares us because he asks questions, *si?* But perhaps he is really an opportunity. Perhaps Christ has sent him to help His Church. After all, it can't be a coincidence that Carlton should appear right when we are facing such a crisis, such a scandal. The question is not whether Carlton is digging. We know he is. Or who he is digging for. But what he is digging for. What he is really digging for. What is his motive?"

"As I said, *Eminenza*, he is on a crusade."

"Yes. But against whom? Against the Church? This man is not a self-serving opportunist. You know what he has done. How he put himself in considerable danger to stop Russkost. I think his crusade is against Waterboer, not the Banco Napolitana or the Church. And he is a Catholic. You saw him praying in the lobby when he was waiting. You saw his respect toward me. Toward my office. No. Just like in the North Sea, I think his motive is to use whatever he can find here against Waterboer."

"But *Eminenza*, whatever he discovers here, no matter the reason, it will hurt the Church."

Cardinal Benedetti shook his head. "Not necessarily. What he finds *could* hurt the Church. It doesn't have to. Unless he is not certain how to use it and misuses it. Like someone who finds a grenade and does not know how it works. But if we help him use what he finds, we can protect the Church and help him in his crusade against Waterboer. Remember, Waterboer is not only Carlton's enemy. It is a corrupt, evil organization. In that, it is the Church's enemy as well. Do you remember the other day? When you and I prayed for faith?"

Felici nodded.

"Faith means trusting God. To trust God, one must listen to Him. One of our theologian brothers said that God speaks to us through other people."

"I'm sorry, *Eminenza*, but I hear nothing."

"I do." The cardinal paused and smiled. "Because Americans are as loud as people can get. God bless them."

68 YALE

Code-named "Yale" by CIA field agents, the colonial-style safehouse sat on over a hundred acres of forest amid the smoky fog of the Blue Ridge Mountains. Agency scuttlebutt had it that the property was once owned by DDI Forbes, a rumor he never expressly denied. Its existence and location was leaked to the KGB by a disgruntled CIA analyst during the cold war, resulting in the loss of ten agents. Its safety cover blown, Yale was now used for a variety of non-clandestine purposes, mainly debriefing, interrogation, and the protection of non-critical Agency assets from dangers in the field.

The interrogation room deep inside the Yale safehouse was nothing like the dank, dark rooms coldly illuminated by bare lightbulbs favored in Hollywood films. The CIA's master psychologists planned the room carefully. Natural light filtered from high above through a series of mirrors and bathed the room in warm sunlight. It was large, comfortable, with polished hardwood floors and sofas covered in blue and white chintz. A mahogany coffee table was heaped with books on horses, French chateaux, tropical island landscapes, and other picture books that depicted the beauty of freedom. Oil landscape paintings hung on the walls.

Yet despite its well-illuminated interior, the room was in fact a deep soundproofed basement, for obvious security reasons. Four men were present in the room. Three of them were CIA agents who wore shoulder holsters from which protruded the black grips of Glock 9mm handguns. One stood by the door and guarded the entrance. Two others, including Thomas Pink, were seated around the coffee table, their attention trained on the fourth man in the room. Blond with blue eyes, severely athletic, unarmed but psychologically armored, dressed in casual clothes, he seemed calm in the presence of the three agents.

"How stupid are you? I told you already. I will say nothing," Ulianov repeated in perfect English.

Pink rose from his overstuffed chair. "Considering the alternative, I think you should reconsider."

"The alternative." Ulianov smiled. "I'm not a *nekulturny* Mafioso. I know how America works. This country is a paradise for me. Bringing me here was stupid. Americans must always do everything by the rules. You can't beat anything out of me. You can't torture me." He laughed at the irony. "Your ACLU would sue you. You'd get fired. You'd be in jail." The Russian sneered at Pink.

"You're right," Pink replied calmly. "We can't do that. We would get fired." *You shit. If it were up to me, I'd nail you to the wall.* "But there are others who won't get fired. In fact, they'd get promoted." The expression of sincere pity on Pink's face confused the Russian. Pink looked at the agent seated next to Ulianov on the sofa and shrugged. "Okay. I'll be back with them." The guard opened the door to let him out. Pink walked into an elevator that took him up six stories to the second floor. He dropped in on Erika, Ramey, and DesJardins. Under the watchful gaze of their heavily armed Company minders, the three were enjoying the chance to rest in safety. Erika read on a sofa, Ramey caught up on action movies he had missed while at sea, and DesJardins alternately watched Emeril and cooked up new recipes for the staff in Yale's bulletproof kitchen.

Seeing they were in good shape and spirits, Pink took the stairs down to the lobby of the stately colonial house. He heard the thump of helicopter rotors far in the distance. Soon a sleek unmarked helicopter appeared over the tall oak trees and flared down into a small clearing at the rear of the house. Four persons jumped out of the side door and walked briskly to the house, bent low to avoid the strong rotor blow. Two more agents materialized from opposite sides of the clearing, accompanied the newcomers after checking their identification. Pink greeted them as they walked through the rear door of the house.

"Agent Bareno." The first man introduced himself first. "This is Agent Starr, and Elena Feodorovna and Yevgeni Tsiolkovsky of the GRU."

"Ma'am. Sir." Pink shook their hands, speaking in perfect, if slightly accented Russian.

"Your Russian is excellent, Mr. Pink," Tsiolkovsky said, in flawless English with a touch of New York accent for good measure.

"Yes. And I must tell you. I never thought I would speak to the CIA in one of its safehouses," Feodorovna said, her English more hesitant, with Russian intonations.

"The feeling is mutual, ma'am." Pink replied, knowing full well that the meeting would not be occurring at Yale had its location not been leaked to the KGB ten years ago, before it had split into the SVR/FSB.

Tsiolkovsky nodded. "Please let me express the gratitude of President Orlov and General Yagoda for your brave actions in the North Atlantic, and for allowing us to help you finish the task you set out to accomplish. It is unfortunate that the diamonds had to sink. Perhaps we will be able to recover them some day," he added, evidencing his skepticism at the notion that the American Navy had truly allowed the Russian stockpile to sink and had not instead taken possession of the diamonds.

"Thank you, *tovarish* Tsiolkovsky. On behalf of DDI Forbes, welcome. Should we begin? Please follow me." Pink led the three into the elevator. As it began its descent to the basement, he turned to the two Russians. "As promised, no recording devices will be on." He did not have to add that the silent electromagnetic storm created by the room's electronic jammers would render any of the GRU's recorders useless as well.

The elevator stopped. Pink walked into the room alone. "Gentlemen. If you please." He motioned to the door. The agents walked to the door and out of the room without a word.

Pink turned to Ulianov. "As I said before, I'm sorry you won't discuss Molotok's whereabouts with us. Or the identity of his main supporters. And as you pointed out quite truthfully, there is no way for us to get that information out of you legally.

However, those American civil rights you find so ridiculous do not apply with as much force in your own country when its national security is threatened."

Tsiolkovsky and Feodorovna walked in and stood before Ulianov silently. For the first time since Carlton's boot had made contact with his private parts aboard the *Pushkin*, Ulianov's eyes grew wide.

"Mr. Tsiolkovsky and Ms. Feodorovna, the United States government hereby places Mr. Ulianov of the Volki in the custody of the Russian government. For the purposes of your interrogation, this room will be temporarily considered the sovereign soil of the Russian Federation. If you need anything, you can ring me with that phone," Pink informed Feodorovna.

"*Spaceba*. But all I need is this." From her jacket pocket she removed a velvet box and opened it. In it was a simple metal bar, the size of a pen, tapered into a flat blade at one end and a hook reminiscent of a dentist's torture instrument at the other. She winked at Ulianov. "I'm an artist. And very creative."

Pink walked out of the room and past the guard into the elevator. Luckily for the guard, the interrogation room, temporarily sovereign Russian soil, was soundproof.

Ulianov had started as Molotok's partner. He would soon end as the megalomaniac's human sacrifice. But not before Feodorovna's artistic talents made him sing like a bird.

69 TRUST

Hotel Hassler
Rome, Italy
1:21 P.M.

For a country that built Ferrari automobiles and Agusta helicopters, the pitiful Italian telephone system was a stunning anachronism. It took four attempts for Carlton to obtain an international line. As instructed by Pink, he placed the telephone handset into the small electronic cover before speaking. The sound impulses generated by his voice were scrambled before their journey, then unscrambled by a master unit seven thousand miles away.

"Forbes."

"It's Carlton."

"Good afternoon. Care to tell me what the hell you're doing in Rome?"

Carlton was stunned. "How did—"

"You forget who you're speaking to. How did the meeting go?"

Carlton took a deep breath in between puffs from his Cohiba Siglo IV Habana. He recounted the meeting with Benedetti nearly word for word.

"I see." Forbes sounded detached. "And despite what he said, you think there still might be a connection between Waterboer and the Vatican Bank?"

"Perhaps."

Forbes permitted himself a dry chuckle. "You're barking up the wrong tree, Carlton."

"I beg your pardon?"

"There's no connection. Not between the Bank and Waterboer. Believe me, I've looked into this before."

"Perhaps the wrong tree. Perhaps not the wrong forest. Benedetti said he'd make inquiries. I'll wait and see. But since you seem to know so much about the Vatican Bank, I need to know something."

"Yes?"

"Can I trust him? Benedetti. Can I—"

"You can." The dry chuckle reappeared. "It's ironic, you know."

"Ironic, sir? How is—"

"That's exactly what Benedetti asked me about you an hour ago."

SAT Analysis
CIA Headquarters
8:10 A.M.

Forbes, Pink, and satellite analyst Elaine Franklin stood in the darkened viewing room, encircled by an array of high-definition monitors. "There we are. Rush hour. Downtown Siberia," Pink announced.

"If you could find Nowhere on a map, that's where it would be," Franklin replied. "Hopefully they'll be on time. We only have a seven-minute viewing window."

Forbes and Pink stood behind her as she dimmed the lights with pudgy fingers, chewing gum less loudly than usual on account of the DDI's presence. One of the monitors, on which she and Pink had determined that the Mirny fire was not an accident, showed a large structure against the black of night. Its outline was traced by the green light of the 8X satellite's infrared detectors, much like looking through night-vision goggles. The image was a live digital feed from four thousand miles up. Pink discerned small variations in the structure as the intensity of sources changed over time. Two other monitors showed the area in wider focus at lower magnification.

"I hope they're targeting the right spot," Pink said. "Ulianov may have been lying."

"I heard the interrogation," Forbes said. "I think he was past his capacity to lie."

"You heard the interrogation?" Pink asked, stunned. "I told them that we—"

"That we wouldn't record anything. We didn't. Listening and recording are two different things. Regardless, I had the information checked out. That house," he pointed to the main screen, "checks out as Molotok's *dacha*. We just didn't have any way of finding it until Ulianov sang. A helicopter Molotok's been known to use landed there less than an hour ago. He's there. Yagoda was only too glad to run this op."

"Here they come," Elaine announced, pointing to the wide-angle monitors. Two white blobs moved eastward from the general direction of Murmansk.

"What do you think?" Elaine asked Pink. "Fulcrums?"

"I'd say MiG-31 Foxbats. They're going supersonic at really low altitude. I don't think Fulcrums would do that. Probably refueled in flight."

Forbes nodded silently, duly impressed by Pink's knowledge.

They moved their gazes to the high-focus monitor as the two jets approached. Nearly immediately after the jets raced past the pale green structure, it exploded into a bright white blotch on the screen. Five more explosions followed. The jets banked north and headed home.

After only a single pass of two Russian Air Force fighters, Molotok was no longer a destabilizing force on the Russian and international political landscape. It would take longer for Yagoda to arrest and eliminate the main *krestnii otets* who had supported Russkost, but within a week, Russkost would be reduced to its former shell of anachronistic imperial ideals.

In Moscow, Colonel Kovanetz stepped out of GRU headquarters into the snow. He waved to his driver, who immediately started the Lada staff car and pulled up to the entrance of the building. Kovanetz stepped inside.

"Take me home, Yevgeni," he said wearily, closing the door and his eyes. "Take me home." He had not heard a word from either Ulianov or Molotok in some time. His telephone calls were not returned. The stress of the unknown exhausted him.

The driver did as he was ordered, drove cautiously on the slushy streets of the Russian capital, headed toward Kuntsevo to the west. Twenty minutes later, they reached a wide avenue lined with birch trees leading to several upper-echelon residential developments newly constructed for high-ranking officers. Kovanetz had the proper connections and cash to secure one of the nicer homes. His driver slowed and pulled over.

Kovanetz opened his eyes wearily and noticed they were not home. "*Shto?* Engine acting up again?" He murmured. "Damn piece of junk."

The driver turned to face him. Kovanetz jerked up in his seat when he saw the man's face. "Who are you? Where is Yevgeni?" He was about to reach for his Makarov pistol when he saw the gun in the driver's hand. A cylindrical silencer was attached to its muzzle.

"General Yagoda despises traitors."

The bullet was faster than Kovanetz's ability to beg for forgiveness.

71 RESEARCH

Main Justice Building
Washington, D.C.
5:58 A.M.

Temporarily released from the Yale safehouse, but still under heavy and thankfully invisible Company guard, Erika and Henri Monet sat in the computer researcher's basement office, drained. The only clue to the time of day was a cuckoo clock that Monet had picked up as a gag during his most recent ski trip in the French Alps.

They were out of steam, with little to show for their twenty straight hours of computer research of Waterboer's control of diamond production. After exhausting five diamond-producing African countries, they had moved on to the war-torn country of Angola. They studied links between Waterboer and Angolan diamond production much the same way archaeologists sift through the petrified remains of a past civilization. As for each of the five other countries they dissected, each electronic sample came up empty.

"I don't know what to try next." Imitating Carlton, his new role model after learning of the North Sea mission, the unshaven Monet propped shiny Nocona cowboy boots near the geological strata of research on his desk, a Gitane firmly screwed in the corner of his mouth. "*Aucune idée*. No idea. We must change our research pattern."

Lying on her back on the floor, head propped up by a stack of books on diamonds, Erika stared up at the low ceiling. It was yellowed by smoke from countless Gitanes cigarettes, illuminated by a halogen torch lamp in the corner of the room near an overworked laser printer. She unwrapped a protein bar. "I don't get it," she mumbled between bites of the bar.

"We must change our—" He removed his feet from the table and sat up. "We've been trying to link Waterboer to Africa."

"Right. And we have. Waterboer controls diamond production just like in the other countries we researched."

"*Exactement*. But maybe we shouldn't be looking at Waterboer's production control."

"You've lost me again."

"*Ecoute.*" Listen. "MacLean suggested we look at African diamond production to see if there could be another stockpile out there. We've been looking at Waterboer's control of African production, now Angola. But how would Waterboer's control of African production show a stockpile?"

"Exactly the way we've been looking: comparing African production and then sales by Waterboer."

"But we know that Waterboer buys more diamonds than it sells," said Monet.

"Right. Hence the stockpiles."

"But those would be Waterboer stockpiles, not African countries' stockpiles. We already know Waterboer has its own stockpiles. We need to look at possible stockpiles that Waterboer doesn't control."

"Right," said Erika. "Because what Waterboer is really afraid of is someone else amassing a stockpile."

"Like the Russians did."

"So maybe someone else operates a mine in Africa?"

"Or someone else buys an African mine's production."

"But we've already looked at that. Waterboer buys all of the African production. Even during all the African civil wars. Even though the mines are controlled by two or more sides in civil wars." She paused momentarily. "Angola's endured civil war for over twenty years. And according to what we found, right now, Waterboer is buying all of the Angolan production, from both the MPLA and UNITA factions. Everyone knows about that after all those articles on 'blood diamonds.'"

"*Oui*. And remember that article we found? It said Churchman convinced the United States Export-Import Bank—now we know it was done through Scott Fress—to finance new technology in the Angolan mines in exchange for an interest payment and the right to market all the stones. They are all sold to Waterboer."

"But that's now. Maybe Waterboer wasn't able to buy all of Angola's diamond production in the past. Maybe…"

"Maybe someone else bought the Angolan diamonds."

They stared at each other for a few seconds before Monet swiveled toward his computer keyboard and typed new search instructions into the mainframe with his tobacco-stained fingers.

"Angola isn't the only African country that's been in civil war in the past ten years," Erika cautioned.

"*Exactement.* Which means we must compare. First we must develop a list of diamond-producing countries. *Très facile.* Very easy." A list of countries appeared on the monitor. "*Voilà.* Now a list of African diamond-producing countries involved in civil war and the length of their civil war." Another list appeared on the screen, much shorter than the original one. Each entry was followed by a number. "*Voilà.*"

"Great. Now let's compare diamond production before and during each country's civil war."

Monet typed the instructions. A tiny green LED light flickered while the computer accessed and organized the stored data. Seconds later, columns of numbers filled the screen.

"Let's see." Erika leaned toward the screen while Monet scrolled down, row by row. Her heart sank. "There's no big difference, civil war or no civil war. Diamond production is almost the same." She pointed a long index finger at the screen. "Here it actually increased. So our theory is—"

"*Elle est bonne.* Our theory is good. It's our search that's bad." He lit another Gitane nervously and inhaled deeply, tapping the screen with his right index finger. "We searched for the difference in diamond production before and after a civil war. But production isn't the key. The key is the amount of purchases by Waterboer."

"Of course." She kissed the top of his head from behind his chair. "You're a genius."

"No. It's simply French Cartesian logic. You know, it was Rene Descartes who invented analyti—"

"That's great, Henri. But please, search first, lecture later."

"Okay, okay." He pursed his lips while typing the new search parameters. New columns of numbers glowed to life on the screen. Erika bent over the screen and pushed strands of red hair away from her eyes. They squinted at each country's figures, comparing the number of carats purchased by Waterboer before and during each civil war.

"There!" Erika exclaimed. "Look at that! Waterboer purchased three million carats annually from Angola in the early '70s, then only 2.5 million carats in 1975, when their civil war started. And it pretty much stayed at that amount during the whole twenty years of civil war, until…1994. Then right back up to over three million carats a year after that, until today."

"But during all that time, Angola still produced three million carats a year."

Erika looked down at Monet, who was already ordering the computer to print the list. A long ash teetered on the tip of the Gitane hanging from his lips. She grabbed the warm page from the laser printer as it came out, stared at it.

"Even if Waterboer bought half of Angola's production from the MPLA and the other half from UNITA during the civil war, it would still have bought about three million carats a year. The drop in purchases by five hundred thousand carats looks like a small drop, but over a period of twenty years, that's one hell of a stockpile."

"The Angolan civil war factions would each have sold as many diamonds as they could, so if Waterboer didn't buy the five hundred thousand carats, someone else must have."

"A half a million carats a year for twenty years. That's ten million carats. Let's assume half of that went to a variety of small purchasers. That's still five million carats. How much is the average price?"

"The computer says the average for each Angolan carat is $230. But remember, the two sides wanted cash as fast as possible, how do you say…*argent rapide?*"

"Fast money?"

"*Oui.* Fast money. So probably they bought them for less."

"At a discount. That makes sense. So let's say $100 per carat, for five million carats. That's $500 million."

Monet whistled. "Who would pay that much money? Who would care so much about diamonds to take a risk like that?"

Erika's lips constricted in concentration. "Big dealers wouldn't take the chance. They'd be locked out of the game if the Waterboer boys ever found out. And it's too big for small purchasers to buy half a million carats a year. Even a large group of them. And a large group would be noticed by Waterboer. And eliminated from the game."

She stared at the sheet of paper in her hand. "Whoever it is, Pat's gotta see this." She fished the handset from under the ocean of paper on Monet's desk, slipped on the scrambler Pink had supplied, and dialed the number of the Hotel Hassler in Rome.

72 DINNER

Hotel Hassler
Rome, Italy
6:31 P.M.

Carlton fumbled for the handset in the dark and managed to answer the telephone on its fifth ring. First Erika and Henri with their Angolan theory, now what? How could anyone get any sleep around here? "Hello?"

"Signore Carlton?"

"Yes." He coughed.

"This is Monsignor Felici. Secretary to Cardinal Benedetti. We met this morning."

Carlton sat up in the darkness, his head light from jet lag. He had fallen asleep. "Yes, of course Monsignor. What—" He coughed again. Too many Cubans. "What can I do for you?"

"I tried to call you earlier, but there was no answer. His eminence asked me to convey that he would enjoy the honor of your company at dinner this evening. He feels the other guests might be able to help you in your search."

"Aces. I mean, please inform his eminence I will be happy to attend."

"His eminence will be pleased. A car will collect you at your hotel at seven."

The black Mercedes with Vatican SCV plates arrived promptly. It was dark outside. A light dusting of snow underscored the cold Roman winter. The doorman respectfully saluted the automobile before opening the rear door adorned with a small yellow and white Vatican crest. Carlton entered. Cardinal Benedetti was seated under a wool blanket.

"*Buona sera*."

"Eminence."

After the car drove off, Benedetti remained silent for a few moments, then looked at his passenger. "You are nervous around me, am I correct? Around all of this." He motioned to the frozen city beyond the window with a wrinkled hand.

"I am," Carlton answered frankly. "I've never been to Rome before, much less to the Vatican. You're the first cardinal I've ever met."

"Then we're even." He smiled. "You're the first Justice Department prosecutor I've met." He turned to stare out the window. Not so much at the city that rushed by, but at his past. "That has been my cross since coming to this palatial prison." His tone was sad, without the morning's confident diplomatic armor.

"Your Eminence?"

"Everyone is nervous around me. Afraid of the weight of official Church authority I carry like a ball and chain."

"You have many important responsibilities, Eminence. Others are always nervous around important people. But with me, it's more than that. I was raised by traditional Catholic parents. They were very good, very generous. We were happy, but poor. We couldn't afford to travel, but I read constantly. About the Church, the saints, the Vatican. All of this is old and new to me. Like meeting a friend for the first time whom I've known all my life. It's so much more impressive than I imagined, seeing it for the first time."

"Yet you are a government lawyer at the political center of the most powerful country on the globe and in history."

"That's true. But if I may be so bold, Eminence, I'd rather sit at home watching an old movie with a good cigar than play politics with bureaucratic windbags at Washington receptions. Perhaps it's my simple upbringing."

Benedetti's face creased into a warm smile. "Then you and I are very much alike, Mr. Carlton."

"Please call me Pat."

"Ah. The American fondness for first names. In Europe we are so formal sometimes even husbands refer to their wives in the formal tense." Another smile. "My parents were also poor. Farmers. But they made sure I received a good education in the local Church school. I studied hard, then I fell in love." Carlton stared at the cleric.

Benedetti laughed. "No, no. Not with a woman. With the

Church. And with a parish. When I became a priest after the war, I was assigned to a small parish in the Tuscany countryside. I fell in love with it the moment I saw it. The parishioners were so simple. So filled with love and humility and happiness, even though they had no money. Nothing but each other and their faith. I celebrated daily mass, heard confessions, performed weddings and baptisms. Funerals. I knew everyone, and everyone knew me. Most were farmers. They invited me to their homes. We would sit on the *terrazzas* in summer, under the stars, discuss the crops, the rain, local politics. Over bottles of Chianti." His eyes half closed as he remembered days long past.

"It sounds wonderful. How did you become a cardinal, if I may ask?"

"Before I arrived at my parish, my predecessors ran the parish at a financial loss, always asking the archdiocese for money. I was the first to balance the books, even save enough money to improve our little school. My local bishop was pleased.

"He didn't have to subsidize the parish anymore. He assigned me to be his secretary. He gave me the opportunity to continue my education. I discovered I was very good with numbers. When I finished my studies, he placed me in the accounting department of the archdiocese. *Santa Lucia*, you should have seen the mess! Priests are good with souls, but most are terrible with numbers. I reorganized the finances, cut costs, invested some of the leftover money in American companies. They did very well after the war. Again, one thing led to another. Finally, I am here. A mobile repository of theology and accounting rules. But I will tell you this, Patrick." He leaned toward Carlton. "I would give it all up to be back in my little stone church in *Toscana* among the vines and the peasants and *bambini* playing football."

Benedetti glanced outside the window as the car passed through the Porta Sant'Anna into Vatican City. "We are almost there. I must tell you about the dinner guests before we arrive."

Monsignor Clemente Rancuzzi of the Office of the Vatican Secretary of State sipped coffee from a tiny espresso cup. Only thirty-five, he was very young to be a monsignor, a papal prelate. Handpicked by the powerful Vatican secretary of state himself for his diplomatic skill only one year before, what the raven-haired Rancuzzi lacked in age, he made up in knowledge and cunning. One of the first lessons of *Romanita* imparted to him by the cardinal secretary was that, to onlookers, silence translates into wisdom rather than ignorance. Rancuzzi learned the lesson well. But his noteworthy trait was that, unlike many other rising stars within the Vatican constellation, Rancuzzi was far more interested in the Church and its mission than in his own power and glory. It made him a powerful ally and a dangerous enemy. Benedetti had invited Rancuzzi to dinner because he knew that the young priest often served as a catalyst in discussions and also because his closeness to the cardinal secretary of state made him close to the Holy Father.

Much to the impatience of both Carlton and Bishop Jean-Chrétien Azimbe, who had recently arrived to plead the case of his impoverished, war-torn homeland of Zaire, now the Democratic Republic of the Congo, dinner conversation was politely limited to other topics. Substantive African matters were not broached until after-dinner liqueurs and cigars were offered in an adjoining salon.

It was Benedetti who opened the discussion. "I wonder if Africa's cross will ever be lifted. And when."

Azimbe jumped in. "It must be lifted soon, Your Eminence. The situation is intolerable. Much worse than the world knows. The news media reports only the most severe tragedies. The West is so accustomed to suffering in Africa it considers African suffering normal. Famine, disease, poverty, drought, corruption, political violence. We cannot allow these tragedies to continue. As our honored guest can attest, corruption and political violence are fought tooth and nail in America. But when they occur in Africa, they are considered normal, ignored. Look at what continues to happen in Rwanda and Uganda. Not thousands, but millions of people. Even by our fellow Catholics!" Tears welled up in the cleric's sad ebony eyes.

"Or in South Africa," Carlton interjected cautiously, attempting to move the discussion closer to the issue of diamonds and

Waterboer. "The Afrikaaner Volksfront and apartheid return to the Orange Free State, with thousands murdered, and the headlines are about who won the Oscars in Hollywood."

"Precisely! It is madness." Azimbe took a deep breath. He liked this man Carlton. The man did not match the loud, brash, uncultured image he had formulated of Americans from popular African thinking. He calmed himself. Outbursts of emotion would get him nowhere in the Vatican, where caution, quiet planning, and patience ruled.

"There are some who believe Africa should take care of its own problems," Benedetti offered. "Every time aid is given, it is sent offshore by corrupt leaders. Every time troops are sent to quell an African civil war, the situation devolves back to civil war after they leave. Every time multinational banks finance development projects, either the anti-globalist ostriches prevent it or the leaders rape the resources and sell them for pennies on the dollar. Must not Africa first change from within?"

"Many Africans blame colonialism, but tribalism and territoriality existed long before. Tribalism is a cultural apology for disunity. And it is disunity that is the central problem."

"The question is," Rancuzzi finally said softly, "how do you achieve unity in such a violent separatist cultural tradition?"

Azimbe looked at him with a look of certainty. "As a cleric, I am biased, of course, but I believe only the Church can lift Africa's cross."

"A lovely proposal, my brother," Benedetti said, "with which I am certain all of us present agree in spiritual terms. But Africa is a Babel of tribes and territorial disputes."

"It is," Azimbe agreed. "But unlike many other battles in the world, I think the one in Africa can be won through the Church. Or through its help, I should say. Most people, and I am sad that I must add to these many of our own brothers in the Church, do not realize that unlike the vast Asian populations, Africans already widely embrace Christianity, even if they sometimes mix in historic cultural beliefs. The problem is that Church teaching has not transcended tribalism to become part of daily life. People believe in Christ, but in Rwanda, for example, Catholics do not think twice about taking up a knife and butchering their brothers and sisters in Christ." He winced.

Rancuzzi listened in silent agreement and wonderment at the outspoken African bishop so blessedly untainted by the Vatican bureaucracy and its ubiquitous power plays. "What you say has great merit, your excellence, but it remains theoretical. How would you propose to wage this campaign? Do you see this as an economic, social, or cultural war?"

"Nothing so complex, Monsignor," responded Azimbe. "Although the African continent contains more than forty states, only a half dozen of those states impact the general economic and political landscape. It is on those countries that we must focus. The rest will follow."

Carlton clipped a Romeo y Julieta Habana and again pushed toward South Africa. He knew the guests had some tie to Waterboer or at least to diamonds, whether they knew it themselves or not. Monsignor Felici had said as much when he had invited Carlton to dinner. "South Africa, for example? Or is that another animal completely?"

"No, no," Azimbe countered. "South Africa is an excellent example."

The shrewd Rancuzzi took note of Carlton's second focus on South Africa and prodded further. "Even if the Church concentrates on a few leading African states, what do you propose? Economic reform? Political reform? Social reform? How can the Church change those countries?"

"I believe the Church must impress upon the African people that the Church and its principles are not theoretical but practical. The Church must show that its teachings have a practical dimension to them. That if they follow the teachings, even though their human instincts tell them otherwise, they will be better off."

Carlton continued to listen in silence, his mind searching for a way to link Waterboer to the discussion.

Azimbe leaned forward. "The Church cannot lead by preaching but by example. This is no longer the colonial period, where what the Church said was taken as the word of God. There are so many media today. Newspapers, television, radio. And so many speakers using those media. No one listens anymore. So the Church can no longer accomplish its function as God's Church merely by preaching. It can only lead by setting an example. Example is the only thing that people follow today. That is what the Church must offer to Africa."

"A wonderful point, your excellence. But exactly what type of example? The people taking up weapons against landowners and businesses preached by our misguided Marxist liberation theologians in the Order?"

"Absolutely not."

Rancuzzi nodded and leaned back with obvious doctrinal relief.

"What I am saying is that day after day, Sunday after Sunday, I see pastors preach against sin, against evil. Do not steal. Do not kill. Do not lie. But then the flock returns to a world where the pressure to kill, to steal, and to lie is almost unbearable. So they kill and steal and lie. Don't you see? It is not enough for the Church to preach good against evil. It must actually show the people that if they do good, they will better their lot in life."

Carlton's impatience continued unabated as he tried hard to formulate how to involve Waterboer in the discussion.

"How do you suggest the Church do this, brother?" asked Cardinal Benedetti.

Azimbe sighed and lowered his eyes. He whispered. "I am uncertain. That is why I came to Rome. I thought perhaps my politically sophisticated brothers inside these halls could find a solution."

Carlton finally saw a link. "I agree with you, excellence. One can only lead by example. If you will pardon a simple American layman's ignorance in such matters, why not start by focusing the leadership—the active, practical, real life leadership of the Church—on a particular conflict? The long road begins with a single, well-placed step."

Rancuzzi smiled. A simple, ignorant layman this American most definitely was not. "An interesting concept, Mr. Carlton. Do you have a particular conflict in mind?"

Carlton observed Rancuzzi carefully. "We mentioned the recent civil war in South Africa earlier. An excellent example of white colonialism versus native blacks, blacks versus those referred to there as coloreds. Civil war, secessionism, and racism. What if the Church ended that conflict? Would that not accomplish the goal Bishop Azimbe proposes? Using the Church's will and example in such an ugly conflict, in such a critically important African country?"

The American still focused on South Africa, Rancuzzi reflected.

"It would," Azimbe replied. "But only partially. It is not enough for the Church merely to accomplish a favorable result. The Church already does this in Africa and around the world on a daily basis. Mother Teresa's Carmelite nuns. Caritas and Catholic Relief Services and missionaries who distribute food, provide medical services, and build classrooms. These things are already being done. They are good things, of course. They do set an example. But people assume the Church will do these things. They take it for granted. It's not news. And other than facing attacks from fundamentalist religious groups, the Church doesn't risk anything by doing it, other than spending money.

"If the Church expects its flock to risk or forgo something tangible for the sake of good, then the Church must also risk something. Look at what the Holy Father accomplished with your President Reagan. The two worked together to dismantle Soviet Communism, first in Poland, then the rest of Eastern Europe followed. Why was this such a victory? Because people in those countries saw they were not risking their lives alone. The Church and the Holy Father himself risked enormous political capital along with the clergy itself, who risked their lives. Such as Father Popieluszko, who was martyred by the Polish secret police. Being together with the Church in risk and fear and suffering. That's what motivated the people to action, that's what gave them courage and hope, not speeches or charity.

"We used to place our lives on the line for Christ and His message. The bones of twenty-five thousand martyrs fill Bernini's columns in St. Peter's basilica. They could merely have preached to their own, in caves. Others closer in time have done the same. Our French brother St. Perboyre, tortured and crucified in China for refusing to renounce the faith just like the priests being tortured in China right now by an inhuman dictatorship that I am sorry to say your government cajoles, Mr. Carlton. Our Polish brother St. Kolbe, who offered his life at Auschwitz for a Jewish family. Our French brother monks tortured in Algeria by Islamic fundamentalists while helping Moslems, not even preaching but giving daily help. Those are examples. Those are witnesses. If the Church is to keep true to her mission, the Church must take real risks. Otherwise, no one will listen."

"But what can the Church risk, excellence?" asked Rancuzzi.

"If I may, Monsignor," Carlton interjected, finally ready to make the crucial link. "I may have an answer to that very question. From my limited knowledge, in South Africa the white supremacist Afrikaaner Volksfront is making a claim for a separate homeland based on the excuse of a nineteenth-century British colonial promise. Because of the disorganized South African troops, they have already managed to secure the Orange Free State." He looked to Benedetti. The cardinal nodded a fraction.

Carlton went for broke. "If the Volksfront invaded the Orange Free State, doesn't it stand to reason they must be dealing with Waterboer?"

"Waterboer?" Azimbe pronounced the word with unmasked trepidation. "Why do you assume this?"

Rancuzzi nodded, finally understanding what Carlton was after.

Carlton wondered if he had overstepped his bounds. Benedetti's minuscule squint of approval and Rancuzzi's rapt attention told him otherwise. "It has been my experience that nearly every political event that occurs in a region containing diamonds has Waterboer behind it. Whether as an active participant, a facilitator, or merely as a neutral observer depends on the situation. Waterboer regularly encourages civil war with the goal of overthrowing regimes counter to Waterboer's interests or keeps civil wars alive by purchasing both rebel-mined and government-mined diamonds.

"The pattern is sadly predictable: rebels take over diamond mines and sell some diamonds through Waterboer, but mostly to dealers and middlemen outside Waterboer's control. Waterboer has so inflated the price of diamonds that both rebel forces and the government can sell the diamonds for a fortune instead of what they are really worth, which is next to nothing. That's why they kill one another for the diamonds, because they are artificially high-priced by Waterboer. Would a small child risk her leg being blown off by a land mine to extract only a ten-cent piece of rock from malaria-infected swampland? Regardless, the rebels use the proceeds to buy weapons to protect the mines and to line their offshore coffers. Waterboer can't allow a flood of diamonds to come onto the market, so it spends fortunes to buy both the rebel-mined and government-mined diamonds that Waterboer itself inflated in price.

"Recently, Waterboer's coffers became so depleted by paying high prices for these diamonds that their marketing geniuses—and they are geniuses—decided to bypass the rebels completely. In my country and others, after reacting negatively to the UN ban on such diamonds, they supported a massive media and legislative campaign calling the diamonds 'blood diamonds' and 'conflict diamonds,' showing how people were being murdered by these diamond-mining rebels. When the story was well-disseminated and the sale of blood diamonds was condemned by political figures around the world, Waterboer turned on their 'good neighbor' light and announced that they would only sell diamonds that were certified as not being 'blood diamonds.' And who else could certify diamonds as being cruelty-free but Waterboer, as if even they could tell a peaceful diamond from a blood-stained diamond? Since no one wants to buy diamonds sold by little African kids being hacked to pieces, the diamond-mining rebels found themselves without a market for their diamonds. And Waterboer once again controls the supply of diamonds without fear of destabilization from civil war. And gets a pat on the back from the innocent yet fully duped consumer. Not to mention that the labeling laws effectively prevent anyone from selling pre-ban diamonds because they are not certified.

"In any event, blood diamonds or no blood diamonds, whether or not you agree with my analysis, it stands to reason that Waterboer would at least be involved in the South African Orange Free State conflict, doesn't it?" He continued. "The Orange Free State has the highest concentration of diamond mines in South Africa. Waterboer is far too powerful to allow the Volksfront to march in and take over the entire area without some agreement on their part. Waterboer can't afford to lose control of its diamond production in the Orange Free State. On the other hand, President Boiko's government has pushed for antitrust legislation that would nationalize certain mines and all but destroy Waterboer's monopoly in South Africa at the very least."

Rancuzzi sat perfectly still, eyes slightly squinted in concentration. "An entirely valid observation, *dottore*. Your conclusion?"

"Waterboer and the Volksfront are fighting the same war."

Rancuzzi straightened himself, genuinely surprised. "Quite honestly, I never thought to make such a connection."

"It's just a calculated guess. I have no evidence to back it up other than logic. But if it's true, the situation poses a fertile field for Bishop Azimbe's proposal."

"In what way?" Azimbe asked.

"South Africa, the Bishop's former Zaire, now Congo, and Angola, Botswana, Ghana, Namibia, Sierra Leone, Tanzania, the Central African Republic. All of those countries produce diamonds. Whether educated or not, their populations are aware of the corruption and misery wrought upon them for the past century not just by the warring factions, but in great part by Waterboer and its artificially high-priced diamonds. If the Church could deal a massive blow to Waterboer, loudly, publicly, and reduce the price of diamonds to where it should really be, that would remove the motivation to mine diamonds and the factions' fight to control the mines. It could fulfill exactly what Bishop Azimbe proposes."

Rancuzzi finally understood why Carlton was here. He waited patiently for him to finish. "An excellent opportunity, Mr. Carlton. But the pivotal question remains: how does the Church neutralize Waterboer? Decrease the price of diamonds? Your impressive Ministry of Justice has tried to bring

Waterboer to justice for a hundred years without success. Waterboer remains a powerful international force. You are among friends, *dottore*. Tell us."

Monsignor Rancuzzi made Carlton feel as though he were speaking with Forbes at CIA rather than with a priest. But the time for diplomacy, hiding the ball, and the art of *Romanita* was over. "I think it's clear from my statements why I am in Rome and why this dinner was organized. My government cannot allow—will not allow—recent events involving Waterboer to continue."

Each of the others understood the statement. The United States government wants to destroy Waterboer.

"To return to Monsignor Rancuzzi's point, I myself had no idea how to go about neutralizing Waterboer." He looked at each of the men around the table. "This afternoon, however, I believe I may have discovered a solution.

"Between the beginning and the end of the Angolan civil war—the original civil war, not the new one—Angola produced approximately sixty million carats of diamonds. Waterboer purchased fifty million of those carats. The remaining ten million carats were sold by both sides of the conflict, the MPLA and UNITA. But not to Waterboer. To whom, then?"

He relit his cigar slowly, adding more tension to the already edgy dinner guests. The thick cloud of smoke shrouded Benedetti's head and concealed the extreme pallor of his face. He wiped his moist palms on his scarlet robe. "What does it matter who purchased the diamonds?" he asked irritably.

"Because someone other than Waterboer purchased the ten million carats. Perhaps five million carats—half—could have been purchased by small operators, but not all. Ten million carats is far too much for small operators to buy up. In addition, our diamond production and sales figures show that those five million carats have never been sold. If they haven't been sold, they're stockpiled somewhere. If those diamonds can be found and dumped on the world diamond market simultaneously, it would cripple Waterboer." He raised his cigar. "I realize the theory's been around for years. But as sure as God made little green apples, given the enormity of the diamond supply purchased secretly during the Angolan civil war, it's now possible."

Azimbe nodded, impressed by the possibility. "And if Waterboer can be crippled?"

"It would end the civil war in South Africa, if Waterboer is in fact the main source of funds for the Volksfront, as we suspect. If the price of diamonds drops like a stone, there is no reason for Waterboer to continue financing the Volksfront's civil war to create an independent Orange Free State for Waterboer."

"But where does the Church fit in?" Benedetti asked. "Is not our purpose to have the Church show Africa and the world the true message of Christ? Assuming we know who holds the Angolan stockpile, how does the Church get to it? You are assuming that it does not legitimately belong to whomever its owner might be. Quite candidly, it is a job more for spies and special forces than Vatican priests."

"Perhaps. As to what the Church might do, I will leave that to the eminent Office of the Vatican Secretary of State and the Vatican Bank."

73 CONFESSION

Wrapped in heavy overcoats, Benedetti and Carlton walked off their dinner along the Colonnade of St. Peter's Square next to the Belvedere Palace. Ice on the columns glistened in the moonlight that bathed the Eternal City in an otherworldly glow.

"I was impressed by the way you shifted the conversation to Waterboer. Very clever, very clever. For all of your claims of simplicity and nervousness, you handled yourself as well as any Vatican diplomat. Particularly with our well-intentioned, but shark-like Rancuzzi. Bravo."

"Thank you."

The cardinal lowered his voice, as if fearful that the ageless columns would hear his words. "He has considerable influence with the secretary of state and the Holy Father."

"He's as sharp as diamond tacks, that one. I wonder what he thought of my theory of the Angolan diamonds. What they all thought."

Benedetti paused for a long moment before responding. "It does not matter what they thought. You planted the seed. For the moment, that is all that matters."

"With all due respect, Eminence, I don't think we have the time for *Romanita* to run its course on this one. The civil war in South Africa continues. Russian nationalism may have been dealt a severe blow in the North Sea, but not Waterboer." And there was still Scott Fress to deal with, but he couldn't tell that to the cardinal, although it wouldn't surprise him if the man already knew.

"Patience, my son. All in God's time. Ah, here we are." Carlton followed him up a flight of marble steps to a set of massive bronze doors. Benedetti could have used the secret side entrance, unguarded and open twenty-four hours, but he wanted Carlton to see the basilica from its main entrance, the way every newcomer should experience its majesty.

A member of the Vigilanza turned to them, gesturing with his arms. "*E chiuso, e chiuso.*" It's closed. He looked annoyed at silly tourists wandering so late before looking more carefully at the man who approached. Then his eyes grew wide. "*Eminenza. Scusi, Eminenza! Scusi, scusi!*" He turned to the bronze doors, unlocked them, pulled one open with great effort, and saluted as the prince of the Church and his guest entered.

"*Grazie.* Saint Peter's Basilica, my son," Benedetti announced.

Carlton and Benedetti dipped the fingers of their right hands in holy water, knelt, and performed the sign of the cross. A series of lights turned on, illuminating the largest church in Christendom. Carlton rose, speechless. The rear altar, a few dozen feet from the entrance of typical churches, was over a football field away. He craned his neck, gaped at the gold coffered ceiling that floated far higher than the spires of many churches.

Benedetti observed Carlton silently with a tinge of envy as the young American walked down the central nave toward the immense *baldachino* supported by Bernini's four curved bronze columns around the massive central altar. The scene transported the elder cardinal to the day, long ago, when he had walked down the nave of St. Peter's Basilica for the first time as a young priest, thunderstruck by the power and immensity of the church. How he had walked around the church for hours and scrutinized every sculpture, every inscription. How the immense jeweled gold crucifix he had expected to find above the altar of the giant church was instead a simple white dove set against a yellow stained-glass background: the symbol of the Holy Spirit bringing forth peace to humanity. Any lingering doubt about his vocation had departed as he had fallen to his knees, in tears.

He followed the young American up the nave until they arrived at the central altar, hundreds of feet under the towering dome. "The altar of Saint Peter," Benedetti explained, anticipating Carlton's question. "Only the successor to Saint Peter, the Holy Father, may celebrate mass here." He pointed down to an ornate gold box encrusted in rock that glowed a deep yellow. "The remains of Saint Peter, the first pope."

In a smaller church, his words would have echoed, but the Basilica's immensity absorbed the words into its imposing silence. He watched as Carlton knelt reverently before the central altar and prayed. Benedetti walked alone to the far altar, knelt in one of the dark wood pews under the white dove, and removed a rosary from his pocket. Crafted of simple pine beads strung together with coarse yarn and worn from years of prayer, it had been with Benedetti since the day of his ordination.

He performed the sign of the cross, bowed his head. *Pater noster. Qui est in caelis. Sanctificetur nomen tuum.*

After reciting five decades of the rosary, Benedetti continued kneeling, prayed in the Basilica's reverent silence. Carlton was right, he reflected. Time was running out. The records and files and vaults of the Banco Napolitana Lucchese would soon be analyzed by the Guarda di Finanza in its search for evidence against Don Arcangelo. They would find the late Altiplano's diamonds in the Order's vault.

Benedetti rose, placed the rosary in his pocket, and returned to the central altar. There, in the same position he had left him over a half hour before, Carlton still knelt on the cold marble floor, hands clasped together, head bowed in humble reverence. Whispers of the Our Father and the Hail Mary and the Glory Be streamed from his lips. He did not hear Benedetti's footsteps. Benedetti was moved by the young American's simple faith. At its core, the Church and its religion were about faith.

As the sight of the white dove above the far altar had done so many years in the past, the sight of Carlton prostrated with such humility erased all remaining traces of doubt from Benedetti's mind. He looked up at the white dove in the distance and nodded.

Gratia Deo.

He knelt beside Carlton and gently touched him on the shoulder.

Carlton turned, startled. "What—? Oh, sorry, Eminence."

The cardinal took a deep breath. "Now that we have both prayed, I have a confession to make."

Carlton smiled. "Isn't it supposed to be the other way around?"

"No." He averted his gaze from Carlton's smiling eyes. He paused. "I lied, my son."

Carlton crooked his head.

"This morning. When you asked me about the diamond stockpile, I told you the Vatican Bank has no connection with any stockpile."

"Yes?"

"It was technically true, but a lie."

Carlton fixed Benedetti with a confused stare.

"The Vatican Bank didn't purchase any diamonds. Nor did it authorize any purchase. But a Church official did. Without authority. The diamonds were purchased from Angola. And not five million carats. Nine."

Carlton's eyes grew wide.

Benedetti nodded slowly, grasped the heavy gold cross that hung around his neck. "Forgive me."

74 EXPLANATION

Piazza del Popolo
Rome
10:01 A.M.

Wrapped in the heavy Loro Piana cashmere overcoat MacLean had supplied, Carlton walked out of the Hotel Hassler, down the Spanish Steps, into the Piazza Spagna, turned right, and walked two blocks to the Piazza del Popolo. As its name suggested, the piazza was filled with people, even on this cold and overcast winter day. He looked around the large plaza and spotted the name "Rosati" on a pink awning next to the church. He walked to the café, hands thrust deep in his pockets to ward off the cold. Both the enclosed outdoor area and indoor rooms were packed with well-dressed patrons who spoke with caffeinated animation. The well-known café smelled of espresso and cigarette smoke. Cardinal Benedetti sat at a corner table, dressed in layman's clothes and surrounded by a protective moat of four empty tables on which were placed small cards that read "*Riservato*."

Carlton rubbed his hands together briskly, cupped them, and blew into them. He sat at Benedetti's right. "Not that I mind the exercise, but it's cold as a popsicle out there." He announced, omitting the honorific "Eminence" to avoid unnecessary attention.

Benedetti leaned toward Carlton. "I'm sorry, but the walls in my house and office have ears." He touched his own. "This is safer."

"Don't these have ears too?" Carlton asked, jutting his chin toward the other patrons, removing his overcoat and handing it to a deferential white-jacketed waiter.

"Less than the Vatican. Stefano here will keep these tables empty." Benedetti announced, looking at the waiter. "*Due espressi per favore*, Stefano."

"*Va bene. Grazie, Eminenza.*" The man bowed slightly to the cardinal, eyeing Carlton curiously before leaving.

Benedetti again leaned forward. "Now. About the stones." The expression on his round face changed from cherubic to nervous. Carlton observed the deep wrinkles that years of worry had etched around Benedetti's eyes. At present, the man before him was neither a cardinal nor the simple country priest he longed to be. He was director of the Institute for the Works of Religion. The Vatican Bank. "You have questions for me. Ask them."

"Why and where is a good place to start," said Carlton. "Although frankly, right now I'm more interested in where."

"The two go hand in hand. Like the stones you sent to the bottom of the North Sea, there was a purpose behind amassing the Vatican stockpile. Not officially sanctioned by the Vatican, of course, that would be madness. But a purpose nonetheless. As you noted, the Angolan civil war discontinued centralized control over the country's mines. Dozens of mines. The MPLA and UNITA both wanted control. The gap between the two allowed miners, dealers, and smugglers to grab stones and sell them outside Angola's original Waterboer contract."

"To someone in the Vatican who was willing to pay."

"Yes."

"Who could want—"

"Cardinal Altiplano, the secretary general of the Order. One of the oldest and most famous orders of the Church. He rerouted funds earmarked for hospitals, universities, and missions to purchase the diamonds."

"But why? And how? I don't understand. You said the Church is already skirting bankruptcy. How did he get the money?"

"He wanted the Order to impose its beliefs on official Church doctrine, believing that those beliefs alone would save the Church. Perhaps believing himself a prophet. In fact, they were the beliefs of a long line of Altiplano's doctrinally questionable predecessors who opposed the Holy Father not only on fundamental doctrine, but on the very legitimacy of the Holy See. For over two hundred years. The difference is that Altiplano's predecessors fought their doctrinal war intellectually. Altiplano wanted to impose his beliefs outright. To do this, he felt he had to become the successor to St. Peter. Pope. His plan was to use the diamonds to bribe the College of Cardinals into voting for him at the next conclave, when the cardinals elect the next pope after the Holy Father passes away. Once he became pope, Altiplano could dismantle the Church's power structure and its doctrine from within. The ranks of the clergy and the faithful laity could disagree and leave the Church, as so many did in the wake of Vatican II, but in any case the Church and its doctrine would be dramatically changed."

Carlton stared at him in disbelief.

"I know it sounds crazy. And it is. Today, at least. But it has been done in the past. During the time of the Borgias, for example, cardinals regularly bribed each other with estates and titles to gain the papacy."

"It's beyond scandalous. And it shocks me, of course. But for our purposes, it is what it is. The question is what lies next. Do you liquidate the diamond stockpile by selling it to Waterboer? That would only strengthen Waterboer. But the Church would recover its money and probably far more if it played its cards right. As director of the Vatican Bank, you'd be able to give it a veneer of legitimacy by saying it was an investment and look how much money you made for the Church." He tested the cardinal.

Benedetti shook his head. "No. As you said, it would only strengthen Waterboer. I may be plagued by a scandal I had nothing to do with, but I will not make a pact with the devil to solve it. No." The chair creaked as he reclined. "I thought long and hard about what Azimbe said last night; have been thinking it for some time. But always without the necessary opportunity. The Church can only set an example if it risks something. The Church must risk this stockpile, this fortune in a way that will do the most good." He also reflected that the Church could save itself from scandal by implying that the diamonds had been purchased for such a purpose.

The waiter arrived with two tiny cups of fragrant espresso and set them on the small table. He folded the bill and placed it under Carlton's saucer, assuming that the cardinal would not be paying.

"*Grazie*, Stefano."

"*A le. Prego, Eminenza.*"

Carlton dumped a white sugar cube in his cup, stirred the oily black coffee with a tiny spoon, and took a sip. "If you don't sell them to Waterboer, your options are to keep them, which serves no immediate purpose, sell them to others, which makes no sense because Waterboer would top anyone else's price, or give them away. Giving them away won't destroy Waterboer, of course. Waterboer is far too strong for nine million carats on the market to destroy it. But it might stop the civil war in South Africa if Waterboer is financing the Afrikaaner Volksfront. Maybe it will stop the dictatorship in the Congo. Maybe also Waterboer's forced child labor in India. Whatever else it accomplishes, it will certainly show that for all the ridicule it receives in the secular world, the Church is not only a powerful force against evil, but it is an institution willing to use that force against evil. For all of humanity, not just for Catholics or other Christians." Carlton finished his espresso, replaced the cup in its saucer, and leaned back in his chair. "For those reasons you must dump the diamonds."

"*Si*. You were correct in mentioning the strategy last night. It is a simple idea, yes," he raised a finger, "but not simplistic. The reason it has been often discussed but never done is that greed prevents it. It always ended with Waterboer buying the diamonds at a premium from whoever planned on flooding the market. The problem is not whether to dump the diamonds, but how."

"So we get them out and flood the market." Carlton felt relieved. He had discovered where the diamonds were, whose control they were in, and the Church had just agreed to dump them on the open market. Mission accomplished. "Compared to the North Sea operation, it's as easy as—"

"No." Benedetti wagged his finger again. "You don't understand. Dumping the diamonds isn't the difficulty, getting them is the difficulty. The diamonds are in a vault at the Banco Napolitana Lucchese, here in Rome. The bank apparently is where Don Arcangelo, the head of a very powerful Sicilian mafia family, transferred a large part of its extortion, drug, and prostitution money. It is also believed to contain computer records of many important mafia transactions. Somehow, one of Sicily's new generation of politicians, a seemingly incorruptible mafia fighter by the name of Orlando Leonida, discovered these transactions. He invoked a law that allowed the GDF—the Guarda di Finanza, similar to a combination of your Treasury Department and FBI—to seal the bank. The diamonds are in that bank. We can't withdraw them because the bank is sealed. Nothing and no one goes in or out without judicial approval. Any day now, Leonida will finish making the proper judicial requests to have the GDF search through the bank's premises and records with a, how do you say, a comb with little teeth."

"A fine-toothed comb." Carlton sighed and took in the enormity of the obstacle. "I understand. The judicial order will allow the GDF to look in all the vaults, and they'll discover the diamonds. Since the diamonds are in a vault belonging to or traceable to Altiplano, the trail will lead to the Church."

"*Exacto*. Not only will this create an enormous scandal, but every cardinal will get involved, each with a different plan. Committees will be organized and so on. It will become politically impossible to appropriate the diamonds and flood the market." Benedetti drank his coffee in a single gulp.

"So we have to get the diamonds out before the GDF searches the vaults. Can't you simply ask the GDF for permission? After all, the Vatican is a sovereign state and you are the director of the sovereign state's bank. Couldn't you just order the withdrawal?"

"In legal theory, yes. But when both the Church and this much money are involved, other demands are made and legal theory, as you say, leaves through the window."

"Goes out the window," Carlton corrected. "I understand. The GDF would demand a huge price in exchange for withdrawing the diamonds."

"*Si*. And many people would know, so a scandal would occur even if the GDF promised confidentiality."

Carlton eyed the cardinal carefully. He did not want to insult him, but he had to ask. Not just to satisfy his own curiosity, but as a matter of political strategy. "It isn't my place to ask, of course, Eminence, but have you informed the Holy Father of all this?"

Benedetti looked down at his tiny empty espresso cup and sighed. "Not yet. But I will have to. I've dreaded the day since I discovered Altiplano's papers. Now it has finally arrived. And I have to deliver the news to the Holy Father in his present medical condition, without a solution." His face creased with sadness, then recovered. "It's ironic, isn't it? The Church finally may have the will to divest itself of such a fortune, but it can't physically get the diamonds because of the mafia. Again, evil preventing good."

Carlton remained in quiet concentration for a moment, his eyes closed. He finally looked up and ran his hands over his chin. "We may have a solution."

Benedetti sat up in his chair. "What is it?"

"Well, the key is to find a way to get the diamonds out without the GDF knowing and before it starts combing through the vaults. But there is another person who wants to get into the bank as much as you do, other than the GDF."

"Don Arcangelo. Of course, but we can't possibly go to him."

"Right. But I may know someone who may wish to play that role."

75 BETRAYAL

Acquasanta, Sicily
1:35 P.M.

Lieutenant Cristina Petronelli of the Guarda di Finanza had ordinary looks and extraordinary greed. Far too much greed for the twenty-something woman to wait for promotions in the ordinary course of merit. Petronelli didn't possess great intelligence, but even she realized the types of bribes she was after could only be obtained after several promotions from her low-level post. Yet the raven-haired woman who bore a perpetual scowl on her face and in her attitude did have one important asset: her present assignment. Cristina Petronelli was guarding the sealed Rome headquarters of the Banco Napolitana Lucchese.

She had left her uniform at home. First, it was her day off. Second, it would be unwise to be seen in her uniform when speaking to one of the most corrupt mafia dons in Europe. She wasn't sufficiently intelligent to fear anything when she ascended the massive stone steps of the Villa Igea Grand Hotel. Two men stared at her as she entered the ornate lobby. She smiled, deluding herself that the two watchers entertained sexual thoughts about her. And also at the notion that the don would pay her handsomely for whatever he wanted her to do. Fifty thousand euros at least. She could buy that diamond ring and necklace she wanted so badly. She saw the man as soon as she entered the inner garden of oleander and jasmine. He sat under a large African palm, surrounded by several men. One of the men, Enzo, the don's head bodyguard, walked toward Petronelli and stopped her with an imposing stare. He frisked her expertly. Feeling no objectionable items, he led her to a seat in front of the square-shouldered don. She stood while the man's cruel eyes appraised her. After what seemed like several minutes, he smiled. "*Buon giorno, signorina,*" he announced, without getting up. He pointed to the chair. "*Prego, signorina.*"

She sat. "*Si, si,*" she responded quickly, making it clear that she wanted to get their meeting over with as quickly as possible. She wanted to return to Rome and enjoy the rest of the afternoon.

The don clearly was not used to being addressed with such disrespect. He frowned at her. Her scowl was no match for his unforgiving gaze. "*Grazie*, Don Arcangelo. *Molto gentile*," he announced slowly, as if teaching a small child.

The man's eyes made her shiver. She was also surprised to find herself repeating the man's words.

Don Arcangelo smiled and leaned back. "*Bene, bene*. So tell me *signorina*, how do you like your job?"

"I do not."

"And why is that?" He turned to the waiter. "Alfredo, bring us some Regaleali, please. And a glass for the *signorina*."

"I don't want—I'm sorry, Don Arcangelo, but I do not drink wine."

The don's frown highlighted his shock at such heresy. "Nonsense. You will enjoy it." It sounded like a prediction, but somehow Petronelli knew it was an order. She began to sweat.

"And so why is it that you dislike your job?"

"I don't make enough money." She paused, then remembered the honorific. "Don Arcangelo."

The don sighed and nodded with seemingly genuine compassion. "*Si, si. Capisco*. Perhaps we can remedy that."

"What can I do for you?" she spat out. "Don Arcangelo."

"So direct, the young generation." He stretched out his palm and waved it back and forth slowly. "*Piano, piano*. You must know how to slow down. All in good time."

"Yes, I've heard that."

"Well, since you are so impatient, here is what you can do for me." He spoke in a low voice and leaned forward.

She leaned forward, licking her lips at the money she knew whatever task she had to do would bring. "Yes?"

"I can only tell you what I need from you if you agree to do it."

"But how can I agree if I don't know what it is?"

"Yes, it is difficult, isn't it? The only thing I can tell you is that you will be paid two hundred and fifty thousand euros."

"Two hundred and fifty thousand?" She gasped in amazement. "I-I thought maybe—"

"Is this acceptable, then? Do I have your word that you will agree to do what we need?"

"Yes, yes. I accept. Absolutely, Don Arcangelo." She could see the diamond ring and necklace very clearly with her mind's eye.

"Very well. You will open the door behind the Banco Napolitana Lucchese. My men will be waiting for you. They will give you several items, including a cellular telephone which you will place in specific locations in the building. You will then leave at the end of your shift, as usual."

She stared at the don. It was so simple. She would have taken far less money for such a job. But she would not tell that to the don. And although she knew that Mayor Orlando Leonida's case against Don Arcangelo was the reason the GDF has sealed BNL headquarters, she would not ask what the items were intended to achieve. She was too cunning for that, she thought, congratulating herself for being so smart. "Very well, Don Arcangelo. When do I do this?"

"Soon, *signorina*. Soon. My men know where you live. They will contact you. Since you are in such a hurry, you may go."

"*Grazie*, Don Arcangelo. *Grazie*." She bent to kiss his hand, but he placed it in his pocket.

"*Buona sera, signorina. Grazie.*"

"*Buona sera*, Don Arcangelo. *E grazie a le.*" She walked away, grinning, knowing that if she did a good job, more jobs and money would follow. If she could do this for a few years, she would be able to retire and do what she wanted to do more than anything else: nothing. She would buy a place on the Amalfi coast somewhere and eat and drink all day. She would not even have to look for men. She would rent them. They would try to use her, but she would use them. She grinned even wider.

Still seated, Don Arcangelo watched Cristina Petronelli disappear through the oleanders, jasmine, and African palms. "What do you think, Enzo?" He asked, without moving his head.

The man paused and thought. "She is a hog, Don Arcangelo. The look in her eyes when you told her how much money you would pay her—she would have done anything you asked. She will never have any loyalty. She can never be trusted."

Don Arcangelo mulled Enzo's words over for a few moments, still looking in the direction where Petronelli had walked away. "You are becoming a wise man, Enzo. *Si*. You are correct. She is a greedy hog. A little greed is acceptable. Reasonable. We are only human. Each of us wants to dip our beaks in more than once. But so much obvious greed. It is dangerous." He shook his head in disapproval. "You know what they say."

"What do they say, Don Arcangelo?"

"The pigs get fed but the hogs get slaughtered."

Enzo understood it was an order.

Arcangelo rose and turned to his chief bodyguard. "But wait until she finishes the job first, eh?"

Villa Forza
Near Palermo, Sicily
11:54 A.M.

The tinted-glass black Alfa Romeo 156 1.6 TS sedan wound up the steep Sicilian escarpments with ease. To avoid attention, its Vatican license plates had been replaced with Italian plates from Palermo. The sedan growled to a lone estate hidden behind an ancient forged iron gate atop Monte Pellegrino. An unshaven man dressed in black peasant garb ordered the driver to stop. He stepped to the passenger window without attempting to hide the Beretta submachine gun slung across his chest.

"Patrick Carlton," Carlton announced calmly.

The guard opened the door, indicated for him to exit the automobile. Carlton complied carefully, blinking uncomfortably in the bright Sicilian sunlight. A backup joined the guard and frisked Carlton with quick, expert hands. With a nod, he pronounced him clean. The other guard opened the massive forged iron gates and waved the car through.

Built by one of the myriad princes, dukes, marquises, counts, and barons who populated eighteenth-century Sicily, the Villa Forza was a stunning example of historic restoration. Behind its sun-baked outer walls, the palazzo appeared exactly as it had over 250 years ago. The ocher yellow edifice was framed in white and dotted by regularly spaced windows hidden behind forged iron lattices. Carlton followed a seemingly mute guard past rows of potted palms that lined the path between lozenges of manicured lawns under tall parasol pines. Water gurgled and dripped in moss-covered fountains. Armed guards mingled with gardeners amid the heat of the neverending Sicilian summer. The guard stopped in front of an ornately sculpted wood door. It appeared thick enough to repel the battalions of Carthaginians, Romans, Byzantine Greeks, Arabs, Normans, Swabians, Frenchmen, and Spaniards who had conquered Sicily over the centuries. The guard handed off his ward to the valet inside, then departed without a word.

"You are expected. Please follow me," the valet announced with a deep Sicilian accent.

Liveried in white tie, tails, and gloves much like the Vatican Bank valet, the man ushered Carlton into the welcome cool of the main hall, led them through an ornate hallway. *The sheep herded into the wolf's lair*, thought Carlton. He admired the collection of Roman sculptures and Italian Renaissance paintings that stood on the polished white marble floors and hung on the scarlet silk walls. Probably all originals, he surmised. The valet knocked once before opening a set of gilded doors, bowed his head slightly to Carlton, who entered the large salon, then closed the doors behind him.

Carlton gazed at the palatial audience chamber. Rococo furniture filled every available space of the room. Gilded mouldings, friezes, and curves glistened in the intense sunlight that streamed from two floor-to-ceiling windows. A man sat in a leather armchair on the far balcony, basking in the sun, squinting at the hazy streets of Palermo far below. His profile displayed a large nose and thinning, nearly white hair. He turned as Carlton walked across the salon. Upon closer scrutiny, Carlton saw that the man was in his mid-seventies. His thick round face and stocky build evident even in his sitting position, and his casual, almost shabby clothes made him look more at home in the fields or in a barn than the intricately distinguished surroundings. The man's face was tan and wrinkled. He was dressed in simple outdoor clothes: old jeans, which struck Carlton as odd for a mafia don, a green plaid wool shirt, an ancient brown wool sweater, and rough brown leather shoes that had not only seen better days, but better decades.

"Signore Carlton. Welcome." He spoke loudly and clearly, without standing. He grasped Carlton's hand in a powerful grip. The genuine smile that creased his face revealed straight rows of brilliant white teeth. "I am Don Forza." His accent was heavy, but his English excellent. "*Per favore*. Sit down." He motioned to a companion armchair next to his. Carlton sat and remained quiet.

After inquiring about Carlton's journey from Rome and

offering him a glass of Chianti, Don Forza moved to the business at hand. "My good friend Don Innocenti—*scusi*, Don MacLean—informs me you have an important proposition for me. He would not tell me what it is over the telephone." He squinted. "A very secretive man, Maximilliano. And any friend of his is a friend of mine. But what can a now-honest man such as myself do for the American Department of Justice? Or the United States Navy? Or the Central Intelligence Agency?" Forza could be described in a variety of ways. Ill-informed was not one of them.

"Mr. Forza," Carlton began, refusing to attach the honorific "Don" to the man, even though MacLean had assured him of Forza's conversion from crime to honest business pursuits. "What do you know about diamonds?"

"They are beautiful, expensive, and cold. Like many women I have known." He chuckled. "Other than that, *niente*. Nothing."

Carlton proceeded with a complete briefing of Waterboer and its history, careful to emphasize Waterboer's use of child labor and its bankrolling of the Soviet Union during the cold war.

"Children? Communists? I had no idea," responded Forza, disgusted. If there was one thing the mafia revered, it was its children. And the political force they despised the most was communism. He breathed deeply. "I still don't see how I fit into all of this."

"For many years, someone in the Vatican has steadily amassed a diamond stockpile. Who is responsible is not import—"

"Altiplano and the Order."

Carlton leaned back, unable to keep his mouth from gaping open in astonishment. "How do you—"

Forza's bright white teeth reappeared. "*Per piacere, signore.* How do you think Altiplano, an Italian, could possibly amass such a vast diamond treasure without the Cosa Nostra? Eh?" He held out his hands, palms up.

Carlton continued staring at him, still in shock, and now very wary of the man, despite MacLean's vetting.

"No, it was not me or my people. But I have big ears and

Sicily is a small place."

Carlton leaned forward. "Since you seem to have a great deal of information, you probably know that the diamonds are in the vaults of the Banco Napolitana Lucchese in Rome."

"*Si.*"

"Do you also know that the bank contains evidence against Don Arcangelo?"

Forza shrugged nonchalantly. "It was in the *jornali*. The newspapers."

"Well since you seem to know everything, I will go straight to the plan the Church proposes." He was not about to use his authority as a representative of the United States to make a deal with the mafia, newly confessed and converted from crime or not. "We believe the GDF will begin sifting through the bank's documents, computers, and vaults very soon. We can't go to the GDF and ask for permission to withdraw the diamonds."

Forza laughed. "Clearly."

Carlton frowned. "So the plan would be for your men to raid the bank and withdraw the diamonds."

"In exchange for what? What do I get out of this other than the satisfaction of helping the Holy Church?"

Carlton leaned back. "MacLean tells me that you went clean a few years ago."

"That is true. MacLean's father, Don Innocenti, set the example for me."

"But some of your former activities have long statutes of limitation."

"Ah. *Capisco.*" Forza nodded. "I understand. You will offer me amnesty in exchange for my help."

Carlton nodded.

"It would be difficult to prosecute me. I have done so many favors for so many people. For judges especially." The rows of white teeth reappeared.

Carlton leaned toward Forza. "How much have you done for federal judges in the United States?"

Forza's smile disappeared. "You are sharp, Signore Carlton."

"There is another reason you should want to participate. And I know you have already thought of it."

"What reason is that?"

"Your family's war with Don Arcangelo. I was informed about it in Rome. You are in a truce, but only because neither family has discovered how to destroy the other. Getting the evidence against Arcangelo in the bank would enable you to ensure Arcangelo's demise, whether through the GDF or other political means if the GDF fails."

"Yes, that is also true."

"We will in fact help you obtain that information in case it later disappears."

"But why would you be willing to give me amnesty?"

"I have to tell you, I am not particularly thrilled to make a deal with you. But as the French say, 'God writes straight with curved lines.' It seems that in the end, justice will be better served by having your men get the diamonds and return them to the Church"—he did not mention the purpose to which the diamonds would be put, but Forza probably already knew, he reasoned—"than by spending the time and money prosecuting you and sending a man of your age, who has already changed his ways, to prison."

"*Bene*. I agree to your plan. But there are two conditions." He counted off on his left hand fingers. "I must have the final say on the operation's tactics. And I must have a signed, original, and notarized amnesty agreement, reviewed and approved by my *consiglieri* before the operation."

"I can see you were raised in the United States. I am certain that can be arranged. On one condition, however. And this is absolute: no one must be killed."

"I cannot foretell the future, Mr. Carlton."

"No one." Carlton stared at him hard. "Or else there is no deal."

Forza shrugged. "*Bene*. But it will make things harder."

"Of course. But if someone were killed and the operation went sour, the repercussions would be devastating."

Forza observed the contents of his glass silently. The wine glowed ruby red in the Sicilian sunlight. He finally nodded and stood. He was taller than Carlton imagined, but still shorter than he. "*Bene*. You have a deal, Signore Carlton."

They shook hands.

77 PONTIFEX

Via Del Pontifice
Financial District
Rome, Italy
9:20 A.M.

The title "bishop of Rome" was often used, but its meaning more often glossed over. Like most, Romans thought of the elderly man in white robes and long pointed miter simply as the pope. Rarely did they think of him as the local leader of the Church in Rome. Yet he was. What happened after the bishop of Rome received Monsignor Rancuzzi and the cardinal secretary of state proved it.

The news traveled fast. But nowhere did it travel faster than in the business center of Rome itself. Telephones, fax machines, email; all relayed the news. Soon it was on everyone's mind and lips. Receptionists abandoned telephones. Secretaries abandoned computers. Lawyers abandoned briefs. Accountants abandoned financial reports. Stockbrokers abandoned electronic boards. A flood of humanity streamed from office buildings and converged into the avenue en masse. Cars destined for meetings were piled two and three deep along frenzied sidewalks. Traffic ground to a standstill. All flocked to see the vicar of Christ who lived among them, whom they saw on television and in newspapers and magazines, but rarely in person. Police trucks carrying emergency crowd-control troops dispatched at the last minute were trapped in the ocean of vehicles.

Although most Romans were Catholic, many were so in name only. Like most Catholic Europeans, they were cultural Catholics. Secular Catholics. They liked Church holidays, bought gifts at Christmas, were proud of their churches, loved the atmosphere of mass. Few obeyed religious tenets or attended mass on Sunday. But this was different. This was unplanned. Today the pope wasn't in a foreign country torn by civil strife or flood or famine. He wasn't in a political meeting with heads of state. He wasn't at an abbey or monastery or cemetery.

He was here.

For them.

A little after nine in the morning, as cars and mopeds and buses ferried people to work, an odd-looking truck had carried the bishop of Rome straight to the center of the financial district. Known to the world as the "popemobile," the white Mercedes 4x4 Gelandewagen with a podium, enclosed in bulletproof glass after the miraculously failed 1981 assassination attempt, was halfway down the Via Della Conziliazione before people realized what was happening. By the time the popemobile and its two-bus convoy filled with priests arrived at the heart of the financial district, it trailed a mile-long line of followers behind it.

More amazing than the spur-of-the-moment papal drive through Rome was the pontiff's exit from the popemobile to a small altar and cross erected between the outline of two trees along the main avenue. Protected by plainclothed Swiss guards who kept the growing crowd at bay, filmed by a half-dozen rooftop and helicopter television crews, accompanied by a contingent of one hundred priests, dressed in white robes and papal miter, leaning painfully against a tall bronze staff that ended in a crucifix, but with eyes sparkling with life and hope as always, the pope traced the sign of the cross high above the crowd.

"*In nomine Patris et Filius et Spiritu Sanctus.*" His frail voice cracked as it lilted through the benediction. Amplified through the remote microphone, it boomed through fifty loudspeakers arranged along the avenue during the previous night. The crowd of twenty-five thousand men and women wrapped in heavy overcoats responded with a collective sign of the cross under the weak winter sun and a resounding "Amen."

The crowd lined both sides of the large avenue. Its members pushed and pulled to get a glimpse of the most outspoken, the most visible, the most traveled, and the most beloved pontiff in modern times. Some stood on the roofs of cars. Others hung from lamp posts.

The crowd-control police troops were enormously outnumbered. *Why didn't the Vatican warn us?* they wondered, confused at the unannounced mass. Despite the relative calm of the crowd as it strained to hear the pontiff's words, it was difficult to control with so few police officers. Outnumbered a thousand to one, they had not been given sufficient time to prepare and were pleased when five army trucks forced their way through the crowd.

The army trucks stopped in front of the six-story limestone Banco Napolitana Lucchese headquarters and backed up against its entrance. Forty green-garbed soldiers armed only with radios and safety batons exited the trucks. Five of them cordoned off the trucks. The remaining thirty-five placed themselves under the orders of a very relieved junior police lieutenant, who directed them to various strategic positions among the crowd.

The rooftop and helicopter television crews were too busy filming the scene below to notice two soldiers hop out of an army truck in the narrow alley behind the limestone building. The soldiers punched an access code into a door keypad and disappeared inside the building's maintenance room.

A dozing member of the Guarda di Finanza inside rose to his feet. His hand was halfway to his holstered Beretta when the invisible mist from a tube in the soldier's hand reached his lungs. He crumpled to the stone floor like a sack of potatoes, alive, but in a deep sleep. A quick glance around the room concluded that the guard was its only human inhabitant.

While one of the soldiers searched among a forest of heating and air-conditioning ducts, his colleague removed a small canister from his backpack and screwed on a short tube ending in a long needle. The first soldier pointed at a ventilation duct. His colleague inserted the needle into the duct's aluminum skin, opened a valve on the canister. Thirty seconds later, he removed the syringe, and both soldiers exited the limestone building by the same door they had entered, leaving only a small pinprick hole in the heating duct.

The crowd could not see the ten soldiers wearing gas masks who exited from one of the truck's rear doors and entered the glass double doors against which it was parked.

As soon as they entered the Banco Napolitana Lucchese's lobby, it was clear their two colleagues had accomplished their mission: a GDF guard lay asleep on the marble floor in a contorted pose. Though his chest rose and fell in regular breathing movements under the strap of his gun holster, the guard would not be awake for at least an hour. The GDF had sealed the bank a week before. There were no employees or clients inside, only GDF guards. Without a word, the ten soldiers split into two groups.

The first group located the stairwell and proceeded to the lower floor, careful not to trip over the bodies of sleeping guards. Once below, the group was confronted by row after row of small rooms, each numbered by a black and white sign and protected from entry by thick shiny metal bars. Beyond the bars were thick columns of armored vaults stacked from floor to ceiling.

The team leader walked to the room labeled "5" and pointed at a small electronic keypad between two of the bars. The soldier behind him punched in a numerical code. The codes were changed daily, but Forza's men had obtained the code earlier that morning. A series of bolts thumped open with heavy metallic thuds. The leader pushed the door open and waited patiently as his men removed two small keys from their pockets. One was supplied by a Forza operative in the bank's administration. The other was Father General Altiplano's key, provided by Benedetti.

The leader checked his watch. They had practiced hard during the past two days. Thirty-seven minutes to go.

His eyes darted around the small room, then into the hallway. Above a desk hung a video surveillance camera. He waved at it defiantly. Who would notice him? Everyone in the building was asleep. By the time the videotapes were analyzed, they would merely reveal the robbery by men wearing Italian Army fatigues, faces hidden by gas masks. He smiled and turned his attention back toward the small room.

On the fifth floor, GDF guard Danieli Romano watched the papal mass through his open window. Unlike most of those who thronged the avenue below to see and hear the Holy Father, Romano was an atheist. He had no particular love for the white-robed man to whom so many looked for moral guidance. Still, he found it entertaining to watch the mass and the crowd, like a theater piece. After watching for a while, the spectacle bored him. He crushed out his cigarette in a black plastic ashtray.

The GDF had a strict no-smoking policy while its guards were on duty, but in Italy, like in the rest of Europe, rules often were merely suggestions. The no-smoking rule was a suggestion Romano opted not to follow. He may not have feared divine retribution, but he still feared his boss. He left the window open, rubbed his hands to ward off the chill, and returned to his video console.

He stared at the images of the men in the vault in disbelief. *Qué?*

His fear subsided as soon as he noticed the men's Italian Army fatigues. Romano had been told the army and police and God only knew how many other government agencies would shuffle through the bank's files and vaults during the next few weeks. He exhaled in relief, only to be surprised a second time.

Why were they wearing gas masks?

The second team of soldiers was made up of only two men. They climbed to the fifth floor and cracked open the stairway door before entering the bank's computer room. Several GDF guards were sprawled on the floor, immobile. The two men proceeded to the main computer terminal, whose monitor displayed the large floating letters of the bank's screen-saver. While his colleague watched their flanks and rear, the other soldier removed a cellular telephone the size of a matchbook from his pocket, attached one end of a cord to its base, and searched for the correct port behind the large computer.

"You have heard the Church speak out against many evils." The supreme pontiff was too weak and physically devastated by Parkinson's disease to deliver his sermon, so it was read by a young monsignor whose voice echoed through the silent crowd outside. Three younger prelates had read the first, second, and gospel readings, all in Italian. Now was the time for the sermon, also delivered in Italian. The pope gazed at the crowd, leaning painfully against his brass staff.

"Against poverty. Against the culture of death. Against violence. Against racism. But there is another evil. An evil to which society has grown accustomed: the evil of materialism. Material goods in themselves are gifts from God. Food. Clothes. Shelter. These are good things. And we labor hard for them. And that labor is good if it is paid for fairly. But society has taken these gifts and transformed them into a struggle for wealth. Not only individuals, but entire organizations are motivated purely by material greed. Society has become accustomed to this. Society's obsession to gain material wealth for its own sake with disregard to people's needs has forced society to abandon its values and morals. It has alienated people from their families. From their neighbors. From their faith.

"That is why I have chosen this place today. Not a slum. Not a hospital. Not a church. But one of the world's financial centers. Our financial center. Banks, stock markets, corporations, and all businesses are made up of people. If these organizations are to change their ways, to move away from greed and blind materialism and environmental harm and unfairness to workers that threaten the spiritual fabric of society, it is the people who make up these organizations that must make that change.

"You must make that change.

"And so I stand here with you to pray for that change. So that you may have the strength to make that change. So that in doing your daily work, you become beacons of Christ's love for all of humanity. It is not enough to curse the darkness. To change the world, each one of us must light a candle. The Church is not just priests and nuns and bishops and popes. You are the Church. You must become the light of love and hope and life within every enterprise."

Baffled more by the gas masks over the soldiers' faces than the pope's statements against runaway capitalism, Romano switched his screen to another camera. His fear returned. This time it didn't go away. He switched to another camera. Then another. And another.

Santa Maria! All of his colleagues lay on the floors. *They look...they look dead.*

Terrified by his coworkers' fates, his heart pounded in his throat. He reached for the telephone.

He punched an automatic dial button.

"*Polizia*," a voice answered.

Down in the bank vault, the team leader looked at his watch. *Twenty minutes.*

The good news was that the little bags of diamonds were light. The bad news was that there were so many of them. Nine million carats, made up mostly of one- to two-carat diamonds. On the outside, the bags were identical to ordinary canvas mail bags. Inside were attached smaller bags, each lined with velvet pockets, each of which in turn contained small white envelopes filled with diamond roughs of the highest quality and color, VS1 F or better. Though well-informed and well-organized, the team leader had not anticipated so many bags. They would never have enough time, he thought. He backed away from his original plan and ordered his men to form a chain from the basement vault to the top of the stairs on the first floor. The bags could be moved more quickly that way. He gazed at his watch again. *Seventeen minutes.*

78 WITHDRAWAL

Banco Napolitana Lucchese Headquarters
Rome, Italy
9:51 A.M.

The impromptu papal mass made access to the bank difficult, but not impossible. Three police cars tore down the narrow alley behind the bank. Twelve police officers leaped from the cars before they had stopped rolling and lined up at the door. Romano had warned them. Each slipped on a gas mask before entering, following their captain's orders.

Fifteen minutes.

The team leader waited impatiently as his men removed the last canvas bags from the armored shelves. Finally, his second-in-command gave him a thumbs-up and began closing the doors. The team leader locked the dual locks while the rest of the men moved the bags from the vault floor up to the entrance lobby and into the truck.

"Hurry," the soldier whispered to his colleague who continued to kneel under the table, looking for the correct computer port.

"I'm still looking. I can't find the damn thing," he whispered back. He finally gave in and removed his flashlight and a telescopic metal rod fitted with an angled circular mirror, like a dentist's tool. He pushed aside the dusty wires behind the computer and was about to insert the metal rod in the opening when he suddenly sneezed.

His colleague slapped him on the head.

Romano couldn't contain his frustration. He was in agony. Armed and fully aware of the situation, he couldn't leave the room for fear that whatever gas had killed his comrades would kill him too.

He had to do something. He looked around the room another time to find some way to protect himself from the gas. Then he heard someone sneeze. He froze. It came from the room next door. He tiptoed to the door and peered through a small peephole placed at eye level. The lens distorted the adjoining room in a bizarre fish-eye view. He would have to open the door. What about the gas?

Then he realized that he had nothing to fear. Thanking his high school science teacher, he remembered that air travels from high to low pressure. The air outside was colder, higher in pressure than the warm air in the room. Clean, cold air would blow in from the outside, saving him from the gas.

Romano dried his sweaty palms on his shirt, removed the Beretta from his holster, cocked it. Slowly, careful not to make any sound, he slid back the door bolt and cracked open the door. As expected, he felt cold outside air breeze through the space in the doorway into the adjoining room. He peered into the next room.

Nothing.

He blinked away the sweat from his eyes and looked again. *There!* Two men wearing army fatigues and masks were crouched next to the main computer terminal. He held his breath and opened the door farther. He raised his Beretta, aimed it at one of the men.

A loud crash erupted behind him as a gust of cold air slammed the window shut. One of the men spun around, saw the Beretta just as Romano fired. The force of the bullet slammed into the soldier's bulletproof kevlar vest and punched him backward onto the computer worktable. The two ducked under the worktable, protected from Romano's fire by a row of low computer tape readers encased in glass.

Romano moved back behind the door, anticipating the soldiers' response. For several seconds he remained behind the safety of the door, panting. But there was no response from the soldiers. Not a bullet. Not a word. He waited for several minutes before opening the door again. Unable to contain his anger, he held his breath again and lunged into the room.

Romano fired repeatedly. The computer tape readers exploded into shards of glass. He moved forward, emptied his magazine, expelled it, then expertly slapped another into the

Beretta's butt. He was about to resume firing when he felt something touch his foot. He looked down. Green smoke billowed from a short metal cylinder on the floor. He kicked the tube away and held his breath, but his vision began to blur, then went black. By the time he crumpled to the floor, Romano was sound asleep.

One soldier kicked the Beretta from Romano's hand while his colleague who continued to search for the appropriate computer port lifted a lid behind the computer. "Got it." He plugged the wire into the port, turned on the cell phone, and hid the tiny device under the jumble of wires. He sneezed again, then motioned to the other guard. "Let's go."

79 CORRUPTION

Banco Napolitana Lucchese Headquarters
Rome, Italy
10:04 A.M.

"He's only asleep," noted police officer Sorrenti, feeling the pulse of the GDF guard in the rear maintenance room. He opened the door that led to the staircase. "Two on each floor. Ricci and I will take the main floor," he ordered in a whisper. "*Avanti!*" He motioned with his Beretta.

Sorrenti waited for the ten officers to climb the staircase, then walked up to the ground level a half-flight up from the maintenance room. He opened the door that led to the main hallway and peeked out. He immediately ducked his head back into the stairwell and cursed.

"What is it?" Ricci asked.

"Soldiers. Wearing gas masks. I count about…ten of them. Except—" He stuck his head out again, not believing what he thought he had seen.

"What?" Ricci pressed.

Sorrenti turned to his partner. "They're not armed."

The team leader watched as the remaining bags were placed in the rear of the truck. With a quick gesture, he ordered the men to get into the trucks, grabbed the last remaining bag, pointed to his mask, then to them.

The team leader waited for the last man to climb into the rear of the truck and was about to step up into it when he heard a noise in the hallway behind him. He turned, only to stare at the Beretta muzzle Sorrenti aimed at his head.

"*Alto! Polizia!* Don't move!"

"I'm unarmed," he responded calmly, silently cursing Forza for not allowing any of his team to carry weapons. He raised his arms, his right hand still clutching the canvas bag full of diamonds. He heard the trucks start their engines behind the entrance door. At least the diamonds and the files are safe, he thought happily, loyal to his don.

"There is nothing you can do, Lieutenant. Everything we came for is gone. If you kill me, I will be of no use to you."

"Shut up! Keep your hands up!" Sorrenti was far more nervous than Forza's seasoned mafia soldier. He had only recently been made a sergeant, and that was only because his cousin was a senator. The Eternal City had changed little over time. His hand trembled.

"If you arrest me, my boss will have me released within an hour," the soldier continued calmly.

His boss? What was he talking ab—? Then Sorrenti remembered why the Banco Napolitana was under surveillance. It was because of Arcangelo's files. *The man must be one of Arcangelo's soldiers,* he reasoned incorrectly, tightening his grip on the Beretta to prevent himself from shaking.

"You see. You can't win."

"In the air!" Sorrenti shouted, quickly losing his wits.

"If you let me go, you'd be doing yourselves a favor." He winked at Ricci who stood behind Sorrenti, pale as a ghost. "I can promise you'll be promoted. Both of you. Officers…" He read the names on their tags, "Sorrenti and Ricci. Good names for detectives, don't you think?" He was alone, but it didn't bother him. He was a professional. His don and the mission came first.

"Why don't you drop those guns? I am unarmed." He continued, his voice soft, gentle. "And take these instead." Without lowering his hands, he dropped the canvas bag and kicked it toward Sorrenti.

"Cover him!" Sorrenti ordered. He bent down, opened the bag. He removed one of the black velour bags, slid out one of the envelopes. The diamond roughs glowed under the bright lobby lights. Sorrenti looked up at Forza's soldier. "Are they real?" he asked, lamely.

"I think you should inspect them."

Sorrenti stared at him for several long seconds. "I think we need to inspect this evidence very carefully indeed." He lowered his weapon. Ricci did the same.

"Take your time." He winked back, dropped his arms, removed his mask, and walked out the door.

The pope and his entourage had returned to the Vatican. Maintenance crews wrapped things up in the large avenue. Police officers shepherded the strays clogging the avenue back to work, pleased no incidents had occurred during their impromptu call to crowd-control duty. The mafia soldier walked out of the bank's lobby past one of the police officers, who saluted with his baton. He walked several blocks, hailed a taxi to the Termini train station, boarded the direct train to Fiumicino airport, then a shuttle flight to Palermo.

Two hours later, the uncut diamonds from the Banco Napolitana Lucchese with a wholesale market value between $900 million and $3 billion and a retail value of over $9 billion were divided. Soon thereafter, fifty emissaries from the Vatican secretary of state's office arrived at Fiumicino airport, hand-picked by Monsignor Rancuzzi and the cardinal secretary of state himself. Each boarded a flight to one of fifty cities around the globe. Each carried an attaché case of little apparent value. As diplomatic couriers from the sovereign Vatican City State, each enjoyed full diplomatic immunity. That immunity extended to the attaché cases, each of which contained between $18 million and $60 million wholesale in uncut diamonds.

Within hours, the contents of those cases would be distributed to the world's poor through the Roman Church's legion charitable organizations. The impoverished recipients would then immediately sell the stones to myriad jewelers throughout the world. As more and more stones were sold, the prices paid would become increasingly low, causing a massive drop in the worldwide price of diamonds. And the number of jewelers who were purchasing diamonds from these impoverished recipients of unorthodox Church aid were so numerous and located in so many places around the globe that it was logistically impossible for Waterboer even to attempt a wholesale buyout of the stones from the jewelers.

Ordinarily, the blow to Waterboer would have been debilitating, but not fatal. But these were far from ordinary times for the monopoly, and the tidal wave of Vatican diamonds on the market did not occur in a vacuum. The civil war between the Afrikaaner Volksfront and the South African government was costing Waterboer a fortune in liquid capital. The enormous increase in prices paid by Waterboer for Russian diamonds under the recent renegotiated contract constituted an additional drain, particularly as it would not change now that Molotok and his nationalist Russkost had been eliminated. The other diamond-producing countries, like sharks, had smelled the blood and soon demanded similar increases in the price of their diamonds.

Waterboer was a company under siege. Alive, but now anemic and hemorrhaging badly. In Johannesburg, Piet Slythe called a special meeting of his top corporate officers to defend the sanctity of diamonds and protect Waterboer and the Slythe family, its keepers.

In the Vatican secretary of state's office, the secretary and Monsignor Rancuzzi each sipped a glass of champagne—smiling and slightly awed by their diplomatic and political skills. Not only had they and the Church turned a political scandal into a great victory by dealing a near fatal blow to a corrupt and evil corporation, they had effectively ended the influence of the Order, the Holy See's internal enemy of two hundred years. Once the banks learned of Altiplano's inability to repay the hundreds of millions of dollars he had borrowed on behalf of the Order, they would not be overwhelmed by charity.

The Church would bail out the Order. But in exchange for doing so, it would reorganize the Order to such an extent that it would not resemble a shadow of its recent self.

The unexpected papal mass had threatened to derail Cristina Petronelli's mission for Don Arcangelo. But she would let nothing stand between her and her 250,000 euros. She had already positioned the ten cubes Don Arcangelo's men had delivered in the alley and turned on their miniature timers when the popemobile arrived. She wasn't sure what happened inside the bank after that, but apparently the members of her shift had been gassed to sleep for some time. Strange, she thought. She hadn't noticed any gas. Perhaps it was because she hid in a bathroom stall and listened to the events outside through an open window. When she exited the bathroom, police officers were swarming inside the bank. Luckily, she had hidden the cubes well. She doubted that the police would find any of them. She took advantage of the confusion to go to the fifth floor, where she quickly installed Arcangelo's cellular telephone to the computer. She was surprised to find another cellular telephone attached to a nearby computer.

Tired after her stressful day, Petronelli signed the daily log and exited the headquarters building nearly three hours before her shift was scheduled to end. A few minutes later, the entire six-story building erupted in flames. She saw the blast before she felt it, but soon felt the waves of heat emanating from the fire. She knew the cubes had caused the inferno and for the first time became afraid. Not guilty or remorseful at having murdered several dozen people, but afraid for herself. People all around her were running and screaming, many shouting instructions. As soon as she saw fire engines, ambulances, and police cars rush to the scene, she started to run to her apartment as fast as her well-exercised legs would take her. It was too bad about the building and her coworkers caught inside, she thought. But the thought of the 250,000 euros soon made her forget their horrible deaths. As she ascended the staircase of her apartment building, she realized that despite having set the timers to go off after her shift ended, the blast had occurred far before her shift was scheduled to end. She stopped on the stairs one story below her floor. But by then it was too late. Enzo intercepted her. As her life ebbed away, she did not regret her acts, only that she had not been smart enough to realize the risk and ask to be paid in advance.

Alitalia Boeing 747SP
35,003 Feet
Atlantic Ocean
11:07 P.M.

Carlton reclined in the soft leather seat of the first-class cabin on the flight from Rome to Washington. Exhausted though he was, he couldn't sleep. Each time he closed his eyes, the events of the past month roiled in his mind.

He gazed about the plush first-class cabin. Except for the minders Forbes had sent to protect him, all the passengers slept soundly. He had no desire to watch a movie on his personal LCD television screen, even though the title of one James Bond selection from the '60s caused an ironic smile. He didn't have the patience for an airline novel. And cigar smoking hadn't been allowed on commercial airliners for years. He restlessly drummed his fingers on the handrest, then buzzed the attractive blond flight attendant to order another Bombay Sapphire and tonic with plenty of ice and lots of lime.

Slipping on the feather-light headset, he selected a Sinatra album named after a song about flying. It made him think of Erika. He had not seen Erika in over three weeks and he longed to be with her. He felt warm as he recalled their lovemaking. He casually leafed through the newspapers and magazines in the seatback compartment in front of him. His favorite headline was POPE OUTSHINES DIAMOND CARTEL. There was no mention of White House Chief of Staff Scott Fress. Forbes must be dealing with him quietly. He coughed up a mouthful of gin as soon as he opened one of the magazines. There on the very first page of the glossy American magazine was a diamond advertisement. Spread across the page was a vivid photograph of a woman's slender neck, circled by a shimmering river of brilliant diamonds. In small white letters were scrawled three words.

"Diamonds Are Beauty."

In tiny letters underneath were the words "Waterboer Mines Limited."

He stared at the ad, enraged and frustrated. The Russian diamonds. The Vatican diamonds. And Waterboer kept on going. How could Waterboer advertise in the American press when it wasn't allowed to do business in the U.S.? Waterboer employees couldn't step into the U.S. without being summarily arrested. He threw the magazine on the floor, gulped down his G&T, and stared out of the window at the starry sky and moonlit clouds. Frank was now singing about high hopes. Hope he had. A plan is what he needed. After another G&T, the gin finally started taking effect and his mind began the free association of ideas. An idea flashed in his mind, then disappeared. He picked up the magazine, found the Waterboer ad and stared at it hard. The thought returned. It was so obvious. He grinned, thinking of the lawsuit he would file.

You're mine now, Slythe.

81 OUTRAGE

Yale Safehouse
Blue Ridge Mountains, Virginia
6:21 A.M.

The navy blue Ford Crown Victoria sedan with tinted windows that collected Carlton at Dulles Airport pulled into the Yale Safehouse's long front drive under gray clouds. The gravel path, coated with a thin layer of snow, cracked under the tires. One of the resident agents walked out to greet the visitors.

Pat Carlton and Tom Pink emerged from the rear doors, protected from the chill wind by heavy overcoats. They were ushered into a large colonial foyer, complete with sweeping staircase and crystal chandelier. "Gentlemen, this is Agent Hargrave. He'll be conducting your debriefing."

Carlton grasped the agent's hand. "I hope this isn't going to take long."

"We've got bedrooms, showers, clothes, and lunch ready for you. Your debriefing shouldn't take more than forty-eight hours."

"Forty-eight hours? I'm thinking more like forty-eight minutes."

"You've got to give these things time, sir."

Something caught Carlton's eye above the staircase. He looked up. Erika bounded down the steps, locked him in her arms. They embraced, kissed, oblivious to the others.

"I missed you so much," she whispered, crying softly.

"Me, too, baby. Me, too." He turned to Pink. "Why didn't you tell me she was here?"

He smiled. "I figured after so many bad surprises, you needed a good one."

Carlton turned to Hargrave, pulling Erika tightly against him. "You know, maybe forty-eight hours isn't so bad after all."

Agent Hargrave was true to his word. Two days later, Carlton had been fully debriefed and was free to go. "I'll be back as soon as I can," he promised Erika.

"He hasn't been arrested?" Carlton bolted upright. "Why on earth not? After everything that scumbag has done? The man murdered Osage and Mazursky and Wenzel and God knows how many others! He took bribes from a foreign monopoly that financed a white supremacist civil war in South Africa and nearly started a civil war in Russia! Not to mention how many times he tried to kill Erika and Tom and me. I can't believe I'm hearing this! Pardon me, but are you out of your fucking mind? Sir?"

Unlike Pink, who cringed at Carlton's monumental disrespect for his boss, Carlton did not work for Forbes. He remained standing, glowering at the man who sat in his wheelchair, unruffled, sending peaceful cherry-scented smoke signals from his pipe.

Ordinarily, Forbes would not have tolerated such insolence, but he knew what Carlton had just accomplished, understood his frustration, and gave him wide latitude. Sensing Carlton had finished his outburst, he removed the pipe stem from his mouth. "I understand your anger, Lieutenant. But no. Fress has not been arrested."

"Why not? You have all the evidence you need! You've had it for a month. Why the hell—"

"I thought it would be eminently clear to you by now, Lieutenant. Think about it for a moment. Not as a Justice Department prosecutor, but as a foreign policy strategist. As you just suggested, there is a good possibility Fress knew about Molotok and Waterboer and their plans for the Russian stockpile. Fress may even have wanted Molotok to start a civil war in Russia so he could play cold warrior in Washington. If we apprehended Fress, it would have tipped off Molotok and Waterboer about the stockpile. We couldn't take that chance."

"I'm not suggesting the CIA should have arrested him. But at the very least you could have given Justice the—"

"Perhaps you should see this," Forbes' straight white teeth clamped down on his pipe. He rolled himself to the side of his desk, reached for a sheet of paper, and handed it to Carlton. "I took the liberty to expand on your initial investigation. Particularly with respect to Fress's cronies on the Waterboer payroll."

Carlton scanned the list. His head pounded and he started to sweat. "My God." He whispered, sitting quietly. "It goes that high at Justice too?"

"And to the bottom. I believe Harry Jarvik is your boss."

Carlton was mute. Stalin. *That pompous prick.*

"So you see, Lieutenant. Even if we had decided to take the risk, it's doubtful anyone at DOJ would have arrested Fress, much less prosecuted him. But they most definitely would have tipped him off."

"And all these people are still free," Carlton whispered.

"Free as the wind."

"This isn't happening," he muttered, running a hand through his hair. He sat silently for a moment, shook his head and stood. "I'm sorry, sir, but I can't let this happen."

"Admirable. What exactly do you propose?"

"It's clear, isn't it?" Carlton grinned without smiling. "I'm going to arrest the bastard."

"Arrest the White House chief of staff?" Forbes dismissed him with a wave of his pipe. "Don't be silly."

"Silly?" Carlton shouted back. "Do you think that—"

"Don't get me wrong, Lieutenant. You're one tough, resourceful, determined son of a bitch. And you've got my admiration. But think about it. What you propose won't fly."

"Why is that, exactly?"

"Politics, Lieutenant. Politics. You can't just arrest the chief of staff. The White House chief of staff. Who's going to give you an arrest warrant?"

"A federal judge."

"Just like that? A federal judge? Do you realize Fress personally handpicked most of the sitting federal judges for nomination by the president?"

"I'll find one appointed by a former administration. There's got to be a few who aren't indebted to Fress."

Forbes nodded. "This isn't a courtroom or a Navy sub. This is Washington. You can't just—"

"Enough! I don't recall you gave a damn about political impossibility when you sent Tom and I on our suicide mission to recover the Russian stockpile. You send us into hell to clean up your mess, and you've got the balls to tell me I can't do my own job as a prosecutor? You know, Tom here may be afraid of you, but I'm not. And with all due respect, sir, fuck you!"

"Revenge does not make for good strategy."

"Revenge?" Carlton stared back hard. "This isn't revenge. This is justice." He glanced at Pink before he turned and walked out of the office, slamming the door.

Pink stood, was about to follow Carlton when Forbes raised his pipe. "Let him go." He hit a speed dial button. "Dirk, get Lieutenant Carlton a car and tail him. Stay invisible, but make sure nothing happens to him. Otherwise let him be."

Pasadena, California
4:10 P.M.

The flight from Washington Dulles to Los Angeles International was long. Carlton's body craved sleep, begged him to check into the nearest airport hotel. He was still furious at Forbes for refusing to arrest Fress, but the anger didn't prevent his mind from being focused on his new objective. As the saying went, he could sleep when he was dead, which might happen sooner rather than later.

Carlton maneuvered the rented Chrysler LHS north on the 405 freeway, then east on the 134 toward Pasadena. He tried to stay awake by puffing on an Upmann 1844 Corona and listening to the news on the radio. More unrest in the Middle East as the Saudi people finally revolted against the corrupt royal family that had kept the wealth of their country from them for so long. More terrorist attacks in Israel. More violent crackdowns and executions of dissenters seeking basic freedoms in China. North Korea had fired another missile toward Japan. The white supremacist Afrikaaner Volksfront still held on tightly to the South African Orange Free State despite heavy fighting with the South African Security Forces and would agree to unbrokered peace negotiations only upon the condition that the Orange Free State remain under self-rule. Supreme Court Justice Daniels was retiring. More reactions to the Vatican's flooding of the diamond market.

The winter sun began its rapid descent below the horizon. Forty minutes after leaving the airport rental lot, he recognized the large 1880s edifice on the edge of Pasadena. First serving as a hotel, then as a psychiatric hospital after World War II, it now housed the Los Angeles branch of the United States Court of Appeals for the Ninth Federal Circuit.

He parked the car and walked to the entrance of the court building. An overweight guard shepherded him through the metal detector and asked for identification. In his exhausted state, he nearly produced his DOJ ID but caught himself in time. He went through the credit cards and other items Pink had temporarily given him upon his return from Rome, produced a driver's license. "Josh Tobias to see Justice Kemsfield."

"Down that hall and to the right."

"Thanks." Adrenaline pumped through his body as he proceeded down the hall and into the federal justice's anteroom. Alicia Kemsfield had been appointed by the previous president. She had little love for President Douglass and his administration. For that reason, Carlton considered her a perfect choice to issue the arrest warrant.

"Josh Tobias to see Justice Kemsfield," he repeated to the judge's assistant.

"I'll inform her you're here. Please have a seat."

Carlton did as he was told, watched the brightly colored fish that swam lazily in a hexagonal tropical aquarium. It reminded him of the palatial penthouse bathroom in Atlantic City. He let his mind drift back to the warm memory, smiled.

A striking woman of forty opened the door near the receptionist's desk. "Mr. Tobias?"

"Yes." Carlton stood.

"I'm Alicia Kemsfield. I hope you haven't been waiting too long."

"No, not at all, Your Honor. I was admiring your fish." He walked to her, shook her hand. She responded to his firm handshake in kind.

"Beautiful, aren't they? Please come this way. Would you like some coffee? You look tired."

"Yes, I would, and yes, I am, Your Honor. Thank you."

"Fred, could you get Mr. Tobias some coffee, please?"

Her assistant complied immediately. Carlton accepted a Ninth Circuit Court mug with a smile and sat opposite the justice's glass and chrome desk. Carlton had always encountered judges in carved oak and leather-lined offices. The stark modern style seemed odd for a federal justice. Justice Kemsfield shut the door and sat behind her desk.

"Out of all the names out there, 'Tobias' isn't the name I would have used," she stated flatly, brushing a strand of blond hair away from her pale blue eyes.

He stared at her in surprise. "I beg your pardon, Your Honor?"

"Save it, Mr. Carlton. I spoke with Randall Forbes this morning. That's how you were able to get an appointment on such short notice. He didn't reveal much. Perhaps you can start by telling me why you're here. I'm always happy to accommodate the good people at Justice, with or without artificial identities. Still, I'm rather busy. So let's make it brief, shall we?"

"Yes, Your Honor. Here is what I have." He pulled a manila folder from his attaché case, placed it on the desk facing her. "And this is what I respectfully request." He pulled a much thinner manila folder from the case, placed it next to the first.

He waited for what seemed like several minutes before Kemsfield looked up from the documents and stared at him with a puzzled expression. She brushed the same strand of hair from her eyes and closed both folders.

"Assuming this information is true, which I will assume for the moment—"

"It is true, Your Honor."

"There is simply no way I can give you what you want."

Carlton sat up in his chair and cocked his head. "Why not, Your Honor?"

"Washington is outside my jurisdiction. You know that. You should get one of my colleagues on the D.C. circuit to issue this."

"You are a federal justice, Your Honor. You have the authority to issue a federal arrest warrant for any jurisdiction in the United States. From Hawaii to Maine."

"Technically, yes. But politically, it would serve you best to speak with a D.C. circuit justice."

Politically? "Thank you for your concern, Your Honor, but I'm willing to take—"

"And that brings me to an even more important reason why I can't grant your request."

"Your Honor?"

"It would be a complete violation of procedure."

"I'm afraid I don't follow."

"Again you surprise me, Mr. Carlton. In a case of this magnitude, the request for an arrest warrant must be made by the attorney general of the United States. Or a United States Attorney at the very least. I can't sign an arrest warrant for a lower level attorney." She held up her hand. "I've pulled your record. I know you're quite the rising star. But that's of no moment here. I'm sorry, get the AG or a USA, otherwise, no warrant."

Carlton waited for her to finish, nodded. "I understand, Your Honor. But this will explain why that's not possible." He removed a third folder from his case and placed it on Kemsfield's desk. "It's classified, strictly need-to-know."

"I need to know." She scanned the documents, then looked back up at him. "This goes all the way to the top."

"It does. That's why I can't produce a request from the AG. Or the Assistant AGs. I don't even want to risk a USA."

"That's an even bigger problem."

"I beg you pardon, Your Honor?"

"The chief of staff alone, perhaps you could arrest with a warrant. But something this pervasive in the federal government can't possibly be handled by a simple arrest warrant."

"Your Honor?"

"This demands a special prosecutor."

"A special prosecutor has to be appointed by the attorney general, Your Honor. That's part of the problem."

"Or Congress."

"Congress?" He nearly laughed. "Your Honor, by the time Congress argues this, Fress will be in South Africa or Russia or God knows where. We can—"

"I'm not a fool. I understand your desire for quick action, and I respect the enormous risks you're willing to take. But for the reasons I stated, I cannot grant your request."

Carlton was about to push harder, but knew that it was no use. "I see." He stood, collected his manila folders. "Thank you for your time, Your Honor. I assume this will remain classified?"

"No one else needs to know. Of course."

By the time Carlton got to his rented car, it was dark. He should have been furious at Kemsfield, but he was too tired for that. Instead, he kicked himself for his political naïveté. Politics. It was always about politics. He hated politics. Why couldn't people just do what was right? Wouldn't that just be easier all around instead of feigning, lying, posturing, and fighting over the meaningless while leaving the meaningful untouched?

Exhausted, he drove the Chrysler carefully and a few minutes later pulled into the Doubletree Hotel. Ironically, it was where he had faced his first real legal battle many years ago: the grueling, three-day, eighteen-hour California bar examination. He continued his charade by checking into the hotel with his Josh Tobias driver's license and credit card, placed an early wake-up call with the operator, and went to sleep without bothering to remove his clothes or undoing the bed.

The following morning, refreshed by a long sleep, a shower, a shave, and a fresh suit of clothes, Carlton stared out of his seventh-floor window. It was one of those rare days, to paraphrase Larry Niven, when God rolls back the smog from Los Angeles to determine if the city is still there, then covers it back up a day later so He doesn't have to bear the sight of the city. Not a wisp of smog obstructed the view of the purple and green mountains to the north and the tight agglomeration of skyscrapers in downtown Los Angeles to the south.

He attacked his room-service breakfast of bacon and eggs, reading the front section of the *Los Angeles Times* between bites of food and sips of coffee. Southern Californian though he was, it seemed an eternity since he had moved away from the sun-drenched Left Coast. He shook his head at some of the headlines. He had forgotten how little the provincial city cared about the rest of the world, how much it obsessed about the inanity of Hollywood, the stars' half-baked political opinions, their forays into weird cults that exchanged money for continued success, their musical-chair divorces. Unless they were so important that even Hollywood would notice, most articles about the real world were mostly buried ten pages deep.

The one that commanded his attention was the article about Thomas Daniels, the retiring Supreme Court Justice. A leader of the civil rights legal reforms in the 1960s and the author of a host of landmark Supreme Court opinions on racial equality, environmental protection, and the safeguarding of the little person against the powerful giants of government and corporate business, Daniels was retiring, he said, while he was still young enough to enjoy life with his wife of fifty-five years. The article went on to describe some of the candidates reported to be on the president's list of replacements.

Alicia Kemsfield was on the list.

Bingo.

Kemsfield had not been appointed by President Douglass, and thus had not been selected by Scott Fress. But she was a moderate U.S. Court of Appeals justice, which meant that she had a chance of filling Daniels' vacant seat, albeit a small one, given her disagreement with the president on several issues. *Improper procedure my ass.*

If Kemsfield wouldn't sign the warrant, it was likely that no other federal judge who hoped to be on the Court would be willing to do so. The others wouldn't want to rock the boat and make waves in a sea that craved the calm of certainty. Oddly, it made Carlton happy. Instead of having to run down a dozen justices for an arrest warrant, his next step was clear. Draining the rest of his coffee, he dialed American Airlines, booked the next flight back to D.C., and left a message on Pink's voicemail.

83 JUSTICE

N Street
Georgetown, Washington, D.C.
3:27 P.M.

Carlton squeezed another rental car into a tiny space between a Cadillac and a 1960s VW bus covered with Grateful Dead, Greenpeace, and "No U.S. War in Afghanistan" stickers. Either would have one heck of a time getting out. Too bad. In D.C., parking was war. Looking at the Cadillac behind his rental car, he wondered what had happened to the Shark.

The Tobias alias appeared to be working. No assassins in his hotel rooms, no shootouts on the Beltway, no threatening letters. Carlton felt safer now, partly because of his cover identity, but mostly because he knew Forbes had assigned an agent to watch his back. He never identified the agent, but sensed he or she was there and allowed himself to relax a little.

The sun had pierced through the gloom of the Washington winter. Though it stopped short of warming the city, it had succeeded in melting what little snow remained along the streets. Its rays filtered through the naked branches of the elms and oaks that lined N Street, the pinnacle of Washington residential neighborhoods. He glanced at the address on a scrap of paper. One more block. Not wanting to be late for his appointment, he walked briskly, admiring the red and painted brick multimillion dollar colonial manors recessed from the avenue behind tall forged iron gates, holly bushes, and long paths.

The serenity stopped abruptly in front of the house bearing the address on Carlton's paper. The place was a zoo. News vans bristling with antennae and satellite feed dishes were jack-knifed in the middle of the street among a jumble of police cruisers. Reporters mobbed the front gate of the blue and white Cape Cod style house, lilliputian beside its behemoth brethren. Carlton fought past the feeding frenzy of reporters to a rotund police officer at the front door.

"Josh Tobias. I have an appointment," he shouted above the clamor of the reporters, some of whom asked if he was from the White House. The officer checked his roster, allowed him inside, and immediately shut the door behind him. Drawn curtains draped the small entryway in darkness. Carlton stood for a few moments, getting his bearings in the hazy darkness.

"Insane, aren't they? At least it's better than in the '60s. Back then it was the Klu Klux Klan," a man's voice said calmly. Carlton had not seen anyone in the entryway. He turned, saw the elderly man on the second step of a narrow staircase. Had Carlton not known the man's identity, he would have assumed that he was a retired physics professor about to invite him for milk and cookies. Dressed in a dark red cardigan and slightly rumpled khakis, the man was tall, slender, with a kind, wrinkled face crowned and a generous tangle of white hair. He leaned against the wooden stairway with a strong grip of his bony left hand. In the other, he held a long cigar, blue smoke curling upward in front of his face, giving the larger-than-life giant of jurisprudence an otherworldly air amid the small beams of light that shot through the drawn velvet drapes.

Carlton found himself speechless before the man. He had read his legal opinions during his constitutional law classes in law school. Some of them had brought him to tears.

His mouth dry, Carlton forced himself to say something. "Justice Daniels. Your...Your Honor. This is a great honor for me, sir. I read your opinions in law school. Your retirement is a great loss for the law." The words sounded so corny, but Carlton meant every one.

Daniels could sense his genuineness. "I appreciate that." He smiled disarmingly; the smile of a child, not of a fearsome judge. "But don't let's turn me into a law school statue before I'm dead, shall we, Mr....Tobias, isn't it?" He winked at the mention of the name, placed his hand to his ear, then motioned to the walls, indicating they had ears.

Forbes must have told him, too. Carlton stuck out his hand. "Yes, Your Honor."

Daniels placed the cigar in his mouth, squeezed Carlton's hand surprisingly tight. "Follow me."

He walked up the creaking stairs slowly, gripping the railing, and ushered Carlton into a study at the rear of the house. A gray Persian cat followed them.

"It's more quiet here. Please sit down. Care for a drink? I could use one myself. The fourth estate is driving me bats."

"I'd love one." For a moment, Carlton's mind placed the purpose of his visit on the fact he, Pat Carlton, was having a drink with Supreme Court Justice Thomas Daniels. In the man's personal study. He felt like a bright-eyed first year law student again and soaked in the surroundings.

A fire crackled in a miniature fireplace underneath an oil painting of Thomas Jefferson, darkened by time and the smoke of countless fires and cigars. Columns of books were stacked six feet high on the hardwood floor. Sheafs of paper were pressed into submission by a wood gavel on a large oak desk. It was exactly what a Supreme Court Justice's private study should look like, Carlton concluded.

Daniels poured two glasses of McCallan twelve-year-old single-malt scotch into cut crystal drams, handed one to Carlton. "I'm afraid scotch is all I have."

He seated himself carefully in a cracked leather button chair next to Carlton and winked. "It's the only thing our housekeeper doesn't drink." He smiled, lifted his glass. "Cheers."

"To your health, Your Honor," said Carlton, lifting his glass in return. The Persian jumped on Daniels' lap as he relit his cigar.

"May I, Your Honor?" Carlton asked politely, slipping an Upmann 1844 Robusto from his suit pocket.

"Ah, a fellow cigar smoker. Please, by all means." Daniels cradled the cat, who half-closed its eyes and purred with contentment.

"I see you received a call from the man in Virginia, Your Honor." Carlton excised the cap of his cigar with a guillotine cutter, lit it slowly with his DOJ Zippo to Daniels' amazement, who considered lighting a cigar with anything but a cedar match barbaric.

"Indeed I did. He didn't tell me exactly what it was about, but I gather it is both important and urgent."

"And politically difficult, Your Honor."

"How so?"

Carlton explained Kemsfield's refusal to sign the arrest warrant, handed him the manila folders with the evidence on Fress and the additional evidence Forbes had dug up on the other Justice Department officials on the Waterboer payroll. He knew he didn't need to insist on total confidentiality.

Daniels donned gold-rimmed spectacles and carefully read each page. When he finished, he closed the manila folders, removed his spectacles, and let them hang from his hand. "I understand Kemsfield's refusal," he stated flatly.

Carlton looked down at the fire. "Unfortunately, so do I, Your Honor. And I assume that the other federal judges would do the same."

"No. Many federal judges were neither appointed by this president nor believe for a second they would be in the running for my seat on the Court. But it would take far too much time for you to sift through individual appointments and the politics of federal judges' opinions vis-a-vis this administration. And the target of your warrant would soon learn of your quest."

"Then you agree with my request, Your Honor?"

"I didn't say that. The problem with the request isn't so much political, but procedural. The people involved in this," he placed his hand on the manila folders, "are too high up for a mere arrest warrant. The proper procedure is to obtain a Congressional special prosecutor."

Failure again washed over Carlton. "So you're not going to sign the warrant, Your Honor?"

"Do you know why I'm retiring from the Court?" Daniels asked, sidestepping the question.

"You want to spend more time with your wife, Your Honor."

"That's the answer I give reporters." He nodded solemnly. "The truth is that I became a lawyer, then a judge, then agreed to be a member of the Court because I wanted to change the status quo. When I grew up, the status quo was segregation and bigotry in a place where the individual had few rights against the giants of government and corporate monoliths. For me, that's not what America is about. Then or now."

"You changed a great many things, Your Honor."

"Yes, I did. And I'm proud of that. The problem is that today, the Court isn't faced with the same opportunities. There are perhaps as many issues as there were back when I started, although I doubt there's anything of the dimension of segregation, except perhaps abortion. The world is truly global now, but no matter how much we change things here, a tweak here, a tweak there, injustices still exist in the rest of the world. There is nothing that the Court can do about it. America is now a small place in a large world, even if it is the only superpower. The Court doesn't have the power to cure as it once did. The Court can only go so far. At some point, its rulings come into conflict with the global world of which America forms a part."

"But it can still set an example that the world can follow, Your Honor. The rule of law. You said it yourself."

Daniels smiled at Carlton for several seconds, then nodded, eyes closed. "Yes, I did. And yes, it can."

He replaced his spectacles, picked up an aged Parker Duofold fountain pen from the leather desktop, unscrewed it, and signed three copies of the arrest warrant with a flourish. He looked up at Carlton. "With cases like yours. As I said, the procedure is wrong. Technically. But then again, workers' strikes were once illegal, too. And what court is going to invalidate my arrest warrant?" He handed the manila folders to Carlton. "You done good, son. Good luck."

84 ARREST

The White House
9:17 A.M.

Carlton wore his Navy uniform. Technically, he was not authorized to wear a uniform except on naval duty, but the fine lines of Navy technicality had become blurred during the past month. On a day like today, every symbol of authority helped.

He pulled the navy blue Chevy Suburban 4x4 on loan from the Company motorpool to the North Gate of the White House and stopped at the pillbox. The entire White House perimeter and entrance gates had been fearsomely reinforced after 9-11.

Carlton was sweating unbearably. He had been to the White House only once, many years earlier, and that was on a tour, not in an official capacity. He wasn't doing this entirely alone. Now that he had secured an arrest warrant, Forbes was passively backing him, but remained in the background, invisible, and would deny involvement if Carlton's crusade turned sour, legally or otherwise. He had ordered Klaus von Engel, the Company man in the White House, to aid Carlton.

"Lieutenant Patrick Carlton, United States Navy Reserves. United States Department of Justice," he announced to the White House security guard, handing the man two pieces of identification. Luckily, von Engel had placed him on the White House roster of authorized entrants, absent which he may as well have attempted to cross the Atlantic in a rowboat.

The sergeant ducked inside the pillbox, consulted his morning list, and reappeared a minute later. "Okay, sir. It checks out. But Mr. von Engel will have to accompany you. And you can't park inside. Please step out of the vehicle. The guards will park it for you." Two guards walked up to the Suburban as Carlton stepped out slowly into the cold. They searched the vehicle and carefully examined its underside with canes that ended in mirrors before one of the guards got behind the wheel and drove the Suburban off-campus. The other guard frisked Carlton, waived an electronic wand over every square inch of his body, walked him through a metal detector, carefully verified both his fingerprints, and again scrutinized both of his pieces of identification. Satisfied that Carlton was fully unarmed, was who he said he was, and had a clean record, the guard gave him a temporary White House ID tag and led him up the driveway toward the stately white house that had originally been called the Executive Mansion. Klaus von Engel, an athletic man of fifty with close-cropped graying hair atop sharply defined features, met him outside the entrance. "Thank you. I'll take him from here." He turned to Carlton, flashed a tight smile, and extended his hand. "Von Engel."

"Carlton. Thanks for meeting me."

"Lucky Malcolm told me about your document or you would never have made it past the first guard." He paused. "You ready for this?"

"I've never been more ready in my life."

"Okay. I'll take you to him." He handed Carlton a pair of handcuffs. "Here. Take these."

They walked into the White House through a side entrance and walked silently through several deceptively plain, muted hallways before arriving at a white doorway blocked by an appointments secretary and her desk.

"Hi, Becky." Von Engel smiled. "We're here to see Scott."

The impeccably dressed brunette looked down at her boss's calendar and shook her head before looking back up at von Engel. "You don't seem to have an appointment, Klaus. I'm sorry, but the chief of staff is in a meeting."

"Please, Becky. Just buzz him. It'll only take a moment. It's urgent." Carlton had stayed behind von Engel and now approached the desk.

"You know how he hates being interrupted. I can't just—"

Carlton leaned over the desk, his blue eyes boring through the secretary. He spoke just above a whisper. "With all due respect, ma'am. I realize you're doing your job. And doing it well. But I don't care if the chief of staff is on the can. You will note the title and signature of Supreme Court Justice Thomas Daniels on this document." He produced an original signed copy of the arrest warrant and slid it toward the secretary. "It is not your job or your decision any longer, ma'am. You must comply with this order and let us inside immediately." He continued staring at her as she read the short document, then looked at von Engel.

He nodded. "It's legit, Becky. I confirmed it earlier. You really want to do as he says."

"Very well," she responded, shaking slightly. "This way, sir." She knocked on the door once, then opened it. Carlton saw Scott Fress seated behind his desk and shivered. *Son of a bitch. This is for real*.

"I'm sorry to interrupt, sir, but this man has an urgent—"

"Goddammit, Becky. I told you 'no one.' What part of that don't you understand?" He pointed to two men in ill-fitting suits seated in front of him. "These are extremely important gentlemen from the Chinese People's Liberation Army and Navy."

Carlton pushed past the secretary, walked into the office. "I'm afraid it can't wait, sir."

"Who the hell are you?" Fress obviously did not recognize him. *Could it be that Fress had never seen a photograph of the man he had tried so hard to eliminate?* Carlton wondered. "Get out of here before I call security."

"I'm afraid that would not do you any good, sir." Carlton's heart pumped madly, awash in adrenaline. "And in response to your legitimate question, my name is Lieutenant Patrick Carlton, United States Navy Reserves, United States Department of Justice." Fress's eyes grew wide, with surprise and anger rather than fear. "By order of U.S. Supreme Court Justice Thomas Daniels, Scott Fress, you are under arrest for treason to the United States of America."

Fress bolted out of his chair and gesticulated madly. "Under arrest?! Are you out of your fucking mind, Carlton? You little prick. Do you think I'm going to allow a little shit lawyer from Justice to arrest me?"

The two Chinese wisely beat a quick retreat from the office. They would have to purchase American military secrets from someone else. Von Engel entered the room and stood behind Carlton.

"Sir, you are under arrest." Carlton stepped up to Fress's desk, placed the warrant in front of him.

"I'm not going anywhere. But you," he leaned forward and wagged a finger at Carlton threateningly, "you are definitely going places, my friend."

Carlton removed the handcuffs from under his uniform jacket and stepped forward.

"You touch me and you're a dead man." Fress stepped back.

"I'm afraid I have no—"

The gun went off without Carlton even seeing it. The bullet grazed his arm and hit von Engel in the chest. As Carlton dropped to the ground for cover, Fress ran through a back door. Carlton kneeled over von Engel. The man lay on his back, his breathing erratic, his shirt stained with blood. He tried to move his head but couldn't. Efficient to a fault, Becky alerted the Secret Service, explained the arrest warrant and events, and summoned the White House EMT unit.

"You'll be okay, Klaus. Just relax. The medics'll be here in a sec." She placed her hand on his forehead.

Von Engel looked at Carlton. "I'll be fine. Take my gun. In my shoulder holster. Take it and go. Get the bastard."

Carlton squeezed the man's hand hard, then removed his Colt Government handgun from its holster. "See you soon." Carlton ran to the rear door. Wherever Fress had gone, he had a two-minute head start. The closest thing to the rear exit was an elevator and a staircase. As good a place to start as any. He hurried down the stairs, which led to a tunnel. He stopped, listened for sounds, heard nothing. He ran down the tunnel. At the end was a guard at a desk in front of a metal door. The guard had been shot at point blank range. Carlton grabbed his radio. A set of keys hung from the door lock. Carlton drew back the Colt with both hands, slammed the door open with his foot. He was surprised to see that it was an entrance to the Old Executive Building parking lot. He pressed down on the radio's "talk" button. "This is Pat Carlton, Department of Justice. I served the arrest warrant on the chief of staff." He stated, in case Becky hadn't made the point clear. "Officer down at the parking entrance from the White House tunnel. Scott Fress has escaped to the OEOB parking lot. Whoever is listening to this, cover the OEOB parking exits. Don't let anyone out." *I can't believe I'm doing this.*

Carlton held close to the wall, then ducked behind the row of parked cars. He looked left and right, inspecting each car as a possible target.

Everyone has their vanity. For Fress, it was cars. Despite the Secret Service–chauffeured car at his disposal twenty-four hours a day, seven days a week, Fress vainly preferred to drive his ostentatious navy blue Rolls-Royce Silver Spur to and from work. It shot out from one of the parking spaces near Carlton and launched toward him. Carlton jumped atop the hood of a black Lincoln an instant before the Rolls crashed into the car's rear bumper. He fell and slammed his knee on the hard cement floor. It hurt like hell. He stood, then ducked instinctively as Fress raised his arm toward him, gun in hand. The shots barely missed Carlton, instead exploded the Lincoln's windshield. Glass rained down on him. A wave of pain traveled through him as he fought to regain a level stance, then fired the Colt at Fress as the Rolls-Royce's tires screamed backward on the smooth concrete amid puffs of burned rubber. It backed up, then shot forward. The first shots pierced the car's trunk. The second round of shots missed the large car as it flew up the parking ramp. It was almost at the top when the barricade system was activated. In an instant, an iron-reinforced concrete cylinder three feet thick rotated up from the driveway. Though solid, the Rolls-Royce was no match for the three-ton barricade. The sedan smashed into it at over thirty miles per hour and came to an immediate halt accompanied by the sound of crushing metal. Two Marine MPs arrived at the scene, each pointing their M-16 semiautomatics at the driver. Apparently unharmed, Fress maniacally tried to restart the engine from behind his airbag. It turned over several times, then died with a whimper.

Carlton limped up the garage ramp, wincing from the pain in his knee. He tried to open the driver side door, but it was locked. He turned to one the Marines. "Open the door, private."

"Yes, sir!" The Marine obeyed the order of the superior officer by flipping over his weapon and ramming its butt hard into the driver's window three times before it cracked into a spider-web of broken safety glass. He turned the weapon back to its normal position and used its steel muzzle to make an opening in the glass, reached inside, opened the door from the inside, then stepped back, ramrod straight at attention. "Sir!"

The airbag deflated while Fress madly groped for his hand-gun on the plush floor carpet. He stopped moving as soon as Carlton shoved the Colt's barrel against his temple. It pressed against him so hard that it tore Fress's skin. Carlton cocked the weapon as a ring of blood appeared around the end of the steel muzzle.

"All right, you son of a bitch. Since you didn't hear me the first time, I'll say it again. You're under arrest, you traitor fuck. You have the right to remain dead silent..."

In strict adherence with his constitutionally mandated rights of due process, Scott Fress, the defeated White House chief of staff, would be given a full jury trial, representation from competent counsel, extensive time to prepare for trial, the opportunity to discover all of the evidence against him in the government's possession, and the right to assert all applicable privileges and defenses. However, it wasn't difficult for Waterboer to locate him as he awaited trial in a federal prison. He did not remain alive long enough for trial.

85 EVIDENCE

Mayor's Residence
Palermo, Sicily
2:02 A.M.

Orlando Leonida still couldn't accept his defeat. He continued to replay the events in his mind's eye. How could he have let it happen? The bank was sealed. Guarded inside and out by twenty GDF troops armed with guns and close-circuit cameras. About to obtain evidence that would put one of most violent mafia dons and his henchmen in cages for the rest of their lives. Avenge the thousands of Italian and other European men, women, and children who had suffered and died through his assassinations, his robberies, his drugs, his prostitution rings. All the critical evidence had disappeared. Strangely, the GDF cyber-forensics team informed Leonida that the evidence had not been destroyed in the fire, but had been sucked out of the bank's mainframe computer database with nothing left but clean, clear disks and tapes which had later burned. How?

He got up from his living room sofa—he did not want to bother his wife while he suffered his bouts of insomnia—and poured himself another whiskey soda. It wasn't personal embarrassment that bothered him. He did all he could and both the media and his voters knew it well. What tortured him were the four years he had invested in the case against Arcangelo at the expense of other cases, other mafia families, now all wasted. He muttered a curse and gulped his fourth drink when he heard a knock at his door. "*Avanti, avanti.*"

His bodyguard opened the door and popped his head in the living room. "Telephone call, sir."

Leonida instinctively looked at his watch. "At two in the morning?" He sighed. "Who the hell is calling at this hour?"

"He says his name is Patrick Carlton. From the American Justice Department in Washington." It was not unusual for him to speak with the U.S. Justice Department, but why would they be calling him at this hour and at home?

Leonida had no desire to speak to anyone, but welcomed the distraction from his frustration and sadness. He picked up the telephone. "This is Leonida. Do you realize what time it is here? What do you want?" he demanded. His accent was heavy, his English quite good.

"Please forgive me for bothering you at this hour, Your Honor. I have wanted to give you certain information for several days, but I haven't been able to."

"What information?"

"The Banco Napolitana's computer information. About Don Arcangelo."

Adrenaline jolted Leonida's body. He put down his glass. "You realize, of course, that the bank exploded in flames and that all the computer evidence we had on Arcangelo was lost."

"That is exactly why I am calling."

"What information exactly do you have?"

"All of it."

The statement made Leonida sit. "All of it? Is this a joke? Because I assure you—"

"I don't have time for jokes, Your Honor."

"Then you will tell me how you obtained the information."

"I'm not at liberty to discuss that, Your Honor. But let's just say that the information was called in. I have to assume that all of your telephone lines are tapped. So a fax and the Internet are out of the question, particularly given the lengths the perpetrators went to destroy the evidence. And I cannot assume that the evidence will be safe with anyone but you. So I will ask you please to go in person to the U.S. embassy to the Vatican in Rome. Ask for special intelligence attaché Tom Pink. He will give you the information you need. He will not give the information to anyone but you."

"Special intelligence attaché? You mean CIA?"

"I have a great deal of respect for you, Your Honor. As a prosecutor, I know you will find the information invaluable. I apologize again for having bothered you at this hour. Good night, sir."

Later that morning, having barely slept through nightmares of American mafia dons in Washington, Leonida sat down with his young wife and two children for breakfast. Bleary-eyed, he sipped his second double espresso as an antidote to the night's four whiskeys and lack of sleep. The bodyguard brought in the morning edition of the *Corriere Della Sera*. The large headline read: WHITE HOUSE CHIEF OF STAFF ARRESTED FOR BRIBERY. Leonida had barely finished the second sentence when he let his coffee cup fall on its saucer. "*Santa Lucia*. It's for real."

"What is it, *amore*?" his young wife inquired.

Leonida continued to read the paper, now out loud. "United States Justice Department antitrust lawyer and Navy Reserves Lieutenant Patrick Carlton made the arrest in Scott Fress's White House office." He looked at the bodyguard. "We need to get to Rome immediately. Make the arrangements." He turned back to his wife and kissed her hard on the lips, then looked up.

Grazie Signore.

United States District Court
District of Columbia
9:14 A.M.

The grand jury was quick to hand down the indictments. The government prosecution against the surviving defendants in the "Diamondgate" scandal progressed with all deliberate speed, first through Congressional indictments, then through federal criminal trials mainly on the charges of treason against the United States of America by accepting bribes from foreign agents and conspiracy with foreign agents to further the Waterboer monopoly of the international diamond market. Carlton and Erika did not participate, except that Carlton served as a witness against Harry Jarvik, a job he thought he would relish but in fact found pathetic and depressing. Never again would "Stalin" terrorize the DOJ antitrust litigators. For them was reserved the most important case of all: the prosecution of Waterboer Mines Limited. The United States could not bring Waterboer to justice directly, for want of jurisdiction against the South African monopoly. But the team would use Carlton's simple legal theory to mete out punishment against Waterboer by prosecuting the companies and other groups in the U.S. who knowingly and intentionally furthered Waterboer's monopoly of diamond supply and demand in the United States: diamond seller associations and the media, which published ads for diamonds under the Waterboer name in print, radio, and television.

During the next three months, Carlton, Erika, and Monet forgot sleep and meals, family and friends. Even before Carlton fully recovered from his injured knee, from dawn to dusk he and Erika researched every applicable federal antitrust case in the books, crafted legal arguments, drafted pleadings and interrogatories, and interviewed and deposed expert witnesses. The chain-smoking Monet relentlessly tracked down a century of advertisements and journalistic corporate ownership chains.

President Douglass had guts. The African-American's famous honesty also made the former general and preacher a class act. The man was personally innocent of any wrongdoing in the Diamondgate scandal, except for his extensive trust and reliance on his chief of staff. But instead of cravenly hiding behind the culprits he had appointed, he took the public blame and confessed his sins to the American people, a people who forgave mistakes but did not tolerate lies. Within days, President Douglass announced a new Executive Order that placed each appointed federal official above a certain rank under financial and personal supervision not just at the time of appointment and Senate confirmation, but randomly throughout their period of appointment. The mandate would be exercised by a special team from the Department of Homeland Defense. It would add to the federal budget, but in light of Diamondgate and 9-11, would likely save billions over the next several administrations. To distance himself from the traitors themselves, Douglass vociferously denounced Waterboer, praised the Church's recent flooding of the international diamond market, and backed his DOJ team in its case against Waterboer's American conspirators, most notably during a speech in the White House Rose Garden at the lawsuit's inception, at which he praised Carlton's and Erika's exposure of the Diamondgate scandal. Under the glare of reporters' cameras, the president bestowed on Carlton the Navy Cross, elevated him to the rank of lieutenant commander, and promoted him to chief of the Department of Justice's Antitrust Litigation Section, directly below Deputy Assistant Attorney General Gail Rothenberg. On Erika he bestowed the DOJ medal of service. Outside the public eye, through Randall Forbes, he bestowed the CIA medal on Pink.

The wily American media knew when it had a story. Soon the press clamored for interviews with Carlton, and to a lesser extent, with Erika. Unable to discuss the case due to the rules of confidentiality, they discussed everything else about the group's ordeals with Scott Fress and his thugs—carefully excising any mention of their role in the Russian and Vatican diamond affairs. On all of the popular news and interview shows. On *Larry King Live*. On *Nightline*. On Charlie Rose.

On Oprah. The press ate it up. So did the American people, who couldn't get enough of the young Justice Department lawyer and Naval Reserve officer. Carlton had become a star.

The federal courthouse was packed with television crews and journalists from nearly every news service, domestic and foreign. Brought by the Department of Justice on behalf of the United States of America, the case named as defendants every newspaper, magazine, radio station, and television station that had ever published an ad on behalf of Waterboer Mines Limited and every company and trade association that had contracted for the ads to be published under license from Waterboer. In fact, so many defendants were named in the lawsuit that their lawyers took up nearly every seat generally reserved for the public. Doggedly, rabidly, the defendants made motion after motion to get the case thrown out. Each was denied. Jury selection was particularly rancorous, the defense wanting to reject any juror who had ever purchased or attempted to purchase a diamond ring to be excluded for cause. Unfortunately for them, Waterboer's hundred-year diamond marketing campaign made it impossible to grant such a request. Defense counsel asked that the media be banned from the courtroom, even though most of the defendants were members of the media. The judge was not about to make the error of barring the media from one of the most explosive cases of the decade.

"All stand!" the large bailiff announced. "The United States District Court for the District of Columbia is now in session. The Honorable Nancy Taggart presiding."

A tall African-American woman of fifty, with graying hair and dressed in a somber black judicial robe appeared behind the bench and sat in the high-backed leather chair. She nodded to the lead attorneys on both sides, smiled at the jury, then leaned forward. "Good morning, counsel. State your names for the record, please."

"Good morning, Your Honor. Patrick Carlton, United States Department of Justice. For the United States," Carlton announced through his microphone, a lump in his throat. For the United States. *God help me.*

"Lester Churchman. Fox, Carlyle, Ashton, Chase, Whitfield & Whyte. Lead counsel for the defense, Your Honor. Good morning."

"The case is docket number 140-1022786," Judge Taggart announced gravely. "United States of America versus Diamond Sellers League, et al. The prosecution may proceed with its opening argument."

Carlton approached the jury. The sound of his cowboy boots on the hardwood floor echoed through the silent chamber. He stopped and looked directly at each juror. *Pay attention, people. This is the real deal. Good versus evil.*

"Ladies and gentlemen, this case is about monopoly," he stated flatly, standing erect. "Not the board game we all played as little kids, but real, live monopoly. The monopoly of the diamond market." *They're as nervous as you are, Carlton.* He relaxed his posture, smiled. "Monopoly. Antitrust law. Conspiracy. Market shares. Sounds complicated, doesn't it? It isn't. It's just about monopoly, pure and simple."

He pulled a small object from his pocket and held it up. "You see this? This is my fiancée's engagement-ring diamond. Actually, I haven't asked her yet, so don't tell her." The jurors laughed and relaxed, now at ease with the Justice Department lawyer. "It's a one-carat diamond. It's real. I checked. I paid $7,000 for it. On my Visa, of course," he added.

"That's pretty much what all the jewelry stores charge for it. Seven thousand dollars. But you know how much this stone is really worth?" He paused, let the diamond fall to the ground, stomped on it with the heel of his cowboy boot. The jury gasped.

"Why are you shocked? Because you think this diamond," he pointed to the floor, "is worth $7,000. Right? Well you're wrong. That diamond," he pointed to the intact stone on the floor, "if prices were not controlled by Waterboer Mines Limited through the willing, knowing, aiding and abetting of the defendants, should sell for about fifty bucks."

He paused as the jurors let out a collective gasp. "That's right, folks. You heard me. Fifty dollars. Five-zero. Now how can that be, you ask? The answer is simple." He leaned toward them, lowered his voice to a whisper. Each member of the jury craned its neck to hear him. "Diamonds aren't rare."

He straightened. "That's right. Diamonds aren't rare. In fact, diamonds are one of the most common gemstones on Earth. Pure carbon." He saw the expression of disbelief in their faces. "You didn't know that either, did you? If you did, you wouldn't have willingly paid such crazy prices for your own engagement rings."

The married or engaged female jurors looked down at their near-worthless diamonds. The male jurors frowned silently.

"Yes. So many people have been ripped off. And that's exactly why monopolies are illegal in the United States. A monopoly controls production, sales, and prices. Waterboer controls diamond production and supply all over the world. By doing that, Waterboer controls the price of diamonds. I'll give you an analogy. If there were only one telephone company in the United States, it could charge you $1,000 a minute per call. Think that's too much?" He grinned.

Perspiring heavily, Lester Churchman finally heaved himself out of his chair. "Objection, Your Honor! The telephone company is not on trial here. Where is counsel going with this?" It was an idiotic objection, but he couldn't let Carlton continue to mesmerize the jury. "I move to strike it from—"

"Sustained." Judge Taggart ruled, then turned to the jury. "The jury will disregard the prosecution's last remark, and it will be stricken from the record." She turned back toward Carlton. "Come to the point or your opening is over, counsel," she snapped.

"Yes, Your Honor." He squinted at the jury. The objection had worked perfectly. "Judge Taggart is right, ladies and gentlemen. I will come to the point. The point is simply this," he said softly. "Waterboer is a monopoly. That's undisputed here. For over a hundred years, Waterboer has used every means at its disposal to control diamond production and diamond prices, including assassination, bribery, torture, and child labor. It supported the Nazis during World War II, communism in the Soviet Union during the cold war, white supremacists, the Russian mafia and Russian nationalists. All to control diamond prices. You don't have to take my word for it. It's a fact, all documented by these unclassified CIA and FBI reports right here." He placed his hands on two stacks of velobound documents so high they hid Erika from the jury, as intended.

"American law—our law—is fair and just. It has prohibited monopolies ever since 1890. I'll read you that law. You don't have to be a lawyer to understand it. It's very simple, very clear." Carlton picked up a book that Donna the DOJ librarian had found, dating back to 1890. He opened it, blew dust off the pages to show how old the law really was and read:

Every contract, combination in the form of trust or otherwise, or conspiracy, in restraint of trade or commerce among the several States, or with foreign nations, is declared to be illegal....Every person who shall monopolize, or attempt to monopolize, or combine or conspire with any other person or persons, to monopolize any part of the trade or commerce among the several States, or with foreign nations, shall be deemed guilty of a felony, and, on conviction thereof, shall be punished.

"You see, the law is simple. Monopolies are illegal. And under the law, anyone who knowingly and willfully aids and abets a monopoly is guilty of the exact same crime. Which comes to the entire reason for this lawsuit: How does Waterboer do it? How does Waterboer keep its monopoly on the $28 billion yearly U.S. market for diamonds? Pretty tough thing to accomplish, don't you think? But Waterboer is tricky, see. They're a South African company. So they're outside the U.S. government's jurisdiction. But the United States is the largest market for diamonds in the world. Waterboer can't ignore it. Waterboer has to sell in the U.S. And to sell in the U.S., Waterboer has to advertise in the U.S. And it has been advertising. For over a hundred years. You've seen the ads. You've heard the ads. 'Diamonds are Beauty.' All of us have seen and heard those words. That's a Waterboer ad. They're all over the place, these ads. Of course, Waterboer itself can't publish these ads because they can't operate in the U.S. So they licensed the Waterboer name to the Diamond Sellers League to run them instead. And those ads are then published by the other defendants. The defendants' newspapers run them. The defendants' magazines run them. The defendants' radio stations play them on the air. The defendants' television stations show them on TV. The defendants are the ones who enable Waterboer to sell their diamonds in the United States and keep their lock on the U.S. diamond market. And that's why you pay $7,000 for this crummy diamond," he pointed to the diamond on the floor, "instead of $50. And remember, under the law, anyone who knowingly and willfully aids and abets a monopoly is guilty of the exact same crime.

"The defendants," he pointed to them, "are conspirators with Waterboer to further an illegal monopoly. If they are conspirators with Waterboer, they should be held accountable for the same crimes as Waterboer."

Carlton paused for what seemed like minutes. The jurors had just become used to the silence when he rushed to the defense counsel's table, pointed at the defendants, and shouted with a conviction he hadn't thought possible.

"The United States of America *accuses* the defendants of actively participating in an international conspiracy to monopolize the United States diamond market!

"The United States of America *accuses* the defendants of being willing, active, and paid participants in an ongoing monopoly of the United States diamond market!

"The United States of America *accuses* the defendants of artificially inflating diamond prices on behalf of Waterboer!

"The United States of America *accuses*…"

The list was long.

87 VERDICT

The trial lasted over a month. Flooded with information about Waterboer through interminable media coverage, the American people, already incensed by Waterboer's corruption of the highest levels of their government in Diamondgate, were outraged. Outraged by Waterboer's support of Russian nationalists, the Russian mafia, and the slimly averted new cold war. Disgusted by Waterboer's financing of the white supremacist Afrikaaner Volksfront in South Africa. Repulsed by Waterboer's historical support of apartheid, Nazism, communism, and child labor. Shocked by the way they had been manipulated like sheep by Waterboer and its media conspirators into willingly forking over thousands of dollars for stones with little inherent value.

And though the American people held sacred their constitutional right to free speech, they disliked the media itself, which they considered biased, elitist, and condescending, just like Waterboer. Particularly when the two had profited for over a century on the backs of hard-working Americans. Combined with Waterboer's misdeeds, to the American people, this was not a mere crime. This was treason against the United States of America.

The feeling was unanimous.

More than in any criminal trial in recent memory, in every state of the Union, in every town and city across the nation, the American people wanted blood.

Would the jury feel the same?

Deliberations lasted an hour. Legal commentators from coast to coast attempted to explain the short length of time.

They must be guilty.
They must be innocent.

Could go either way.

The commentators' babble died down as soon as the television screens showed the jurors exit the deliberation room and take their seats in the carved wood jury box.

"Mr. Foreman. Has the jury reached its verdict?" Judge Taggart inquired. She too had become the darling of the press.

An elderly Korean American man rose solemnly from his position at the end of the jury box. "It has, Your Honor."

"What find you?"

Slightly trembling with nervousness, the man unfolded a piece of paper and adjusted his round, gold-rimmed spectacles. "In the matter of The United States of America versus Diamond Sellers League, et al, we, the jury, find the defendants guilty on all counts criminal and civil. We hereby—"

The shouts of vindication that streamed in through the windows drowned out the moans and gasps of the defendants in the courtroom.

Carlton raised his eyes upward and clasped his hands. *Thank you, God. Thank you.*

Judge Taggart's gavel repeatedly slammed against its mahogany coaster. "Order! Order! Order!"

The room fell silent.

"Thank you, Mr. Foreman. The Court thanks all of the jurors for their patience, dedication, and hard work. Please remain in the jury box until after sentencing and the award of damages."

Carlton looked over to the defeated Churchman, who shared his shock at the judge's statement. *Sentencing? An award? Already?*

It made sense. Sentencing and the determination of a monetary award would normally have come later. But Judge Taggart was no media fool. If she didn't pronounce sentences and announce the award of damages immediately, it would get lost in the press. She too wanted her moment of glory.

"As the prosecution mentioned, the Sherman Antitrust Act provides for a maximum penalty of $10 million dollars for corporations. In this suit, it was alleged that each published advertisement constituted a separate violation of the Act. The statute of limitations under the Act is three years. Therefore, the penalties can be assessed only for advertisements published during the three years prior to the date of the filing of this case. Based on the jury's verdict of guilty on all counts, this court hereby sentences the defendant Diamond Sellers League Inc. to pay the fine of $523 million. This court orders defendant American Publications Inc. to pay the fine of $1.327 billion. This court orders defendant…"

Judge Taggart continued to read the staggering sums one by one in a sanitized monotone.

The bankruptcy lawyers had prepared the defendants' bankruptcy filings long before verdict and sentencing were announced. Each was filed within an hour of the sentence. Each defendant would seek reorganization under Chapter 11 of 10 U.S.C., the federal bankruptcy code. The Justice Department's objective was fulfilled. Never again would any member of the American media agree to run a Waterboer diamond advertisement.

Not in print.

Not on the radio.

Not on television.

Not ever again.

Without advertisements to create and bolster the appeal and value of diamonds, Waterboer could not maintain its high level of sales in the U.S. and thus would never regain control of the international diamond market.

CNN carried the judgment live and beamed it around the world, including South Africa. Nine thousand miles east of the courtroom, a shot reverberated through the financial district of Johannesburg.

Slythe's head fell against his otherwise immaculate desk next to a small mound of cocaine. The desktop was soon also covered with a pool of blood.

The Waterboer monopoly was dead.

EPILOGUE

Macon Grove, Arkansas
11:34 A.M.

Neither Carlton nor Erika had ever been to Arkansas, the original loose end that had unraveled the Waterboer monopoly. They admired the bright green landscape in silence as they drove on the rural road. Spring had arrived to the Arkansas countryside. Flora and fauna had awakened from their winter slumber and now reveled in the rebirth of spring.

Two hours after leaving Little Rock, they arrived to the town of Macon Grove, as small as it was quaint. Despite its size and location in the remote countryside, the town buzzed with an activity generally seen only in the big city. Construction crews were busy extending Main Street and constructing a series of one-story buildings. A large sign proudly proclaimed that an office center and retail stores were coming soon. Men and women walked through the two-block center of town with a tangible sense of purpose. Mostly new pickup trucks and SUVs drove along the town's few but newly paved streets. Storefronts were bright with fresh coats of paint. Sidewalks were clean and newly landscaped with trees.

Carlton and Erika continued on the rural road, which workers were expanding from two to four lanes. They understood why when traffic slowed to a halt behind a slow line of cargo trucks carrying everything from crates and oil drums to pipe and tractors. A half hour later, they turned right under a white entry gate that proclaimed: "Osage-Wenzel Mine." In small letters below was written "Operated by MacLean Arkansas, LLC." A guard stopped them, politely asked their names, identification, and nature of their visit, gave them passes, and directed them to a low, white building. They parked next to a mud-splattered, black four-door Hummer with fat tires and stretched in the bright sun. The compound was composed of a large circular courtyard, in the center of which three tall flagpoles proudly flew the flags of the United States, Arkansas, and the Osage-Wenzel Mine. Mining equipment, offices, and warehouses surrounded the courtyard, where men and women, dressed in hardhats, overalls, heavy jackets, and gloves, walked to and from their duties amid loud mechanical noises and the thumping rotors of a departing helicopter.

A loud voice boomed from behind Carlton and Erika. "Mr. Carlton and Ms. Wassenaar. I thought you'd never make it!"

They both turned as the large helicopter took off and flew away. A man of forty with a tan face stood in front of the little office, dressed in a navy blue blazer with a pale yellow silk pocket square, a pale blue shirt of Sea Island cotton fastened with bright yellow diamond cufflinks, pleated khaki trousers, and black leather moccasins, all by Ralph Lauren. With his brown hair slicked back, slightly tanned face, and bright white smile, the man looked more like a movie star from the 1930s than the owner of a mining concern. He walked up to them.

"I can't tell you how happy I am finally to meet you. I'm Max MacLean." He extended his hand in a warm greeting to both.

"It's an honor, Mr. MacLean. Thank you for everything you did for us," responded Carlton, appreciating the strong handshake.

"And thank you so much for inviting us," announced Erika, who blushed slightly as MacLean kissed her hand.

"Please call me Max and come in out of the sun. I hope you haven't already had lunch. Follow me." MacLean ushered them through the doorway. The air inside was pleasantly cooler and less humid than outside. The squat building was larger than Carlton had expected. The front office gave way to a hallway with administrative offices and restrooms, and led to a spacious office. It was brightly illuminated from skylights and furnished mostly with Le Corbusier black leather, glass, and chrome resting on a deep-pile pale green carpet. A bright red and black lacquered bar stood in the corner.

MacLean waited for them to wash up before bringing them to the conference room, where they enjoyed an exquisite lunch of crab and shrimp salad, spicy velvet corn soup, penne pasta, and chocolate and marzipan cake accompanied by a crisp South African Stellenbosch white wine. MacLean's curiosity was ravenous. He knew the general outlines of the missions to

Murmansk, the Vatican, and the White House, but he wanted to know all the details, step by step. Except for Carlton's and Pink's mission aboard the *Seawolf*, Carlton and Erika left little out and again thanked MacLean for the invaluable assistance he had provided at each step of the way. The introduction to Colonel Saunders, the escape to Atlantic City, the trip to Murmansk, the tip about Angola, and the introductions to Cardinal Benedetti at the Vatican and Don Forza in Palermo.

After lunch, MacLean prepared espressos for himself and Carlton and a nonfat cappuccino for Erika in an ancient Lavazza machine in the corner. "This was Dan Wenzel's machine. His wife said he would have wanted me to have it." MacLean stared ahead, visualizing his friend and counselor's face through the steam of the man's adored hand-press espresso machine.

"I'm so sorry about your friend." Erika said softly.

"Thank you."

"It was a nice touch for you to name the mine after him and Theodore Osage."

"It was only fair. They were the ones who brought the diamond deposits to my attention in the first place. And they paid for it with their lives."

An awkward silence ensued while MacLean finished preparing the coffee. After several minutes, MacLean handed Carlton and Erika their cups, each with a crescent-shaped chopped almond biscotti on the saucer.

"Just like in Rome. Thank you, Max."

"*Prego*. May I offer you a cigar?" He opened a blue-lacquered Elie Bleu humidor to reveal an impressive selection of Cuban, Dominican, Jamaican, and Honduran cigars. "Don't worry, Erika, I'll open the skylight so the smoke doesn't bother you."

She smiled with her green eyes behind the oversized cup.

Carlton selected a CAO maduro robusto Dominican. MacLean was about to select a Cohiba Siglo IV Habana, but instead chose a Padron Anniversario in deference to Carlton's well-known aversion to illegal Cuban cigars in the U.S. Carlton watched the smoke billow upward. "What puzzles me is why you decided to build this mine. After everything that happened, the price of diamonds is at an all-time low. So low and politically incorrect that I hear it isn't even economically efficient to pick them off of some old river beds, let alone mine them."

MacLean extinguished his match and reclined in his chair. "This may seem strange to you, but from the moment Dan Wenzel told me about the diamond deposits here, I never focused on the mine as a money maker. I may be slightly extravagant, but I'm not greedy. I wanted the mine merely for the beauty of the diamonds themselves."

Over the past month, Carlton had become keenly aware of MacLean's obsession with the esthetic. "I see."

"Waterboer and Scott Fress prevented me from opening the mine, as you well know. But after they were silenced, the Justice Department rescinded the forced purchase of the land, as you also know, so I was free to open the mine."

"I understand that, but if you can't sell the diamonds, then what—"

"No, no. I'm selling them. They're going like hot cakes. And they're making a fortune."

Carlton was puzzled. A quick glance confirmed that Erika shared the emotion. "You've lost us, Max. If diamonds aren't worth anything anymore, how—"

MacLean raised his cigar. "You are right to say that diamonds are no longer worth much. But that only applies to common white diamonds; the engagement ring and bracelet diamonds Waterboer convinced society were necessary. But the fancy diamonds—the yellows, the blues, the pinks—those diamonds truly are rare. Their prices haven't dropped. In fact, they've skyrocketed now that no one wants white diamonds anymore.

"When Wenzel told me about the diamonds, we talked about the quantity and general quality of the diamonds, but Waterboer stopped the mine from moving forward before we could focus on the color of the diamonds. I had always assumed that the diamonds would be white, perhaps with a few fancies thrown in. But when we performed additional tests, we discovered something incredible." He grinned, clearly enjoying the suspense. He walked to the credenza and carefully lifted a silver container the size of a shoe box. "These are the diamonds that are buried under your feet." He spilled the contents on the glass table.

Carlton and Erika gasped. Spread before them was a mound of brilliant-cut yellow diamonds of inexplicable beauty.

"Three hundred carats." MacLean announced. "Not just stones, but gems. Cut here on the premises by a team of unemployed cutters I hired. The geologists expect a yield of five million carats within the next ten years."

"I've never seen anything so beautiful in my life," Erika whispered, leaning close to the table, pushing the little stones with her slender fingers. Each stone's fifty-eight facets refracted the sunlight in bright shards of light in a variety of different yellows. "They look like they're winking." Erika laughed, giddy with excitement.

"After costs are recovered, the profits will go first to fund a small hospital, a school, a sports facility, and a park for the people of Macon Grove. Then to establish national scholarships in legal ethics in Dan Wenzel's name and in geology in Theodore Osage's name. The rest will go to a fund for infrastructure and health care projects in Africa, under the direction of Bishop Azimbe, who you met in Rome, Pat. And one other thing." MacLean stood and removed a keychain from his pocket. "I may have helped you, Pat, but you also helped me. You avenged my friend and my honor by arresting Scott Fress and destroying Waterboer. I will always be grateful. Please accept this as a small token of my appreciation." He handed the keys to Carlton.

Carlton looked at the keys, then back up at MacLean, once again puzzled. "What are they for?"

"For the fully restored white 1958 Cadillac Biarritz convertible parked behind your apartment in Virginia."

Carlton stared at the keys, wide-eyed. "Max, I can't—"

"I insist."

He remained silent for a moment, staring at the keys to the restored Shark. "Thank you, Max. So you won't refuse what Erika has for you."

Now it was MacLean's turn to be intrigued as Erika pulled a

small black velvet bag from her purse and handed it to him. "We found it in the Russian icebreaker before Russkost took over. It's the only remaining diamond of the Russian stockpile. *Mazal u'bracha.*"

MacLean let the content of the bag fall into his hand. His jaw fell open in wonderment as the sunlight illuminated a brilliant-cut blue diamond the size of a golf ball.

"Thanks for getting us there safely, Max," said Erika.

As they each admired the beauty around them, Carlton leaned back into his chair and looked at Erika and MacLean through the wisps of blue smoke from his cigar. "You know, after all is said and done, maybe Waterboer was right after all."

"How is that?" MacLean asked.

"Diamonds are beauty."

NOTE FROM THE AUTHOR

Diamonds are not as rare as the cartel deceives well-meaning consumers into believing. Global deposits are enormous. New diamond mines are coming on line every few months. In a free market for diamonds, diamonds would not be expensive. If you don't believe this, try selling your diamond to a jeweler. You'll be surprised at how few dollars you're offered. The cartel hoards and stockpiles diamonds to prevent such a free market.

Far more disturbing is the crisis brought to light in recent years by groups such as Global Witness: international terrorism and bloody civil wars, mostly in diamond-rich Africa, are fueled and funded by diamonds. Diamonds are used as untraceable and easily hidden currency to fund terrorism outside regular banking conduits. Impoverished, terrified, and enslaved men, women, and children are forced at gunpoint to dig through filth, disease, and live land mines to obtain diamonds for rebel groups of all political stripes. These stones are called "conflict diamonds" or "blood diamonds." Incensed, well-meaning legislatures the world over, including the United States Congress, are attempting to restrict the import and sale of diamonds not labeled as "conflict-free." Labeled by whom, one wonders. The cartel has stated its support of such labeling. Not a difficult decision to make, since banning the sale of conflict diamonds ensures that diamonds not under the cartel's control cannot be sold, thus reinforcing the cartel's monopoly. Sadly, these lawmaking bodies completely miss the point. The culprit is not the sale of illegal unlabeled diamonds, but the cartel's monopoly. As long as the cartel singlehandedly keeps diamond prices artificially high by regulating diamond supply and demand, terrorists will continue to enjoy an untraceable flow of funds, and our fellow brothers and sisters in Africa will continue to lose limbs and lives to obtain the shiny stones. How long will civilized men and women allow this to continue by buying pressed-coal engagement rings when so many other beautiful, monopoly-free gemstones exist? Everlasting love cannot be symbolized by a diamond for which an orphan child has lost a limb. The solution is only as far as our pocketbooks.

Despite the foregoing, *The Diamond Conspiracy* is a work of fiction. Regardless of any similarities, Waterboer Mines Limited is not De Beers. The Slythe family is not the Oppenheimer family. None of Waterboer Mines Limited, the Slythe family, and the Banco Napolitana Lucchese exist. Although the Vatican hierarchy and many religious orders within the Catholic Church disagree over certain issues, the Order does not exist, but merely represents certain conflicts within the large Church family.

The Vatican Bank, its low cash liquidity, the Vatican Office of the Secretary of State, the GRU, the *Rossiya* icebreaker (named differently), and the U.S. Senate underground tramway are real. So too are the National Security Agency, the National Reconnaissance Office, the CIA Directorate for Intelligence, the NATO air base in Keflavik, Iceland, the U.S. 8X intelligence satellite, the USS *Seawolf* attack submarine, the USS *Ronald Reagan* aircraft carrier, and the USN F/A-18E Super Hornet fighter, whose hardware and personnel daily protect the United States and her allies from their all too real enemies. *Mazal u'bracha*.

Nicolas Kublicki
www.thediamondconspiracy.com

ACKNOWLEDGMENTS

The Diamond Conspiracy is my first novel. It took nine years to write, from initial concept to publication. I wrote it mostly on weekends, vacations, and at night while I practiced law during weekdays. It was a long and often rocky road, but I wouldn't trade it for any other experience.

The Diamond Conspiracy has my name on the cover, yet I could not have written it without the help of Providence and of those named below.

My parents, for instilling in me the belief that I could achieve whatever I set out to do, provided that I work hard enough for it. My father, for reading the manuscript untiringly and his suggestions. The rest of my family, for its support.

Molly Gould for her love and patience.

Elisa Celli-Wallace, for her constant optimism and encouragement, for teaching me my first steps in the book business, and for introducing me to Ed Stackler. Her husband, the late Trevor Wallace, for teaching me the essential duty of a principal character. Nick F., for suggesting that I write the ending while I lingered in the midway doldrums.

Ed Stackler, editor extraordinaire, for his enthusiasm about the story, for his invaluable help and patience in editing the manuscript, and for introducing me to Natasha Kern.

Natasha Kern, my agent, for her faith in the manuscript and in me, for her patience and suggestions, for guiding me through the publishing labyrinth and for protecting me against its minotaurs. Her crack assistants Ruth Widener and Laura Conner, for their kind and efficient help.

Lesley Kellas Payne, for her fine-tuning and point-of-view suggestions.

Alex Lubertozzi, my publishing editor at Sourcebooks, for having the guts to bet on the manuscript and on me, and for his comments and patience. They who state that all authors dislike their editors utter lies.

Sourcebooks marketing director Judith Kelly, publicist Megan Casper, event coordinator Heidi Kent, and all the other people at Sourcebooks who believed in the book and who worked so diligently to make it a success.

Robert D. Billings, for his friendship, for introducing me to Capitol Hill, and for guiding me through the House, the Senate, and the Senate tramway. Mr. Billings, aye!

Daniel L. Casey, for giving me my first job, for so clearly understanding and legitimating my desire to write this book when the odds and conventional wisdom were against it, and for his help in marketing the book.

Todd Samovitz, fellow scribe, for his friendship, for being such a good sounding board, and for having the guts to blaze the "write" path.

Peter Riebling, fellow jurist, for his friendship, for blazing the path to Washington, D.C., and for sharing those lonely spaghetti law nights with me while on the other side of town and, later, on the other side of the country. Uh-rah!

Ann Bengele and Louis Bareno, for their friendship and for their untiring efforts at the trusty Macintosh laptop computer during tedious hours. More than any of my friends, Ann and Louis understand that in writing a novel, rewriting and editing outweigh writing at least tenfold.

Therese Wilson, my assistant, for making work much easier. Cynthia Kaiser, for helping me with marketing and invitations. Darius Baghai, Christina Carlson, Orlando Cartaya, Rick Cipra, Bari Cooper, Tina Crowe, Michelle Flores, Gerhard Heusch, Steve Istock, Vanina Marsot, Richard Marshall, Max Netty, Colm O'Ryan, Yvette Patko-Coffin, Tanya Rothman, Todd Shollenbarger, and Milo Stevanovich for helping me through the difficult times.

William Gray, for the maps and his artistic skill. Georgana Millican, for her photography and her willingness to help. Chris Netty, for his uncanny ability to locate items, particularly loose cubic zirconium stones.

Tom Clancy, Clive Cussler, and Peter Mayle, for their extraordinary books, which made law school and other hard times bearable and encouraged me not only to dream, but to pursue the dream.

The men and women of Ervin, Cohen & Jessup LLP of Beverly Hills, the best law firm in California, for creating and managing a work environment that allows lawyers to have personal lives, interests, and pursuits outside of the practice of law while demanding only the best in the service of their clients.

My fellow members and the staff of the Grand Havana Room in Beverly Hills, for providing a haven away from it all.

All my other friends, thankfully too many to name, without whose kindness, support, encouragement, faith, and friendship, even when they may not have known I was writing this book, without which I could not have completed this work. You know who you are. Diamonds ye be.

And finally, you, the reader, for your interest and time. This book is for you. I am honored by your decision to read it. I hope you enjoy it as much as I enjoyed writing it.